Edited by

Ed Gorman and
Martin H. Greenberg

RoC
A ROC BOOK

ROC
Published by the Penguin Group
Penguin Books USA Inc., 375 Hudson Street,
New York, New York 10014, U.S.A.
Penguin Books Ltd, 27 Wrights Lane,
London W8 5TZ, England
Penguin Books Australia Ltd, Ringwood,
Victoria, Australia
Penguin Books Canada Ltd, 2801 John Street,
Markham, Ontario, Canada L3R 1B4
Penguin Books (N.Z.) Ltd, 182–190 Wairau Road,
Auckland 10, New Zealand

Penguin Books Ltd, Registered Offices:
Harmondsworth, Middlesex, England

First published by Roc, an imprint of New American Library,
a division of Penguin Books USA Inc.

ROC is a trademark of New American Library, a division of Penguin Books
USA Inc.

ISBN 0-451-45048-5

Printed in the United States of America

PUBLISHER'S NOTE
This is a work of fiction. Names, characters, places, and incidents either are the product
of the author's imagination or are used fictitiously, and any resemblance to actual
persons, living or dead, events, or locales is entirely coincidental.

CONTENTS

INTRODUCTION

Movies have given the stalker subgenre a bad name. All those close-ups of big plodding male shoes stalking cute little female feet. All those foggy, back-lit angle-on shots of a tall meaty guy tugging on the leather gloves he is about to wrap around the throat of the woman half a block ahead of him. Or (my favorite) the guy with the nylon pulled down over his head so that his features are all mashed up.

You know the movies I mean. And you know how lame and predictable they've become.

It is the intention of this anthology to offer readers a group of variations on the stalker theme, not a one of them using heavy breathing on the sound track or a heroine so stupid she goes into the old mansion alone after midnight.

There is nothing wrong with fiction that frightens and disturbs. Indeed, one can make a serious case that for healthy minds such fiction is a healthy way to work through subconscious fears. But can't we perform therapy with a little style and grace?

We hope you'll find the stories here not only interesting but instructive in some small human way. A few of them you may even find yourself thinking about down the days ahead.

—Ed Gorman

Dean R. Koontz is one of the two dominant voices in contemporary popular fiction, the other being of course Stephen King. From the start— even when he was doing one half of Ace doublebooks—Koontz wrote in a style and voice all his own. He used to write (variously) science fiction, suspense, horror, and romantic suspense novels. Today, having fused all of them, he writes what can only be called Koontzes, the last one of which (*Midnight*) shot immediately to the top of all the national bestseller lists. He can virtually do it all. You can count on the fingers of one hand the writers about whom that can be said. He wrote what many consider to be the most accomplished novel of this decade, *Watchers*.

Introduction to "Trapped"

Stories rarely need introductions. Introductions are boring. Introductions are intrusive. I know, I know. But bear with me, and you'll see why I want to provide an introduction for this tale.

A major national magazine, which shall remain nameless, asked my agent if I would be willing to write a two-part novella dealing with genetic engineering, scary but not too bloody, incorporating a few of the elements of *Watchers* (my novel that dealt with the same subject). They offered an excellent word rate; furthermore, the appearance of the piece in two successive issues would reach many millions of readers, providing considerable exposure. I'd long had the idea for "Trapped"; in fact, it predated *Watchers*, and after writing the novel, I figured I'd never do the novella because of the similarities. Now someone wanted the piece precisely *because* of those similarities.

Well, hey, kismet. I seemed destined to write the story. It would be a nice break between a couple of long novels. Nothing could be easier, huh?

Every writer is an optimist at heart. Even if his work trades in cynicism and despair, even if he is genuinely weary of the world and cold in his soul, a writer is always sure that the end of the rainbow will inevitably be found on the publication date of his next novel. "Life is crap," he will say, and seem to mean it, and a moment later will be caught dreamily ruminating on his pending elevation by critics to the pantheon of American writers *and* to the top of the *New York Times* bestseller list!

The aforementioned magazine had certain requirements for the novella. It had to be between 22,000 and 23,000 words. It had to divide naturally into two parts, slightly past the midpoint. No problem. I set to work, and in time I delivered to specifications, without having to strain or contort the tale.

The editors loved the piece. Couldn't wait to publish it. They virtually pinched my cheeks with pleasure, the way your grandma does when she hears that you received a good report card and that you aren't into satanic rock and roll or human sacrifices, the way other eight-year-old kids are.

Then a few weeks passed, and they came back and said, "Listen, we like this so much that we don't want the impact of it to be diluted by spreading it over two issues. It should appear in a single issue. But we don't have *room* for quite this much fiction in one issue, so you'll have to cut it." Cut it? How much? "In half."

Having been commissioned to produce a two-parter of a certain length, I might have been justified if I had responded to this suggestion with anger and sullen refusal to discuss the matter further. Instead, I banged my head against the top of my desk, as hard as I could, for . . . oh, for about half an hour. Maybe forty minutes. Well, maybe even forty-five minutes, but surely no longer. Then, slightly dazed and with oak splinters from the desk embedded in my forehead, I called my agent and suggested an alternative. If I put in another week or so on the piece, with a great deal of effort, I might be able to pare it down as far as 18,000 to 19,000 words, but that would be as much as I could do if I were to hold fast to the story values that made me want to write "Trapped" in the first place.

The magazine editors considered my proposal and decided that if the story could be printed in slightly smaller type than they usually employed, the new length would fit within their space limitations. I sat down at the word processor again. A week later the work was done—but I had even more oak splinters in my head, and the top of the desk looked like hell.

When the new version was finished—and just as it was being submitted—the editors decided that 18,000 to 19,000 words were still too many, that the solution offered by a smaller than usual type size was too problematic, and that about four or five thousand *more* words would have to come out. "Not to worry," I was assured, "we'll cut it for you."

Fifteen minutes after that, my desk collapsed from all of the additional pounding (and to this day, it is necessary for me to make an application of lemon-oil polish to my forehead once a week, as the ratio of wood content to flesh is now so high that the upper part of my facial structure is required, by federal law, to be classified as furniture).

Apparently, major magazines often fiddle with writers' prose, and writers don't care much. But I sure care, and I can't bear to relinquish such authorial control to anyone. Therefore, I asked that the script be returned, told them they could keep their money, and put "Trapped" on the shelf, telling myself that I had not really *wasted* weeks and weeks of my time but had, in fact, come out of the affair with a valuable lesson; *nota bene*—never write for a major national magazine, on commission, unless you are able to hold the editor's favorite child hostage through publication date of the issue that contains your work.

Shortly thereafter, Ed Gorman, one of the editors of this anthology, called to say he needed stories about stalkers or people being stalked. "Trapped" instantly came to mind.

Kismet.

Maybe it makes sense to be an eternal optimist.

Anyway, that's how this piece came to be written, and

that's why it contains elements familiar to readers of *Watchers*, and that's why, if you see me some day, you'll notice that my forehead has a lovely, oaken luster. I write different types of short stories when I have the time between novels. Some, such as "Twilight of the Dawn," are pretty much mainstream fiction in their style and intentions. Some, like "Graveyard Highway," are strange and sometimes even didactic (not surprising, since three of the writers whose work had the strongest influence on me were didactic to one degree or another—John D. MacDonald, Robert Heinlein, and Charles Dickens.) Others, like this novella, are old-fashioned yarns, stories written purely for the sake of story-telling. But regardless of the degree of their complexity, *none* of them comes easily.

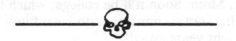

TRAPPED

Dean R. Koontz

On the night it happened, a blizzard swept across the entire Northeast. Creatures that preferred to venture out only after sunset were therefore doubly cloaked by darkness and the storm.

Snow began to fall at twilight, as Meg Lassiter drove home from the doctor's office with Tommy. Powdery flakes sifted out of an iron-gray sky and at first fell straight down through the cold, still air. By the time she covered eight miles, a hard wind swept in from the southwest and harried the snow at a slant through the Jeep station wagon's headlights.

Behind her, sitting sideways on the rear seat to accommodate his cast-encumbered leg, Tommy sighed. "I'm going to miss a lot of sledding, skiing—ice skating too."

"It's early in the season," Meg said. "You ought to heal up in time to have some fun before spring."

"Yeah, maybe." He had broken his leg two weeks ago, and during today's follow-up visit to Dr. Jacklin, they had learned he'd be in a cast six more weeks. The fracture was splintered—"minor but complicating comminution"—impacted as well, and it would knit more slowly than a simple break. "But, Mom, there's only so many winters in a person's life. I hate to waste one."

Meg smiled and glanced at the rearview mirror, in which she could see him. "You're only ten years old, honey. In your case the winters ahead are countless—or darn close to it."

"No way, Mom. Soon it'll be college, which'll mean a lot more studying, not so much time to have fun—"

"That's eight years away!"

"You always say time goes faster the older you get. And after college I'll have a job, and a family to support."

"Trust me, kiddo, life doesn't speed up till you're thirty."

Though he was as fun-loving as any ten-year-old, he was also occasionally a strangely serious boy. He'd been that way even as a toddler, but he had become increasingly solemn after his father's death two years ago.

Meg braked for the last spotlight at the north end of town, still seven miles from their farm. She switched on the wipers, which swept the fine, dry snow from the windshield.

"How old are you, Mom?"

"Thirty-five."

"Wow, really?"

"You make it sound as if I'm ancient."

"Did they have *cars* when you were ten?"

His laugh was musical. Meg loved the sound of his laughter, perhaps because she had heard so little of it the past two years.

On the righthand corner two cars and a pickup were

filling up at the Shell station's pumps. A six-foot pine tree was angled across the bed of the truck. Christmas was only eight days away.

On the lefthand corner was Haddenbeck's Tavern, set before a backdrop on hundred-foot spruces. In the burnt-out gray twilight, the falling snow looked like millions of specks of ash descending from an unseen celestial blaze, though in the amber light of the roadhouse windows, the flakes resembled not ashes but gold dust.

"Come to think of it," Tommy said from the rear seat, "how could there have been cars when you were ten? I mean, gee, they didn't invent the wheel till you were eleven."

"Tonight for dinner—worm cakes and beetle soup."

"You're the meanest mother in the world."

She glanced at the mirror again and saw that in spite of his bantering tone, the boy was not smiling any longer. He was staring grimly at the tavern.

Slightly more than two years ago, a drunk named Deke Slater had left Haddenbeck's Tavern at the same time Jim Lassiter had been driving toward town to chair a fund-raising committee at St. Paul's Church. Traveling at high speed on Black Oak Road, Slater's Buick ran head-on into Jim's car. Jim died instantly, and Slater was paralyzed from the neck down, for life.

When they passed Haddenbeck's—and when they rounded the curve where Jim had been killed—Tommy sometimes tried to conceal his enduring anguish by involving Meg in a jokey conversation.

"Light's green, Mom."

She went through the intersection, across the township line. Main Street became a two-lane county route: Black Oak Road.

Tommy had adjusted intellectually—and for the most part emotionally—to the loss of his father. In the year following the tragedy, Meg had often come upon the boy as he sat quietly at a window, lost in thought, with tears slipping down his face. She hadn't caught him weeping for ten months.

Reluctantly he had accepted his father's death. He would be okay.

That did not mean he was *whole*. Still—and perhaps for a long time to come—there was an emptiness in Tommy. Jim had been a wonderful husband but an even better father, so devoted to his son that they essentially had been a part of each other. Jim's death left a hole in Tommy as real as any a bullet might have made, although it would not scar over as fast as a gunshot wound.

Meg knew that only time could knit him completely.

She slowed the Jeep wagon because snow began to fall faster and dusk surrendered to night, reducing visibility. Hunching over the wheel, she could see ahead only twenty yards.

"Getting bad," Tommy said tensely from the rear seat.

"Seen worse."

"Where? The Yukon?"

"Yep. Gold Rush, winter of 1849. You forgetting how old I am? I was mushing Yukon dog sleds before they'd invented *dogs*."

Tommy laughed but only dutifully.

Meg could not see the broad meadows on either side, or the frozen silver ribbon of Seeger's Creek off to the right, though she could make out the gnarled trunks and jagged, winter-stripped limbs of the looming oaks that flanked that portion of the country road. The trees were a landmark by which she judged that she was a quarter of a mile from the blind curve where Jim had died.

Tommy settled into silence.

Then, when they were seconds from the curve, he said, "I don't really miss sledding and skating so much. It's just . . . I feel so helpless in this cast, so . . . so *trapped*."

His use of the word "trapped" wrenched Meg because it meant that his uneasiness at being immobilized was linked to his dad's death. Jim's Chevy had been so mangled by the impact that the police and coroner's men had required more than three hours to extract his corpse from the overturned car; his body had been ensnared by tangled metal and had to be cut loose with acetylene torches. At the time, she had tried to protect Tommy from the worst details of the accident, but when eventually he returned to his third-grade class, his schoolmates had insisted on sharing the grisly facts with him, motivated by a morbid curiosity about death and by an innocent cruelty peculiar to some children.

"You're not trapped in the cast," Meg said, as she piloted the Jeep into the long, snowswept curve. "I'm here to help."

Tommy had come home early from his first day of school after the funeral, bawling: "Daddy was trapped in the car, he couldn't move, all tangled up in twisted metal, they had to cut him loose, he was *trapped*." Meg soothed him and explained that Jim had been killed on impact, in an instant, and had not suffered: "Honey, it was only his body, his poor empty shell, that was trapped. His mind and soul, your *real* daddy, had already gone up to heaven."

Now Meg braked as she approached the midpoint of the curve, *that* curve, which would always be a frightening place no matter how often they navigated it.

Tommy had come to accept Meg's assurances that his father had not suffered. Nevertheless he was still haunted by the image of his dad's body in the clutch of mangled metal.

Suddenly, as they turned the blind point of the long curve, oncoming headlights seared Meg's eyes. A car rushed at them, moving too fast for road conditions, not out of control but not stable either; it was starting to fishtail, partly straddling the double line down the center of the road. Meg pulled the steering wheel to the right, swinging onto the hard shoulder, pumping the brakes, afraid of putting two wheels in a ditch and rolling the station wagon. She held it all the way around the curve, however, as the tires churned up chunks of gravel that rattled against the undercarriage, the oncoming car skinned past with no more than an inch to spare, vanishing in the night and snow.

"Idiot!" she said angrily.

When she had driven around the bend into a straightaway, she pulled to the side of the road and stopped. "You okay?"

Tommy was huddled in one corner of the back seat, with his head pulled down turtlelike into the collar of his heavy winter coat. Pale and trembling, he nodded, "Y-Yeah. Okay."

The night seemed strangely still in spite of the softly idling Jeep, the thump of windshield wipers, and the wind.

"I'd like to get my hands on that irresponsible jerk." She struck the dashboard with the flat side of her fist.

"It was a Biolomech car," Tommy said, referring to the large research firm located on a hundred acres half a mile south of their farm. "I saw the name on the side. 'Biolomech.' "

She took several deep breaths. "You okay?"

"Yeah. I'm all right. I just . . . want to get home."

The storm had intensified. They seemed to be beneath the snowy equivalent of a waterfall, as millions upon millions of flakes poured over them in churning currents.

Back on Black Oak Road, they crawled along at twenty-five miles an hour. Weather conditions wouldn't permit greater speed.

Two miles farther, at Biolomech, strange lights filled the night. Beyond the nine-foot-high, chain-link fence that ringed the place, sodium-vapor security lamps glowed eerily atop twenty-foot poles, their light diffused by the thickly falling snow. Although the lamps were positioned at hundred-foot intervals across the expansive grounds that surrounded the single-story offices and research labs, they were rarely switched on; Meg had seen them burning on only one other night in the past four years.

The buildings were set back from the road, beyond a screen of trees. Even in good weather and daylight, they were hard to see. Currently they were invisible in spite of the hundred or more pools of queer yellow light that surrounded them.

Pairs of men in heavy coats moved along the perimeter of the property, sweeping flashlights and the intense beams of hand-held spotlights over the fence, as if looking for a breach, focusing especially on the snow-mantled ground along the chain link.

"Somebody must've tried to break in," Tommy said.

Biolomech cars and vans were clustered at the main gate. Sputtering red emergency flares flickered and smoked along both shoulders of Black Oak Road, leading to a roadblock at which three men held flashlights. Three others had shotguns.

"Wow!" Tommy said. "Something really big must've happened."

Meg braked, stopped, and rolled down her window. Cold wind knived into the car.

She expected one of the men to approach her. Instead, a man in boots, gray uniform pants, and a black coat with the Biolomech logo moved toward the Jeep from the other side; he carried a long pole at the base of which were attached a pair of angled mirrors and a light. He was accompanied by a much taller man, similarly dressed, who had a shotgun. The shorter guard thrust the lighted mirrors beneath the Jeep and squinted at the reflection of the undercarriage that the first mirror threw onto the second.

"They're looking for bombs!" Tommy said from the rear seat.

"Bombs?" Meg said disbelievingly. "Hardly."

The man with the mirror moved slowly around the Jeep wagon, and his armed companion stayed close. Even in the obscuring whirl of snow, Meg could see their faces were lined with anxiety.

When the pair had circled the Jeep, the armed guard waved an all-clear to the other four at the roadblock, and at last one of those men approached the driver's window. He was wearing jeans and a bulky, brown leather flight jacket with sheepskin lining, without a Biolomech patch. A dark blue toboggan cap, caked with snow, was pulled halfway over his ears.

He leaned down to the open window and said, "Sorry for the inconvenience, ma'am."

He was handsome, with an appealing—but false—smile.
The smile on his lips did not extend to his gray-green eyes.
"What's going on?" she asked.

"Just a security alert," he said, the words steaming from
him in the icy air. "Could I see your driver's license, please?"

He was evidently a Biolomech employee, not a police
officer, but Meg saw no reason to decline to cooperate.

As the man was holding her wallet, studying the license,
Tommy said, "Russian spies try to sneak in there tonight?"

That same insincere smile accompanied the man's response. "Most likely just a short circuit in the alarm system,
son. Nothing here that Russians would be interested in."

Biolomech was involved in recombinant-DNA research
and the application of their discoveries to commercial enter-
prise. Meg knew that in recent years genetic engineering
had produced a manmade virus that threw off pure insulin
as a waste product, a multitude of wonder drugs, and other
blessings. She also knew the same science could engender
biological weapons—new diseases as deadly as nuclear
bombs—but she always avoided pondering the frightening
possibility that Biolomech, half a mile from their house,
might be engaged in such dangerous work. In fact a few
years ago rumors had surfaced the Biolomech had landed a
major defense contract, but the company had assured the
county that it would never perform research related to bac-
teriological warfare. Yet their fence and security system
seemed more formidable than necessary for a commercial
facility limited to benign projects.

Blinking snow off his lashes, the man in the sheepskin-
lined jacket said, "You live near here, Mrs. Lassiter?"

"Cascade Farm," she said. "About a mile down the road."

He passed her wallet back through the window.

From behind her Tommy said, "You think terrorists with
bombs are gonna drive in there and blow the place up or
something?"

"Bombs? Whatever gave you that idea, son?"

"The mirrors on the pole," Tommy said.

"Ah! Well, that's just part of our standard procedure in a

security alert. Like I said, it's probably a false alarm. Short circuit, something like that." To Meg he said, "Sorry for the trouble, Mrs. Lassiter."

As the man stepped back from the station wagon, Meg glanced past him at the guards with shotguns and at more distant figures combing the eerily lighted grounds. These men did not believe they were investigating a false alarm. Their anxiety and tension were visible not only in the faces of those nearby but in the way that all of them stood and moved in the blizzard-shot night.

She rolled up the window and put the car in gear.

As she pulled forward, Tommy said, "You think he was lying?"

"It's none of our business, honey."

"Terrorists or Russians," Tommy said with the enthusiasm for a good crisis that only young boys could muster.

They passed the northernmost end of Biolomech's land. The sodium-vapor security lights receded into the gloom behind them, while the night and snow closed in from all sides. More leafless oaks thrust spiky arms over the lane; among their thick trunks, the Jeep wagon's headlights stirred brief-lived, leaping shadows.

Two minutes later, Meg turned left off the county route, into their quarter-mile driveway. She was relieved to be home.

Cascade Farm—named after three generations of the Cascade family who once lived there—was a ten-acre spread in semirural Connecticut. It was not a working farm any more. She and Jim had bought the place four years ago, after he had sold his share in the New York ad agency that he'd founded with two partners. The farm was to have been the start of a new life, where he could pursue his dream of being a writer of more than just ad copy, and where Meg could enjoy an art studio more spacious and in a more serene environment than anything she could have had in the city.

Before he died, Jim had written two moderately successful suspense novels at Cascade Farm. There, also, Meg found new directions for her art: first a brighter tone than she previously had employed; then after Jim's death, a style so brooding and grim that the gallery handling her work in New York had suggested a return to the brighter style if she hoped to continue to sell.

The two-story fieldstone house stood a hundred yards in front of the barn. It had eight rooms, plus a spacious kitchen with modern appliances, two baths, two fireplaces, and front and back porches for sitting and rocking on summer evenings.

Even in this stormy darkness, its eaves bedecked with ice, battered by wind and lashed by whips of snow, with not a single front window warmed by a lamp's glow, the house looked cozy and welcoming in the Jeep's headlights.

"Home," she said with relief. "Spaghetti for dinner?"

"Make a lot so I can have cold leftovers for breakfast."

She said, "Yuch."

"Cold spaghetti makes a *great* breakfast."

"You're a demented child." She pulled alongside the house, stopped next to the rear porch, and helped him out of the wagon. "Leave your crutches; lean on me," she said over the whistling-hooting wind. The crutches would be of no use on snow-covered ground. "I'll bring them in after I put the Jeep in the garage."

If the heavy cast had not encased his right leg from toes to above the knee, she might have been able to carry him. Instead he leaned on her and hopped on his good leg.

She had left a light in the kitchen for Doofus, their four-year-old black Labrador. The frost-rimmed windows shimmered with that amber glow, and the porch was vaguely illuminated by it.

At the door Tommy rested against the wall of the house while Meg disengaged the lock. When she stepped into the kitchen, the big dog did not rush at her, wagging his tail with excitement, as she expected. Instead he slunk forward with his tail between his legs; he kept his head down and looked at her warily.

She pushed the door shut behind them and helped Tommy to a chair at the kitchen table. Then she took off her boots and stood them on a rag rug in the corner by the door.

Doofus was shivering, as though cold. But the oil furnace was on; the place was warm. The dog made an odd, mewling sound.

"What's the matter, Doofus?" she asked. "What've you been up to? Knock over a lamp? Huh? Chew up a sofa cushion?"

"Ah, he's a good pooch," Tommy said. "If he knocked over a lamp, he'll pay for it. Won't you, Doofus?"

The dog wagged his tail but only tentatively. He glanced nervously at Meg, then looked back toward the dining room—as if someone lurked there, someone he feared too much to bark at.

Suddenly apprehension clutched Meg.

Ben Parnell left the roadblock near the main gate and drove his Chevy Blazer to lab number three, the building deepest in the Biolomech complex. Snow melted off his toboggan cap and trickled under the collar of his sheepskin-lined flight jacket.

All across the grounds anxious searchers moved through the sulfur-yellow glow of the security lamps. In deference to the stinging wind, they hunched their shoulders and held their heads low, which made them appear less than human, demonic.

In a strange way he was glad the crisis had arisen. If he had not been there, he would have been at home, alone, pretending to read, pretending to watch TV, but brooding about Melissa, his much-loved daughter, who was gone, lost to cancer. And if he could have avoided brooding about Melissa, he would have brooded instead about Leah, his wife, who had also been lost to . . .

Lost to what? He still did not fully understand why their marriage had ended after the ordeal with Melissa was over. As far as Ben could see, the only thing that had come between him and Leah had been her grief, which had been so great and dark and heavy that she had no longer been capable of harboring any other emotion, not even love for him. Maybe the seeds of divorce had been there for a long

time, sprouting after Melissa succumbed, but he had loved
Leah; he still loved her, not passionately any more, but in
the melancholy way that a man could love a dream of
happiness even knowing the dream could never come true.
That's what Leah had become during the past year: not
even a memory, painful or otherwise, but a dream, and not
even a dream of what might be but of what could never be.

He parked the Blazer in front of lab three, a windowless
single-story structure that looked like a bunker. He went to
the steel door, inserted his plastic ID card in the slot,
reclaimed the card when the light above the entrance changed
from red to green, and stepped past that barrier as it slid
open with a hiss.

He was in a vestibule that resembled the airlock of a
spaceship. The outer door hissed shut behind him, and he
stood before the inner door, stripping off his gloves, while
he was scanned by a security camera. A foot-square wall
panel slid open, revealing a lighted screen painted with the
blue outline of a right hand. Ben matched his hand to the
outline, and the computer scanned his fingerprints. Seconds
later, when his identity was confirmed, the inner door slid
open, and he went into the main hall off which led other
halls, labs, offices.

Minutes ago Dr. John Acuff, head of Project Blackberry,
had returned to Biolomech in response to the crisis. Now
Ben located Acuff in the corridor of the east wing, where he
was conferring urgently with three men, researchers working on Blackberry.

As Ben approached, he saw that Acuff was half sick with
fear. The chief scientist—stocky, balding, a salt-and-pepper
beard—was neither absent-minded nor coldly analytic, in
no way a sterotypical man of science, and in fact he possessed a splendid sense of humor; there was usually a merry,
positively Clausian twinkle in his eyes. No twinkle tonight,
however. And no smile.

"Ben! Have you found our rats?"

"Not a trace. I want to talk to you, get some idea of
where they might go."

Acuff put one hand against his forehead, as if checking for a fever. "We've *got* to get our hands on them, Ben. If we don't recover them . . . the possible consequences are terrifying."

The dog tried to growl at whoever was in the darkness beyond the archway, but the growl softened into another whine.

Meg moved reluctantly yet boldly to the dining room, fumbled along the wall for the light switch, clicked it. The eight chairs were spaced evenly around the Queen Anne table; plates gleamed softly behind the beveled panes of the big china cabinet; nothing was out of place. She had expected to find an intruder.

Doofus remained in the kitchen, trembling. He was not an easily frightened dog, yet something had spooked him. Badly.

"Mom?"

"Stay there," she said.

"What's wrong?"

Turning on lamps as she went, Meg searched the living room and book-lined den. She looked in closets and behind the larger pieces of furniture. She kept a gun upstairs but didn't want to get it until she was sure no one was downstairs with Tommy.

Since Jim's death Meg had been paranoid about Tommy's health and safety. She knew it, admitted it, but could do nothing about her attitude. Every time he got a cold, she was sure it would become pneumonia. When he cut himself, no matter how small the wound, she feared the bleeding, as if the loss of a mere teaspoon of his blood would be the death of him. When, at play, he had fallen out of a tree and broken his leg, she'd nearly fainted at the sight of his twisted limb. If she lost Tommy, whom she loved with all her heart, she would not only be losing her son but the last living part of Jim, as well. More than her own death, Meg Lassiter had learned to fear the deaths of those she loved.

She had been afraid that Tommy would succumb to disease or accident—but although she had bought a gun for protection, she had not given much thought to the possibility that her boy might fall victim to foul play. *Foul play:* That sounded melodramatic, ridiculous. After all, this was the country, uninfected by the violence that had been such a part of life in New York City.

But something had shaken the usually boisterous Labrador, a breed prized for gameness and courage. If not an intruder—what?

She stepped into the front hall, peered up the dark stairs. She flicked a wall switch, turning on the second-floor lights.

Her own courage was draining away. She had stormed through the first-floor rooms, driven by fear for Tommy's welfare, giving no consideration to her safety. Now she began to wonder what she would do if she actually encountered an intruder.

No sound descended from the second floor. She could hear only the keening and susurrant wind. Yet she was overcome by an eerie feeling that she should not venture into the upper rooms.

Perhaps the wisest course would be to return with Tommy to the station wagon and drive to the nearest neighbors, who lived more than a quarter of a mile north on Black Oak. From there she could call the sheriff's office and ask them to check the house.

On the other hand, in a rapidly escalating blizzard, travel could be hazardous even in a four-wheel-drive Jeep.

Surely if an intruder was upstairs, Doofus would be barking furiously. The dog was somewhat clumsy, but he was no coward.

Maybe his behavior had not been indicative of fear; maybe she had misinterpreted his symptoms. His tucked tail, hung head, and trembling could have been signs of illness.

"Don't be such a *wimp*," she said angrily, and she hurriedly climbed the stairs.

The second-floor hall was deserted.

She went to her room and took the 12-gauge, pistol-grip, short-barreled Mossberg shotgun from under the bed. It was the ideal weapon for home protection: compact yet powerful enough to deter an assailant. To use it, she didn't have to be a marksmen, for the spread pattern of the pellets guaranteed a hit if she aimed in the general direction of an attacker. Furthermore, by using lightly loaded shells, she could deter an aggressor without having to destroy him. She didn't want to kill anyone.

In fact she hated guns and might never have acquired the Mossberg if she'd not had Tommy to worry about.

She checked her son's room. No one there.

The two bedrooms at the back of the house had been connected with a wide archway to make one studio. Her drawingboard, easels, and white-enameled art-supply cabinets were as she had left them.

No one lurked in either of the bathrooms.

Jim's office, the last place she searched, was deserted too. Evidently she *had* misinterpreted the Labrador's behavior, and she felt a bit sheepish about her overreaction.

She lowered the shotgun and stood in Jim's office, composing herself. After his death Meg had left the room untouched, so she could use his computer to write letters and do bookkeeping. In fact she'd also had sentimental reasons for leaving his things undisturbed. The room helped her to recall how happy Jim had been with a novel under way. He'd had a charmingly boyish aspect that was never more visible than when he was excited about a story, elaborating on a kernel of an idea. Since his funeral she sometimes came to this room to sit and remember him.

Often she felt trapped by Jim's death, as if a door had slammed shut and locked after him when he had stepped out of her life, as if she were now in a tiny room behind that door, with no key to free herself, with no window by which she could escape.

How could she build a new life, find happiness, after losing a man she had loved so deeply? What she'd had with Jim had been perfection. Could any future relationship equal it?

She sighed, turned off the light, and closed the door on her way out. She returned the shotgun to her own room.

In the hall, as she approached the head of the stairs, she suddenly had the peculiar feeling that someone was watching her. The uncanny awareness of being under observation was so powerful that she turned to look back down the hall. Empty. Besides, she had searched everywhere. She was certain she and Tommy were alone.

You're just jumpy because of that maniac who almost hit you on Black Oak Road, she told herself.

When she returned to the kitchen, Tommy was sitting in the chair where she'd left him. "What's wrong?" he asked worriedly.

"Nothing, honey. The way Doofus was acting, I thought maybe we had a burglar, but no one's been here."

"Did old Doofus break something?"

"Not that either," she said. "Not that I noticed."

The Labrador was no longer slinking about with his head held low. He wasn't trembling. He was sitting on the floor beside Tommy's chair when Meg entered the room, but he got up and padded to her, grinned, nuzzled her hand when she offered it. Then he went to the door and scratched at it lightly with one paw, which was his way of indicating he needed to go out to relieve himself.

"Take off your coat and gloves," she told Tommy, "but don't you get out of that chair until I come back with your crutches."

She pulled her boots on again and went outside, taking the dog with her, into a storm that had grown more fierce. The snowflakes were smaller and harder, almost sandlike; they made millions of tiny, ticking sounds as they struck the porch roof.

Undaunted by the storm, Doofus dashed into the yard.

Meg parked the wagon in the barn, which served as a garage. When she got out of the Jeep, she looked up at half-seen rafters in the gloom above; they creaked as gusts of wind slammed into the roof. The place smelled of oil drippings and grease, but the underlying aroma of hay and livestock had not entirely dissipated even after all these years.

As she took Tommy's crutches out of the wagon, she felt again that creepy prickling at the back of her neck: the physical manifestation of the awareness of being watched. She surveyed the dim interior of the barn, which was illumined only by the weak bulb on the automatic door opener. Someone could have been lurking behind one of the dividers that separated the area along the south wall into horse stalls, or crouching in the loft above, but she saw no evidence of an intruder to justify her suspicion.

"Meg, you've been reading too many mysteries lately," she said aloud, seeking reassurance in the sound of her own voice.

Carrying Tommy's crutches, she stepped outside, pushed the automatic door button, and watched the segmented metal panels roll down until they met the concrete sill with a solid *clunk.*

When she reached the middle of yard, she stopped, struck by the beauty of the winter nightscape. The scene was revealed primarily by the ghostly radiance of the snow on the ground, a luminescence akin to moonlight but more ethereal and, in spite of the ferocity of the storm, more serene. Marking the northern end of the yard were five leafless maples, black branches spearing the night; windhammered snow had begun to plate the rough bark.

By morning she and Tommy might be snowbound. A couple of times every winter, Black Oak Road was closed for a day or two by drifts. Being cut off from civilization for short periods was not particularly inconvenient and, in fact, had a certain appeal.

Though strangely lovely, the night was also hard; the tiny pellets of snow stung her face.

When she called Doofus, he appeared around the side of the house, half-seen in the dimness, more a phantom than a dog. He seemed to be *gliding* over the ground, as if he were not a living creature but a dark revenant. He was panting, wagging his tail, unbothered by the weather, invigorated.

Meg opened the kitchen door. Tommy was still sitting at

the table. Behind her, Doofus had halted on the top porch step.

"Come on, pooch, it's cold out here."

The Labrador whined, as if afraid to return to the house.

"Come on, come on. It's suppertime."

He climbed the last step and hesitantly crossed the porch. He put his head in the open door and studied the kitchen with inexplicable suspicion, sniffed the warm air. He shuddered.

Meg playfully bumped one boot against the dog's bottom.

He looked at her reproachfully and did not move.

"Come on, boy. You going to leave us in here unprotected?" Tommy asked from his chair by the table.

As if he understood that his reputation was at stake, the dog reluctantly slunk across the threshold.

Meg entered the house, too, and locked the door behind them.

Taking the dog's towel off a wall hook, she said, "Don't you dare shake your coat until I've dried you, pooch."

Doofus shook his coat vigorously as Meg bent to towel his fur, spraying melted snow in her face and over nearby cabinets.

Tommy laughed, so the dog looked at him quizzically, which made Tommy laugh harder, and Meg had to laugh, too, and the dog was buoyed by all the merriment. He straightened up from his meek crouch, dared to wag his tail, and went to Tommy.

When she and Tommy had first come home, perhaps they had been tense and frightened because of the crash they had narrowly avoided at the blind curve on Black Oak Road, and maybe their residual fear had been communicated to Doofus, just as their laughter now lifted his spirits. Dogs were sensitive to human moods, and there was no other explanation for his behavior.

The windows were frosted over, and the wind was wailing outside, and the house seemed all the cozier by contrast.

Meg and Tommy ate spaghetti at the kitchen table.

Doofus was not acting as strange as he had earlier, but he was not himself. More than usual, he sought companionship, even to the extent that he didn't want to eat by himself. Meg watched with surprise and amusement as the dog pushed his dish of Alpo across the floor with his nose, to a spot beside Tommy's chair.

"Next thing you know," Tommy said, "he's going to want to sit in a chair and have his plate on the table."

"First," Meg said, "he'll have to learn now to hold a fork properly. I hate it when he holds a fork backward."

"We'll send him to charm school," Tommy said, twirling long strands of spaghetti onto his fork. "And maybe he can learn to stand on his hind feet and walk like a real person."

"Once he can stand erect, he'll want to learn to dance."

"He'll cut a fine figure on the ballroom floor."

They grinned at each other across the dinner table, and Meg relished that special kind of closeness that came only from being silly together. In the past two years Tommy had too seldom been in the mood for frivolity.

Lying on the floor by his dish, Doofus ate his Alpo but didn't gobble it as usual. He nibbled, as if he was not hungry, and he frequently lifted his head and raised his floppy ears to listen to the wind moaning at the windows and in the eaves.

Later, as Meg was washing the dinner dishes and as Tommy was sitting at the table, reading an adventure novel, Doofus suddenly let out a low *woof* of alarm and sprang to his feet. He stood rigidly, staring at the cabinets on the other side of the room, between the refrigerator and the cellar door.

As she was about to say something to soothe the dog, Meg heard what had alarmed him: a rustling inside the cabinets.

"Mice?" Tommy said hopefully, for he loathed rats.

"Sounds too big for mice."

They'd had rats before. After all, they lived on a farm that had once been attractive to rodents because of the livestock feed in the barn. Though the barn housed only a car and a Jeep now, and though the rats had sought better scavenging elsewhere, they returned once every winter, as if the long-ago memory of Cascade Farm as a rat haven still stirred in each new generation.

From within the closed cabinet came the frenzied scratching of claws on wood, then a thump as something was knocked over, and the unmistakable sound of a rat-thick, sinuous body slipping along one of the shelves, rattling the stacks of canned goods as it passed between them.

"*Really* big," Tommy said, wide-eyed.

Instead of barking, Doofus whined and padded to the other end of the kitchen, as far from the rat-inhabited cabinet as he could get. At other times he had been eager to pursue rats, thought he was not very successful at catching them.

As she dried her hands on the dishtowel, Meg wondered again about the dog's loss of spirit. She went to the cabinet. There were three sets of double doors, and she put her head against the middle set, listening. Nothing.

"It's gone," she said after long seconds of silence.

"You're not going to *open* that, are you?" Tommy asked when she put her hand on one of the door handles.

"Well, of course I am. I have to see how it got in, if maybe it's chewed a hole in the cabinet backing."

"But what if it's still in there?" the boy asked.

"It's not, honey. Anyway, it's disgusting and filthy, but it's not dangerous. Nothing's more cowardly than a rat."

She thumped the cabinet with one fist, to be sure she scared off the foul thing if in fact it was in there. She opened the middle doors, saw everything was in order, got on her hands and knees, and opened the lower doors. A few cans were knocked over. A new box of Saltines was chewed open, the contents plundered.

Doofus whimpered.

She reached into the lower cupboard and pushed some of the canned goods aside, removed several boxes of macaroni and put them on the floor beside her, trying to get a look at the back wall of the cabinet. Just enough light from the kitchen seeped into that secluded space to reveal the ragged-edged hole in the plywood backing, where the rat had chewed through from the wall behind. A vague, cool draft was flowing out of the hole.

She got up, dusting her hands together, and said, "Yep, it's definitely not Mickey Mouse stopping by for a visit. This is a genuine capital R, capital A, capital T. Better get the traps."

As Meg stepped to the cellar door, Tommy said, "You're not leaving me alone?"

"Just till I get the traps, honey."

"But . . . but what it the rat comes around while you're gone?"

"It won't. They like to stay where it's dark."

The boy was blushing, embarrassed by his fear. "It's just . . . with this leg . . . I couldn't get away if it came after me."

Sympathetic but aware that coddling him would encourage his irrational fear, she said, "It won't come after you, kiddo. It's more scared of us than we are of it."

She switched on the cellar lights and went down the stairs, leaving him with Doofus. The shadowy basement was lit by two bulbs dimmed by dust. She found six heavy-duty traps on the utility shelves, rat breakers with steel hammers, not flimsy mousetraps—and a box of Warfarin poisoned food pellets—and took them upstairs without seeing or hearing the unwelcome houseguest.

Tommy sighed with relief when she returned. "There's something weird about these rats."

"There's probably only one," she said as she put the traps down on the counter by the sink. "What do you mean—weird?"

"They've got Doofus jumpy, like he was when we came home, so it must've been rats that spooked him then too. He doesn't spook easy, so what is it about these rats that has him so nervous?"

"Not rats, plural," Meg corrected. "We've only seen one. There's probably just the one. And I don't know what's gotten under that pooch's skin. He's just being silly. Remember how he used to be scared witless by the vacuum cleaner?"

"He was just a puppy then."

"No, he was scared of it until he was almost three," she said as she took from the refrigerator a packet of Buddig dried, smoked beef, with which she intended to bait the traps.

Sitting on the floor beside his young master's chair, the dog rolled his eyes at Meg and whined softly.

In truth she was as unnerved by the Labrador's behavior as Tommy was, but by saying so, she would feed the boy's anxiety.

After filling two dishes with the poisoned pellets, she put one in the cupboard under the sink, the other in the cabinet with the Saltines. She left the ravaged crackers as they were, hoping the rat would return for more and take the Warfarin instead.

She baited four traps with beef. She put one in the cabinet under the sink, another in the cabinet with the Saltines and the dish of Warfarin, but on a different shelf. She placed the third trap in the walk-in pantry and the fourth in the basement.

When she returned to the kitchen, she said, "Let me finish washing the dishes. Then we'll move into the living room. We might nail it tonight, but certainly by tomorrow morning."

Ten minutes later, on leaving the kitchen, Meg turned off the lights behind them, hoping the darkness would lure the rat out of hiding and into a trap before she retired for the night. She and Tommy would sleep better knowing the thing was dead.

She built a fire in the living-room fireplace, and Doofus settled in front of the hearth. Tommy sat in an armchair, put his crutches nearby, propped his castbound leg on a footstool, and opened his adventure novel. Meg programmed the compact-disc player with some easy-listening music, and repaired to her own chair with a new novel by Mary Higgins Clark.

The wind sounded cold and sharp, but the living room was cozy. In half an hour Meg was involved in the novel when, in a lull between songs, she heard a hard *snap!* from the kitchen.

Doofus lifted his head.

Tommy's eyes met hers.

Then a second sound. *Snap!*

"Two," the boy said. "We caught two at the same time!"

Meg put her book aside and armed herself with an iron poker from the fireplace in case the prey needed to be struck once each to finish them off. She *hated* this part of rat catching.

She went to the kitchen, switched on the lights, and looked first in the cabinet beneath the sink. In the dish, the poisoned food was almost gone. The beef was gone from the big trap too; the steel bar had been sprung, but no rat had been caught.

However, the trap was not empty. Caught under the bar was a six-inch-long stick of wood, as if it had been used to spring the trap so the bait could be taken safely.

No. That was ridiculous.

Meg took the trap from the cupboard to have a closer look. The stick was stained dark on one side, natural on the other: a strip of plywood. Like the plywood backing in all the cabinets, the kind through which the rat had chewed to get at the Saltines.

A shiver shook her, but she was reluctant to consider the frightening thought that had given rise to her tremors.

In the cupboard by the refrigerator, the poisoned bait had been taken from the other dish. The second trap had been sprung, too. With another stick of plywood. The bait had been stolen.

What kind of rat was smart enough . . . ?

She rose from her knees and opened the middle doors of that cabinet. The canned goods, packages of Jell-O, boxes of raisins, and boxes of cereal looked undisturbed at first.

Then she noticed the darkish brown, pea-sized pellet on the shelf in front of an open box of All-Bran: a piece of

Warfarin bait. But she had not put any bait on the shelf with the cereal; all of it had been in the dish below, or under the kitchen sink. So a rat had carried a piece of it onto the higher shelf.

If she hadn't been alerted by the pellet, she might not have noticed the scratch marks and small punctures on the package All-Bran. Heart hammering, she stared at the box for a long time before she took it off the shelf and carried it to the sink.

She put the poker on the counter and, with trembling hands, opened the cereal box. She poured some into the sink. Mixed in with the All-Bran were scores of poisoned grain pellets. She emptied the entire box into the sink; all the missing bait from both plastic dishes had been transferred to the cereal.

Her heart was racing, pounding so hard that she could feel the throb of her own pulse in her temples.

What's going on here? she wondered.

Something screeched behind her. A strange, angry sound. She turned and saw the rat. A hideous white rat.

It was on the shelf where the All-Bran had been, standing on its hindquarters. The shelf was fifteen inches high, and the rat was not entirely erect because it was about eighteen inches long, six inches longer than an average rat, exclusive of its tail. But it's size wasn't what iced her blood. The scary thing was its head: twice the size of a rat's head, big as a baseball, out of proportion to its body—and oddly shaped, bulging toward the top of the skull, eyes and nose and mouth squeezed in the lower half.

It stared at her and made clawing motions with its upraised forepaws. It bared its teeth and hissed—actually *hissed* like a cat—then shrieked again, and there was such hostility in its shrill cry and in its demeanor that she snatched up the fireplace poker that moments ago she had put down on the kitchen counter.

Though its eyes were beady and red like any rat's, there was a difference about them that she could not immediately identify. The way it stared at her so boldly was terrifying.

She looked at its enlarged skull—the bigger the skull, the bigger the brain—and suddenly realized that what she saw in the scarlet eyes was an unthinkably high, unratlike degree of intelligence.

It shrieked again, challengingly.

Wild rats weren't white. *Lab* rats were white.

She knew now what they had been searching for at the roadblock at Biolomech. She didn't know *why* their researchers would have wanted to create such a beast as this, and though she was a well-educated woman and had a layman's knowledge of genetic engineering, she didn't know *how* they had created it, but she knew beyond a doubt that they *had* created it, for there was no place else on earth from which it could have come.

Clearly, it had not ridden on the undercarriage of their car. Even as Biolomech's security men had been searching for it, this rat had been here, out of the cold, setting up house.

On the shelf behind it and on the three shelves below it, other rats pushed through cans and bottles and boxes. They were repulsively large and pale like the mutant that still challenged her from the cereal shelf.

Behind her, claws clicked on the floor.

Meg did not even look back, and she didn't delude herself into thinking she could handle them with the poker. She threw that useless weapon aside and ran for her shotgun upstairs.

Ben Parnell and Dr. Acuff crouched in front of the cage that stood in one corner of the windowless room. It was a six-foot cube with a sheet-metal floor that had been softened with a layer of silky, dry, yellow-brown grass. The food and water dispensers could be filled from outside but were operable from within, so the occupants could obtain nourishment as desired. One third of the pen was equipped with an array of miniature wooden ladders and climbing bars for exercise and play. The cage door was open.

"Here, see?" Acuff said. "It locks automatically every

time the door is shut, so it can't be left unlocked by mistake. And once shut, it can only be opened with a key. Seemed safe to us. I mean, we didn't think they'd be smart enough to pick a lock!"

"But surely they didn't. How could they—without hands?"

"You ever take a close look at their feet? A rat's feet aren't like hands, but they're more than just paws. There's an articulation of digits that allows them to grasp things. It's true of most rodents. Squirrels, for instance: You've seen them sitting up, holding a piece of fruit in their forepaws."

"Yes, but without an opposable thumb—"

"Of course," Acuff said, "they don't have great dexterity, nothing like we have, but these aren't ordinary rats. Remember, these creatures have been genetically engineered. Except for the shape and size of their craniums, they aren't physically much different from other rats, but they're *smarter*. A lot smarter."

Acuff was involved in intelligence-enhancement experiments, seeking to discover if lower species—rats—could be gentically altered to breed future generations with drastically increased brain power, in the hope that success with lab animals might lead to procedures that would enhance human intelligence. His research was labeled Project Blackberry in honor of the brave, intelligent rabbit of the same name in Richard Adam's *Watership Down*.

At Acuff's suggestion, Ben had read and immensely enjoyed Adam's book, but he had not yet decided whether he approved or disapproved of Project Blackberry.

"Anyway," Acuff said, "whether they could have picked the cage lock is debatable. And maybe they didn't. Because there's *this* to consider." He pointed to the slot in the frame of the cage door where the stubby, brass bolt was supposed to fit when engaged. The slot was packed full of a grainy brown substance. "Food pellets. They chewed up food pellets, then filled the slot with the paste, so the bolt couldn't automatically engage."

"But the door had to be open for them to do that."

"Well, there's this flexible maze we constantly reconfigure, half as big as this whole room. It's made of clear plastic tubes with difficult obstacles. We attach it to the front of the cage, then just open their door, so they go straight from the cage into the maze, and we were doing that yesterday, so the cage was open a long time. If some of them paused at the door before entering the maze, if they sniffed around the lock slot for a second or two, we might not have noticed. We were more interested in what they did *after* they entered the maze."

Ben rose from a crouch. "I've already seen how they got out of the room itself. Have you?"

"Yeah." Acuff stood, too, and they went to the far end of the room. Near floor level, an eighteen-inch-square intake duct to the building's ventilation system had been tampered with. The grille, held in place only by light tension clamps, had been torn loose. Acuff said, "Have you looked in the exchange chamber?"

Because of the nature of the work done in lab number three, all air was chemically decontaminated before being vented to the outside. It was forced, under pressure, through multiple chemical baths in a five-tiered exchange chamber as big as a pickup truck.

"They couldn't get through the exchange chamber alive," Acuff said. "Might be eight dead rats in those chemical baths."

"There aren't. We checked. And we can't find vent grilles distrubed in other rooms, where they might have left the ducts— "

"You don't think they're still in the ventilation system?"

"No, they must've gotten out at some point, into the walls."

"But how? PVC pipe is used for the duckwork, pressure-sealed with a high-temperature bonding agent in all joints."

Ben nodded. "We think they chewed up the adhesive at one of the joints, loosened two sections of pipe just enough to squeeze out. We've found rat droppings in the crawlspace attic . . . and a place where it looks like they gnawed through the subroof and the overlying shingles. Once they got onto the roof, they could get off the building easily, by gutters and downspouts."

John Acuff's face had grown whitier than the salt part of his salt-and-pepper beard. "Listen," Acuff said, "we have got to get them back tonight, no matter what. *Tonight.*"

"We'll try."

"Just trying isn't good enough. We've *got* to do it. Ben, there are three males and five females in that pack. And they're fertile. If we don't get them back, if they breed in the wild . . . ultimately they'll drive ordinary rats into extinction, and we'll be faced with a menace unlike any we've known. Think about it: *smart* rats, able to recognize and elude traps, quick to detect poison bait, virtually ineradicable. Already, the world loses a large portion of its food supply to rats, as much as ten or fifteen percent in developed countries like ours, fifty percent in many third-world countries. Ben, we lose that much to *dumb* rats. What'll we lose to these? We might eventually see famine even in the United States—and in less advanced countries, starvation deaths in numbers beyond imagination."

Frowning, Ben said, "You're overstating the danger."

"Absolutely not! Rats are parasitical. They're competitors, and these will be competing much more vigorously and aggressively than any rats we've ever known."

Ben felt as if a wad of chill, wet leaves was pressed to his spine. "Just because they're a bit smarter than ordinary rats—"

"More than a bit. Scores of times smarter."

"But not as smart as we are, for heaven's sake."

"Maybe half as smart as the average man," Acuff said.

Ben blinked in surprise.

"Maybe even a little smarter than that," Acuff said, his fear evident in his lined face and eyes. "Combine that level of intellect with their natural cunning, size advantage—"

"Size advantage? But we're much bigger—"

Acuff shook his head. "No, small can be better. Because they're smaller, they're faster than we are. And they can vanish through a chink in the wall, down a drain pipe.

They're bigger than the average rat, about eighteen inches long instead of twelve, but they can move unseen through the shadows because they're still relatively small. Size isn't their only advantage, however. *They can also see at night as well as in daylight.*"

"Doc, you're starting to scare me."

"You better be scared half to death. Because these rats we've made, this new species we've engineered, is hostile to us."

Finally Ben was forming an opinion of Project Blackberry. It wasn't favorable. Not sure he wanted to know the answer to his own question, he said, "What exactly do you mean by that?"

Turning away from the wall vent, walking to the center of the room, planting both hands on the marble lab bench, leaning forward with his head hung down and his eyes closed, Acuff said, "We don't know why they're hostile. They just are. Is it some quirk of their genetics? Or have we made them just intelligent enough so they can understand that we're their masters—and resent it? Whatever the reason, they're aggressive, fierce. A few researchers were badly bitten. Sooner or later someone would've been killed if we hadn't taken extreme precautions. We handle them with heavy bite-proof gloves, wearing Plexiglas face masks, suited in specially made Kevlar coveralls with high, rolled collars. *Kevlar!* That's the stuff they make bulletproof vests out of, and we needed something that tough because these little beasts were determined to hurt us."

Astonished, Ben said, "But why didn't you destroy them?"

"We couldn't destroy a success," Acuff said.

Ben was baffled. "Success?"

"From a scientific point of view, their hostility wasn't important because they were also *smart*. What we were trying to create was smart rats, and we succeeded. Given time, we figured to identify the cause of the hostility and deal with it. That's why we put them all in one pen—'cause we thought their isolation in individual cages might be partly to blame for their hostility, that they were intelligent enough to need a communal environment, that housing them together might . . . mellow them."

"Instead it only facilitated their escape."

Acuff nodded. "And now they're loose."

Hurrying along the hall, Meg passed the wide archway to the living room and saw Tommy struggling up from his chair, groping for his crutches. Doofus was whining, agitated. Tommy called to Meg, but she didn't paused to answer because every second counted.

Turning at the newel post, starting up the stairs, she glanced back and could see no rats following her. However, the light wasn't on in the hallway itself, so something could have been scurrying through the shadows along the baseboard.

She climbed the steps two at a time and was breathing hard when she reached the second floor. In her room she took the shotgun from under the bed and chambered the first of the five rounds in the magazine: *clackety-clack*.

A vivid image of rats swarming through the cabinet flickered across her mind, and she realized she might need additional ammo. She kept a box of fifty shells in her clothes closet, so she slid open that door—and cried out in surprise when two large, white rats scuttled across the closet floor. They clambered over her shoes and disappeared through a hole in the wall, moving too fast for her to take a shot at them even if she had thought to do so.

She had kept the box of shells on the closet floor, and the rats had found it. They had chewed open the cardboard carton and stolen the shells one at a time, carrying them away through the hole in the wall. Only four rounds were left; she scooped them up and stuffed them into the pockets of her jeans.

If the rats had succeeded in making off with all of the shells, would they then have tried subsequently to find a way to remove the last five rounds from the shotgun's magazine, as well, leaving her defenseless? Just how smart *were* they? But she knew the answer to that last one: too smart, much too smart.

Tommy was calling for her, and Doofus was barking angrily.

Meg left the bedroom at a run. She went down the steps so fast that she risked twisting an ankle.

The Labrador was in the first-floor hall, his sturdy legs planted wide, blocky head lowered, ears flattened against his skull. He was looking toward the kitchen, no longer barking but growling menacingly, even though he was also trembling with fear.

Meg found Tommy in the living room, standing with the aid of his crutches, and she let out a wordless cry of relief when she saw that no rats were swarming over him.

"Mom, what is it? What's wrong?"

"The rats . . . I think . . . I *know* they're from Biolomech. That's what the roadblock was all about. That's what those men were looking for with their spotlights, with the angled mirrors they poked under the car." She swept the room with her gaze, looking for furtive movement along the walls and beside the furniture.

"How do you know?" the boy asked.

"I've seen them. You'll know it, too, if you see them."

Doofus remained in the hall, but Meg took small comfort from the warning growl he directed toward the kitchen. She realized the dog was no match for these rats. They'd trick or overpower him without difficulty, as soon as they were ready to attack.

They *were* going to attack. Her awful certainty about their intentions arose from simple observation. They were genetically altered, with large skulls and brains, but they were different from ordinary rats in other ways, primarily in their behavior. By nature rats were scavengers, not hunters, and they thrived because they skulked through shadows, living secretively in walls and sewers; they never dared to assault a human being unless he was helpless—an unconscious wino, a baby in a crib. But the Biolomech rats she had seen in the kitchen were bold and hostile, hunters as well as scavengers, and their scheme to steal her shotgun shells and disarm her was in preparation for an attack.

His voice quaverous, Tommy said, "But if they aren't like ordinary rats, what *are* they like?"

She remembered the hideously enlarged skull, the scarlet eyes informed with malevolent intelligence, the pale and plump and somehow obscene white body. She said, "I'll tell you later. Come on, honey, we're getting out of here."

They could have gone out the front door, all the way around the house, and across the rear yard to the barn, where the Jeep was parked, but that was a long way through driving snow for a boy on crutches. Meg decided they would have to go through the kitchen and out the back. Besides, their coats were drying on the rack by the rear door, and her car keys were in her coat.

Doofus bravely led them along the hall to the kitchen, though he was not happy about it.

Meg stayed close to Tommy, holding the pistol-grip, pump-action 12-gauge ready in both hands. Five shells in the gun, four in her pockets. Was that enough? How many rats had escaped Biolomech? Six? Ten? Twenty? She would have to avoid shooting them one at a time, save her ammunition until she could take them out in twos or threes. Yes, but what if they didn't attack in a pack? What if they rushed at her singly, from several different directions, forcing her to swivel left and right and left again, blasting at them one at a time until her ammunition was all gone? She *had* to stop them before they reached her or Tommy, even if they came singly, because once they were on her or climbing over the boy, the shotgun would be useless; then she and Tommy would have to defend themselves with bare hands against sharp teeth and claws. They'd be no match for even half a dozen large, fearless—and smart—rats intent on tearing out their throats.

But for the wind outside and the tick of granular snow striking the windows, the kitchen was silent. The cupboard stood open, as she had left it, but there were no rats on the shelves.

This was *crazy*! For two years she had worried about her ability to raise Tommy on her own, without Jim's help. She had been concerned about how to instill in him the right values and principles. His small injuries and illnesses had scared her. She had worried about how she would handle unexpected crisis if they arose, but she had never contemplated anything as unexpected as *this*. Sometimes she had taken comfort in the thought that she and Tommy lived in the country, where crime was not a concern, for if they still lived in the city, she would have had even more to worry about; but now bucolic Cascade Farm, at the hayseed end of Black Oak Road, had been swallowed up by the Twilight Zone.

"Put on your coat," she told Tommy.

Doofus's ears pricked. He sniffed the air. He turned his head from side to side, surveying the base of the cupboards, the refrigerator, the unlit open cabinet under the sink.

Holding the Mossberg in her right hand, Meg speared her own coat off the rack with her left, struggled until she got her arm into it, then took the shotgun in her left hand, shrugged her right arm into the second sleeve. She used just one hand to pull on her boots, refusing to put down the shotgun.

Tommy was staring at the rat trap that she had left on the counter, the one that had been under the sink. The stick that the rats had used to trip the mechanism was still wedged between the anvil and the hammer bar. Tommy frowned at it.

Before he could ask questions or have more time to think, Meg said, "You can do without a boot on your good foot. And leave your crutches here. They're no good outside. You'll have to lean on me."

Suddenly Doofus went rigid.

Meg brought up the gun and scanned the kitchen.

The Labrador growled deep in his throat, but there was no sign of the rats.

Meg pulled open the back door, letting in the frigid wind, and said, "Let's move, let's go, now."

Tommy lurched outside, holding on to the door frame,

then balancing against the porch wall. The dog slipped out after him. Meg followed, closing the door behind them.

Holding the Mossberg in her right hand, using her left arm to support Tommy, she helped the boy across the porch, down the snow-covered steps, into the yard. With the wind-chill factor, the temperature must have been below zero. Her eyes teared, and her face went numb. She hadn't paused to put on gloves, and the cold sliced through to the bones of her hands. Still, she felt better outside than in the house, safer; she did not think the rats would come after them, for the storm was a far greater obstacle to those small creatures than it was to Meg and her son.

Conversation was impossible because the wind keened across the open land, whistled under the eaves of the house, and made the bare branches of the maples clatter against one another. She and Tommy progressed silently, and Doofus stayed at their side.

Though they slipped several times and almost fell, they reached the barn quicker than she had expected, and she hit the switch to put up the electric door. They ducked under the rising barrier before it was entirely out of their way. In the weak light of the lone bulb, they went directly to the station wagon.

She fished her keys out of her coat pocket, opened the door on the passenger's side, slid the seat back all the way on its tracks, and helped Tommy into the front of the car because she wanted him beside her now, close, not in the back, even if he would have been more comfortable there. When she looked around for the dog, she saw that he was standing outside the barn, just beyond the threshold, unwilling to follow.

"Doofus, here, quick now," she said.

The Labrador whined. Surveying the shadows in the barn, he let the whine deepen into a growl.

Remembering the feeling of being watched when she had parked the Jeep in the barn earlier, Meg also scanned the murky corners and the tenebrous reaches of the loft, but she saw neither small, pale, slinking figures nor the telltale red shine of rodent eyes.

The Labrador was probably just tense, excessively cautious. His condition was understandable, but they had to get moving. More forcefully, Meg said, "Doofus, get in here, right now."

He entered the barn hesitantly, sniffing the air and floor, then came to her and jumped into the back seat of the wagon.

She closed the door, went around to the other side, and got in behind the wheel. "We'll drive back to Biolomech," she said. "We'll tell them we've found what they're looking for."

"What's wrong with Doofus?"

In the back seat the dog was moving from one side window to the other, peering out at the barn, making thin, anxious sounds.

"He's just being Doofus," Meg said.

Huddled in his seat, angled awkwardly to accommodate his cast, Tommy looked younger than ten, frightened and vulnerable.

"It's okay," Meg said. "We're out of here."

She thrust the key in the ignition, turned it. Nothing. She tried again. The Jeep would not start.

At the fence along the northeast flank of the Biolomech property, Ben Parnell crouched to examine the rat-sized tunnel in the half-frozen earth. Several of his men gathered around him, and one directed the beam of a powerful flashlight on the patch of ground in question. Luckily the hole was in a spot where the wind scoured most of the snow away instead of piling it up in drifts, but the searchers had still not spotted it until they'd made a second circuit of the perimeter.

Steve Harding raised his voice to compete with the wind: "Think they're in there, curled up in a burrow?"

"No," Ben said, his breath smoking in the arctic air. If he'd thought they were in a burrow at the end of this entrance tunnel, he would not have been crouched in front

of the hole, where one of them might fly out at him, straight
at his face.

Hostile, John Acuff had said. Exceedingly hostile.

Ben said, "No, they weren't digging a burrow. They came
up somewhere on the other side of the fence, and they're
gone now."

A tall, lanky young man in a county sheriff's department
coat joined the group and said, "One of you named Parnell?"

"That's me."

"I'm Joe Hockner." He was half-shouting to be heard
above the skirling wind. "Sheriff's office. I brought the
bloodhound you asked for. What's happenin' here?"

"In a minute," Ben said, returning his attention to the
tunnel that went under the fence.

"How do we know it was them that dug here?" asked
George Yancy, another of Ben's men. "Could've been some
other animal."

"Bring the light closer," Ben said.

Steve Harding shone the beam directly into the five-inch-
diameter tunnel.

Squinting, leaning closer, Ben saw what appeared to be
snippets of white thread adhering to the moist earth just far
enough inside the hole to be undisturbed by the wind. He
took off his right glove, reached carefully into the mouth of
the tunnel, plucked up two of the threads. White hairs.

Tommy and the dog stayed in the station wagon, while
Meg got out with the shotgun—and with a flashlight from
the glove compartment—to open the hood. The light revealed a mess of torn and tangled wires inside the engine
compartment; all the lines from the spark plugs to the
distributor cap were severed. Holes had been gnawed in the
hoses; oil and coolants dripped onto the barn floor under
the Jeep.

She was no longer just scared. She was flat-out terrified.
Yet she had to conceal her fear to avoid panicking Tommy.

She closed the hood, went around to the passenger's side,

and opened the door. "I don't know what's wrong, but it's dead."

"It was all right a while ago, when we came home."

"Yes, well, but it's dead now. Come on, let's go."

He allowed her to help him out of the car, and when they were face to face, he said, "The rats got to it, didn't they?"

"Rats? The rats are in the house, yes, and they're ugly things, like I said, but—"

Interrupting her before she could lie to him, the boy said, "You're trying not to show it, but you're afraid of them, really afraid, which must mean they're not just a little different from ordinary rats but a whole lot different, because you don't scare easy, not you. You were scared when Dad died, I know you were, but not for long, you took charge real quick, you made me feel safe, and if Dad's dying couldn't make you fall to pieces, then I guess pretty much nothing can. But these rats from Biolomech, whatever they are, *they* scare you more than anything ever has."

She hugged him tight, loving him so hard it almost hurt—though she did not let go of the shotgun.

He said, "Mom, I saw the trap with the stick in it, and I saw the cereal in the sink all mixed up with the poison pellets, and I've been thinking, and I guess one thing about these rats is . . . they're awful smart, maybe because of something that was done to them at the laboratory, smarter than rats should ever be, and now they somehow zapped the Jeep."

"They're not smart enough. Not smart enough for us, kiddo."

"What're we going to do?" he whispered.

She whispered, too, though she had seen no rats in the barn and was not sure they had remained after disabling the station wagon. Even if they were nearby, watching, she was certain that they could not understand English. Surely there were limits to what the people at Biolomech had done to these creatures. But she whispered anyway. "We'll go back to the house—"

"But maybe that's what they want us to do."

"Maybe. But I've got to try to use the telephone."

"They'll have thought of the phone."

"Maybe but probably not. I mean how smart can they be?"

"Smart enough to think of the Jeep."

Beyond the fence was a meadow about a hundred yards across, and at the end of the meadow were woods, deep and dark.

The chance of finding the rats now was slim, but the men fanned out across the field in teams of two and three, not sure what signs of their quarry could have survived the storm. Even in good weather, on a dry and sunny day, it would be virtually impossible to track animals as small as rats across open ground.

Ben Parnell took four men directly to the far side of the meadow, where they began searching the perimeter of the forest with the aid of the bloodhound. The dog's name was Max. He was built low and broad, with huge ears and a comical face, but there was nothing funny about his approach to the case at hand: He was eager, serious. Max's handler, Deputy Joe Hockner, had given the dog a whiff of the rats' spoor from a jarful of grass and droppings that had been taken from their cage, and the hound hadn't liked what he smelled. But the scent was apparently so intense and unusual that it was easy to follow, and Max was a game tracker, willing to give his best in spite of wind and snow.

Within two minutes, the hound caught the scent in a clump of winter-dried brush. Straining at his leash, he pulled Hockner into the woods, and Ben and his men followed.

Meg let Doofus out of the station wagon, and the three of them headed toward the big open door of the barn, past which the wind drove whirling columns of snow like dervish ghosts. The storm had accelerated, raising a noisy clatter on the roof as it tore a few shingles off and spun them away in the night. The rafters creaked, and the loft door chattered on its loose hinges.

"Tommy, you'll stay out on the porch, and I'll go into the kitchen as far as the phone. If it's out of order . . . we'll walk the driveway to the county road and flag down a car."

"No one's going to be out in this storm."

"Someone will be. A county snowplow or cinder truck."

He halted at the threshold of the open barn door. "Mom, it's three-quarters of a mile to Black Oak. I'm not sure I can walk that far with the cast, in this storm, not even with you helping. I'm already tired, and my good leg keeps buckling. Even if I can do it, it'll take a long, long time."

"We'll make it," she said, "and it doesn't matter how long we take. I'm sure they won't pursue us outside. We're safe in the storm—safe from *them* at least." Then she remembered the sled. "I can pull you to the county road!"

"What? Pull me?"

She risked leaving Tommy with Doofus long enough to run back into the barn, to the north wall, where the boy's sled—*Midnight Flyer* was the legend in script across the seat of it—hung on the wall beside a shovel, a hoe, and a leaf rake. Without putting the Mossberg down, she unhooked the sled and carried it, in one hand, to the open door where Tommy waited.

"But, Mom, I'm too heavy for you to pull."

"Haven't I pulled you back and forth over this farm on at least a hundred snowy days?"

"Yeah, but that was years ago, when I was little."

"You're not so huge now, buckaroo. Come on."

She was pleased that she had remembered the sled, and she thought, *I've got one great advantage over this high-tech Hamlin plague; I'm a mother with a child to protect, and that makes me a force to be reckoned with.*

She took the sled outside and helped him onto it. He sat with his shoe-clad left foot braced against the guide bar. His right foot was covered with the cast, except for his toes, and both his toes and the lower part of the cast were sheathed in a thick woolen sock that was now wet and half frozen; nevertheless he managed to wedge even that foot into the space in front of the guide bar. When he held onto the sides of the sled with both hands, he was in no danger of falling off.

Doofus circled them anxiously as they got Tommy settled on the sled. Several times he barked at the barn behind them, but each time that Meg looked back, she saw nothing.

Picking up the sturdy nylon tow rope, Meg prayed that when they got to the house the phone would work, that she would be able to call for help. She dragged Tommmy across the long back yard. In some places the runners cut through the thin layer of snow, digging into the frozen ground beneath, and the going was tough. In other places, however, where the snow was deeper or the ground icy, the sled glided smoothly enough to give her hope that, if they had to, they would be able to make the county road before the relentless gales hammered her to her knees in exhaustion.

The brush in the forest was not too dense, and the rats evidently took advantage of deer trails to make greater speed, for the bloodhound plunged relentlessly forward, leading the searchers where the creatures had gone. They were fortunate that the interlaced trees kept most of the snow from reaching the forest floor, which made their job easier and was a boon to the stumpy-legged dog. Ben expected Max to bay, for he had seen all the old jailbreak movies in which Cagney or Bogart had been pursued by baying hounds, but Max made a lot of chuffing and snuffling sounds, barked once, and did not bay at all.

They had gone a quarter of a mile from the Biolomech fence, stumbling on the uneven ground, frequently spooked by the bizarre shadows stirred by the bobbling beams of the flashlights, when Ben realized the rats had not burrowed into the forest floor. If that had been their intention, they could have tunneled into the ground shortly after entering the cover of the trees. But they had raced on, searching for something better than a wild home, and of course that made sense because they were *not* wild, far from it. They had been bred from generations of tame lab rats, and they had lived all their lives in a cage, with food and water constantly available. They would be at a loss in the woods, even as smart as they were, so they would try to press ahead in hope of finding some human habitation to share, travel as far as they could before exhaustion and the deepening cold stopped them.

Cascade Farm.

With a jolt Ben remembered the attractive woman in the Jeep wagon: chestnut hair, almond-brown eyes, a porcelain complexion just saved from perfection by an appealing spatter of freckles. The boy in the back seat, his leg in a cast, had been nine or ten and had reminded Ben of his own daughter, Melissa, who had been nine when she had lost her hard-fought war with cancer. The boy had that look of innocence and vulnerability that Melissa had possessed and that had made it so hard for Ben to witness her decline. Peering at mother and son through the open car window, Ben had envied them the normal life he imagined they led, the love and sharing of a family unscathed by the whims of fate.

Now, crashing through the woods behind the dog and Deputy Hockner, Ben was seized by the horrible certainty that the rats—having escaped from Biolomech hours before the snow began to fall—had made it to Cascade Farm, the nearest human habitat, and that the family he had envied was in mortal danger. Lassiter . . . that was their name. With a surety almost psychic in intensity, Ben knew the rats had taken up residence with the Lassiters.

Hostile, Acuff had said. Exceedingly hostile. Mindlessly, unrelentingly, demonically hostile.

"Hold up! Wait! Hold up!" he shouted.

Deputy Hockner reined in Max, and the search party came to a halt in a clearing encircled by wind-shaken pines. Explosive clouds of crystallized breath plumed from the nostrils and mouths of the men, and they all turned to look questioningly at Ben.

He said, "Steve, go back to the main gate. Load up a truck with men and get down to Cascade Farm. You know it?"

"Yeah, it's the next place along Black Oak Road."

"God help those people, but I'm sure the rats have gone

there. It's the only warm place near enough for them to reach. If they didn't stumble on Cascade Farm and take refuge there, then they'll die in this storm—and I just don't think we're lucky enough to count on the weather having done them in."

"I'm on my way," Steve said, turning back.

To Deputy Hockner, Ben said, "All right, let's go. And let's hope to God I'm wrong."

Hockner relaxed the tension on Max's leash. This time the hound bayed once, long and low, when he caught the rats' scent.

By the time Meg drew the sled across the long yard to the foot of the porch steps, her heart was thudding almost painfully, and her throat was raw from all the frigid, hard-drawn air she'd had to pull into her lungs. She was far less sanguine about her ability to haul Tommy all the way out to the county road. The task might have been relatively easy after the storm had passed; however, now she was not just fighting the boy's weight but the vicious wind as well. Furthermore, the sled's runners had not been sanded, oil-polished, and soaped in preparation for the season, so there was some rust on them, which created friction.

Doofus stayed close to the sled, but in spite of his fur, he was beginning to suffer from the effects of the blizzard. He was shuddering uncontrollably. His coat was matted with snow. In the vague amber light that radiated from the kitchen windows to the yard at the bottom of the porch steps, Meg could see tiny, glistening icicles hanging from the fur on the Labrador's throat.

Tommy was in better shape than the dog. He had pulled up the hood on his coat and had bent forward, keeping his face down, out of the punishing wind. But neither he nor Meg was wearing insulated underwear, and they were both dressed in jeans rather than heavy outdoor pants. On the longer trek from the house to Black Oak Road, the wind would leech a lot of heat from them.

Again she prayed that the telephone would work.

Looking up at her, Tommy was bleak-faced within the cowl of his coat. All but shouting against the cacophonous babble of the storm, she told him to wait there (as if he could do anything else), told him she would be back in a minute (though they both knew that something terrible could happen to her in the house).

Carrying the 12-gauge Mossberg, she went up the porch steps and cautiously opened the back door. The kitchen was a mess. Packages of food had been dragged out of the cabinets, torn open, and the contents scattered across the floor. Several kinds of cereal, sugar, flour, corn starch, corn meal, crackers, cookies, boxes of macaroni and spaghetti were mixed together and laced with the shattered glass and wet contents of a score of broken jars of spaghetti sauce, applesauce, cherries, olives, pickles.

The destruction was unnerving because it was so unmistakably an expression of the mindless rage that, in a man, would be called psychotic. The rats had not torn these packages to obtain sustenance. The creatures seemed so inimicable to humankind that they destroyed people's property for the joy of it, reveling in the ruin and waste in much the way that gremlins of age-old myth were supposed to revel in the trouble that they caused.

These gremlins, of course, were manmade. What kind of world had it become when men created their own goblins? Or had that always been the case?

She could see no signs of the rats that had caused the ruin in the kitchen, no furtive movement in the shadowy cupboards, no sinuously slinking forms along the walls or in the rubble. Cautiously she stepped across the threshold, into the house.

The icy wind came with her, exploding through the door, as if it were water under high pressure. White clouds of flour and sparkling miniature tornadoes of sugar granules were spun across the room, and some of the heavier debris—Cheerios and broken bits of spaghetti—took flight as well.

Garbage and shattered glass crunched underfoot as she edged warily to the telephone, which hung on the wall on the far side of the room, near the refrigerator. Three times she saw movement from the corner of her eye and was sure it was purposeful—the rats—and she swung the muzzle of the shotgun to bear on it, but it was always just an empty raisin box or the torn wrapper from a package of cookies, stirring in the invasive wind.

She reached the phone and lifted the handset. No dial tone. The line was dead, either because of the storm or the rats.

As Meg regretfully returned the handset to its cradle, the wind subsided outside, withdrawing from the kitchen as well, and in the suddenly still air, she smelled fumes. Natural gas. No, not natural gas. Something else. More like . . . gasoline.

Heating oil.

All of her internal alarm bells began to clang.

Now that cold wind was no longer sweeping through the room, Meg realized that the house reeked of heating-oil fumes, which must be rising from the basement where the lines between the big oil tank and the furnace had been breached. She had walked into a trap. These ratlike gremlins were so hostile, so demonic, that they were willing to destroy the house that provided them with shelter if, in leveling it, they could kill one human being.

She took one step away from the telephone, toward the door, when through the ventilation duct she heard the soft, hollow, echoy, familiar thump-click-whoosh of the electronic pilot light on the basement furnace, the sparking of an electric arc to ignite the heating coils. A fraction of a second later, before she could even take a second step, the house exploded.

Following Max the bloodhound and Deputy Hockner, followed in turn by three of his own men, Ben Parnell reached the northern perimeter of the woods and saw the faint lights of the house at Cascade Farm, dimly visible through the heavily falling snow, perhaps two hundred yards away across a sloping field.

"I *knew* it," he said. "That's where they've gone."

He thought of the woman and the boy in the station wagon, and he was overcome by a powerful sense of responsibility for them that went beyond his duties at Biolomech. For two years he felt that he had failed his own child, Melissa, by not saving her from cancer, which was irrational, of course, because he was not a doctor and did not have the knowledge to cure her. But his profound feeling of failure couldn't be assuaged. He had always had an unusually strong sense of responsibility to and for others, a virtue that sometimes could be a curse. Now, as he looked down on Cascade Farm, he was gripped by a powerful and urgent need to ensure the safety of that woman, her boy, and whatever other members of their family shared the farmhouse.

"Let's move," he said to his men.

Deputy Hockner was unfolding a lightweight blanket made from one of those space-age materials with a high insulation factor in spite of its thinness. "You go ahead," he said, dropping to his knees and wrapping Max in the blanket. "My dog has to warm up. He isn't built for prolonged exposure to this kind of weather. Soon as he's thawed out a bit, we'll follow you."

Ben nodded, turned, and took only two steps when, out on the lowlands, the farmhouse exploded. There was a yellow-orange flash of light. That flare was followed by the shockwave, a low and ominous *wham* that was felt as much as heard. Flames leaped from the shattered windows, flapped like bright banners in the wind, raced up the walls.

The floor bucked, throwing Meg off her feet; then it fell into place, and she fell with it, face down in the torn packages, scattered food, and glass. The breath was knocked out of her, and she was temporarily deafened by the blast. But she was not so disoriented that she was unaware of the fire, which licked up the walls and spread across the floor with frightening speed, as if it were alive and intent upon cutting her off from the door.

As she pushed up onto her knees, she saw that blood

slicked her hand, and she realized that she had sustained a cut from the broken glass. It was not life-threatening, just a gash across the meaty part of her left palm, but deep enough to hurt. She felt no pain, probably because she was in a state of shock.

Still holding the shotgun tightly in her right hand, she rose to her feet. Her legs were shaky, but she stumbled toward the door. Fire spread over all four walls, across the ceiling. In seconds she would be enshrouded in a blazing cocoon.

She made it through the door just as the kitchen floor began to crack apart behind her. The porch was badly damaged by the blast, and the roof sagged toward the middle. When she moved off the bottom step, into the yard, one of the corner posts snapped from the strain of dislocation. The porch collapsed in her wake, as if her passage had been sufficient to disturb its delicate balance, and her temporary deafness ended with that crash.

Tommy had been thrown off the sled by the shockwave of the explosion, and he had either rolled or crawled about twenty feet farther from the burning house. He was sprawled in the snow, and the Labrador was attending him solicitously. Meg raced to him, certain he had been hurt, though there was nothing that could have fallen on him, and though he was beyond the reach of the fire. He was all right—frightened, crying, but all right. She said, "It's okay, everything's going to be fine, baby," but she doubted that he could hear her reassurances above the howling of the wind and the roar of the flames that consumed the house.

Hugging him, feeling him alive against her, Meg was relieved and grateful—and furious. Furious with the rats and with the men who had made those gremlins.

She had once thought that her career as an artist was the most important thing in her life. Then for a while, when she and Jim were first married and struggling to build the ad agency into a thriving business, financial success seemed ever so important. But long ago she had realized that the most important thing in life was family, the caring relationships between husbands and wives, parents and children.

Yet in this world beneath heaven and above hell, it seemed that irresistible forces were bent on the destruction of the family; disease and death tore loved ones apart; war, bigotry, and poverty dissolved families in the corrosive acids of violence, hatred, want; and sometimes families brought themselves to ruin through base emotions—envy, jealousy, lust. She had lost Jim, half her family, but she had held on to Tommy and to the house that had harbored the memory of Jim. Now the house had been taken from her by those ratform, manmade gremlins, but she was not going to let them take Tommy, and she was determined to make them pay for what they had already stolen.

She helped Tommy move farther away from the house, well out into the open where the full force of the wind and cold would probably protect him from the rats. Then she set out alone for the barn at the back of the yard.

The rats would be there. She was certain that they had not immolated themselves. They had left the house after tampering with the furnace and setting the trap for her. She knew they would not huddle in the open, which left only the barn. She figured they had constructed a tunnel between the two structures. They must have arrived midafternoon, which gave them time to scout the property and to dig the long, connecting, subterranean passage; they were big, stronger than ordinary rats, so the tunnel would not have been a major project. While she and Tommy had struggled from house to barn to house again, the rats had scampered easily back and forth, through the ground beneath them.

Meg went to the barn not just to blast away at the rats out of a need for vengeance. More important, it was the only place where she and Tommy had a hope of surviving the night. With the cut in her left hand, she was limited to one arm with which to pull the sled. She was also in a mild state of shock, and shock was draining. Previously she had realized that pulling the sled out to Black Oak Road in sixty-mile-an-hour winds and subzero cold, then waiting for perhaps hours until a road crew came by, was a task at the extremity of her endurance; in her current condition, she would not make it, and neither would Tommy. The house was gone, which left only the barn as a shelter, so she would have to take it back from the rats, kill all of them and reclaim her property, if she and her son were to live.

She had no hope that anyone would see the glow of the fire from afar and come inquiring as to the cause. Cascade Farm was relatively isolated, and the cloaking effect of the blizzard would prevent the flames from being seen at much of a distance.

At the open barn door, she hesitated. The lone bulb still burned inside, but the shadows seemed deeper than before. Then, with the wind and the orange light of her burning home at her back, she entered the gremlins' lair.

Ben Parnell discovered that the sloping meadow was cut by a series of natural, angled drainage channels that made progress difficult. In the nearly blinding whirl of snow, the ground was dangerous, for he often realized a ditch lay ahead only when he fell into it. Rapid progress across the field was sure to result in a sprained ankle or broken leg, so he and his three men were forced to maintain a cautious pace, although the sight of the burning house terrified him.

He knew the rats had caused the fire. He did not know how or why they had done it, but the timely eruption of the flames could not be a coincidence. Through his mind throbbed horrible images of the woman and the boy, their rat-gnawed bodies aflame in the middle of the house.

She was scared, though it was an odd kind of fear that did not weaken her but contributed to her strength and determination. A cornered rat would freeze up in panic; but a cornered woman was not always easy prey. It depended on the woman.

Meg walked to the middle of the barn, in front of the Jeep. She looked around at the shadowy stalls along the south wall, at the open loft suspended from the front wall, and at the large, empty, long-unused feed bin in the northeast corner. She sensed that the rats were present and watching her.

They were not going to reveal themselves while she was armed with the shotgun, yet she had to lure them into the open in order to shoot them. They were too smart to be enticed with food. So . . . if she could not lure them, perhaps she could force them into the open with a few well-placed rounds from the 12-gauge.

She walked slowly down the center of the barn, to the end farthest from the door. As she passed the stalls that had once housed livestock, she peered intently into the shadows, seeking the telltale gleam of small red eyes. At least one or two gremlins must be crouched in those pools of darkness.

Although she saw none of the enemy, she began to fire into the stall as she moved again toward the front of the barn: *blam, blam, blam,* three rounds in three of those narrow spaces, a yardlong flare spurting from the muzzle with each hard explosion, the thunderous roar of gunfire echoing off the barn walls. When she fired the third shot, a squealing pair of rats burst from the fourth stall, into the better-lit center section of the barn, sprinting toward the cover offered by the disabled Jeep. She pumped two rounds into them, and both were hit, killed, tossed end over end as if they were balls of rags in a typhoon.

She had emptied the Mossberg. Wincing, she dug in her pockets with her injured hand and extracted the four shells, reloading fast. As she jammed the last of the rounds into the magazine, she heard several high shrieks behind her. She turned. Six large, white rats with misshapen skulls were charging her.

Four of the creatures realized they were not going to reach her fast enough; they peeled off from the pack and disappeared under the car. Unnerved by the swiftness with which the last two closed the gap, she fired twice, decisively eliminating them.

She hurried around the Jeep in time to see the other four scurry out from under the vehicle and across the floor toward the old feed bin. She fired once, twice, as they vanished into the shadows at the base of that big, wooden storage box.

She was out of ammunition. She pumped the Mossberg anyway, as if by that act she could make another shell appear magically in the chamber, but the *clackity-clack* of the gun's action had a distinctly different sound when the magazine was empty.

Either because they knew what that sound meant as well as she did, or because they knew she had been left with only nine rounds—the five in the shotgun and the four they had not managed to steal from the carton in her bedroom closet—the rats that had vanished under the bin now reappeared. Four pale forms slinked into the wan fall of light from the single, dusty bulb overhead.

Meg reversed her hold on the shotgun, gripping it by the barrel, making a club of it. Trying to ignore the pain in her left palm, she raised the gun over her head.

The rats continued to approach slowly . . . then more boldly.

She glanced behind, half expecting to see a dozen other rats encircling her, but evidently there were no more. Just these four. They might as well have numbered a thousand, however, for she knew she would not be able to club more than one of them before they reached her and crawled up her legs. When they were on her, biting and clawing, at her throat and face, she would not be able to deal with even three of them, not with her bare hands.

She glanced at the big open door, but she knew that if she threw the gun down and ran for the safety of the mean winter night, she would not make it before the rats were on her.

As if sensing her terrible vulnerability, the four creatures began to make a queer, keening sound of triumph. They lifted their grotesque, malformed heads and sniffed at the air, lashed their thick tails across the floor, and in unison let out a short shriek more shrill than any that Meg had heard from them before.

Then they streaked toward her.

Though she knew that she could never make the door in time, she had to try. If the rats killed her, Tommy would be helpless out there in the snow, with his broken leg. He would freeze to death by morning . . . if the rats didn't risk the fury of the storm to go after him.

She turned from the advancing pack, dashed toward the exit, and was startled to see a man silhouetted in the fading but still bright glow of the burning house. He was holding a revolver, and he said, "Get out of the way!"

Meg flung herself to one side, and the stranger squeezed off four quick shots. He hit only one of the rats, because they made small targets for a handgun. The remaining three vanished again into the shadows at the base of the feed bin.

The man hurried to Meg, and she saw he wasn't a stranger, after all. He had spoken to her at the roadblock. He was still wearing his sheepskin-lined jacket and snow-crusted tobaggan cap.

"Are you all right, Mrs. Lassiter?"

She ignored his concern and said, "How many of them are there? I killed four, and you killed one, so how many are left?"

"Eight of them escaped."

"So just those three are left?"

"Yes. Hey, your hand's bleeding. Are you sure you're—"

"I think maybe they've got a tunnel between the barn and the house," she said urgently. "And I've got a hunch the opening to it is around the bottom of that feed bin." Speaking through clenched teeth and with a fury that surprised her, she said, "They're foul, an abomination, *monsters,* and I want to finish them, all of them, make them pay for taking my home from me, for threatening Tommy, but how can we get at them if they're down there in the ground?"

He pointed to a large truck that had just pulled into the driveway. "We figured when we found the rats, we might have to go after them in a burrow. So among a lot of other things, we have the necessary equipment to pump gas down in their holes."

"I want them dead," she said, frightened by the purity of the anger in her own voice.

Men were pouring out of the back of the big truck, coming toward the barn. Snow—and wind-born ashes from the collapsing house—slanted through their flashlight beams.

"We'll need the gas," the man in the toboggan cap shouted.

One of the other men answered him.

Shaking with anger and with fear to which she had not dared give herself until now, Meg went outside to find her son.

She and Tommy and Doofus shared the warmth and safety of the truck cab while the men from Biolomech attempted to eradicate the last of the vermin. The boy huddled against her, trembling even after the warm air from the heater had surely chased the chill from his bones. Doofus was blessed with the greater emotional resilience that arose from being a lower animal without a dark imagination, so eventually he slept.

Though they did not think the rats would follow the tunnel back to the ruined house, some of the Biolomech security men established a cordon around the still burning structure, ready to kill any creature that appeared from out of the conflagration. Likewise, a cordon was thrown up around the barn to prevent any escape from that building.

Several times Ben Parnell came to the truck, and Meg put down the window, and he stood on the short running board to report on their progress.

Wearing respirators to protect themselves, they pumped a lethal gas into the mouth of the rats' tunnel, which had indeed been located by the feed bin. "We gave 'em a generous dose," Parnell said during one of his visits. "Enough to saturate a burrow ten times larger than any they've had the time to dig. Now we've got to excavate the tunnel until we find the bodies. Shouldn't be too difficult. They won't have gone deep while boring out a passage between the house and the barn, because going deep wouldn't been wasted effort. So we'll start stripping the surface off the ground, the top few inches, digging backwards from the barn wall, across the yard, sheering the top off the tunnel, you see, until we turn them up."

"And if you don't turn them up?" she asked.

"We will. I'm sure we will."

Meg wanted to hate all of the men, and she especially wanted to hate Parnell because he was in charge of the search and was therefore the only figure of authority on whom she could vent her anger. But speaking harshly to him—and maintaining her rage in the face of his obvious concern for her and Tommy—was difficult, for she realized that these were not the men responsible for the creation of the rats or for letting them escape. This was just the cleanup crew, ordinary citizens, just like all the ordinary citizens who, down through all the centuries, had been called in to clean up when the big shots screwed up. It was the ordinary citizen who always made the world safe for peace by fighting the current war to the end, always the ordinary citizen whose taxes and labors and sacrifices paved the way for those advancements of civilization for which the politicians stole credit.

Furthermore, she was touched by the genuine sympathy and understanding Parnell showed when he learned her husband had died and that she and Tommy were alone. He spoke of loss and loneliness and longing as if he had known his share of them.

"I heard of this woman once," he said rather enigmatically, leaning in the open truck window, "who lost her only daughter to cancer, and she was so crushed by grief that she had to change her entire life, move on to totally new horizons. She couldn't bear to look at her own husband any more, even though he loved her, because they *shared* the experience of their daughter, you see, and every time she looked at him . . . well, she saw her little daughter again, and was reminded again of the girl's suffering. See, that shared experience, that shared tragedy, was like a trap their relationship just couldn't escape. So . . . divorce, a new city, new state . . . that was the only solution for her, drastic as it was. But you seem to've handled grief better than that, Mrs. Lassiter. I know how hard it must've been for you these past couple years, but maybe you can take some heart in the fact that, for certain people who don't have your strength, life can be harder."

At ten minutes past eleven that night, two-thirds of the way across the yard from the barn to the ruined house, they scraped off another couple of feet from the top of the tunnel and found the three dead rats. They put the bodies side by side on the barn floor, next to the other five that had been shot.

Ben Parnell came to the truck. "I thought maybe you'd want to see them—that we've got all eight of them, I mean."

"I would," she said. "Yes. I'll feel safer."

Meg and Tommy got out of the truck.

"Yeah," the boy said, "I want to see them. They thought they trapped us, but it was the other way around." He looked at Meg. "As long as we've got each other, we can get out of any scrape, huh?"

"Bet on it," she said.

Parnell scooped the weary boy in his arms to carry him to the barn.

As the raw wind nipped at Meg, she jammed her hands into her coat pockets. She was relieved. At least for the moment, not all of the burden was hers.

Looking over his shoulder, Tommy said, "You and me, Mom."

"Bet on it," she repeated. And she smiled. She felt as if the door to a cage, of which she'd been only dimly aware, had opened now, giving them access to a new freedom.

John Coyne started his career at the top (*The Legacy*) and has, even more remarkably, managed to stay there, his latest novel (*The Hunting Season*) having been a bona-fide paperback bestseller. Coyne's fiction is filled with people afraid of the dark—the dark all around them but most especially the dark inside them. A good example is the following story.

FLIGHT

John Coyne

My son slept. He slept without moving—without breathing, it seemed—and several times I reached over in the dark front seat of the car to feel for the tiny warm puffs of his breath on my palm. My terrifying fear was that he would die right there and then, on the back roads of Virginia, after everything I had done to steal him from his mother.

It was three A.M., but still he slept. He hadn't even awakened when I leaned over his small crib, wrapped him gently in the wool blanket, and lifted him into my arms. His weight had nearly staggered me, there in the dark house. It wasn't his fifteen pounds, that I knew. It was my fear of taking him from his crib, taking him from his mother.

She could have the house, have everything we owned together, have everything I owned before we were married. But she couldn't have my son. Timmy was mine, now and forever. I had told her so when I walked out of her life.

It might have been different, I guess, if we had had a girl. Lynne had been expecting, planning on a girl. "What do I know about boys?" she had said, once she got pregnant.

A girl would have made everything a lot easier, all the

way around. Women know about girls. I would have been
happy with visiting rights. But a boy belongs with his father.
That's what I think. That's what I told her. Told the judge.
Told everyone. It's only right, whatever the law says. Her
mother called me crazy. And then Lynne wouldn't even let
me see my kid. She said I had no rights, not after what I had
put her through.

Okay. I'll give her that much. I had gone a little crazy after
she sprang it on me. I mean, she thought it was wonderful,
great news, her getting pregnant. She phoned me at work
with the news the same day I was let go from TGRA.

McClintock had just come down to my cubicle and told
me. With the cutbacks in the federal budget, there wouldn't
be any more funding for our solar-energy research. Our task
force was the first to get the federal ax. Bob felt bad about
it, sorry, he said. Sure! But he wasn't out of work. I went a
little wild thinking of where my next job would come from.
Not in Washington, that was for sure, not while the Repub-
licans were in office.

So I was in no mood to learn that Lynne was pregnant. A
few of us went out and tied one on. I admit it. I told the
judge that much. And when I got home, there she was,
grinning and telling me, "Well, Nelson, I guess you weren't
shooting blanks after all."

I swore at her, broke her favorite vase. That sort of thing.
And I'm sorry about it. But that had more to do with getting
the pink slip than her having a kid. I mean, I think I wanted
a kid. We never talked about it, but heck, after six years you
stop thinking of having one, about it being your turn. You get
a little careless when it comes to preventing one. I hadn't
expected it would happen to me. Having a family, I mean.

I glanced at the dashboard clock and saw that I would
have to stop soon. The baby should have been fed at 3:00.
I knew that from the notebook Lynne kept on his feedings. I
had taken that with me, too, slipped it into my belt before
I reached down into the crib and picked him up. When I
lifted him, he turned, like, into my arms. It was as if he

suddenly knew he was being held by his old man.

I held my breath and listened. Lynne was only a dozen feet away, on the other side of the wall. But she was bad when it came to hearing anything. I was the one who always heard Timmy. He'd turn over in his bed and I'd hear him. It didn't matter how tired I was, I was the one who got out of bed and went to him in the middle of the night. After the first few weeks, Lynne said she couldn't. She just couldn't function without a good nine hours of sleep. Poor Timmy, I thought. He must have learned to live with a wet diaper.

Well, those days were over, I told myself. He was with his dad now. For the rest of his life. And I knew how to take care of him.

It had felt wonderful, holding him. I hadn't held him, or seen him, since October. He wasn't even eight weeks old when I left. It was one o'clock and we were all up screaming: the baby, Lynne, me. It was a dumb thing, fighting in the middle of the night, yelling about her going back to work, and how dumpy she looked since having the kid. And she was yelling at me for not getting a job, for feeling sorry for myself and never helping with the baby. "We're going to lose this place, Nelson. Don't you understand? And I'm not going to ask my parents again for the mortgage payment."

I don't know what was wrong with us, but it seemed as if we could only fight late at night. I kept thinking that it must have to do with the building tension up all day, thinking of how hurt and rotten we felt toward each other, and then— wow!—it had to come out, and with us, it was always the middle of the night, feeding Timmy.

I was sitting in the rocker trying to make him take the bottle, but he kept screaming, red in the face, gasping in that helpless way he had, as if he couldn't get his next breath. I kept thinking: he's going to die on me. I worried about that a lot. Lynne wouldn't shut up. She kept talking about the mortgage, about my getting a job. Kept pacing through the baby's room, and talking about what some of the guys had done. "You saw how long it took Logan to find work! He went straight off to Chattanooga and got

hired by TVA. No, don't tell me you can't find anything.
There are plenty of jobs in the paper, but you won't take
anything less than what fits your goddamn qualifications.
Oh, God!" She kept pacing, straightening up the nursery as
she went on ranting. She always tidied things up when she
got mad. It was an obsession.

I just snapped.

I didn't hit her or throw anything. I just took Tim—he was
still screaming—stood, and went to her. She looked up, suddenly frightened, I think, after blaming me for everything, and
she shouted over his noise, "Can't you even feed your child?"

I didn't say anything, I just gave her Timmy. I went back
to our room, dressed, tossed a handful of clothes into my
gym bag, and left the house. I could still hear Timmy crying.
I never heard a kid with such lungs. It made me kinda
proud, hearing him scream.

I know Lynne didn't hear me leave. She even said so. I
drove out the Pike awhile, stopped at an all-night diner, had
something to eat, then called Stan downtown in D.C. and
asked if I could crash for the night.

"What happened?" he asked, trying to pull himself awake.
"Is something wrong?"

"I left my family," I told him. But it wasn't true. I left
Lynne. I didn't leave Timmy. I knew it then, even as I gave
Timmy to Lynne. I would never leave my son. Never. And
now they all know it.

That night, two months later, in the dark kitchen, on the
way out the door with my baby, I stopped at the fridge and
took out the bottles. I can't believe I was that casual. I
mean, it's one thing to sneak back into my house after
leaving my wife, and take my child from his crib, but then to
remember the bottles . . . It made me feel good, knowing I
hadn't panicked. I had to get through the first twenty-four
hours, I told myself. After that I'd know his feeding schedule. I could start my own notebook and know how many
ounces of formula he had taken.

I reached over and touched his thick body and he cried.

He was suddenly awake in the front seat, screaming with hunger. I felt beneath the wool blanket, felt the warm wetness of his stretch pajamas. He needed to be changed. Diapers I had. I had stopped at Toys R Us on Rockville Pike and filled the trunk with Huggies, plastic baby bottles, cans of Enfamil, a traveling crib, some toys. I had already stopped at a drug store for Tylenol, wipes, Desitin, cotton balls, everything Lynne had had neatly arranged on the shelf over Timmy's changing table.

I paid it all with our Mastercard. That was it for the card, I knew. I had reached the credit limit, and once Lynne and the police realized what I was using to finance my escape, they'd have every cop in the Middle Atlantic states looking for that number.

From now on it was cash only, and no expressways with tolls. I had to keep to the back roads, and I had to keep moving, at least until I got to North Carolina. In the mountains, I'd be okay. In Blowing Rock, I could stop worrying about Lynne catching up to me. Stop worrying about the police.

I wasn't too worried about the cops. Lynne wouldn't be smart about that. She'll tell them I had taken Timmy. That would do it. A family matter, something for the divorce courts. The cops had more to worry about than some father taking his son. Besides, they were men. They'd understand. The kid was in no danger, not if he was with his father.

Kramer vs. Kramer proved that. And *Ordinary People*. It was the fathers in those movies who hung in there when the going got tough; the fathers who took care of their sons while the mother split. It's all a lot of nonsense that mothers make the best parents. I told the judge that in family court. But I knew I didn't have a chance, not when I saw the judge was a woman. Forget it. There'd be no appeal. No throwing good money after bad. The odds were stacked against me. I didn't have a chance at custody after that judge heard I had hit Lynne.

Let them find me. Even with back roads, and stopping to feed Timmy, I'd be two hundred miles from Rockville by daybreak. By evening, I'd be hidden away in the Great

Smokeys. Hidden away in one of those hollows that don't even appear on maps.

The car hit a bump and the baby screamed, flared his arms, his tight little fists.

"Okay, son, I hear you. I hear you," I said gently as I eased off the gas and with one hand reached forward and searched through my gym bag for the bottles. I could change him later, once I had a place to park. But I didn't want to stop here, on the side of the road, in the middle of nowhere. It would just be inviting trouble. I realized it was almost as if men, even fathers, were suspect if they were caught alone with an infant.

The last sign said Warrenton was ten miles ahead. I could stop in town and buy gas. A full tank would take me into the North Carolina mountains.

"When you're older, Timmy, we'll go fishing in these mountains. And white-water rafting. How'd you like that?" I kept talking over his screams.

The bottle was cold and I wondered if Lynne was still warming them up first. I remembered those first weeks, getting up every two hours, rushing into the kitchen to get a bottle out of the fridge, then heating it while the baby kept screaming. We'd both gotten up those first weeks. We had a little routine between us, and even with us both half asleep, she'd get him changed while I warmed the bottle. Then Lynne would sit in the rocker with the baby and feed him. She'd always test the milk first against her wrist, as if she didn't believe me when I told her the formula wasn't too hot. She never totally trusted me with the baby. That was just another one of our problems.

And I'd stand there watching them, like some sort of intruder. It didn't seem he was alive at all, not those first weeks. I kept thinking: where did he come from? It was as if he was really ET.

"Okay, son, here we go." I kept one hand on the steering wheel as I slipped the bottle nipple into his mouth. He began to choke at once, formula spilling from his mouth. "Oh, God!" I hit the brake and bounced the car off the country road and onto the grassy apron, skidding to a stop. I was holding Timmy down with one hand. His tiny body was trembling beneath my palm as he screamed.

I slid over to the passenger side, lifting him up. "Please, sweetheart, be still. Shhh." I pulled him in a tight embrace. He was hungry and cold. No wonder he was screaming. "I'm sorry, Timmy. I'm sorry. But everything will be okay soon. I'll have you safe and sound again."

I set him down on the seat beside me and stripped off the blankets, the stretchy, and his diaper. I flipped on the reading light and worked fast, as if he were a small bomb ready to explode, and stripped him naked. His face was scarlet and twisted as if in pain. I knew he didn't know who I was. I had read how babies know their parents by their smell and touch. I had been gone half of his life, over two months. Who did he think I was? Would he remember any of this? Our midnight escape?

I kept wispering to him, bent down over his tiny, trembling body as I taped on the Huggies. I never heard the county cop until he tapped his flashlight on the car window and then shone it in my face as if I were some sort of pervert.

I hadn't locked the door; when he spotted the naked baby, he jerked open the door and shoved his service revolver in my face.

"What the fuck are you doing?" he shouted at me.

Timmy screamed and I picked him up, and said softly, to answer the cop without upsetting the baby more, "He's mine. My son."

"What are you doing?" he asked again, but lowered his voice. Now he wasn't sure what to do.

Before he could say more, I went on quickly. "I'm simply changing his diaper," I whispered. I told him that the baby had wakened, I had to change him, give him a bottle. "Do you have children, officer?" I asked nicely.

The man nodded, still staring at Timmy. I had gone back to diapering the baby, as if to show the cop I knew what I was doing.

"Well, you know how it is when they need to be fed. He's only four months old. My wife . . ."

"Where's she?" the cop said quickly, seizing on her absence. He was a big Southern boy, with the sharp, clean features of a kid.

I stopped diapering, held a tube of Desitin in one hand, and looked up at him. "She died. In childbirth. It was a C-section, and there were complications. The baby was early—it was our first—and Sue, my wife . . ." I looked away.

"Oh, man," the cop said. The breath went out of him. "That's tough, you know . . ." He stopped, not knowing what more to say. I knew I was safe then. Lynne hadn't gotten to the police, no alarm had been issued for my arrest, the missing child. I suddenly thought she probably didn't even know Timmy was gone. I felt bad then, imagining her coming into the dark baby's room and seeing the empty crib. Timmy and his blanket gone. She'd go wild at first, not realizing what had happened. Only when she thought about if for a moment would she know it was me and not some crazy nut.

"You take care now," the cop spoke up, backing off. He had snapped off his flashlight, and was embarrassed by his intrusion, my story. "I mean, there's not anything I can do for you, is there?"

"No, officer. Thank you." I had Timmy changed and was wrapping him up again in his blue blanket. I slipped my hands beneath his head and body and lifted my sleeping son to my chest.

It was the only evidence this cop needed, seeing the sleeping child snuggled against me. He tipped his cap and hurried to his car. I waved, kept being friendly, and wondered what he'd think when he heard a baby boy was missing in Rockville, Maryland.

He'd know it was me, that there had been no mother lost in childbirth. I felt a small satisfaction at how easily the story had come to me. I began thinking I could get away with it. It was just that the notion of taking Timmy from Lynne was more frightening than the fact of it was. The baby was fine with me.

And then he threw up again.

The formula gushed out in a milky flow, wet his clothes and the blue blanket, and soaked my shirt.

"Dammit, Timmy!" My voice startled me on the empty back road. "Okay! Okay!" I kept talking, reassuring myself, trying to quiet the baby. He was screaming, frightened by me and the cold wind that was shaking the car. And he was hungry, I knew.

I had to get off this road. I had to get going. At home, Lynne would be waking, wondering why the baby wasn't crying. She would be going to his room right about now, glancing at my watch. I could almost hear her cries of alarm.

I tried to force the bottle into Timmy's mouth. If he got the taste of the formula he would drink again. I knew that from the first month of his life. But now he turned his head away, his little body squirming in my arms.

"All right! All right!" I shouted. "Take the goddamn bottle!" My nerves were shot, I couldn't keep going like this. I was exhausted. And it was doing no good screaming at Timmy.

I slid back into the car, strapped Timmy into the baby seat, then ran around the car and got in behind the wheel. Timmy kept screaming, his cries bouncing off the interior. I couldn't hear myself think.

On the road again, I raced the car as if I was trying to speed away from his screaming. I had forgotten how loud it was, how insistent. I hadn't lived at home for two months. I hadn't had to get up every night at his waking. I had forgotten what it was like.

Still racing the car, I gave Timmy the bottle again, but this time he reached up with his tiny hand and knocked it away. It was involuntary, I know, but I smiled, pleased at his anger.

"That's a boy, Timmy, you don't let anyone push you around. You're my boy, okay. No one fucks with you."

That was part of Lynne's and my problem. Our personalities. Our stubbornness. We had gotten married late, both of us over thirty. And even then we didn't know each other. It would have been better if we had lived together for a while, gotten to see if we could get along.

It was a crazy time right after Lynne came home with the baby. Lynne was sick and crying a lot, and I couldn't get a job. Any couple, I guess, would start thinking of splitting. But it was worse with us. We didn't have any reserve of good will, you see, between us. Things started getting bad as soon as Lynne learned she was pregnant, and then she was always sick. She told me she would have quit her job at the Office of Education if I had been working. She held that against me, my getting fired.

Timmy stopped crying, as if the life had gone out of him. My heart seized up and I let the car coast to a stop as I leaned over in the seat. He had fallen asleep again, exhausted from crying. It wouldn't last long, not without a bottle. The poor kid. I had to get something into him.

I stepped on the gas. Warrenton was ahead. I could see the light of a gas station at the intersection. I'd fill up there, I thought, and park, get Timmy to take a bottle. When I left home, he was only taking four ounces, but now, I saw, Lynne was using eight-ounce bottles. When did that happen? I wondered.

That's what drove me crazy. Every day he was changing on me, and I was cut out of his life.

Well, not any more.

He started crying again when I pulled up to the station. It was deserted. I could see a man, a kid really, inside the office. He looked up, but didn't move from behind the desk.

This had to be quick, I told myself. I didn't need more people seeing Timmy, remembering my car. I jumped out and pulled the gas nozzle from the pump and filled the tank while I watched Timmy in the front seat. He was still crying, struggling to get free of the car seat.

I was torturing my son, putting him through all this. I hated to have him crying. I just couldn't stand it, seeing him suffer.

"He's all right, Warren! He's all right!" Lynne would yell at me when I complained.

"He's not okay if he's crying," I'd shout back. And I was right. But what drove me nuts was that neither one of us knew how to shut him up, once he started. I got into a pattern, first his diaper, then a bottle. I'd try to get him to sleep, rock him in the chair. Still he cried. For a while I thought it was that his T-shirts were too small for him.

I topped off the tank then walked over to the station office to pay.

When I pushed open the door I could hear the CB radio. The kid had it tuned to the highway patrol. The radio crackled with static.

"Morning," the attendant said. He was wearing a John Deere cap that he pushed up on his head when he reached for my cash.

I nodded and held my breath as I listened to the police band. They were putting out an alert for my arrest.

"That's eleven twenty," the kid said, not picking up on the state alert.

WHITE BLOND MALE, AGE 37, HEIGHT 6'1". GLASSES. DRIVING A WHITE '85 PONTIAC. TRAVELING WITH A FIVE-MONTH-OLD BABY BOY. CONSIDERED DANGEROUS. HOLD FOR QUESTIONING. WANTED IN MARYLAND FOR KIDNAPPING.

Considered dangerous! What in the world had Lynne told the cops?

"Looks like snow. Get a morning sky like that out west and it means snow before night," the kid said, handing me change for the twenty. My fingers were trembling. "Cold, ain't it?" the kid grinned.

I nodded, stuffed the money into my pocket, and headed out. If I could get away in time, I kept telling myself, I'd be okay. They won't get me; I'd keep away from gas stations, main highways. I wasn't but five hours from the mountains of North Carolina. Once up on the Blue Ridge, I knew I'd be okay.

"Where are you heading?" the kid called after me. He had come to the office door.

"South," I said, backing away and smiling. I didn't want him to suddenly think I was behaving oddly.

"Keep out of the hills, then. Storm coming."

"I'll do that."

I was in the car and out of the station while he still stood inside the office door, watching me leave. The highway patrol bulletin hadn't meant anything to him.

I headed west out of Warrenton, toward Amissville and Sperryville, where I knew I could get up on the Skyline Drive. It would be slower, but it would take me into North Carolina and keep me away from Route 81 into Bristol. Up on the Blue Ridge, I'd be less likely to be spotted by the cops.

In the seat, Timmy had fallen asleep. Still driving, I reached around and pulled the blanket up to his chin. He didn't move.

I kept glancing back at him as I drove. Now I wished I had left him strapped down next to me in the front seat so I could watch him. I couldn't look at him enough, couldn't get enough of him. All I had were the photos from his infancy. He had changed so much in two months. It was almost like a different child. But he was still mine, all mine.

On the long stretch of empty highway, I pressed down on the pedal and raced for the hills. The sun was up. I made out the outline of the ridge, the bank of snow clouds. The kid was right, I thought. There would be snow today. But that was okay. Better for me. The cops would have more to worry about than me if it snowed.

It began snowing when I went through Sperryville. Very light, blowing snow that whipped around the car. I kept my headlights on because even with dawn, it wasn't much brighter. I felt the wind buffeting the car and I slowed some as I climbed toward the Skyline Drive. The road was narrower and twisting as I climbed, and the rocking motion woke Timmy, frightening him again. He woke crying.

I pulled the car off onto the shoulder and stopped.

"Okay, sweetheart. Everything is okay."

He began to sob, rubbing his tiny fists into his eyes, then he fell back into the warmth of his blanket and kicked out in wild rage.

I reached over the back seat and lifted him into my lap. He was flailing at me with his small arms, banging his fists against my face and chest as he raged. Lynne had done this, I kept telling myself. If she had let Timmy have a relationship with his father, this would never have happened. He wouldn't be treating me like a stranger, a kidnapper.

I kept whispering to Timmy, holding him tight, and gradually, more from exhaustion than anything else, he calmed down, though he kept weeping. I set him on my lap and smiled at him. "All right, Timmy. You're all right." He leaned forward, as if to fill his vision and his whole world with my face.

He studied me a moment, tilted his head. It was Lynne's gesture, whenever she was being thoughtful. I suddenly thought: would I be always seeing my ex-wife in my son's face?

Timmy turned his head away and stared out the front window, lost in the secret world of children. Then he grinned and raised his hand, as if to point.

I looked up myself at the thick, wet snow blowing across the road. Already there was a white film covering the road surface.

"Yes, snow, Timmy." I tried to sound pleased, but the snow, I saw at once, would make it tough going, especially up on the Blue Ridge. Well, I told myself, there was no turning back.

He kept pointing, but he couldn't quite point; his tiny fingers curled up on him and went astray. I found that I had to pull my attention away from him. I wanted only to watch him, as if he were something totally unique, a creature from another planet.

"We have to go ahead, Timmy," I said, stirring myself, happy now that he was awake. I moved Timmy off my lap

and strapped him into the seat. "Here, how 'bout a cookie?"
I smiled, pleased to give him something.

I was happy to feed him. It was a treat, just being able to
feed him. I reached into the bag and pulled out a cookie.
His blue eyes sparkled as he grabbed for it. He could have a
dirty face the rest of his life, as far as I was concerned.

I pulled the car back onto the access road and started up
again toward the Skyline Drive. The car skidded at once on
the new snow, fishtailing as I pressed on the gas. It was
going to be a long trip and I was suddenly afraid. It wasn't
the weather that I minded, but Timmy. How would he
handle being kept strapped into the chair all day? I was
afraid to let him loose in the back seat, where I couldn't
reach him.

I had reached the mountain drive in twenty minutes. The
weather was suddenly bright and clear. I had passed through
the clouds, gone above the snow, as you do in a plane. It
was pretty and bright, and I smiled at Timmy, immensely
happy to be with my son and on the road, all alone with
him, after all this time.

"It's going to get better," I told him, "once you're older,
and have things to say. Right?" I kept grinning.

He stared at me, his round pink face smeared with the
chocolate.

I reached for the bag and fed him another. "You can have
one every day of your life, how's that? We both will. Okay?"
I laughed at my silliness. I wasn't making any sense, but it
didn't matter. Timmy didn't understand what I was saying. I
was just happy he wasn't crying. He had forgotten his
mother, I decided, feeling better about that too. He had
forgotten all about her. I pressed down on the accelerator.
Yet he kept turning his head, trying to look around, as if he
expected to see her in the back seat. Well, what could I
expect? She had been with him every day of his life. He
didn't know better.

And then he cried.

"Jesus Christ, Timmy!" I shouted and immediately felt

like shit. Goddamn, I thought, why am I yelling at Timmy? It wasn't his fault. What did he know?

I kept glancing over at him, marveling that he was even alive, marveling that I had him with me, all alone. There we were inside the warm car, driving up into the Blue Ridge. I got out the bottle again and gave it to him, and this time, thank God, he took it, sucked hungrily though it was cold. I took a deep breath.

It was now quiet in the car. Timmy had the bottle in his tiny fists and I was helping him, steadying it. I could only hear the slapping of the windshield wipers and the sound of the heater blowing air against my legs, against Timmy's face. The world outside was silent and white. I had driven into more clouds and all there was to my world was the inside of the car. I felt safe and warm.

I could see just the thin sliver of the dividing line, nothing else. I liked being lost inside this white world. I wished Timmy and I could live in it forever. I slowed. The snow was coming down heavier and I flipped up the speed of the wipers, let the rubber flip wildly back and forth across the wet glass. This was crazy, I told myself, driving on this mountan road. I grinned and whispered, "Crazy like a fox, right, Timmy?"

I glanced at my son. He had fallen asleep. The rubber nipple had slipped from his pink mouth, leaving a bubble of formula on his pulsed lips. He slept like a toy doll, his tiny hands poised in the air, his eyes closed tight in a round, soft face.

The car skidded. I spun the wheel against the turning and brought it back under control, stalling it.

"Shit," I whispered, dropping my head against the steering wheel. I could feel my body give way, feel the tiredness of my bones and muscles. I hadn't slept all night, and now I couldn't stop, not until I reached North Carolina. I'd get a motel room then, someplace cheap and out of the way where they wouldn't ask a lot of questions about me and the baby.

I turned the engine over and touched the gas. The car

skidded and went sideways on the steep incline. I gunned the engine and the wheels squealed, then caught on gravel, and the Pontiac jumped forward, fishtailing on the hillside. I kept the gas pedal against the floor, kept hunched forward in the seat, kept my hands squeezed on the wheel, and nursed the car forward, through the sheets of blinding snow, up and around the Skyline Drive turn.

We came out of the fog of snow clouds, higher on the ridge. I saw into a valley. There were houses in the distance and lighted windows. I dropped back into the seat and kept driving.

When I looked over again at Timmy he was awake and watching me.

"Hi, darling," I said, smiling, blowing him a kiss. He kept watching me, as if he were seeing me for the first time.

"We're going to make it now," I told him, feeling confident. This was the only way to escape, I told myself. Only a goddamn fool would be driving up on the ridge. I passed an exit with a road sign for Elkton, and another said that the Skyline Drive was closed for winter. I drove on, kept going up on the ridge. It was suddenly bright and shiny again. The clouds lay below me like endless pillows, stretching to the horizon.

"This will be a piece of cake," I told Timmy, grinning at him.

Timmy had closed his eyes.

"Sleep, sweetie," I whispered, "please sleep."

He never needed sleep when he was first born. Some babies are like that, Lynne's doctor had told her. But that wasn't it. It was Lynne's fault that Timmy didn't get enough sleep. She was a bad mother, that was all. I'm sorry now I never told her that. She was always the one after me, lecturing about how to do this, do that. She didn't even think I knew how to diaper the kid.

But now I knew her game. She was afraid I knew too much, more than her. I was the goddamn natural parent, not her. What she knew, she learned in books, or talking on the phone. She was always calling the pediatrician. She couldn't make a decision about Timmy until the doctor said okay. It cost me a fortune.

"No more, doctor, right, Timmy?" I glanced at my son. In the bright morning light above the clouds, his face glowed. He looked like an angel, one of those cherubs you see on Christmas cards.

When I looked out the front window again, I could see the storm clouds. They had come over the mountains beyond Shenandoah Park. The storm was rising out of the southwest and it wasn't like the pillowy cloud below me in the valley. This one was massive and black, and ugly. It consumed the mountaintop, came tumbling over like it was the hand of God. I could see ahead to where the snowy Skyline Drive turned and disappeared into the enormous blackness. The cloud was moving fast, like a black racehorse, and bearing down on me. "Shit," I said out loud, and then, to Timmy, "It looks like trouble, right?" I was trying to pump myself up. Since leaving Lynne, since I started to live in the motel in Washington on New York Avenue, that's the way I was. Always jabbering to myself, answering myself back, as if I were some sort of never-ending talk show.

There was something suddenly in Timmy's mouth. He had moved, and there it was. Not much. It had bubbled up like that trace of formula. But it wasn't formula. It felt sticky, and yellow, like a dab of paint, at the corner of his lips. It stood out against his soft pink face, his dark eyelashes.

My heart shot through the roof of my mouth. "Oh, God, no!" I screamed, and forgot where I was, what I was doing, and reached for him. The car went into a great slow slide. I had Timmy in my hands, had him squeezed between my fingers, and I knew even as I was doing that, that I should be watching the road, getting the Pontiac parked. I looked again and I saw the Drive, saw the menacing cloud approaching, and saw, too, that I was looking out the side window. The car was spinning, picking up speed. I grabbed at the wheel, with Timmy in my grasp, and then the little baby vomited into my face.

And he kept vomiting up this yellow shit. It kept coming

from deep inside his little body, and I thought at once: he is going to die. He's going to die in my arms.

The car hit the guard rail and bounced off, then spun a half turn and hit the low rail a second time, and this time the weight and speed were enough to break through, and the car tumbled over onto itself.

It was all happening so slowly. I could have filmed it in my mind. I saw everything, all my efforts to save Timmy, how I clung to his little body; and the car's movement, how the machine tumbled through the snowy embankment. The car had a life of its own; its own destiny.

I held onto the steering wheel with one hand, vainly tried to steer, to pull the machine under my control, but we were in space, floating off, disappearing into the white billowing clouds that spread across the wide valley.

"Timmy," I heard myself shouting, "Timmy, I love you."

I was cold and Timmy was silent. He lay against my chest and on top of me. We were squeezed together, trapped in the wreckage of the Pontiac. The windshield was broken. Snow fell into my face. I could taste the water, taste my own blood. Or was it Timmy's blood?

"Timmy?" I whispered, struggling to move, to free myself. My son lay against me like a broken doll. "Timmy!" I shouted, trying to wake him, and then he did scream into my face, and I started to weep for joy at the sound of his voice. I would never again be angered by his crying, I promised myself.

I got my one hand free and reached up and had hold of the back seat. It was above us, and both of us were jammed beneath the dashboard. My head was caught between the brake and accelerator.

Shit, I said. I was going to live now, I knew. I could feel my body hurting.

I could move, I realized, with great effort and great pain, but not while I had hold of Timmy. And there was no place to put the baby. The front seats had slammed down over us, like a makeshift tent. I raised one arm and pushed up against the cushiony seat, but the little effort left me dizzy, and I dropped my head back into the tight space between the pedals.

Timmy had stopped crying. His eyes were open and he was watching me. We would die like this, I suddenly thought. He would die in my arms, watching me, waiting for his father to save him.

"We're going to be okay, Timmy. I promise," I told him, and tried to move the edge of his blanket up and across his face. Trapped as we were, we weren't protected from the heavy snow. Flakes landed on his face and clung to his cheek like cake icing. Why didn't the snow melt, I thought to myself, and then I whispered, "Help." My breath fogged in my face. I knew what was coming next. My body temperature would drop, I'd begin to shiver, and then at some point I'd simply drop off to sleep and never wake. Timmy would die first, I guessed. There was so little to him, and he'd freeze once he wet himself, once he cried himself into exhaustion.

Now he just stared at me. He had developed his mother's look, I saw for the first time. The same sort of quizzical gaze, as if he thought I was somehow putting him on. I had once thought it was Lynne's most endearing expression. I looked away from him, and shouted help, and when I did, Timmy cried, startled by my voice.

I reached up and managed to touch the car horn. I hit it once and the simple, clear blast of sound was loud inside my ears, but how far, I wondered, would the noise carry in the snowy woods? I kept hitting the horn until I could no longer hold up my arm, and then I slumped down further and hugged my son to my chest. He had fallen asleep, and I had the sudden, terrifying feeling that he would never wake up.

"Timmy! No!" I said shaking his tiny body.

He woke crying and I smothered his tiny face with kisses. Already, I could feel his body losing warmth. He would be shivering in a few minutes, crying from pain, and then he'd fall asleep and I wouldn't be able to save him.

I started swearing then, screaming into the fog and snow, and once more I fought with the jammed seat, until it exhausted me and I slumped down again, still trapped between the brake and gas pedal.

I closed my eyes and started to pray, wild and disjointed words of prayer, as I begged for God's help. It wasn't my fault, I told God. I only wanted my little boy. He was mine, not just his mother's. She had taken him away from me, and it wasn't my fault. What had I done wrong? I was crying hysterically, sobbing into Timmy's blue blanket. I didn't even hear the old man. Perhaps the deep snow muffled his footsteps, I don't know, but when I looked up he was there, staring down through the broken front window, his beard and eyebrows thick with snow, his breath fogging in his face. But I could see his eyes, blue, bright, and sparkling, and he was smiling.

Thank God, I thought, Timmy has been saved, and the breath went out of me. I began crying, like a child.

"The baby," he said, and for a moment I didn't understand what he meant, but he reached down through the broken glass and seized Timmy. "Give me the child," he told me, and I did, realizing that Timmy was safe now, and so was I.

When I had time again to think and sort out what had happened, I was in the old man's cabin, wearing his clothes and with a blanket wrapped about me. I was sitting before the cast-iron stove and I had Timmy in my arms. He was changed and wrapped up, too, in a quilt, and I was telling the old man that he had saved our lives.

He waved away my thanks and kept fiddling with the stove, making coffee for me, heating up a bottle of milk for Timmy.

"I heard the crash, you know, but wasn't sure," he said, and then he said something else, but I didn't catch all of it. He was an old man used to talking to himself, I guessed, and in the mountains of western Virginia the old-timers spoke with their distinctive accent. I'd get used to it in time, I knew.

"Here now, feed the lad," he told me, shuffling over to me with the warm bottle of milk.

The old man shuffled off again, went back to the stove and poured two cups of coffee into tin mugs. I glanced around the cabin. It was nothing more than a small room, with a makeshift bed, made, I saw, of crude lumber, and a few pieces of handmade furniture. The table was pine, as was the clothes chest. There were no closets. He had his few pieces of clothes hanging from wood pegs on the wall and behind the door. There was real poverty here, I thought.

"You farm?" I asked the old man, raising my voice so he'd hear me, even if it was a small, tight room.

"I do a bit of everything," he said, returning from the stove with the cups of coffee and sitting down. He needed to pull over a wooden box and make use of that. I had the rocker, his chair. "A man my age, you learn to do what you can do." He sipped his hot coffee, smiled.

I liked his smile. Even with his full gray beard it managed to light up his face and give off warmth. For the first time since taking Timmy from his crib, I felt safe.

"Have you lived here long?" I asked, wanting to talk, needing to talk. I felt as if I had been pulled back from the edge of death, gained another life.

The old man nodded, staring into the red glow of the stove window. "A long time," he said, "some say too long." Then he glanced over at me, shifted just his bright blue eyes and asked, "Where you all going with the little one?"

"South," I answered abruptly, immediately wary, and then to soften my reply, I added, "Home to his mother. We live in Georgia.

"Visiting relatives," I said next, still lying. It was getting so easy to live this fictional life. I now felt as if I had a whole new existence, that Timmy and I were creatures of our own, without history, and what lay ahead for us was just blank pages in our own book.

"Well, you better figure you'll spend a few days here," he

said, nodding toward the window and the blowing snow. "It'll be two, three days before the county clears the Skyline. Come 'morrow we'll see about getting your vehicle out that ditch. I've got a tractor out back. Don't have no phone. Can't call the missus, I'm afraid."

"That's okay," I told him. I was thankful he didn't have a phone, nor a radio or television, not that I could see, anyway. It was better this way, the perfect hiding spot. Like hiding in the open. Again, I was silently thankful for my good luck.

"I think you and the little one should sleep in there," he said next, pulling himself up and motioning behind him.

I turned away from the stove and noticed, beside the hanging clothes, a small door, crudely cut into the side wall. There was, after all, an extra room.

"I don't want to put you out," I told the old man.

"No trouble. No trouble at all. Don't use the room myself. It was for the kid, when my wife was living."

"Oh, you've had a family?" I said, pleased that we had something in common.

"Yes," he said, quietly, then added, as if for explanation, "once."

He went ahead of me, pushing open the door, flipping on lights, and showing me the extra room, built sometime after the cabin itself, I could see.

"It's a boy's room," I said, surprised by the small, neatly kept addition. There was a child's bed, made of brass, and made up with sheets and a quilt. The walls had a pinned-up poster of Superman, black-and-white photos of cowboy movie stars, and World War II posters of Eisenhower and MacArthur. On the shelves of a bookcase were model airplanes, Tinker-toys, dozens of tiny cars, and old-fashioned mechanical toys. It was a child's room from the forties.

"Your son's room?" I asked.

The old man nodded, and stepped aside. "Your baby will be fine here," he said, not looking into the room, and I realized that it pained him.

"Your son is dead?" I asked softly.

He shook his head, and this time, he did permit himself to glance inside, to look at the tiny bed, all the toys. There was a flash of tears in his eyes and he said simply, "His mother took him. It was back aways." And then, catching himself from saying more, he showed me where there were towels, a basin. "I'll heat up some water. You'll want to wash him," he nodded to Timmy, who, like a forgotten angel, slept on in the cradle of my arm.

The old man had gone to the ditch and brought in what he could from the back seat of the car: my jacket, and the bag of baby stuff, the wipes, Desitin, and diapers. I lay Timmy gently on the bed, took off his blue stretchy as he slept, and changed his diaper. There was yellow shit in his diapers. He was sick, I thought. Something was wrong with him, but I couldn't focus on it. I didn't want to know. I was afraid in my heart that I really couldn't take care of him. That I wasn't ready to be his real Dad, not any more.

When I had cleaned and changed Timmy, I arranged him in the bed so he couldn't roll off, then took the diaper back with me to the other room. The old man was sitting again by the stove fire, and had poured himself another cup of black coffee.

"Are you a drinking man?" he asked.

"Yes, I could use a drink."

"I have scotch wiskey, that's all."

"Scotch is perfect."

I threw away the dirty diaper and, accepting his drink, sat down with him by the stove, neither of us speaking for the moment. I was thinking of Lynne, wondering what she was doing, who she might be calling. The edge of my anger had gone, I realized, and I was feeling some guilt, like giant whitecap waves.

"You got yourself a fine boy, Nelson," the old man announced.

I sat forward, startled by him saying my name, and said at once, "You know who I am?"

"Heard it a while back, on the CB." He didn't look at

me. He seemed embarrassed, knowing my identify. Then
added, to make his point, "You're safe here with me."

"Where's your CB?" I wanted to know.

He reached out and flipped up the blanket that covered a
small table and there, shiny and black, was a small CB, and
as if to prove he had information on me, he flipped on the
switch. Between bursts of static were police calls and highway accident reports.

"Shit," I said.

"You're safe here," he said again, glancing at me, making
his point.

In the soft light of the stove, he didn't seem so much the
grandfatherly type. I could see how well built he was under
his flannel shirt, in his old trousers.

"What are you saying?"

The old man shrugged, "Nothing much. They say you
took your kid. You're wanted in Maryland." Again he gestured toward the outside, the blowing snow. "They'll never
find you here, not for a while, not with two feet of new
snow," and then as he sipped the scotch, he added, "not if
you want."

Old codgers like him are cagey, I knew. They didn't
survive so long in the mountains of Virginia without knowing how to read a man.

"What do you want?" I finally asked.

"When my wife, she took my boy, I should have gone
after her, you know, gotten him back, but I didn't. You
know why?" He glanced my way, raising his thick eyebrows.
The skin around his eyes was tight and wrinkled.

I didn't reply. I let him tell his own story, because he was
a man who lived alone, and I could tell he liked to talk to
himself.

"I didn't go for him because I wasn't right in the head,
that's why. They kept taking me away, you know, over to
Lynchburg. They had a place there for the likes of my
kind."

"Your kind?" I could feel my fear. It started way off, in
the tips of my fingers, in my toes, and was sweeping through

me as I sat still there beside the old man, trapped as I felt now, inside his snowbound cabin.

"I was only a lad myself when I went to war, over there in Europe, the Second World War, it was." He shook his head. "I ain't been right since," he said, almost apologizing. And then he grinned.

His smile gave away the truth of the man. It was a loony smile, lopsided and warped, as if he had suffered electric shock, over there in Lynchburg, a few too many times.

"Jesus Christ," I swore out loud, and all my strength went out of me.

"And they killed him, too," the old man said, and then he giggled.

I realized now how he had held it together, kept himself under control for a few hours, until I was safely settled, locked up inside his isolated farmhouse.

"Hey," I said, talking fast, "what gives? You want some money, or what?" I leaned foward, as if to prove I wouldn't harm him, that I didn't want anything myself except for maybe a night's rest. In the morning I could be off. I'd walk to North Carolina if I had to.

"Arthur Lee was my boy's name. He and his mother, you know, they didn't have to run off like that, middle of the goddamn night, leaving me pissed in the head, sick and all. Oh, it ain't the boy's fault. He loved me, that one. The mother, though, she was one of those McGraffs, came from Scotland, and I swear to God there wasn't a good one among them. I buried two myself out back. Goddamn trespassers coming onto my land.

"And you!" He had his fist up and then he was pointing his finger at me. "You come driving out here in the middle of the winter, no one in his right mind would be up on Skyline Drive this time of year, storm coming and all." He nodded his head. "I know why you're coming. Can't fool me, even with that kid of yours. I know. I saw."

"What? You saw what?" I was still leaning forward, trying to catch what the old man was saying. He was speaking to himself now, rambling on, like another homeless crazy living on a bench in Union Station, downtown in Washington. "Electrodes!" he said, shouting at me, and he pointed to his nose. "They put those electrodes in my nose over there in Lynchburg. I cut them, once I come home again." He raised his left hand and showed me two of his fingers that were curled up tight. "Electrodes did this, years ago."

"Say, sir, I don't know anything about this," I whispered.

"Course you know. You work for the government, don't you?" He glared at me.

He had been through my wallet, I realized.

"I was a consultant, yes, but I didn't have anything to do with electrodes, or—"

"They put this electrode in my nose," he went on, "put it into me, all kinds of poor people to cause us pain, give us illness. You know what it did to Billy Wright?" He turned on me, and those blue eyes bulged in his bearded face. He looked like Santa Claus gone mad.

"Those electrodes just blew him apart. He was out there, this side of Slide Mountain, putting in his spring corn, and he just blew apart. Never did find all of him. Did it by radio. A plane was flying over. I saw it." He tore off the heavy rug that covered his CB. "You know why I keep it covered? It hears! It listens! They know." Then he tossed the rug over the box and sat back in the rocker. He was breathing fast now; he had frightened himself with his talk.

I would keep calm, I told myself. I would agree with him. I would do anything I had to until morning, until I had a chance to get away with Timmy.

"You may be right," I said calmly.

"You're damn right I am!" He shook his fist, stared fiercely ahead, and for a moment was locked up with his own demons.

Why was everything going wrong, I asked myself. I couldn't even kidnap my own kid. The storm. Now this. I should have stayed in the valley, taken my chances on the interstate.

"I know why you're here," he said at last. "I know why

they sent you." He wasn't looking at me, but was instead watching the bedroom door.

"Why?" I asked, holding my breath. I knew I couldn't convince him otherwise, whatever he believed.

"You've come to get me, haven't you? Ain't enough that you killed my only friend, now you want me, don't you?" He kept watching the bedroom, looking into the dark room where Timmy was sound asleep.

I kept nodding, not fully comprehending.

"We got to get rid of him," he whispered, leaning closer.

"What?" I asked, still not understanding what he meant.

He jerked his head toward the little bedroom. "Him!" he said.

"Hey, what are you talking about?" I stood up and he was on his feet at once, moving faster than I would have imagined.

"He's sending radio signals back to Washington. They'll be here with their SWAT team. I've read about them."

I was sweating now, and felt the perspiration under my arms and down my chest.

"Hey, wait, old man! What are you talking about?"

"This!" He was pointing to his nose. "In '42 they put that in my nose. A tiny electrode. I didn't know it then. Over there in Lynchburg, they slipped it into my nose, beneath the skin, you see, and since then, every time they want, they throw a switch, or something, and it goes click, click-click and it tortures me. I get pains in my chest, my muscles jerk. I itch all over my body." He was shaking his head, and crying. "All of my life that's all I've had, pain and illness, because of this electrode. I went to see a doctor, and you know what he said?" The old man paused. He was staring up at me, his head cocked. I shook my head. "He said he couldn't remove it. Hear that? Couldn't remove it, and him a medical doctor!" The old man waved his arm, said with a long sigh, "They're all in it together, all them medical doctors. What can I do?" He sat back into his rocker.

I sat down carefully on the small wooden box and said gently to the old man, "I'm not one of them. I mean,

Timmy and I. You heard yourself. We're wanted by the police in Maryland."

"The only good people in this country are wanted by the police," he said finally.

I took a deep breath and glanced at the small bedroom. I had left the door open so I could see Timmy, but the room was dark. I couldn't even see the bed.

"That's all right," I said finally, not knowing what to say.

"I'll do it," the man responded, looking up, nodding.

"Do what?" I asked, but I knew what he meant.

"They took your own flesh and blood, just like they did with me."

I raised both my hands, gestured for him to keep still. I was afraid I might have to hurt him if he went near Timmy.

"I'll prove it to you," he said, grinning.

"Prove it?"

He reached into his worn trousers and pulled out a Buck knife and snapped it open. "We'll cut the kid, see if he draws blood."

"Hey, are you crazy or something?" I yelled at him, backing off.

He kept waving the Buck knife. How in God's name did all of this happen to me, I kept thinking.

"He ain't human, that little one. I looked into his eyes." The old man was glaring at me, his eyes wild in his gray head. He kept coming, backing me into the corner. I suddenly realized I couldn't stop him. He was too crazy for me.

"Okay," I said quickly. "We'll do it. I'll do it! I'll cut his finger, okay?" I was panicky now, and sweating. I could feel the sweat on my T-shirt, between my legs, Jesus, I thought, had I pissed my pants?

He handed me the small bladed knife, nodding, motioned for me to go into the small room, to my sleeping baby, and he followed, still grinning and pleased with himself.

I knelt beside the bed. Timmy was turned on his side, hidden in the quilts. I could hear his soft breath, felt the warmth of his small body when I gently touched his smooth cheek.

The old man nudged me from behind.

It was going to be okay, I thought. I'd just nip his fingertip, draw a bubble of blood, that was all. He would scream and wake, I know, but his finger would be fine; he'd heal within minutes.

I pulled his chubby fingers out from beneath the warm quilt. At once his fingers circled my thumb. I can't do this, I told myself.

"Hurry!" the old man shouted, poking me, "or give me that blade."

I reached out, took his tiny thumb in my fingers, pinched it, and then squeezing my eyes I laced the knife across the flesh.

"See! See!" the crazy hermit shouted in my face. I opened my eyes. Timmy's fingers had not bled. I could see a thin silver spring. It had popped through the fleshy skin. I squeezed Timmy's hand and another silver spring, like the insides of a delicate watch, came into sight. Behind me the old man kept shouting, hitting me in the shoulder.

I ripped off the tight blanket and pulled at his stretchy. He was crying now, hiccuping for breath. I grabbed him and lifted him, squeezing hard. I could feel the thin frame of machinery, and I squeezed all the metal and bolts, enraged. Timmy's doll's-blue eyes bulged in the soft flesh. I watched the blue irises, wanting them to pop out. The eyes fell onto the bed, two round pieces of glass. Inside the empty sockets I could see the intricate wiring, all the tiny microchips.

"Goddamnit!" I shouted, screaming. "She tricked me!" Timmy was still with her.

I turned and heaved the worthless baby at the opposite wall, where its head bounced against the rough legs, then the body slid down to the floor, leaving a smear of wet blood.

Then I fled the room, ran for my coat and shoes. The old man came after me, hobbling on his bad leg, telling me to wait until morning, telling me to stay with him.

I wasn't listening. I wanted Lynne now. I wanted to get to

her for stealing my kid. I opened the front door as I buttoned my jacket and felt the blast of cold and blowing snow.
"You're crazy!" the old man shouted after me.

I slammed the door behind me. I wasn't crazy. I just wanted my son.

I made it to the Skyline Drive, back to where my overturned car lay buried in the snow. I got a lift from the crew of a county snowplow, then reached 340 and at a truckstop hitched a ride back to Washington. It took over forty hours. When I reached the city, I took the Metro out to Rockville, getting off after dark, two days from when I had first come home and taken my son.

It had snowed in Rockville and my tracks were clear as I climbed over some backyard fences and came up behind my house. I stood shivering there in the cold, watching through the dark windows as my wife made dinner for Timmy.

They were both in the kitchen. Timmy was in the high chair and Lynne was talking to him, smiling, going back and forth between his chair and the stove. I could see the steam off the oven, almost feel the warmth and coziness of the scene. Mother and child.

Lynne had lost weight, I saw. After the baby she had been plump and I had got onto her about it, told her she looked like those fat women you see on the bus sometimes, the ones who can only fit into sweat suits, and feed themselves with hamburgers from McDonalds.

She didn't look bad, I thought. I got kind of a half erection, watching her. She wasn't wearing much, just her housecoat, no bra, and no panties, I knew. I slipped my tongue around my lips, wetting them.

It wasn't fair. Nothing was ever fair, not to men, not to me at least. I hadn't been warm in two days. My wet clothes had frozen on my body. My pant legs were stiff, my shoes and socks were soaked. I could feel water between my toes. She had done this to me, I thought. She had tricked me, driven me out into the snow like some homeless person.

I went over to the garage and took the extra key down from the ledge, unlocked the side door and slipped inside. It was warmer there, out of the wind, but I didn't need the warmth. I was too excited. I could feel my heart again, felt the rush of blood through my body. I grinned in the darkness at my own adrenaline.

The car took up all the space in the garage and I had to crawl over the lawnmower to reach the other side and the door to the breezeway that led to the house. Lynne always left it open, so I slipped inside, then ran across the breezeway. I didn't want her looking out the kitchen window, seeing me coming to get her.

When I opened the house door, I felt the warmth, smelled chicken cooking. She was making lemon chicken. She knew it was my favorite dinner.

It was dark in the entrance hallway. I could see Lynne's overcoat, and little Timmy's snowsuit, both hanging from the old-fashioned tree stand Lynne had found somewhere, at one of her goddamn garage sales. I slipped off my gloves and coat. I was shivering. I needed a drink, but I wasn't going to risk going into the living room, opening the cabinets. Besides, Lynne had gotten rid of the booze, ever since I started drinking.

"Honey? Is that you?" Her voice stunned me, knocked me back against the hallway mirror. I could see my hand in front of me, trembling with fear. I tried to make a fist, to imagine my fingers gripping her throat, ending her life. I could do it, I told myself. It would be easy once I got close to her and had hold of her neck. I'd give her a friendly kiss, a welcome-home kiss, and then I'd end her life, end all my misery, and take my son away.

Maybe I wouldn't leave the house, not with her gone, at least. Maybe I'd just get rid of her, bury her in the basement or somewhere, and stay there with Timmy. I grinned at myself in the dark mirror, excited by that sudden notion.

I put both hands in my pocket, felt the damp stickiness of the cloth.

"Aren't you going to come in and say hello to Timmy?"

she asked next, still cheery, as if there was nothing at all
wrong in the world, wrong between the two of us.

I shuffled around the hallway, leaving damp spots on the
hardened floor. I moved through the shadows and toward
the light of the kitchen doorway. Lynne was sitting at the
kitchen table and feeding Timmy. I thought to myself: can I
kill her with Timmy in the room? Would he remember?

"Hi, darling," she glanced at me. "How was the job
search?"

I slumped down across from her, keeping my hands hidden. They were trembling beneath the table, knocking against
my knees. I nodded, saying nothing. If I spoke now, I knew
I'd scream.

"Bert Lynch called, remember him? He and I worked
together at HUD. He says that maybe you should check
personnel at HUD. They're hiring." She glanced at me, still
smiling.

"Okay," I whispered, nodding.

Lynne had turned her attention back to Timmy. She was
cleaning off his face where he had spit up the apple sauce. I
stared at him and he looked back, grinning. I smiled, happy
for the first time in days.

"What did you do all day?"

"What?" I shouted back.

"Honey, there's no need to snap." Lynne glanced at me,
frowning. "I just asked you a simple question: where were
you all day, that's all."

"Out!"

"Yes, I know you were out!" She sighed.

I hated it when she sighed like that, as if I had done
something irrevocably wrong.

"I was . . ." I stopped talking and stared across the room,
trying to focus. I didn't know where I had been all day. I
shook my head, trying to clear my mind.

"Honey, are you okay?" She looked at me, worried now.
"Did you get everything at the store, the diapers?"

I nodded, then managed to say with great difficulty. "I
got what we needed."

"Thanks, I'm sorry I forgot them today, but the interview went on longer than I thought. I think I'm going to get this job, honey, and then we won't have to worry about anything for a while. And you'll find work, I know." She kept talking, glancing over as she cleaned up Timmy, took off his bib.

"I'll take him," I told her, avoiding her question.

"Oh, no, that's okay. He needs his bath. Why don't you start dinner, put on some potatoes?" She left the kitchen, never letting me close to my kid. When she passed me, I could smell her body. It almost made me throw up. I hated the smell of her vagina.

Timmy began to cry, once he was out of the kitchen. I could hear Lynne talking to him, cooing. All she cared about was him, not me, not any longer. I remembered when we used to make love, she'd coo like that to me, as if I were her only love, but not any more.

My mind was jumping fast, popping ahead, making plans. I started to grin, just at the pleasure of knowing what I'd do next, later.

I glanced around the kitchen. It was brighter than I had remembered. There were more lights and they were burning me, like sun lamps. It felt as if I were down at the beach, sitting in the sun. I felt the sweat on my forehead, under my arms. I had too many clothes on, sweaters and shirts. I stripped down to my T-shirt and even then the heat of the kitchen lights burned my skin. Looking at my forearm, I could see that there were already bubbles of flesh, blisters under my skin.

I turned off all the lights, turned off the stove, and stood there in the fresh darkness of the house. When I felt cool again, I went over to the drawer and took out the knife, the thick heavy one that Lynne used to cut up chicken, and felt its weight. I loved this knife. I loved how heavy it was. Using it, I wouldn't even have to work up a sweat.

I went into our bedroom and stood behind the door and away from the light that spread out onto the carpeted floor. When I looked up, I was standing in front of the full-length mirror. I could not see myself in the mirror. I could not see myself in the mirror, and I grinned.

"Honey, what are you doing?"

Lynne was beside me, speaking softly, as if I were just another child to attend to.

"And what are you doing with that soup spoon?" She was amused, and kept smiling quizzically at me.

I stared down at my hand. I had grabbed hold of the wooden ladle, not the black-handled knife.

"Honey, what's the matter?" She came closer to me, worried now. I couldn't stand to breathe. The reek of her genitals consumed the room. When I didn't answer, she said quickly, "I can't leave the baby," and dashed back to the bathroom. "Come with me!" she ordered.

I followed after her obediently, still staring at the wooden spoon. It was a mistake, that's all. In my haste I had grabbed the wrong instrument. I could still kill her, I thought next, spill her brains over the bathroom tile, let her blood drain in the tub. Then I'd clean out the basement freezer, throw away all the meat, and stuff her inside. I might have to cut her up some, but that wouldn't be much of a problem. I'd tell the neighbors she was out of town, traveling on business. She wouldn't be missed. She's just be frozen stiff, that's all. I grinned at the thought.

"Aren't you going to shower?" Lynne asked next. She had her back to me and was drying off Timmy, wiping him with baby oil.

"Why?" I asked, surprised by the question.

Lynne turned around at me. "Honey, we're having dinner with the McCafferys." Her voice had risen.

I didn't answer her. It was best not to answer her when she had an edge on her. I had learned my lesson well. I knew how to handle my wife.

I went back into the living room and stood there for a moment, trying to decide what to do next. I had forgotten about the dinner with the McCafferys. In fact, now that I thought about it, I didn't know who she was talking about. McCaffery who?

I was standing there for only a few minutes when the woman came back to me. She just wouldn't leave me alone. "Honey, what are you doing? You've been standing in here for fifteen minutes. Why aren't you taking a shower? The sitter will be here in half an hour." She came around and stared at me, her eyes bulging again. I couldn't look at her eyes. "What's the matter? Are you okay?" She reached up and touched my face. "Honey, you're freezing." She sounded alarmed.

I wondered then who she was and why she was bothering me, asking me questions. I stepped away, not wanting this person to touch me.

"I'm going to telephone the doctor," she said with some urgency, "and we're not going out tonight. You're coming down with something, I know. Oh, dear God, and the baby will have it next."

She went off by herself into the kitchen. I could see her on the phone, talking to someone, and then she turned around and told me to look after the baby.

What baby? I wondered, turning slowly. I couldn't see a baby. I tried to speak, to tell this woman so, but my tongue felt thick in my mouth. It was gagging me and I stopped trying to speak and instead walked toward the bathroom. I needed to pee, I realized. That's all I wanted to do, just pee, and I was afraid that I'd do it in my pants, as I once did in school, years ago, far away.

In the bathroom I saw the baby. He was on the counter, sitting up in a little contraption. He had his arms up, waving or something, and grinning at me.

I told him not to look at me that way, but he kept grinning, even while I pissed, and I missed the toilet bowl and sprayed the seat, then the wall. I turned my body and sprayed the shower curtain. It sounded like rain hitting the plastic and I laughed, pleased with myself.

The baby started to giggle, laughing too, and I turned around and looked at him while I was still holding my pecker. I told him not to laugh at me, and he giggled again. When he smiled, his whole face lit up, like a clown. "I don't like you laughing at me," I told the baby, but then he giggled.

I zipped up my pants and went after him, grabbing his tight blue stretchy.

"Don't laugh at me!" I shouted.

My voice startled him. His blue eyes bright in his face. Then his face twisted up and he turned red and screamed.

I picked him up with one hand and shook his fat little body, shouting at him to stop. His crying filled my mind. I couldn't think.

Out of the corner of my eye I saw the woman. She was suddenly in the doorway, blocking my way, her thin face white and frightened. I liked that, seeing her so afraid.

"What are you doing, Nelson?" she yelled, reaching for the baby. I had held him up high, holding him at arm's length, like a fat football. When she dove for him I kneed her in the stomach and she gasped and tumbled over, falling forward through the shower curtain, and landed face-down in the tub.

I got away from her, ran into the living room, laughing at her, still holding the screaming baby. I told the little brat I'd smash his head if he didn't stop screaming, and I whirled around to face the woman who was after me, screaming out a name, telling me to give her the kid.

She dove for the baby and I swung him around, tucked him under my arm, as if he were a bag of potatoes. She slashed me with her nails, drawing blood.

"Goddammit," I yelled, and swung at her, hitting her face with my elbow, bashing her nose. I saw a flow of rich blood spread over her face.

She hit the floor, skidding on the hardwood, and when she got up again, she didn't come toward me, but ran into the bedroom, ran, I somehow knew, for the pistol that was in the top drawer of the dresser. I went after her, cutting through the other living room door, then vaulting the bed, with the baby tucked up under my arm like I was some kind of football player.

She had her hand deep inside the drawer, reaching for the

pistol. I kicked out and slammed it on her wrist, breaking her arm.

She screamed and screamed, hanging there, choking on her tears and sobs of pain. I let her suffer a little, let her feel the pain. Then I pulled open the drawer, let her drop to the bedroom floor, clutching her arm beneath her and bleeding from her nose and mouth.

I reached inside the top drawer with my one free hand, took out the heavy pistol, looked down at her, aimed, and blew a hole in the side of her head. She jerked like a snake.

When I went back into the living room the old man was sitting there on the couch. He was grinning at the television, watching *Family Feud.* He glanced over at me and said, "What did you do with the woman?"

I shook my head. I couldn't remember right off, though I knew I had done something to her. I told him I had sent her to the store to buy a dress.

"Good!" He told me. "And what about it?"

I looked at my hand. I had forgotten that I had the kid in my hand. I had him around the neck and he hung there, dead as a chicken. I tossed him away, tossed him into an enmpty chair, where he bounced and then lay sprawled like a stuffed toy, abandoned by a child.

Then I sat down beside the old man, who asked me if I liked *Family Feud.*

I shook my head, not knowing what to say.

Then he told me I wasn't going to get away, told me they'd follow me, the woman, too, because I had electrodes in my nose. He had seen them.

I reached up and tentatively felt the soft skin of my right nostril. He was right. I could feel the tiny microchip.

"What do I do?" I asked the man, trying to keep calm. It was important, I knew to keep calm.

"You can't run away," he told me. "You thought about that, didn't you?"

I nodded, but I wasn't sure. I had a memory, but maybe it was a dream, of being on a cold dark Virginia highway, speeding south. Someone was with me, I think, or I was talking to myself. I like to talk to myself.

"They'll track you," the old man told me, nodding toward the television. "They know."

"Who?" I wanted to know.

He kept nodding to the television, then reached forward and switched the channel. "Him!" he said. "He knows."

I saw Dan Rather watching me.

"See!" He pointed to the screen, to the small earplug in the anchorman's ear. "He's listening to us. He knows. They all know." He glanced at me, grinning. It seemed to please him, showing the connection.

"Shit," I said, remembering the pistol, I reached up and blew a hole in Dan Rather's forehead. The screen hissed and blew up before us, and the both of us started laughing, seeing Dan Rather go black before our eyes. I hadn't thought about that before. I hadn't realized it would be so simple, getting rid of him, I mean.

We sat there for a while, just the two of us, and after midnight, when it started to get cold, I went into the bedroom and grabbed the quilt and pulled it over me. The woman was still there, sitting in the dark black spot of her own blood. I told her to go wash up, but she didn't respond.

When I came back into the living room, the old man was gone. I had half expected that. I was sorry now that I had put a bullet in Dan Rather's forehead. I missed him. I missed the kid and the woman, too. They'd been company at least.

I crawled up on the couch and fell asleep and when I woke it was daylight and the sun was in my eyes. I looked up and saw it had snowed overnight but now the sun was out and it was a bright day. A nice day. I saw my Pontiac in the driveway and I guessed the old man had done that, driven it up from Virginia, and then I remembered the electrodes he had told me about and I tentatively touched them. I felt oddly reassured that someone was monitoring me, looking after me, almost like, you know, an angel.

"Hello," I said, to whoever was listening.

I got up and went into the kitchen. The kid was still sprawled out crazy-legged on the chair, and I could see the woman's feet in the doorway of the bedroom.

I opened the frige and took out some juice, some eggs, and made myself breakfast, standing up and eating it by the table. I wanted coffee but I was too tired to go to all the trouble of making it.

I was still standing when the phone rang. I think it was the phone. Myabe it was the electrodes, I couldn't tell. But when the phone rang, my teeth hurt.

When I answered the phone a woman said, happy and friendly like, "Nelson? Is that you, Nelson? Are you home again?"

I hung up the phone, but I was shaking so I couldn't take my hand off the receiver. Again my teeth began to buzz and I picked up the receiver.

"Nelson? Is Lynne there, Nelson?" Now the voice sounded worried.

"This is not Nelson," I answered coolly, "my name is Kellogg," I said, reading the name off the cereal box. Then I hung up the phone again.

It rang at once, buzzing my teeth, hurting my ears. I went back to the living room, found the pistol buried in the blankets and then realized I had no shirt on, no shoes. I got dressed fast, hurrying, for they would be here soon, come to find Nelson and Lynne, to find the people who lived here.

Dressed, I went to the door, and then I remembered my son. The image of his happy face came back to me, burned a hole in my heart, and I went back to him, back to where he had fallen asleep in the chair. I wrapped him up in a blanket, carried him easily with me out to the car.

Down the street I could see that the neighbors were up, and that a woman I seemed to know was hurrying toward the house, crossing the snowy street. She was wearing boots and her husband's heavy coat.

I think she was calling to me, but I got into the car, put the baby in the back seat, and jumped into the driver's seat.

She was hurrying now, running, calling a name. I could see the fog of her breath, see the fear in her eyes.

"Nelson!" she shouted. "Nelson, what is wrong?" I gunned the car, whipped it out into the cul-de-sac, and nearly clipped her legs as she jumped aside and then fell into the bank of snow.

"Did you see that, Timmy? Do you see that?" I shouted, as I gunned the engine and skidded away from the house, down the suburban street and onto the highway, free at last. "Free at last," I shouted.

My son slept. He slept without moving.

F. Paul Wilson is probably best known for *The Keep*, the first major novel to fuse Nazis and vampires and make the fusion a statement instead of a hash. Though he started out as a science fiction writer, he has since published horror, his own version of the Yellow Peril novel (*Black Wind*), and a new bead on the hardboiled science fiction tale (*Dydeetown World*). He is never less than surprising and always good.

A DAY IN THE LIFE

F. Paul Wilson

When the cockroach made a right turn up the wall, Jack flipped another *shuriken* across the room at it. The steel points of the throwing star drove into the wallboard just above its long antennae. It backed up and found itself hemmed in on all sides now by four of the stars.

"Did it!" Jack said from where he lay across the still-made hotel bed.

He counted the *shuriken* protruding from the wall. A dozen of them traveled upward in a gentle arc above and behind the barely functioning TV, ending in a tiny square where the roach was trapped.

Check that. It was free again. It had crawled over one of the *shuriken* and was now continuing on its journey to wherever. Jack let it go and rolled onto his back on the bedspread.

Bored.

And hot. He was dressed in jeans and a loose, heavy sweater under an oversized lightweight jacket, both dark blue; a black and orange knited cap was jammed on the top of his head. He had turned the thermostat all the way down but the room remained an oven. He didn't want to risk taking anything off because, when the buzzer sounded, he had to hit the ground running.

He glanced over at the dusty end table where the little Walkman-sized box with the antenna sat in silence.

"Come on, already!" he mumbled to it. "Let's do it!"

Reilly and his sleazos were due to make their move tonight. What was taking them so long to get started? Almost one A.M. already—three hours here in this fleabag. He was starting to itch. There was only so much TV he could watch without getting drowsy. Even without the lulling drone of Johnny Carson interviewing some actor he had never heard of, the heat was draining him.

Fresh air. Maybe that would help.

Jack got up, stretched, and stepped to the window. A clear night out there, with a big almost-Halloween moon rising over the city. He gripped the handles and pulled. Nothing. The damn thing wouldn't budge. He was checking the edges of the sash when he heard the faint crack of a rifle. The bullet came through the glass two inches to the left of his head, peppering his face with tiny sharp fragments as it whistled past his ear.

Jack collapsed his legs and dropped to the floor. He waited. No more shots. Keeping his head below the level of the windowsill, he rose to a crouch, then leapt for the lamp on the end table at the far side of the bed, grabbed it. He rolled to the floor with it. Another shot spat through the glass and whistled through the room as his back thudded against the floor. He turned off the lamp.

The other lamp, the one next to the TV, was still on— sixty watts of help for the shooter. And whoever was shooting had to know Jack would be going for it next. He'd be ready.

On his belly, Jack slid along the industrial-grade carpet toward the end of the bed until he had an angle where the bulb was visible under the shade. He pulled out his next-to-last *shuriken* and spun it toward the bulb. With an electric pop it flared blue-white and left the room dark except for the flickering glow from the TV.

Immediately Jack popped his head above the bed and looked out the window. Through the spider-webbed glass he caught sight of a bundled figure turning and darting away across the neighboring rooftop. Moonlight glinted off the long barrel of a high-powered rifle, flashed off the lens of a telescopic sight, then he was gone.

A high-pitched beep made him jump. The red light on the signal box was blinking like mad. Kuropolis wanted help. Which meant Reilly had struck.

"Swell!"

Not a bad night, George Kuropolis thought, wiping down the counter in front of the slim young brunette as she seated herself. Not a great night, but still to have half a dozen customers at this hour was good. And better yet, Reilly and his creeps hadn't shown up.

Maybe they'd bother somebody else tonight.

"What'll it be?" he asked the brunette.

"Tea, please," she said with a smile. A nice smile. She was dressed nice and had decent jewelry on. Not exactly overdressed for the neighborhood, but better than the usual.

George wished he had more customers of her caliber. And he *should* have them! Why not? Didn't the chrome inside and out sparkle? Couldn't you eat off the floor? Wasn't everything he served made right here on the premises?"

"Sure. Want some pie?"

"No, thank you."

"It's good. Blueberry. Made it myself."

The smile again. "No, thanks. I'm on a diet."

"Sure," he mumbled as he turned away to get her some hot water. "Everyone's on a goddam diet. Diets are gettin' hazardous to my health!"

Just then, the front door burst open and a white-haired man in his mid-twenties leaped in with a sawed-off shotgun in his hands. He pointed it at the ceiling and let loose a round at the fixture over the cash register. The *boom* of the blast was deafening as glass showered down on everything.

Matt Reilly was here.

Four more of his gang crowded in behind him. George recognized them: Reece was the black with the white fringe leather jacket; Rafe had the blue Mohican, Tony had the white; and Cheeks was the baby-faced skinhead.

"Aw*right!*" Reilly said, grinning fiercely under his bent nose, mean little eyes, dark brows, and bleached crewcut. "It's ass-kickin' time!"

George reached into his pocket and pressed the button on the beeper there, then raised his hands and backed up against the wall.

"Hey, Matt!" he called. "C'mon! What's the problem?"

"You know the problem, George!" Reilly said.

He tossed the shotgun to Reece and stepped around the counter. Smiling, he closed with George. The smile only heightened the sick knot of fear coiling in George's belly. He was so fixed on that empty smile that he didn't see the sucker punch coming. It caught him in the gut. He doubled over in agony; his last cup of coffee heaved but stayed down.

He groaned. *"Christ!"*

"You're late again, George!" Reilly said through his teeth. "I told you last time what would happen if you didn't stick to the schedule!"

George struggled to remember his lines.

"I can't pay two protections! I can't afford it!"

"You can't afford *not* to afford it! And you don't have to pay two. Just pay me!"

"Sure! That's what the other guy says when *he* wants *his!* And where are *you* then?"

"Don't worry about the other guy! I'm taking care of him tonight! But *you!*" Reilly rammed George back against the wall. "I'm gonna hafta make an example outta you, George! People saw what happened to Wolansky when he turned pigeon. Now they're gonna see what happens to a shit who don't pay!"

Just then there was a scream from off to George's right. He looked and saw Reece covering the five male customers from booths two and four, making them empty their pockets onto one of the tables. Farther down the counter, Cheeks was waving a big knife with a mean-looking curved blade at the girl who'd wanted the tea.

"The ring, babe," he was saying. "Let's have it."

"It's my engagement ring!" she said.

"You wanna look nice at your wedding, you better give it quick."

He reached for it and she snapped his hand away.

"No!"

Cheeks straightened up and slipped the knife into a sheath tucked into the small of his back.

"Ooooh, you shouldna done that, bitch," said Reece in oily tones.

George wished he were a twenty-five-year-old with a Schwarzenegger build instead of a wheezy fifty with pencil arms. He'd wipe the floor with these creeps!

"Stop him," he said to Reilly. "Please. I'll pay you."

"Couldn't stop him now if I wanted to," Reilly said, grinning. "Cheeks *likes* it when they play rough."

In a single smooth motion, the skinhead's hand snaked out, grabbed the front of the woman's blouse, and ripped. The whole front came away. Her breasts were visible through a semi-transparent bra. She screamed and swatted at him. Cheeks shrugged off the blow and grappled with her, dragging her to the floor.

One of the men in the booth near Reece leapt to his feet and started toward the pair, yelling, "Hey! Whatta y'think you're doin'?"

Reece slammed the shotgun barrel across his face. Blood spurted from his forehead as he dropped back into his seat.

"Tony!" Reilly said to the Mohican standing by the cash register. "Where's Rafe?"

"Inna back."

George suddenly felt his scalp turn to fire as Reilly grabbed him by the hair and shoved him toward Tony.

"Take George in the back. You and Rafe give him some memory lessons so he won't be late again."

George felt his sphincters loosening. Where was Jack?

"I'll pay! I told you I'll pay!"

"It's not the same, George," Reilly said with a slow shake of his head. "If I gotta come here and kick ass every month just to get what's mine, well, I got better things to do, y'know?"

As George watched, Reilly hit the "NO SALE" button on the cash register and started digging into the bills.

Thick, pincer-like fingers closed on the back of George's neck, then he was propelled into the rear of the diner. He saw Rafe off to the side, playing with the electric meat grinder where George mixed his homemade sausage.

"Rafe!" said Tony. "Matt wants us to teach Mr. Greasyspoon some manners!"

Rafe didn't look up. He had a raw chicken leg in his hand. He shoved it into the top of the meat grinder. The sickening crunch of bone and cartilage being pulverized rose over the whirr of the motor, then ground chicken leg began to extrude through the grate at the bottom.

"Hey, Tone!" Rafe said, looking up and grinning. "I got a great idea!"

Jack pounded along the second floor hallway. He double-timed down the flight of stairs to the lobby, sprinted across the carpet tiles that spelled out "The Lucky Hotel" in bright yellow on dark blue, and pushed through the smudged glass doors of the entrance. One of the letters on the neon sign above the door was out. *The ucky Hotel* flashed fitfully in hot red.

Jack leapt down the three front steps and hit the pavement running. Half a block to the left, then another left down an alley, leaping puddles and dodging garbage cans until he came to the rear of the Highwater Diner. He had his key ready and shoved it into the deadbolt on the delivery door. He paused there long enough to draw his .45 automatic, a Colt Mark IV, and to stretch the knitted cap down over his face. It then became a Holloween decorated ski mask, and he was looking out through a bright orange jack-o-lantern. He pulled the door open and slipped into the storage area at the rear of the kitchen.

Up ahead he heard the sound of a scuffle, and George's terrified voice crying, "No, don't! *Please* don't!"

He rounded the corner of the meat locker and found Tony and Rafe—he'd know those Mohicans anywhere—from Reilly's gang forcing George's hand into a meat grinder and George struggling like all hell to keep it out. But he was losing the battle. His fingers would soon be sausage meat.

Jack was just reaching for the slide on his automatic when he spotted a steel meat hammer on a nearby counter. He picked it up and hefted it. Heavy—a good three pounds, most of it in the head. Pocketing the pistol, he stepped over to the trio and began a sidearm swing toward Tony's head.

"Tony! Trick or treat!"

Tony looked up just in time to stop the full weight of the hammer head with the center of his face. It made a noise like *smoonch!* as it buried itself in his nose. He was halfway to the floor before Rafe even noticed.

"Tony?"

Jack didn't wait for him to look up. He used the hammer to crunch a wide part in the center of Rafe's blue Mohican. Rafe joined Tony on the floor.

"God, am I glad to see you!" George said, gasping and fondling his fingers as if to reassure himself that they were all there. "What took you so long?"

"Can't be more than two minutes," Jack said, slipping the handle of the hammer through his belt and pulling the automatic again.

"Seemed like a *year!*"

"The rest of them out front?"

"Just three—Reilly, the skinhead, and Reece."

Jack paused. "Where's the rest of them?"

"Don't know."

Jack thought he knew. The older three had probably been on that rooftop trying to plug him in his hotel room. But

how had they found him? He hadn't even told George about
staying at the Lucky.

One way to find out . . .

"Okay. You lock the back door and stay here. I'll take
care of the rest."

"There's a girl out there—" George said.

Jack nodded. "I'm on my way."

He turned and almost bumped into Reilly coming through
the swinging doors from the front. He was counting the
fistful of cash in his hands.

"How we doin' back—?" Reilly said and then froze when
the muzzle of Jack's automatic jammed up under his chin.

"Happy Halloween," Jack said.

"Shit! You again!"

"Right, Matt, old boy. Me again. And I see you've made
my collection for me. How thoughtful. You can shove it in
my left pocket."

Reilly's face was white with rage as he glanced over to
where Tony and Rafe writhed on the floor.

"You're a dead man, pal. Worse than dead!"

Jack smiled through the ski mask and increased the pressure of the barrel on Reilly's throat.

"Just do as you're told."

"What's with you and these masks, anyway?" he said as
he stuffed the money into Jack's pocket. "You that ugly? Or
do you think you're Spiderman or something?"

"No, I'm Pumpkinman. And this way I know you but you
don't know me. You see, Matt, I've been keeping close tabs
on you. I know all your haunts. I stand in plain view and
watch you. I've watched you play pool at Gus's. I've walked
up behind you in a crowd and bumped you as I passed. I
could have slipped an ice pick between your ribs a dozen
times by now. But don't try to spot me. You won't. While
you're trying too hard to look like Billy Idol, I'm trying
even harder to look like nobody."

"You *are* nobody, man!" His voice was as tough as ever,
but a haunted look had crept into his eyes.

Jack laughed. "Surprised to see me?"

"Not really," Reilly said, recovering. "I figured you'd show up."

"Yeah? What's the matter? No faith in your hit squad?"

"Hit squad?" There was a genuine bafflement in his eyes. "What the fuck you talkin' about?"

Jack sensed that Reilly wasn't faking it. He was as baffled as Jack.

He let his mind wander an instant. *If not Reilly's bunch, then who?*

No time for that now. Especially with the muffled screams coming from the front. He turned Reilly around and shoved him back through the swinging doors to the front of the diner. Once there, he bellied Reilly up against the counter and put the .45 to his temple. He saw Reece covering half a dozen customers with a sawed-off shotgun. But where was that psycho, Cheeks?

"Okay, turkeys!" Jack yelled. "Fun's over! Drop the hardware!"

Reece spun and faced them. His eyes widened and he raised the scattergun in their direction. Jack felt Reilly cringe back against him.

"Go ahead," Jack said, placing himself almost completely behind Reilly. "You can't make him any uglier."

"Don't, man!" Reilly said in a low voice.

Reece didn't move. He didn't seem to know what to do. So Jack told him.

"Put the piece on the counter or I'll blow his head off."

"No way," Reece said.

"Don't try me, pal. I'll do it just for fun."

Jack hoped Reece didn't think he was bluffing, because he wasn't. He'd already been shot at once tonight and he was in a foul mood.

"Do what he says, man," Reilly told him.

"No *way!*" Reece said. "I'll get outta here, but no way I'm givin' that suckuh my piece!"

Jack wasn't going to allow that. As soon as Reece got outside he'd start peppering the big windows with shot. He was about to move Reilly out from behind the counter to block the aisle when one of the men Reece had been covering stood up behind him and grabbed the pump handle of the scattergun. A second man leapt to his side to help him. One round blasted into the ceiling, and then the gun was useless—with all those hands on it, Reece couldn't pump another round into the chamber. Two more men jumped up and overpowered him. The shotgun came free as a fifth man with a deep cut in his forehead shoved Reece back onto the seat of the booth and began pounding at his face. More fists began to fly. These were *very* angry men.

Jack guided Reilly toward the group. He saw two pairs of legs—male and female, struggling on the floor around the far end of the counter. He shoved Reilly toward the cluster of male customers.

"Here's another one for you. Have fun. Just don't do anything to them that they wouldn't do to you."

Two of the men smiled and slammed Reilly down face first on the booth's table. They began pummeling his kidneys as Jack hurried down to where Cheeks was doing his dirty work.

He looked over the edge of the counter and saw that the skinhead held the woman's arms pinned between them with his left hand and had his right thrust up under her bra, twisting her nipple, oblivious to everything else. Her right eye was bruised and swollen. She was crying and writhing under him, even snapping at him with her teeth. A real fighter. She must have put up quite a struggle. Cheeks' face was bleeding from several scratches.

Jack was tempted to put a slug into the base of Cheeks' spine so he'd not only never walk again, he'd never get it up again, either. But Cheeks' knife was in the way, and besides, the bullet might pass right through him and into the woman. So he pocketed the pistol, grabbed Cheeks' right ear, and ripped upward.

Cheeks came off the floor with a howl. Jack lifted him by the ear and stretched his upper body across the counter. He could barely speak. He really wanted to hurt this son of a bitch.

"Naughty, naughty!" he managed to say. "Didn't you ever go to Catholic school? Didn't the nuns tell you that bad things would happen to you if you ever did that to a girl?"

He stretched Cheek's right hand out on the counter, palm down.

"Like warts?"

He pulled the meat hammer from his belt and raised it over his head.

"Or worse?"

He put everything he had into the shot. Bones crunched like breadsticks. Cheeks screamed and slipped off the counter. He rolled on the floor, moaning and crying, cradling his injured hand like a mother with a newborn baby.

"Never hassle a paying customer," Jack said. "George can't pay his protection without them!"

He grabbed Reece's scattergun and pulled him and Reilly free from the men. Both were battered and bloody. He shoved them toward the front door.

"I told you clowns about trying to cut in on my turf! How many times we have to do this dance?"

Reilly whirled on him, rage in his eyes. He probably would have leapt at Jack's throat if not for the shotgun.

"We was here *first*, asshole!"

"Maybe. But *I'm* here now, so scrape up your two wimps from the back room and get them out of here."

He oversaw the pair as they dragged Rafe and Tony out the front door. Cheeks was on his feet by then. Jack waved him forward.

"C'mon, loverboy. Party's over."

"He's got my ring!" the brunette cried from the far end of the counter. She held her torn dress up over her breasts. There was blood at the corner of her mouth. "My engagement ring."

"Really?" Jack said. "That ought to be worth something! Let's see it."

Cheeks glared at Jack and reached into his back pocket with his good hand.

"You wanna see it?" he said. Suddenly he was swinging a big Gurkha *kukri* knife through the air, slashing at Jack's eyes. "Here! Get a close look!"

Jack blocked the curved blade with the short barrel of the sawed-off, then grabbed Cheeks' wrist and twisted. As Cheeks instinctively brought his broken hand up, Jack dropped the shotgun. He grabbed the injured hand and squeezed. Cheeks screamed and went to his knees.

"Drop the blade," Jack said softly.

It clattered to the counter.

"Good. Now find that ring and put it on the counter."

Cheeks dug into the left front pocket of his jeans and pulled out a tiny diamond on a gold band. Jack's throat tightened when he saw the light in the brunette's eyes at the sight of it. Such a little thing . . . yet so important.

Still gripping Cheeks' crushed hand, he picked up the ring and pretended to examine it.

"You went to all that trouble for this itty-bitty thing?" Jack slid it down the counter. "Here, babe. Compliments of the house."

She had to let the front of her dress drop to grab it. She clutched the tiny ring against her with both hands and began to cry. Jack felt the black fury crowd the edges of his vision. He looked at Cheeks' round baby face, glaring up at him from seat level by the countertop, and picked up the *kukri*. He held it before Cheeks' eyes. The pupils dilated with terror.

Releasing the broken hand, Jack immediately grabbed Cheek's throat and jaw, twisted him up and around, and slammed the back of his head down on the counter, pinning him there. With two quick strokes he carved a crude "X" in the center of Cheeks' forehead. He howled and Jack let go. He grabbed the shotgun again and shoved Cheeks toward the door.

"Don't worry, Cheeks. It's nothing embarrassing—just your signature."

Once he had them all outside, he used the shotgun to prod them into the alley between the diner and the vacant three-story Borden building next door. They were a pitiful bunch, what with Tony and Rafe barely able to stand, Cheeks with a bloody forehead and a hand swollen to twice normal size, and Reece and Reilly nursing cracked ribs and swollen jaws.

"This is the last time I want to do this dance with you guys. It's bad for business around here. And besides, sooner or later one of you is really going to get hurt."

Jack was about to turn and leave them there when he heard tires squeal in the street. Headlights lit the alley and rushed toward him. Jack dove to his left to avoid being hit as the nose of a beat-up Chrysler rammed into the mouth of the alley. His foot slipped on some rubble and he went down. By the time he scrambled to his feet, he found himself looking into the business ends of a shotgun, a 9mm automatic, and a Tec-9 assault pistol.

He had found the missing members of Reilly's gang.

Even though it made his ribs feel like they were breaking, Matt couldn't help laughing.

"Gotcha! *Gotcha*, scumbag!"

He picked up the fallen scattergun and jabbed the barrel at Ski-mask's gut. The guy deflected the thrust and almost pulled it from his grasp. Fast hands. Better not leave this guy any openings.

"The gun," he said. "Take it out real slow and drop it."

The guy looked at all the guns pointed at him, then reached into his pocket and pulled out his own by the barrel; it fell to the alley floor with a thud.

"Turn around," Matt told him, "lean on the wall, and spread 'em, police style. And remember—one funny move and you're full of holes."

Matt patted down his torso and legs and told him, "You musta thought I was a stupid jerk to hit this place without backup. These guys've been waiting the whole time for you to show. Never figured you'd come in the back, though. But that's okay. We gotcha now."

The frisk turned up nothing, not even a wallet. The blue

jacket had nothing in the pockets except the cash from the register. He'd get that later. Right now, though, it was game time.

"All right. Turn around. Let's see what you look like."

When the guy turned, Matt reached up and pulled off the pumpkin-headed ski mask. He saw an average-looking guy about ten years older than he—mid-thirties—with dark brown hair. Nothing special. He shoved the mask back on the top of the guy's head where it perched at a stupid-looking angle.

"What's your name, asshole?"

"Jack."

"Jack what?"

"O'Lantern. It's an old Irish—"

Suddenly Cheeks was at Matt's shoulder, brandishing the special services knife they kept in the car.

"He's *mine!*" he screeched. "Lemme make his face into a *permanent* jack-o'-lantern!"

"Cool it, man."

"Look what he did to me! Look at my fuckin' hand! And look at this!" He pointed the knife at the bloody "X" on his forehead. "Look what he did to my face! He's *mine*, man!"

"You get firsts, okay? But first we're gonna take Mr. Jack here for a ride, and then we're all gonna get a turn with him." He held the shotgun out to Cheeks. "Here. Trade ya."

Matt took the heavy, slotted blade and placed the point against one of the guy's lower eyelids. He wanted to see him squirm.

"Some knife, huh? Just like the one Rambo uses. Even cuts through *bone!*"

The guy winced. His tough-guy act was gone. He was almost whining now.

"Wha . . . what are you going to do?"

"Not sure yet, Mr. Jack. But I'm sure Cheeks and me can think up a thousand ways to make you wish you'd never been born."

The guy slid along the wall a little, pressing back like he

was trying to seep into it. His right hand crept up and covered his mouth.

"You're not gonna t-torture me, are you?"

Behind him, Cheeks laughed. Matt had to smile. Yeah, this was more like it. This was going to be *fun*!

"Who? Us? Torture? Nah! Just a little sport. 'Creative playtime,' as my teachers used to call it. I've got this *great* imagination. I can think of—"

Matt saw the guy twist his arm funny. He heard a *snikt*! and suddenly there was this tiny pistol in the guy's hand and the big bore of the stubby barrel was staring into his left eye from about an inch away. And the guy wasn't whining anymore.

"Imagine *this*, Matt!" he said through his teeth. "You do a lousy frisk."

Matt heard his boys crowding in behind him, heard somebody work the slide on an automatic.

"You got no way out of this," he told the guy.

"Neither do you," the guy said. "You want to play Rambo? Fine! You've got your oversized fishing knife? I've got this Semmerling LM-4, the world's smallest .45. It holds four three-hundred-grain hollowpoints. You know about hollowpoints, Matt? Imagine one of those going into your skull. It makes a little hole going in but then it starts to break up into thousands of tiny pieces that fan out as they go through your brain. When those pieces leave your head they'll take most of your brain—not a heavy load in your case—and the back half of your skull with them, spraying the whole alley behind you."

Without turning, Matt could sense that his boys were moving away from directly behind him.

He dropped the knife. "Okay. We call this one a draw."

The guy grabbed the front of his shirt and dragged him deeper into the alley, to a doorless doorway. Then he shoved Matt back and dove inside.

Matt didn't have to tell the others what to do. They charged up and began blasting away into the doorway. Jerry, one of the new arrivals, stood right in front of the opening and emptied his Tec-9's thirty-six-round clip in one long, wild, jittery burst. He stopped and was grinning at Matt when a single shot came from inside. Jerry was thrown back like someone had jerked a wire. His assault pistol went flying as he spun and landed on his face. There was this big red hole where the middle of his back used to be.

"Shit!" Matt said. He turned to Cheeks. "Go around the other side and make sure he doesn't sneak out."

Reece nudged him, making climbing motions as he pointed up at the rusty fire escape. Matt nodded and boosted him up. It creaked and groaned as Reece, his scattergun clamped under his arm, headed for the second floor like a ghost in white fringed leather. Matt hoped he got real close to the bastard before firing—close enough to make hamburger out of his head with the first shot.

Everybody waited. Even Rafe and Tony had come around enough to get their pieces out and ready. Tony was in bad shape, though. His nose was all squished in and he made weird noises when he breathed. His face looked *awful*, man.

They waited some more. Reece should have found him by now.

Then a shotgun boomed inside.

"Awright, *Reece!*" Rafe shouted.

Matt listened a moment to the quiet inside. "Reece! Y'get him?"

Suddenly someone came flying out the door, dark blue jacket and jack-o'v-lantern ski mask, stumbling like he was wounded.

"Shit, it's *him!*"

Matt opened up and so did everyone else. They pumped that bastard so full of holes that a whole goddamn medical center couldn't patch him up even if they got the chance. And then they kept on blasting as he fell to the rubble-strewn ground and twisted and writhed and jolted with the slugs. Finally he lay still.

Cheeks came running back from the other side of the building.

"Y'get 'im?" he said. "Y'get 'im?"

"Got him. Cheeks!" Rafe said. "Got him *good!*"

Matt held the guy's own .45 on him as he approached the body. No way he could be alive, but no sense in taking chances. That was when he noticed that the guy's hands were tied behind his back. He suddenly had a sick feeling that he'd been had again. He pulled off the ski mask, knowing he'd see Reece's face.

He was right. And there was a sock shoved in his mouth.

Behind Matt, Cheeks howled with rage.

Abe ran his fingers through the shoulder fringe of the white leather jacket.

"So, Jack. Who's your new tailor? Now that Liberace's gone, you're thinking maybe of filling his sartorial niche? Or is this Elvis you're trying to look like?"

Jack couldn't help smiling. "Could be either. But since I don't play piano, it'll have to be Elvis. You can tour with me as Jackie Mason since you sound just like him. You write for him?"

"What can I say?" Abe said with an elaborate shrug. "He comes to me, I give him material."

Jack pulled off the jacket. He'd known he'd get heat from Abe for it, but it was a little too cold out tonight for just a sweater. But he was glad Abe was still in his store. He kept much the same hours as Jack.

Jack rolled up the right sleeve of his sweater and set the little Semmerling back into the spring holster strapped to his forearm. Not the most comfortable rig, but after tonight he ranked it as one of the best investments he'd ever made.

"You had to use that tonight?"

"Yeah. Not one of my better nights."

"*Nu?* You're not going to tell me how such a beautiful and stylish leather coat fits in?"

"Sure. I'll tell you downstairs. I need some supplies."

"Ah! So this is a for-buying visit and not just a social call. Good! I'm having a special on Claymores this week."

Abe stepped to the front door of the Isher Sports Shop, locked it, making sure the "SORRY, WE ARE CLOSED" sign faced toward the street. Jack waited as he unlocked the heavy steel door that led to the basement. Below, light from overhead lamps gleamed off the rows and stacks of pistols, rifles, machine guns, bazookas, grenades, knives, mines, and other miscellaneous tools of destruction.

"What'll it be?"

"I lost my forty-five, so I'll need a replacement for that."

"Swishy leather jackets and losing guns. A change of life, maybe? How about a nine-millimeter parabellum instead? I can give you something nice in a Tokarev M213, or a TT9, or a Beretta 92F. How about a Glock 17, or a Llama Commander?"

"Nah."

" 'Nah'. You never want to change."

"I'm loyal."

"To a person you can be loyal. To a country maybe you're loyal. But loyal to a caliber? Feh!"

"Just give me another Colt like the last."

"I'm out of the Mark IV. How about a Combat Stallion? Cost you five-fifty."

"Deal. And maybe I should look into one of those Kevlar vests," Jack said, glancing at a rack of them at the far end of the basement.

"For years I've been telling you that. What makes a change of mind now?"

"Somebody tried to kill me tonight."

"So? This is new?"

"I mean a sniper. Right through the hotel room window. Where nobody but me knew I was staying. I didn't even use Jack in the name when I called in the reservation."

"So maybe it wasn't you they were after. Maybe it was just anybody who happened to walk by a window."

"Maybe," Jack said, but he couldn't quite buy it. "Lousy shot, too. I spotted a telescopic sight on it and still he managed to miss me."

Abe made a disgusted noise. "They sell guns to anybody these days."

"Maybe I'll take a raincheck on the vest," Jack said, then quickly added, "Oh, and I need another dozen *shuriken*."

Abe whirled on him. "Don't tell me! Don't *tell* me! You've been spiking cockroaches with my *shuriken* again, haven't you? Jack, you promised!"

Jack cringed away. "Not exactly spiking them. But Abe, I got bored."

Abe reached into a square crate and pulled out one of the six-pointed models, wrapped in oiled paper. He held it up and spoke to heaven.

"Oy! Precision weapons made of the finest steel! Hones to a razor's edge! But does Mr. *Macher* Repairman Jack appreciate? Does he show respect? Reverence? Of course not! For pest control he uses them!"

"Uh, I'll need a about a dozen."

Muttering Yiddish curses under his breath, Abe began pulling the *shuriken* out of the crate and slamming them down on the table one by one.

"Better make that a dozen and a half," Jack said.

First thing the next morning, Jack called George at the diner and told him to meet him at Julio's at ten. Then he went for his morning run. From a booth on the rim of Central Park, he called the answering maching that sat alone in the fourth-floor office he rented on Tenth Avenue. There were a couple of requests for appliance repairs, which he fast-forwarded through, and then came a tentative Oriental voice, Chinese maybe:

"Mistah Jack, this is Tram. Please call. Have bad problem. People say you can help." He gave a phone number, a downtown exchange.

Tram. Jack had never heard of him. There was nothing else on the tape. Jack reset it, then called this Tram person. He was hard to understand, but Jack decided to see him. He told him where Julio's was and to be there at 10:30.

After a shave and a shower, he headed to Julio's for some breakfast. He was on the sidewalk, maybe half a block away, when he heard someone shout a warning. He glanced left, saw a man halfway across the street, pointing above him. Something in his expression made Jack dive for the nearest doorway. He was halfway there when something brushed his ankle and thudded against the pavement in an explosion of white.

When the dust finally cleared, Jack was staring at what was left of a fifty-pound bag of cement. The man who had shouted the warning was standing on the other side of the mess.

"That maniac could've killed you!"

"Maniac?" Jack said, brushing the white powder off his coat and jeans.

"Yeah. That didn't fall. Somebody dropped it. Looked like he was aiming for your head!"

"Thanks!"

Jack spun and raced around the corner to the other side of the building. This was the second time since midnight that someone had tried to off him. Or maim him. The cement bag probably wouldn't have killed him, but it easily could have broken his neck or his back.

Maybe there was a chance he could catch the sniper.

He found the stairs to the upper floors, but by the time he reached the roof his assailant was gone. Another bag of cement sat on the black tar surface next to a pile of bricks. Someone was planning to repair a chimney.

Warily, he hurried the rest of the way to Julio's. He didn't like this at all. Because of the nature of his business, he had carefully structured it for anonymity. He did things to people that they didn't like, so it was best that they not know who was doing it to them. He did a cash business and worked hard at being an average-looking Joe. No trails. Most of the time he worked behind the scenes. His customers knew his face, but their only contact with him was over the phone—and he never called his answering machine from home—or in brief meetings in places like Julio's.

But somebody seemed to know his every move. How?

"Yo, Jack!" said Julio, the muscular little man who ran the tavern. "Lon' time no see!" He began slapping at Jack's jacket, sending white clouds into the air. "Wha's all this whi' stuff?"

He told Julio about the two near misses.

"Y'know," Julio said, "I see' to remember hearing abou' some guy asking aroun' for you a coupla wee's ago. I'll fin' ou' who he was."

"Thanks, Julio. Give it a shot."

It probably wouldn't pan out to anything, but it was worth a try. *Anything* was worth a try at this point.

Jack had finished his roll and was on his second coffee when George Kuropolis came in. He handed George a wad of cash.

"Here's what Reilly's boys took from you last night—minus your portion of the next installment on my fee. Tell the rest of your Merchants' Association to ante in their shares."

George avoided his eyes.

"Some of them are saying you cost as much as Reilly."

Jack felt the beginning of a surge of anger but it flattened out quickly. He was used to this. It always had happened with a number of his customers, but more often since that damn stupid TV show hit the air. Before that, people who called him never expected him to work for free. Now a fair percentage thought it was his civic duty to get them out of jams. He had been expecting some bitching from the group.

This particular merchants' association had had it rough lately. They ran a cluster of shops on the lower west side. With the Westies in disarray, they'd thought they'd have some peace. Then Reilly's gang came along and began bleeding them dry. Finally one of them, Wolansky, went to the police. Not too long after, a Molotov cocktail came through the front door of his greengrocer, blackening most of his store; and shortly after that his son was crippled in a hit-and-run accident outside their apartment building. As a result, Wolansky developed acute Alzheimer's when the police asked him to identify Reilly.

That was when George and the others got together and called Repairman Jack.

"You going to tell me you don't see the difference?"

"No, of course not," George said hurriedly.

"Well, let me refresh your memory," Jack said. *"You came to me,* not the other way round. This isn't television and I'm not *The Equalizer.* Don't get reality and make-believe confused here. This is my work. I get paid for what I do. I was around before that do-gooder came on the air and I'll be around after he's off. Those knives Reilly and his bunch carry aren't props. Their guns aren't loaded with blanks. This is the real thing. I don't risk my neck for kicks."

"All right, all right," George said. "I'm sorry—"

"And another thing. I may be costing you, but I'm just temporary, George. Like purgatory. Reilly is hell, and hell is forever. He'll bleed you until he's stopped."

"I know. I just wish it was over. I don't know if I can take another night like last night." George began rubbing his right hand. "They were gonna—"

"But they didn't. And as long as they see me as a competitor, they'll save their worst for me."

George shuddered and looked at his fingers. "I sure hope so."

Shortly after George left, an Oriental who looked to be on the far side of fifty showed up at the door. His face was bruised and scraped, his left eye was swollen half shut. Julio intercepted him, shook his hand, welcome him to his place, clapped him on the back, and led him toward the rear of the tavern. Jack noticed that he walked with a limp. A bum right leg. By the time he reached Jack's table, he had been thoroughly frisked. If Julio found anything, he would lead him right past Jack and out the back door.

"Tram," Julio said, stopping at Jack's table, "this is the man you're looking for. Jack, this is Tram."

They had coffee and made small talk while Tram smoked unfiltered Pall Malls back-to-back. Jack led the conversation around to Tram's background. His fractured English was hard to follow but Jack managed to piece together the story.

Tram was from Viet Nam, from Quang Ngai, he said. He had fought in a string of wars for most of his life, from battling the French at Dien Bien Phu through the final civil war that had ravaged what was left of his country. It was during the last one that a Cong finger charge finished his right leg. Along with so many others who had fought on the losing side, Tram became a refugee after the war. But things improved after he made it to the States. Now an American-made prosthesis of metal and plastic took up where his own flesh left off above the knee. And he now ran a tiny laundry just off Canal Street, on the interface between Little Italy and Chinatown.

Finally he got around to the reason he had called Jack.

His laundry had been used for years as a drop between the local mob and some drug runners from Phnom Penh. The setup was simple. The "importers" left a package of Cambodian brown on a given morning; that afternoon it was picked up by one of the local Italian guys, who would leave a package of cash in its place. No one watching would see anything unusual. The laundry's customers ran the ethnic gamut of the area—white, black, yellow, and all the shades between; the bad guys walked in with bundles of dirty clothes and walked out with packages wrapped in brown paper, just like everyone else.

"How'd you get involved in this?" Jack asked.

"Mr. Tony," Tram said, lighting still another cigarette.

Sounded like a hairdresser. "Mr. Tony who?"

"Campisi."

"Tony Campisi?" That was no hairdresser.

Tram nodded. "Yes, yes. Knew very good Mr. Tony nephew Patsy in Quang Ngai. We call him 'Fatman' there. Was with Patsy when he die. Call medic for him but too late."

Jack had heard of Tony "the Cannon" Campisi. Who hadn't? A big shot in the dope end of the Gambino family. Tram went on to say that "Fatman" Pasquale had been one of Tony's favorite nephews. Tony learned of Tram's friendship with Patsy and helped Tram get into the States after the U.S. bailed out of Nam. Tony even set him up in the laundry business.

But there was a price to pay. Natch.

"So he put you in business and used your place as a drop."

"Yes. Make promise to do for him."

"Seems like small time for a guy like Campisi."

"Mr. Tony have many place to drop. No put all egg in one basket, he say."

Smart. If the narcs raided a drop, they never got much, and didn't affect the flow through all the other drops around the city. Campisi was slick. Which was probably why he had rarely seen the inside of a federal courtroom.

"So why the change of heart?"

Tram shrugged. "Mr. Tony dead."

Right. The Gambino family had pretty much fallen apart after old Carlo's death and a deluge of federal indictments. And Tony "the Cannon" Campisi had succumbed to the Big C of the lung last summer.

"You don't like the new man?"

"No like dope. Bad."

"Then why'd you act as a middle for Campisi?"

"Make promise."

Jack's gaze locked with Tram's for an instant. The brown eyes stared back placidly. Not much more needed to be said in the way of explanation.

"Right. So what's the present situation?"

The present situation was that the hard guy who had made the drops and pickups for Campisi over the years was now running that corner of the operation himself. Tram had tried to tell him that the deal was off—"Mr. Tony dead . . . promise dead," as Tram put it. But Aldo D'Amato wasn't listening. He had paid Tram a personal visit the other day. The result was Tram's battered face.

"He belted you around *himself*?"

A nod. "He like that."

Jack knew the type—you could take the guy off the street, but you couldn't take the street out of the guy.

Obviously, Tram couldn't go the police or the DEA about Aldo. He'd had to find some unofficial help.

"So you want me to get him off your back."

Another nod. "Have heard you can do."

"Maybe. Don't you have any Vietnamese friends who can help you?"

"Mr. Aldo will know it is me. Will break my store, hurt my family."

And Jack could imagine how. The Reillys and the D'Amatos . . . bully boys, pure and simple. The only difference between them was the size of their bank accounts. And the size of their organizations.

That last part bothered Jack. He did *not* want to get into any rough-and-tumble with the mob. But he didn't like to turn down a customer just because the bad guys were too tough.

There was always a way.

Central to the Repairman Jack method was shielding himself and the customer by making the target's sudden run of bad luck appear unrelated to the customer. The hardest part was coming up with a way to do that.

"You know my price?"

"Have been saving."

"Good." Jack had a feeling he was going to earn every penny of this one.

The brown eyes lit with hope. "You will help?"

"I'll see. When's the next pickup?"

"This day. At four."

"Okay. I'll be there."

"It will not be good to shoot him dead. He has many friends."

Jack had to smile at Tram's matter-of-fact manner.

"I know. Besides, that's only a last resort. I'll just be there to do research."

"Good. Want peace. Very tired of fight. Too much fight in my life."

Jack looked at Tram's battered face, thought of his missing leg below the knee, of the succession of wars he had fought in since age fifteen. The man deserved a little peace.

"I read you."

Tram gave him the address of his laundry and a down payment in twenty-dollar bills that were old yet clean and crisp—like he had washed, starched, and pressed them. Jack in return gave him his customary promise to deduct from his fee the worth of any currency or valuables he happened to recover from D'Amato & Co. during the course of the job.

After bowing three times, Tram left him alone at the table. Julio took his place.

"The name 'Cirlot' mean anything to you?" he asked.

Jack thought a moment. "Sure. Ed Cirlot. The blackmailer."

A customer named Levinson—Tom Levinson—had come to Jack a few years ago asking to get Cirlot off his back. Levinson was a high-end dealer in identities. *Primo* quality. Jack had used him twice in the past himself. So Levinson had called him when Cirlot had found a screw and begun turning it.

Cirlot, it seemed, had learned of a few high-placed foreign mobsters who had availed themselves of Levinson's services. He threatened to tip the feds to the ersatz ID the next time they came Stateside. Levinson knew that if that ever happened, their boys would come looking for him.

Cirlot had made a career out of blackmail. He was always looking for new pigeons. So Jack set himself up as a mark—supposedly a crooked coin dealer running a nationwide scam from a local boiler room. Cirlot wanted ten large down and one a month to keep quiet. If he didn't get it, the FTC would come a-knockin' and not only close Jack down, but take him to court.

Jack had paid him—in bogus twenties. Cirlot had been caught with the counterfeit—enough of it to make a charge of conspiracy to distribute stick. When he had named Jack's coin operation as his source, no such operation could be found. He got ten years soft fed time.

"Don't tell me he's out already."

"*Sí.* Good behavior. And he was asking around about you."

Jack didn't like that. Not at all. Cirlot wasn't supposed to know anything about Repairman Jack. The coin dealer who had stiffed the blackmailer with bogus twenties was gone like he had never existed. Because he hadn't.

So why was Cirlot looking for Repairman Jack? There was no connection.

Except for Tom Levinson.

"I think I'll go visit a certain ID dealer."

Jack spotted Levinson up on East 92nd Street, approaching his apartment house from the other side. Levinson spotted him at the same time. Instead of waving, he turned and started to run. But he couldn't move too fast because his foot was all bandaged up. He did a quick hop-skip-limp combination that made him look like a fleeing Walter Brennan. Jack caught up to him easily.

"What's the story, Tom?" he said, grabbing Levinson's shoulder.

He looked frightened, and his spiked black hair only heightened the effect. He was a thin, weasely man in his early forties trying to look younger than he was. He was panting and his eyes were darting left and right like those of a cornered animal.

"I couldn't help it, Jack! I had to tell him!"

"Tell him what?"

"About you!" His mouth began running at breakneck speed. "Somehow he connected me and that coin dealer you played. Maybe he had lots of time to think while he was inside. Maybe he remembered that he first heard about a certain coin dealer from me. Anyway, the first time he does when he gets out is come to me. I was scared shitless, but he doesn't want me. He wants you. Said you set him up for a fall and made him look like a jerk."

Jack turned away from Levinson and walked in a small circle. He was angry at Levinson, and disappointed as well. He had thought the forger was a stand-up guy.

"We had a deal," Jack said. "When I took you on, you were to keep quiet about it. You don't know Repairman Jack—never heard of him. That's part of the deal. Why didn't you play dumb?"

"I did, but he wasn't having any."

"So tell him to go squat."

"I did." Levinson sighed. "Jack . . . he started cutting off my toes."

The words stunned Jack. "He *what*?"

"My toes!" Levinson pointed to his bandaged left foot. "He tied me up and cut off my fucking little toe! And he was going to cut off another and another and keep on cutting until I told him how to find you!"

Jack felt his jaw muscles tighten. "Jesus!"

"So I told him all I knew, Jack. Which ain't much. I gave him the White Pages number and told him we met at Julio's. I don't know much more so I couldn't tell him much more. He didn't believe me, so he cut off the next one."

"He cut off *two* toes?" Jack was still having trouble believing it.

"With a big shiny meat cleaver. You want to see?"

"Hell no." He shook off the revulsion. "I took Cirlot for the white-collar type. He never seemed the kind to mix it up."

"Maybe he used to be, but he ain't that way now. He's *crazed*, Jack. And he wants to bring you down real bad. Says he's gonna make you look like shit, then he's gonna ice you. And I guess he's already tried, otherwise you wouldn't be here."

Jack thought of the shot through the hotel window and the falling cement bag."

"Yeah. Twice."

"I'm sorry, Jack, but he really *hurt* me."

"Christ, Tom. Don't give it another thought. I mean, your toes . . . *Damn*"

He told Levinson he'd take care of things and left him there. As he walked away, he wondered how many toes he'd have given up for Levinson.

He decided he could muddle through life without ever knowing the answer to that one.

*   *   *

As soon as the car pulled to a stop in front of the laundry, Aldo reached for the door handle. He felt Joey grab his arm.

"Mr. D. Let me go in. You stay out here."

Aldo shrugged off the hand. "I know where you're comin' from, Joey, but don't keep buggin' my ass about this."

Joey spread his hands and shrugged. "Ay. You're the boss. But I still don't think it's right, know what I mean?"

Joey was okay. Aldo knew how he felt. He was Aldo D'Amato's driver and bodyguard, so *he* should be doing all the rough stuff. And as far as Aldo was concerned, Joey could have most of it. But not all of it. Aldo wasn't going to hide in the background all the time like Tony C. Hell, in his day Tony could walk through areas like this and hardly anyone would know him. He was just another *paisan* to these people. Well, that wasn't going to be Aldo's way. *Everybody* was going to know who he was. And when he walked through it was going to be, "Good morning, Mr. D'Amato!" "Would you like a nice apple, Mr. D'Amato?" "Have some coffee, Mr. D'Amato!" "Right this way, Mr. D'Amato!" People were going to know him, were going to treat him with respect. He deserved a little goddamn respect by now. He'd be forty-five next month. He'd done Tony the Cannon's scut work forever. Knew all the ins and outs of the operation. Now it was *his.* And everybody was going to know that.

"I'll handle this like I did yesterday," he told Joey. "Like I told you: I believe in giving certain matters the *personal* touch."

What he didn't tell Joey was that he *liked* the rough stuff. That was the only bad thing about moving up in the organization—you never got a chance for hands-on communication with jerks like the gook who owned this laundry. Never a peep out of the little yellow bastard all the years Tony C. was running things, but as soon as he's gone, the gook thinks he's gonna get independent with the new guy. Not here, babe. Not when the new guy was Aldo D'Amato.

He was hoping the gook gave him some more bullshit

about not using his place for a drop anymore. Any excuse to work him over again like the other day.

"Awright," Joey said, shaking his head with frustration, "but I'm comin' in to back you up. Just in case."

"Sure, Joey. You can carry the laundry!"

Aldo laughed, and Joey laughed with him.

Jack had arrived at Tram's with a couple of dirty shirts at about 3:30. Dressed in jeans, an army fatigue jacket, and a baseball cap pulled low on his forehead, he now sat in one of the three chairs and read the *Post* while Tram ran the shirts through the machine. It was a tiny hole-in-the-wall shop that probably cost the little man most of his good leg in rent. A one-man operation except for some after-school counter help, which Tram always sent on an errand when a pickup or delivery was due.

Jack watched the customers flow in and out. They were a motley group of mostly lower-middle-class downtowners. Aldo D'Amato and his bodyguard were instantly identifiable by their expensive topcoats when they arrived at 4:00 on the button. Aldo's was dark gray with a black felt collar, a style Jack hadn't seen since the Beatles' heyday. He was mid-forties, with a winter tan and wavy blow-dried hair receding on both sides. Jack knew he was Aldo because the other guy was a side of beef and was carrying a wad of dirty laundry.

Jack noticed the second guy giving him a close inspection. He might as well have had *Bodyguard* stenciled on his back. Jack glanced up, gave the two of them a disinterested up-and-down, then went back to the sports page.

"Got something for me, gook?" Also said, grinning like a shark as he slapped the knuckles of his right fist into his left palm.

Jack sighed. He knew the type. Most tough guys he knew wouldn't hesitate to hurt somebody, even ice them if necessary, but to them it was like driving a car through downtown traffic in the rain: You didn't particularly like it but you did it because you had to get someplace; and if you had the means, you preferred to have somebody else do it for you.

Not this Aldo. Jack could tell that mixing it up was some kind of fix for him.

Maybe that could be turned around. Jack didn't have a plan here. His old Corvair was parked outside. He intended to pick up Aldo and follow him around, follow him home if he could. He'd do that for a couple of days. Eventually, he'd get an idea of how to stick him. Then he'd have to find a way to work that idea to Tram's benefit. This was going to be long, drawn-out, and touchy.

At the counter, Tram sullenly placed a brown-paper-wrapped bundle on the counter. The bodyguard picked it up and plopped the dirty laundry down in its place. Tram ignored it.

"Please, Mr. Aldo," he said. "Will not do this anymore."

"Boy, you're one stupid gook, y'know that?" He turned to his bodyguard. "Joey, take the customer for a walk while I discuss business with our Vietnamese friend here."

Jack felt a tap on his shoulder and looked up from his paper into Joey's surprisingly mild eyes.

"C'mon. I'll buy you a cup of coffee."

"I got shirts coming," Jack said.

"They'll wait. My friend wants a little private talk with the owner."

Jack wasn't sure how to play this. He wasn't prepared for any rough-and-tumble here, but he didn't want to leave Tram to Aldo's tender mercies again.

"Then let him talk in the back. I ain't goin' nowhere."

Joey grabbed him under the arm and pulled him out of the chair. "Yeah. You are."

Jack came out of the chair quickly and knocked Joe's arm away.

"Hands off, man!"

He decided that the only way to get out of this scene on his terms was to pull a psycho number. He looked at Joey's beefy frame and heavy overcoat and knew attacking his body would be a waste of time. That left his face.

"Just stay away!" Jack shouted. "I don't like people touching me. Makes me mad! *Real* mad!"

Joey dropped the brown-paper bundle onto a chair. "All right. Enough of this shit." He stepped in close, gripped Jack's shoulders, and tried to turn him around.

Jack reached up between Joey's arms, grabbed his ears, and yanked the bodyguard's head forward. He had a fleeting glimpse of Joey's startled face as he lowered his head and butted. There was a sick look there. He hadn't been expecting anything like this, but he knew what was coming.

When Jack heard Joey's nose crunch against the top of his skull, he pushed him away and kicked him in the balls. Joey dropped to his knees and groaned. His bloody face was slack with pain and nausea.

Jack next leapt on Aldo, who was gaping at him with a stunned expression.

"You want some of me, too?" he shouted.

Aldo's overcoat was unbuttoned and he was leaner than Joe. Jack went for the breadbasket: right-left combination jabs to the solar plexus, then a knee to the face when he doubled over. Aldo went down in a heap.

But it wasn't over. Joey was reaching a hand into his overcoat pocket. Jack jumped on him and wrestled a short-barreled Cobra .357 revolver away from him.

"A gun? You pulled a fucking *gun* on me, man?" He slammed the barrel and trigger guard across the side of Joe's head. "*Shit* that makes me mad!"

Then he spun and pointed the pistol at the tip of Aldo's swelling nose.

"You!" he screamed. "You started this! You didn't want me to get my shirts! Well, you can have them! They're old anyway! I'll take *yours*! All of them!"

He grabbed the bundle of dirty shirts from the counter and then went for the brown-paper package on the chair.

"Jesus, no!" Aldo said. "No! You don't know what—"

Jack leapt on him and began pistol-whipping him, screaming, "Don't tell me what I don't know!"

As Aldo covered his head with his arms, Jack glanced at

Tram, motioned him over. Tram got the idea. He came out from behind the counter and shoved Jack away, but not before Jack had managed to open Aldo's scalp in a couple of places.

"You get out!" Tram cried. "Get out or I call police!"

"Yeah, I'll get out, but not before I put a couple of holes in this rich pig here!"

Tram stood between him and Aldo. "No! You go! You cause enough trouble!"

Jack made a disgusted noise and ran out with both bundles. Outside he found an empty Mercedes 350 SEL idling at the curb by a fire hydrant. *Why not?*

As he gunned the heavy car toward Canal Street, he wondered at his screaming psycho performance. Pretty convincing. And easy, too. He'd hardly stretched at all to take the part and really get into it.

That bothered him a little.

"Fifty thousand in small bills," Abe said after he'd finished counting the money that had been wrapped inside the dirty laundry. He had it spread out in neat piles on a crate in the basement of his store. "If I were you, I shouldn't complain. Not so bad for an afternoon's work."

"Yeah. But it's the ten keys of cocaine and the thirty of Cambodian brown." The wrapped package had housed some of the heroin. The cocaine and the rest of the heroin had been in a duffle bag in the trunk. "What am I going to do with *that?*"

"There's a storm drain outside. Next time it rains . . ."

Jack thought about that. The heroin would definitely go down the drain. Any alligators or crocs living down in the sewers would be stoned for life. But the cocaine . . . that might come in handy in the future, just like the bogus twenties had come in handy against Cirlot.

Cirlot! Something about him was perking in the back of Jack's mind.

"I've always wanted a Mercedes," Abe said.

"What for? You haven't been further east than Queens

and further west than Columbus Avenue in a quarter century."

"Someday I might like maybe to travel. See New Jersey."

"Yeah. Well, that's not a bad idea. No doubt about it, the best way to see New Jersey is from the inside of a Mercedes. But it's too late. I gave the car to Julio to dispose of."

Abe sagged. "Chop shop?"

Jack nodded. "He's going to shop it around for quick cash. Figures another ten grand, minimum, maybe twenty."

A take of sixty-seventy K so far from one visit to Tram's laundry. Which meant that Jack would be returning Tram's down payment and giving him a free ride on this job. Which was fine for Tram's bank account, but Jack didn't know what his next step was. He had shaken things up down there. Now maybe it would be best to sit back and watch what fell out of the trees.

He headed for Gia's. It was dark and windy as he walked along. He kept to the shadows, kept looking over his shoulder. Cirlot seemed to know where he was going, and when he'd be there. Was he watching him now?

Jack didn't like being on this end of the game.

But how did Cirlot know? That was what ate at him. Jack knew his apartment wasn't bugged—the place was like a fortress. Besides, Cirlot didn't know where he lived. And even if he did, he couldn't get inside to place a bug. Yet he seemed to know Jack's moves. How, dammit?

Jack made a full circuit of Gia's block and cut through an alley before he felt it was safe to enter her apartment house.

There were two fish-eye peepholes in Gia's door. Jack had installed them himself. One was the usual height, and one was Vicky-height. He knocked and stood there, pressing his thumb over the lower peephole as he waited.

"Jack, is that you?" said a child's voice from the other side.

He pulled his thumb away and grinned into the convex glass.

"Ta-daaa!"

The deadbolt slid back, the door swung inward, and suddenly he was holding a bony eight-year-old girl in his arms. She had long dark hair, blue eyes, and a blinding smile.

"Jack! Whatcha bring me?"

He pointed to the breast pocket of his fatigue jacket. Vicky reached inside and pulled out a packet of bubblegum cards.

"Football cards! Neat! You think there's any Jets in this one?"

"Only one way to find out."

He carried her inside and put her down. He locked the door behind them as she fumbled with the wrapper.

"Jack!" she said, her voiced hushed with wonder. "They're all Jets! *All* Jets! I even got Jo-jo Townsell! Oh, this is so neat!"

Gia stepped into the living room. "The only eight-year-old in New York who says 'neat.' Wonder where she got that from?"

She kissed him lightly and he slid an arm around her waist, pulling her close to him. She shared her daughter's blue eyes and bright smile, but her hair was blond. She brightened up the whole room for Jack.

"I don't know about you," he said, "but I think it's pretty neat to get five—*five*—members of your favorite team in a single pack of bubblegum. I don't know anybody else who's got that kind of luck."

Jack had gone through a dozen packs of cards before coming up with those five Jets, then he had slipped them into a single wrapper and glued the flaps back in place. Vicky had developed a thing for the Jets, simply because she liked their green-and-white jerseys. Which, considering the consistency of their play, was probably as good a reason as any to be a Jets fan.

"Start dinner yet?" he asked.

Gia shook her head. "Just getting ready to. Why?"

"Have to take a raincheck. I've got a few things I've got to do tonight."

She frowned. "Nothing dangerous, I hope."

"Nah."

"That's what you always say."

"Well, sure. I mean, after surviving the blue meanies last year, everything else is a piece of cake."

"Don't mention those things!" Ga shuddered and hugged him. "Promise you'll call me when you're back home?"

"Yes, mother."

"I'm serious. I worry about you."

"You just made my day."

She broke away and picked up a slim cardboard box from the couch. "Land's End" was written across one end.

"Your order arrived today."

"Neat." He pulled out a bright red jacket with navy blue lining. He pulled off the fatigue jacket and tried it on. "Perfect. How do I look?"

"Like every third person in Manhattan," Gia said.

"Great!"

Jack worked at being ordinary, at being indistinguishable from everybody else, at being just another face in the crowd. To do that, he had to keep up with what the crowd was wearing. Since he didn't have a charge card, Gia had ordered the jacket for him on hers and he had paid her cash.

"I'd better turn off the oven," Gia said.

"I'll treat tomorrow night. Chinese. For sure."

"Sure," she said. "I'll believe it when I smell it."

Jack stood there in the tiny living room, watching Vicky spread out her football cards, listening to Gia move about the kitchen over the drone of *Eyewitness News,* drinking in the rustle and bustle and noises and silence of a *home.* The domestic feel of this tiny apartment—he wanted it. But it seemed so out of reach. He could come and visit and warm himself by the fire, but he couldn't stay. As much as he wanted to, he couldn't gather it up and take it with him.

His work was the problem. He had never asked Gia to marry him because he knew the answer would be no. Because of what he did for a living. And he *wouldn't* ask her for the same reason: Because of what he did for a living. Marriage would make him vulnerable. He couldn't expose Gia and Vicky to risk like that. He'd have to retire fast. But

he wasn't even forty. Besides go crazy, what would he do for the next thirty or forty years?

Became a citizen? Get a day job? How would he do that? How would he explain why there was no record of his existence up till now? No job history, no social security hours, no file of income tax. The IRS would want to know if he was an illegal alien or a Gulag refugee or something. And if he wasn't, they'd ask a lot of questions he wouldn't want to answer.

He wondered if he had started something he couldn't stop.

And then he was looking out through the picture window in Gia's dining room at the roof of the apartment house across the street and remembering the bullets tearing through the hotel room less than twenty-four hours ago. His skin tingled with alarm. He felt vulnerable here. And worse, he was exposing Gia and Vicky to his own danger. Quickly he made his apologies and goodbyes, kissed them both, and hurried back to the street.

He stood outside the apartment house, slowly walking back and forth before the front door.

Come on, you son of a bitch! Do you know I'm here? Take a shot! Let me know!

No shot. Nothing fell from the roof.

Jack stretched his cramped fingers out from the tight fists he had made. He imagined some vicious bastard like Cirlot finding out about Gia and Vicky, threatening them, maybe hurting them . . . it almost put him over the edge.

He began walking back toward his own apartment. He moved quickly along the pavement, then broke into a run, trying to work off the anger, the mounting frustration.

This had to stop. And it was going to stop. Tonight, if he had anything to say about it.

Jack stopped at a pay phone and called Tram. The Vietnamese told him that Aldo and his bodyguard had limped out and found a cab, swearing vengeance on the punk who had busted them up. Tram was worried that Aldo might

take his wrath out on him if he couldn't find Jack. That worried Jack, too. He called his answering machine but there was nothing of interest on it.

As he hung up he remembered something: Cirlot and phones. *Yes!* That was how the blackmailer had got his hooks into his victims. He was an ace wiretapper!

Jack trotted back to his brownstone. But instead of going up to the second floor where he rented his apartment, he slipped down to the utility closet. He pulled open the phone box and spotted the tap immediately: jumper wires attached to a tiny high-frequency transmitter. Cirlot probably had a voice-activated recorder stashed not too far from here.

Now things were starting to make sense. Cirlot had learned from Levinson that Jack met customers at Julio's. He had hung around outside until he had spotted Jack, then tailed him home.

Jack clucked to himself. He was getting careless in his old age.

Soon after that, Cirlot had shown up, probably as a phone man, inserted the tap, and sat back and listened. Jack had used his apartment phone to reserve the room at the Lucky Hotel . . . and he had called Julio this morning to tell him he'd be over by ten thirty. It all fit.

Jack closed the phone box, leaving the tap in place.

Two could play this game.

Jack sprawled amid the clutter of Victorian oak and bric-a-brac that filled the front room of his apartment and called George at the diner. This was his second such call in half an hour, except that the first had been made from a public phone. He had told George to expect his call, and had told him what to say.

"Hello, George," he said when the Greek picked up the other end. "You got the next payment together from your merchants' association?"

"Yeah. We got it. In cash like usual."

"Good deal. I'll be by around midnight to pick it up."

"I'll be here," George said.

Jack hung up and sat there, thinking. The bait was out. If Cirlot was listening, there was a good chance he'd set up another ambush somewhere in the neighborhood of the Highwater Diner at around midnight. But Jack planned to be there first to see if he could catch Cirlot setting up. And then they would settle things. For good. Jack wasn't going to have anybody dogging his steps back to Gia and Vicky, especially someone who had chopped a couple of toes off a former customer.

On his way downtown an hour later, Jack called his answering machine again. He heard a message from George asking him to call right away. When he did, he heard a strange story.

"I asked you to *what?*" Jack said.

"Meet you in the old Borden building next door. You said there'd been a change of plans and it was probably safer if you didn't show up at the diner. So I was to meet you next door at ten thirty and hand over the money."

Jack had to smile. This Cirlot was slicker than he'd thought.

"Did it sound like me?"

"Hard to say. The connection was bad."

"What did you say?"

"I agreed, but I thought it was fishy because it wasn't the way we had set it up before. And because you said you'd be wearing a ski mask like last night. That sounded fishy, too."

"Good man. I appreciate the call. Call me again if you hear from anyone who says he's me."

"Will do."

Jack hung up. Instead of hailing a cab to go downtown, he ducked into a nearby tavern and ordered a draft of Amsterdam.

Curiouser and curiouser.

Cirlot seemed more interested in ripping him off than knocking him off tonight. Tom Levinson's words came back: *Gonna make you look like shit, then he's gonna ice you.*

So that was it. Another piece fell into place. The bag of cement had missed him. Okay—no one could expect much accuracy against a moving target with a heavy, cumbersome object like that. But the shooter outside the Lucky Hotel had had a telescopic sight. Jack had been a sitting duck. The guy shouldn't have missed.

Unless he'd wanted to. That had to be it. Cirlot was playing head games with him, getting him off balance until he had a chance to humiliate him, expose him, make him look like a jerk. He wanted to pay Jack back in kind before he killed him.

Ripping off one of his fees would be a good start.

Jack's anger was tinged with amusement.

He's playing my own game against me.

But not for long. Jack was the old hand here. It was his game. He'd invented it, and he'd be damned if he'd let Cirlot outplay him. The simpliest thing to do was to confront Cirlot in that old wreck of a building and have a showdown.

Simple, direct, effective, but lacking in style. He needed to come up with something very neat here. A masterstroke, even.

And then, as he lifted his glass to drain the final ounces of his draft, he had it.

Reilly was waiting his turn at the pool table. He didn't feel like shooting much. With Reece and Jerry dead, everybody was down and pissed. All they'd talked about since last night was finding that jack-o'-lantern guy. The only laugh they'd had all day was when they learned that Reece's real name was *Maurice*.

Just then Gus called over from the bar. He was holding the phone receiver in the air.

"Yo! Reilly! You're wanted!"

"Yeah? Who?"

"Said to tell you it's Pumpkinhead."

Reilly nearly tripped over his stick getting to the phone. Cheeks and the others were right behind him.

"Gonna find you, fucker!" he said as he got the receiver to his head.

"I know you are," said the voice on the other end. "Because I'm gonna tell you where I am. We need a meet. Tonight. You lost two men and I almost got killed last time we tangled. What do you say to a truce? We can find some way to divide things up so we both come out ahead."

Reilly was silent while he controlled himself. Was this fucker crazy? A *truce*? After what he did last night?

"Sure," he managed to say. "We can talk."

"Good. Just you and me."

"Okay." *Riiiiight.* "Where?"

"The old place we were in last night—next to the Highwater. Ten thirty okay?"

Reilly looked at his watch. That gave him an hour and a half. Plenty of time.

"Sure."

"Good. And remember, Reilly: Come alone or the truce is off."

"Yeah."

He hung up and turned to his battered boys. They didn't look like much, what with Rafe, Tony, and Cheeks all bandaged up, and Cheeks' hand in a cast. Hard to believe only one guy had done all this. But that one guy was a mean dude, full of tricks. So they weren't going to take any chances this time. No talk. No deals. No hesitation. No reprieve. They were going to throw everything they had at him tonight.

"That really him?" Cheeks asked.

"Yeah," said Reilly, smiling. "And tonight we're gonna have us some punkin pie!"

"Aldo, this man insists on speaking to you!"

Aldo D'Amato glared at his wife and removed the ice pack from his face. He had a brutal headache, bruises and stitches in his scalp. His nose was killing him. Broken in two places. The swelling made him sound like he had a bad cold.

He wondered for the hundredth time about that punk in the laundry. Had the gook set them up? Aldo wanted to believe it, but it just didn't wash. If he'd been laying for Aldo, he'd have had his store filled with some sort of gook

army, not one white guy. But Christ the way that one guy
moved! *Fast.* Like liquid lightning. A butt and a kick and
Joey was down and then he'd been on Aldo, his face crazy.
No. It hadn't been a setup. Just some crazy *stunad* punk.
But that didn't make it any easier to take.

"I told you, Maria, no calls!"

Bad enough that he'd be laughed at all over town for
being such a *gavone* to allow some nobody to bust him up
and steal his car, and even worse that his balls were on the
line for the missing money and shit, so why couldn't Marie
follow a simple order? He never should have come home
tonight. He'd have been better off at Franny's loft on Greene
Street. Franny did what she was told. She damn well better.
He paid her rent.

"But he says he has information on your car."

Aldo's hands shot out. "Gimme that! Hello!"

"Mr. D'Amato, sir," said a very deferential voice on the
other end. "I'm very sorry about what happened today at
that laundry. If I'da known it was someone like you, I
wouldn'a caused no trouble. But I didn't know, y'see, an I
got this real bad temper, so like I'm sorry—"

"Where's the car?" Aldo said in a low voice.

"I got it safe and I wanna return it to you along with the
money I took and the, uh, other laundry and the, uh, stuff
in the trunk, if you know what I mean and I think you do."

The little shit was scared. Good. Scared enough to want
to give everything back. Even better. Also sighed with relief.

"Where is it?"

"I'm in it now. This car phone is really neat. But I'm
gonna leave it somewhere and tell you where you can find
it."

"Don't do that!" Aldo said quickly.

His mind raced. Getting the car back was number-one
priority, but he wanted to get this punk, too. If he didn't
even the score, it would be a damn long time before he
could hold his head up with the family.

"Don't leave it *anywhere*! Someone might rip it off before
I get there, and that'll be on your head! We'll meet—"

"Oh, no! I'm not getting plugged full of holes!"

Yes, you are, Aldo thought, remembering the punk pointing Joey's Magnum in his face.

"Hey, don't worry about that," Aldo said softly. "You've apologized and you're returning the car. It was an accident. We'll call it even. As a matter of fact, I like the way you move. You made Joey look like he was in slow motion. Actually, you did me a favor. Made me see how bad my security is."

"Really?"

"Yeah. I could use a guy like you. How'd you like to replace Joey?"

"Y'mean be your bodyguard? I don't know, Mr. D'Amato."

"Think about it. We'll talk about it when I see you tonight. Where we gonna meet?"

"Uuuuh, how about by the Highwater Diner. It's down on—"

"I know where it is."

"Yeah, well, there's an old abandoned building right next door. How about if I meet you there?"

"Great. When?"

"Ten thirty."

"That's kinda soon—"

"I know. But I'll feel safer."

"Hey, don't worry! When Aldo D'Amato gives his word, you can take it to the bank!"

And I promise you you're a dead man, punk!

"Yeah, well, just in case we don't hit it off, I'll be wearing a ski mask. I *figure* you didn't get a real good look at me in that laundry and I don't want you getting a better one."

"Have it your way. See you at ten thirty." *Gabidose!*

He hung up and called to his wife. "Maria! Get Joey on the phone. Tell him to get over here now!"

Aldo went to his desk drawer and pulled out his little Jennings .22 automatic. He hefted it. Small, light, and loaded with high-velocity longs. It did the job at close range. And Aldo intended to be real close when he used this.

* * *

A little before ten, Jack climbed up to the roof of the Highwater Diner and sat facing the old Borden building. He watched Reilly and five of his boys—the whole crew—arrive shortly afterwards. They entered the building from the rear. Two of them carried large duffel bags. They appeared to have come loaded for bear. Not too long after them came Aldo and three wiseguys. They took up positions outside in the alley below and out of sight on the far side.

No one, it seemed, wanted to be fashionably late.

At 10:30 sharp, a lone figure in a dark coat, jeans, and what looked like a knit watch cap strolled along the sidewalk in front of the Highwater. He paused a moment to stare in through the front window. Jack hoped George was out of sight like he had told him to be. The dark figure continued on. When he reached the front of the Borden building, he glanced around, then started toward it. As he approached the gaping front entry, he stretched the cap down over his face. Jack couldn't see the design clearly but it appeared to be a crude copy of the one he'd worn last night. All it took was some orange paint . . .

Do you really want to play Repairman Jack tonight, pal?

For an instant he flirted with the idea of shouting out a warning and aborting the setup. But he called up thoughts of life in a wheelchair due to a falling cement bag, of Levinson's missing toes, of bullets screaming through Gia and Vicky's apartment.

He kept silent.

He watched the figure push in through the remains of the front door and disappear. Below in the alley, Aldo and Joey rose from their hiding places and shrugged to each other in the moonlight. Jack knew what Aldo was thinking: *Where's my car?*

But they leapt for cover when the gunfire began. It was a brief roar, but very loud and concentrated. Jack picked out the sound of single rounds, bursts from a pair of assault pistols, and at least two, maybe three shotguns, all blasting away simultaneously. Barely more than a single prolonged flash from within. Then silence.

Slowly, cautiously, Aldo and his boys came out of hiding, whispering, making baffled gestures. One of them was carrying an Uzi, another held a sawed-off shotgun. Jack watched them slip inside, heard shots, even picked out the word "car."

Then all hell broke loose.

It looked as if a very small, very violent thunderstorm had got itself trapped on the first floor of the old Borden building. The racket was deafening, the flashes through the glassless windows like half a dozen strobe lights going at once. It went on full force for what seemed like twenty minutes but ticked out to slightly less than five on Jack's watch. Then it tapered and died. Finally there was quiet. Nothing moved.

No. Check that. Someone was crawling out a side window and falling into the alley. Jack went down to see.

It was Reilly. He was bleeding from his mouth, his nose, and his gut. And he was hurting.

"Get me a ambulance, man!" he grunted as Jack crouched over him. His voice was barely audible.

"Right away, Matt," Jack said.

Reilly looked up at him. His eyes widened. "Am I dead? I mean . . . we offed you but good in there."

"You offed the wrong man, Reilly."

"Who cares . . . You can have this turf . . . I'm out of it . . . Just get me a fucking ambulance! Please?"

Jack didn't even try to dredge up any compassion for the man. He knew there wouldn't be any.

"Sure," he said.

Jack got his arms under Reilly and lifted him. The wounded man nearly passed out with the pain of being moved. But he was aware enough to notice that Jack wasn't carrying him toward the street.

"Hey . . . where y'takin' me?"

"Around back."

Jack could hear the sirens approaching. He quickened his pace toward the rear.

"Need a doc . . . need a ambulance."

"Don't worry," Jack said. "I'm getting you one."

He dumped Reilly in the rearmost section of the Borden building's back alley and left him there.

"Wait here for your ambulence," he told him. "It's the same one you called for Wolansky's kid when you ran him down last month."

Then Jack headed for the Highwater Diner to call Tram and to tell George that they didn't need him anymore.

Almost from the beginning of his career back in the late seventies, Robert R. McCammon has been a major figure on the horror scene. He writes the sort of fat, complex book favored by the contemporary reader and most devoutly sought by editors— i.e., the rarely seen but often alluded to "breakthrough book." You never know what McCammon is going to write next. All you know for sure is that it's going to be good. In case you haven't read his novels, start with *Stinger*. It's everything a novel of any kind should be.

LIZARDMAN

Robert R. McCammon

The lizardman, king of his domain, rode on air into the swamp and gnashed his teeth against the night.

He had a feeling in his bones. A mighty feeling. He was old and wise enough to know the power of such feelings. Tonight—yes, tonight—he would find the beast he sought. Out there amid the cypresses and on the mud flats, somewhere betwixt moonrise and dawn, the Old Pope waited for him, in robes of gnarled green. Tonight he would pay his respects to the Old Pope, that chawer of bones and spitter of flesh, and then he would sail his lasso around the Old Pope's throat and drive his gaffhook into the white bellyflesh to pierce a heart as tough as a cannonball.

The lizardman chewed on his unlit cigar, the wind streaming his long white hair back from his leatherbrown face, and powered the airboat over a sea of weeds. The light of a single battery lamp, mounted on the frame behind his seat, speared a direction for him, but he could have found his way in the dark. He knew the sounds of the swamp—the chirrs, croaks, and whispers—and he knew the smells of the swamp, the stale wet odors of earth caught between dry land and sea. The lizardman had navigated this place in drought and monsoon; he knew it as a man knows the feel of a well-worn shirt, but in all these many years the Old Pope had found a secret pocket and would not come out to play.

"You'll come out," the lizardman growled. The wind ate his words. "You'll come out tonight, won't you? Yessir, you'll come out tonight and we'll dance us a little dance."

He had said those same words every night he'd left the shore and ventured into the swamp. Saying those words was a habit now, a ritual, but tonight . . . tonight he could feel the true power in them. Tonight he felt them prick the hide of the Old Pope, like darts thunking into treebark, and the Old Pope stirring in his underwater cavern, opening one red eye and exhaling a single bubble from the great, gruesome snout.

The lizardman changed his direction, a wrinkled hand nudging the tiller. South by southwest, into the sweet and rancid heart of the swamp, where honeysuckle covered the hulks of decaying boats and toads as big as dinner platters sang like Johnny Cash. Some of those boats had belonged to the lizardman's friends: other lizardmen, who had sailed the sargasso seas of the swamp in search of Old Pope, and found their eternity here. Their corpses had not been recovered. The lizardman knew where they were. Their guts and gristle had nourished Old Pope, had rushed through the reptilian bulk in bloody tides to be expelled into the dark mud thirty feet down. Their bones had moldered on the bottom, like gray castles, and slowly moss had streamed from their ramparts and consumed them in velvet slime. The lizardman knew. His friends, the old braggers and bastards and butchers, had made their living from the swamp, and the swamp now laid new foundations on their frames.

"Gonna dance a little dance," the lizardman said. Another correction of the tiller, the fan rotor roaring at his back. "Gonna prance a little prance."

He had seen sixty-three summers; this sweltering August was his sixty-fourth. He was a Southern man, burned dark by the Florida sun, his skin freckled and blotched, his eyes dark brown, almost black, revealing nothing. He lived alone, drank rotgut whiskey straight from the moonshiner's still, played a wicked game of five-card stud, had two ex-wives who couldn't stand the sight or smell of him, and he made his money off gator skins. He'd done his share of poaching, sure, but the gators were growing wild in Florida now and it was open season. He'd read in the paper last week that a gator had chomped three fingers off a golfer's hand when he'd reached into the bushes for his ball on a Sarasota course. That didn't surprise the lizardman. If it moved or used to move, a gator would go after it. Mean sonsofbitches, they were. Almost as mean as he was. Well, the lizardman figured, it took mean and ugly to kill mean and ugly.

A slight nudge of the tiller sent the airboat heading straighter south. He could smell honeysuckle and Indian weed, the sweet tang of wild persimmons and the musky fragrance of cypress. And the odor of death in the night air, too: rot and fungus, putrifying gas from the muddy bottom, something lond dead caught in a quicksand pool. The wind took those aromas, and he arrowed on, following the beam of light. Wasn't too far now; maybe a mile or so, as the buzzard flew.

The lizardman did not fear the swamp. That didn't mean, of course, that he came in asking to be gator bait. Far from it: in his airboat he carried two gaffhooks, a billyclub with nails driven into it and sticking out like porcupine quills, a double-barreled shotgun, a bangstick, and his rope. Plus extra food, water, and gasoline. The swamp was a tricky beast; it lulled you, turned you into false channels and threw a mudbar up under your keel when you thought you were in six feet of water. Here, panic was death. The lizardman made a little extra money in tourist season, guiding the greenhorns through. It always amazed him how soft the

tourists were, how white and overfed. He could almost hear
the swamp drool when he brought the tourists in, and he
made sure he stayed in the wide, safe channels, showed the
greenhorns a few snakes and deer and such, and then got
them out quick. They thought they'd seen a swamp; the
lizardman just smiled and took their money.

The Seminoles, now, they were the tall-talers. You get a
Seminole to visit the little hamlet where the lizardman lived,
and his stories would make curly hair go straight. Like how
Old Pope was a ghost gator, couldn't be killed by mortal
man but only by God himself. Like how Old Pope had
ridden on a bolt of lightning into the heart of the swamp,
and any man who went looking for him was going to end up
as nuggets of gator dung.

The lizardman believe that one, almost. Too many of his
friends had come in here and not come out again. Oh yeah,
the swamp had teeth. Eat you up, bury you under. That was
how it was.

He cut his speed. The light showed a green morass ahead:
huge lilypads, and emerald slime that sparkled with irides-
cence. The air was heavy, humid, pungent with life. A mist
hung over the water, and in that mist glowed red rubies: the
eyes of gators, watching him approach. As his airboat neared,
their heads submerged with thick *shuccccking* sounds, then
came back up in the foamy wake. The lizardman went on
another hundred yards or so, then he cut off the rotor and
the airboat drifted, silent through the mist.

He lit his cigar, puffed smoke, reached for his rope, and
began to slip-knot a noose in it. The airboat was drifting
over the lilypads, making toads croak and leap for safety.
Just beyond the area of lilypads was a deeper channel that
ran between glades of rushes, and it was at the edge of this
channel that the lizardman threw his anchor over the side, a
rubber boot full of concrete. The airboat stopped drifting, in
the midst of the rushes on the rim of the deep channel.

The lizardman finished knotting the rope, tested it a few
times and found it secure. Then he went about the business
of opening a metal can, scooping out bloody chunks of

horseflesh, and hooking them onto a fist-sized prong on the end of a chain. The chain, in turn, was fixed to the metal framework of the airboat's rotor and had a little bell on it. He tossed the bait chain out, into the rushes, then he sat on his perch with a gaffhook and the lasso near at hand, switched off the light, and smoked his White Owl.

He gazed up at the stars. The moon was rising, a white crescent. Off in the distance, toward Miami, heat lightning flared across the sky. The lizardman could feel electricity in the night. It made his scalp tingle and the hairs stand up on the backs of his sinewy, tattooed arms. He weighed about a hundred and sixty pounds, stood only five feet seven, but he was as strong as a Dolphins linebacker, his shoulders hard with muscle. The lizardman was nobody's kindly old grandpap. His gaze tracked a shooting star, a red streak spitting sparks. The night throbbed. He could feel it, like a pulse. To his right somewhere a nightbird screeched nervously, and a gator made a noise like a bass fiddle. Tonight the swamp seethed. Clouds of mosquitoes swirled around the lizardman's face, but the grease and ashes he'd rubbed onto his flesh kept them from biting. He felt the same powerful sensation he'd experienced when he was getting ready to cast off from shore: something was going to happen tonight, something different. The swamp knew it, and so did the lizardman. Maybe the Old Pope was on the prowl, mean and hungry. Maybe. Laney Allen had seen Old Pope here, in this channel a year ago. The big gators cruised it like submarines, placid in the depths, angry on the surface. Laney Allen— God rest his soul—said the biggest gator paled beside the Old Pope. Said the Old Pope had eyes that shone like Cadillac headlamps in the dark, and his ebony-green hide was so thick cypress roots grew out of it. The Old Pope's wake could drown an airboat, Laney had said, and from grinning snout to wedge-shaped tail the Old Pope looked like an island moving through the channel.

Laney and T-Bird Stokes had come out here, in late April, armed with shotguns, rifles, and a few sticks of dynamite, to root Old Pope out of his secret pocket. In May, a

Seminole had found what was left of their airboat: the rotor and part of the splintered stern.

The bell dinged. The lizardman felt the boat shudder as a gator took the bait.

Teeth clenched around the cigar's butt, he picked up a high-intensity flashlight from its holder beside his seat and flicked it on. The gator was thrashing water now, turning itself over and over on the end of the chain. The lizardman's light found it, there in the rushes. It was a young gator, mabye four feet long, not very heavy but it was madder than hell-cast Lucifer and ready to fight. The lizardman got down off his perch, put on a pair of cowhide gloves, and watched the gator battle against the prongs jabbed in its jaws. Foamy water and dark mud splattered him, as the beast's tail smacked back and forth. The lizardman couldn't help it; though he and the gators were always on opposite ends of the chain, he found a savage beauty in the saw-toothed grin, the red-filmed eyes, the heaving, slime-draped body. But money was more beautiful, and the hides kept him alive. So be it. The lizardman waited until the gator lifted its head to try to shake the prongs loose, then he let fly with the lasso.

His aim, born of much practice, was perfect. He snared the gator's throat, drew the beast in closer, the muscles standing out in his arms and the boat rocking underneath him. Then he picked up the gaffhook and speared the white belly as the gator began to turn over and over again in the frothy gray water. Blood bloomed like a red flower, the heart pierced. But the gator still fought with stubborn determination until the lizardman conked it a few times on the skull with the nail-studded billyclub. The gator, its brain impaled, expired with a last thrash that popped water ten feet into the air, then its eyes rolled back into the prehistoric head and the lizardman hauled the carcass over the side. He gave the skull another hard knock with the billyclub, knowing that gators sometimes played possum until they could get hold of an arm or leg. This one, however, had given up the ghost. The lizardman slipped the chain out of the prongs, which were deeply imbedded and would have to be pulled out with pliers at a later date. He had a cardboard box full of prongs, so he attached another one to the chain, baited it with horseflesh, and threw it over the side.

He freed his lasso from around the bleeding, swamp-smelling carcass, turned off his flashlight, and climbed again onto his perch.

This was what his life was all about.

An hour passed before the bait was taken again. This gator was larger than the first, heavy but sluggish. It had one claw missing, evidence of a fight. The lizardman hauled it in some, rested, hauled it in the last distance with the lasso and the gaffhook. Finally, the gator lay in the bottom of the airboat with the first, its lungs making a noise like a steam engine slowly losing power.

The lizardman, slime on his arms and his face glistening with sweat, waited.

It was amazing to him that these creatures had never changed. The world had turned around the sun a million times, a hundred times a million, and the gators stayed the same. Down in the mud they dwelled, in their secret swamp caverns, their bodies hard and perfect for their purpose. They slept and fed, fed and bred, slept and fed, and that was the circle of their existence. It was weird, the lizardman thought, that jet airplanes flew over the swamp and fast cars sped on the interstate only a few miles from here while down in the mud dinosaurs stirred and crept. That's what they were, for sure. Dinosaurs, the last of their breed.

The lizardman watched shooting stars, the dead cigar clamped in his teeth. The hair prickled on his arms. There was a power in the night. What was it? Something about to happen, something different from all the other nights. The swamp knew it too, and wondered in its language of bird-calls, gator grunts, frog croaks, and whistles. What was it?

The Old Pope, the lizardman thought. The Old Pope, on the move.

The moon tracked across the sky. The lizardman brought in his bait—found a water moccasin clinging to it—then he pulled up anchor and guided the boat through the weeds with a gaffhook. The water was about five feet deep, but nearer the channel the bottom sloped to twelve or more. He found what he thought might be a good place next to a clump of cypress, a fallen tree angled down into the depths and speckled with yellow crabs. He let the anchor down again, threw out the bait chain, got up on his perch, and sat there, thinking and listening.

The swamp was speaking to him. What was it trying to say?

Ten minutes or so later, the bell dinged.

Water foamed and boiled. A big one! the lizardman thought. "Dance a little dance!" he said, and turned on the flashlight.

It was a big gator, true, but it wasn't Old Pope. This beast was seven feet long, weighed maybe four hundred pounds. It was going to be a ballbreaker to get in the boat. Its eyes flared like comets in the light, its jaws snapping as it tried to spit out the prongs. The lizardman waited for the right moment, then flung his rope. It noosed the gator's muzzle, sealing the jaws shut. The lizardman pulled, but the gator was a powerful bastard and didn't want to come. Careful, careful, he thought. If he lost his footing and went overboard, God help him. He got the gaffhook ready, the muscles straining in his shoulders and back, though he already knew he'd have to use the shotgun on this one.

He started to pick up the shotgun when he felt the airboat rise on a pressure wave.

He lost his balance, came perilously close to slipping over, but the rubber grips of his boots gripped to the wet deck. He was surprised more than anything else, at the suddenness of it. And then he saw the gator on the end of the chain thrash up and almost leap out of the foaming water. If a gator's eyes could register terror, then that was what the lizardman saw.

The gator shivered. There was a ripping noise, like an axed tree falling. Bloody water splashed up around the reptile's body. Not only bloody water, the lizardman saw in another second, but also ropy coils of dark green intestines, billowing out of the gator's belly. The beast was jerked downward with a force that made the rope and the chain crack taut, the bell dinging madly. The lizardman had dropped his light. He fumbled for it, amid the gator carcasses, the rope scorching his cowhide glove. The airboat lifted up again, crashed down with a mighty splash, and the lizardman went to his knees. He heard terrible, crunching noises: the sounds of bones being broken.

And just that fast, it was all over.

He stood up, shaking. The airboat rocked, rocked, rocked, a cradle on the deep. He found the light and turned it on the beast at the chain's end.

The lizardman gave a soft gasp, his mouth dry as Sahara dust.

The gator had been diminished. More than half of it had been torn away, guts and gore floating in the water around the ragged wound.

Bitten in two, the lizardman thought. A surge of pure horror coursed through him. Bitten by something from underneath . . .

"Good God A'mighty," he whispered, and he let go of the rope.

The severed gator floated on the end of the chain, its insides still streaming out in sluggish tides. On the fallen tree trunk, the crabs were scrambling over each other, smelling a feast.

The lizardman realized that he was a long way from home.

Something was coming. He heard it pushing the reeds aside on the edge of the deep channel. Heard the swirl of water around its body, and the suction of mud on its claws. Old Pope. Old Pope, risen from the heart of the swamp. Old Pope, mean and hungry. Coming back for the rest of the gator, caught on the chain's end.

The lizardman had often heard of people bleating with fear. He'd never known what that would've sounded like, until that moment. It was, indeed, a bleat, like a stunned sheep about to get its head smashed with a mallet.

He turned toward the airboat's engine, hit the starter switch, and reached for the throttle beside his seat. As soon as he gave the engine some gas, the rotor crashed against the frame, bent by the force of Old Pope on the chain, and it threw a pinwheel of sparks and crumpled like wet cardboard. The airboat spun around in a tight circle before the engine blew, the flashlight flying out of the lizardman's grip as he fell onto the rough hides of the dead gators. He looked up, slime dripping from his chin, as something large and dark rose up against the night.

Swamp water streamed from Old Pope's armored sides. The lizardman could see that Laney had been right: roots, rushes, and weeds grew from the ebony-green plates, and not only that but snakes slithered through the cracks and crabs scuttled over the leathery edges. The lizardman recoiled, but he could only go to the boat's other side and that wasn't nearly far enough. He was on his knees, like a penitent praying for mercy at Old Pope's altar. He saw something—a scaled claw, a tendril, something—slither down and grasp the snared gator's head. Old Pope began to pull the mangled carcass up out of the water, and as the chain snapped tight again the entire airboat started to overturn.

In another few seconds the lizardman would be up to his neck in deep shit. He knew that, and knew he was a dead man one way or the other. He reached out, found the shotgun, and gave Old Pope the blast of a barrel.

In the flare of orange light he saw gleaming teeth, yellow eyes set under a massive brow where a hundred crabs clung like barnacles to an ancient wharf. Old Pope gave a deep grunt like the lowest note of a church organ, and that was when the lizardman knew.

Old Pope was not an alligator.

The severed gator slid into Old Pope's maw, and the teeth crunched down. The airboat overturned as the lizardman fired his second barrel, then he was in the churning water with the monster less than fifteen feet away.

His boots sank into mud. The flashlight, waterproof,

bobbed in the turbulence. Snakes writhed around Old Pope's jaws as the beast ate, and the lizardman floundered for the submerged treetrunk.

Something oozing and rubbery wound around his chest. He screamed, being lifted out of the water. An object was beside him; he grabbed it, held tight, and knew Old Pope had decided on a second meal. He smelled the thing's breath—blood and swamp—as he was being carried toward the gaping mouth, and he heard the hissing of snakes that clung to the thing's gnarled maw. The lizardman saw the shine of an eye, catching the crescent moon. He jabbed at it with the object in his grip, and the bangstick exploded.

The eye burst into gelatinous muck, its inside showering the lizardman. At the same time, Old Pope roared with a noise like the clap of doom, and whatever held the lizardman went slack. He fell, head over heels, into the water. Came up again, choking and spitting, and half-ran, half-swam for his life through the swaying rushes.

Old Pope was coming after him. He didn't need an eye in the back of his head to tell him that. Whatever the thing was, it wanted his meat and bones. He heard the sound of it coming, the awful suction of water and mud as it advanced. The lizardman felt panic and insanity, two Siamese twins, whirl through his mind. Dance a little dance! Prance a little prance! He stepped in a hole, went in over his head, fought to the surface again and threw himself forward. Old Pope— swamp-god, king of the gators—was almost upon him, like a moving cliff, and snakes and crabs rained down around the lizardman.

He scrambled up, out of the reeds onto a mudflat. Hot breath washed over him, and then that rubbery thing whipped around his waist like a frog's tongue. It squeezed the breath out of him, lifted him off his feet, and began to reel him toward the glistening, saw-edged jaws.

The lizardman had not gotten to be sixty-four years old by playing dead. He fought against the oozing, sticky thing that had him. He beat at it with his fists, kicked and hollered and thrashed. He raged against it, and Old Pope held him tight and watched him with its single eye like a man might watch an insect struggling on flypaper.

It had him. It knew it had him. The lizardman wasn't far gone enough in the head not to know that. But still he beat at the beast, still he hollered and raged, and still Old Pope inspected him, its massive gnarly head tilted slightly to one side and water running through the cracks on the skull-deep ugly of its face.

Lightning flashed. There was no thunder. The lizardman heard a high whine. His skin prickled and writhed with electricity, and his wet hair danced.

Old Pope grunted again. Another surge of lightning, closer this time.

The abomination dropped him, and the lizardman plopped down onto the mudflat like an unwanted scrap.

Old Pope lifted its head, contemplating the stars.

The crescent moon was falling to earth, in a slow spiral. The lizardman watched it, his heart pounding and his arms and legs encased in mire. The crescent moon shot streaks of blue lightning, like fingers probing the swamp's folds. Slowly, slowly, it neared Old Pope, and the monster lifted claw-fingered arms and called in a voice that wailed over the wilderness like a thousand trumpets.

It was the voice, the lizardman thought, of something lost and far from home.

The crescent moon—no, not a moon, but a huge shape that sparkled metallic—was now almost overhead. It hovered, with a high whine, above the creature that had been known as Old Pope, and the lizardman watched lightning dance around the beast like homecoming banners.

Dance a little dance, he thought. Prance a little prance.

Old Pope rumbled. The craggy body shivered, like a child about to go to a birthday party. And then Old Pope's head turned, and the single eye fixed on the lizardman.

Electricity flowed through the lizardman's hair, through his bones and sinews. He was plugged into a socket of unknown design, his fillings sparking pain in his mouth. He took a breath as the Old Pope stepped toward him, one grotesque, ancient leg sinking into the earth.

Something—a tendril, a third arm, whatever—came out of Old Pope's chest. It scooped up mud and painted the lizardman's face with it, like a tribal marking. The touch was sticky and rough, and it left the smell of the swamp and reptilian things in the lizardman's nostrils.

Then Old Pope lifted its face toward the metallic crescent, and raised its arms. Lightning flared and crackled across the mudflats. Birds screeched in their trees, and the voices of gators throbbed.

The lizardman blinked, his eyes narrowed against the glare.

And when the glare had faded, two seconds later, the lightning had taken Old Pope with it.

The machine began to rise, slowly, slowly. Then it ascended in a blur of speed and was gone as well, leaving only one crescent moon over the cacophonous swamp.

The Seminoles had been right, the lizardman thought. Right as rain. Old Pope had come to the swamp on a bolt of lightning, and was riding one home again too.

Whatever that might be.

He rested awhile, there in the mud of his domain.

Sometime before dawn he roused himself, and he found a piece of his airboat floating off the mudflat. He found one of his gaffhooks too, and he lay on the splintered remnant of his boat and began pushing himself through the downtrodden rushes toward the far shore. The swamp sang around him, as the lizardman crawled home on his belly.

PILOTS

Joe R. Lansdale and Dan Lowry

Micky was at it again. His screams echoed up the fuselage, blended with the wind roaring past the top gunner port. The Pilot released Sparks from his radio duty long enough to send him back to take care of and comfort Micky.

The day had passed slowly and they had passed it in the hanger, listening to the radio, taking turns at watch from the tower, making battle plans. Just after sundown they got into their gear and took off, waited high up in cover over the well-traveled trade lanes. Waited for prey.

Tonight they intended to go after a big convoy. Get as many kills as they could, then hit the smaller trade lanes later on, search out and destroy. With luck their craft would be covered with a horde of red kill marks before daybreak. At the thought of that, the Pilot formed the thing he used as a mouth into a smile. He was the one who painted the red slashes on the sides of their machine (war paint), and it was a joy to see them grow. It was his hope that someday they would turn the craft from black to red.

Finally the Pilot saw the convoy. He called to Sparks.

In the rear, Micky was settled down to sobs and moans, had pushed the pain in the stumps of his legs aside, tightened his will to the mission at hand.

As Sparks came forward at a stoop, he reached down and patted Ted, the turret gunner, on the flight jacket, then settled back in with the radio.

"It's going to be a good night for hunting," Sparks said to the Pilot. "I've been intercepting enemy communiqués. There must be a hundred in our operational area. There are twelve in the present enemy convoy, sir. Most of the state escorts are to the north, around the scene of last night's sortie."

The Pilot nodded, painfully formed the words that came out of his fire-gutted throat. "It'll be a good night, Sparks. I can feel it."

"Death to the enemy," Sparks said. And the words were repeated as one by the crew.

So they sat high up, on the overpass, waiting for the convoy of trucks to pass below.

"This is the Tulsa Tramp. You got the Tulsa Tramp. Have I got a copy there? Come back."

"That's a big 10-4, Tramp. You got the L.A. Flash here."

"What's your 20, L.A.?"

"East bound and pounded down on this I-20, coming up on that 450 marker. How 'bout yourself, Tramp?"

"West bound for Dallas town with a truck load of cakes. What's the Smokey situation? Come back?"

"Got one at the Garland exit. Big ole bear. How's it look over your shoulder?"

"Got it clear, L.A., clear back to that Hallsville town. You got a couple County Mounties up there at the Owentown exit."

"Where's all the super troopers?"

"Haven't you heard, Tramp?"

"Heard what, L.A.? Come back."

"Up around I-30, that Mount Pleasant town. Didn't you know about Banana Peel?"

"Don't know Banana Peel. Come back with it."

"Black Bird got him."

"Black Bird?"

"You have been out of it."

"Been up New York way for a while, just pulled down and loaded up at Birmingham, heading out to the West Coast."

"Some psycho's knocking off truckers. Banana Peel was the last one. Someone's been nailing us right and left. Banana Peel's cab was shot to pieces, just like the rest. Someone claims he saw the car that got Banana Peel. A black Thunderbird, all cut down and rigged special. Over-long looking. Truckers have got to calling it the Black Bird. There's even rumor it's a ghost. Watch out for it."

"Ghosts don't chop down and rerig Thunderbirds. But I'll sure watch for it."

"10-4 on that. All we need is some nut case messing with us. Business is hard enough as it is."

"A big 10-4 there. Starting to fade, catch you on the flip-flop."

"10-4."

"10-4. Puttin' the pedal to the metal and gone."

The Tramp, driving a White Freight Liner equipped with shrunken head dangling from the cigarette-lighter knob and a men's magazine foldout taped to the cab ceiling, popped a Ronny Milsap tape into the deck, sang along with three songs, and drowned Milsap out.

It was dead out there on the highway. Not a truck or car in sight. No stars above. Just a thick black cloud cover with a moon hidden behind it.

Milsap wasn't cutting it. Tramp pulled out the tape and turned on the stereo, found a snappy little tune he could whistle along with. For some reason he felt like whistling, like making noise. He wondered if it had something to do with the business L.A. had told him about. The Black Bird.

Or perhaps it was just the night. Certainly it was unusual for the Interstate to be this desolate, this dead. It was as if his were the only vehicle left in the world . . .

He saw something. It seemed to have appeared out of nowhere, had flicked beneath the orangish glow of the up-coming underpass lights. It looked like a car running fast without lights.

Tramp blinked. Had he imagined it? It had been so quick. Certainly only a madman would be crazy enough to drive that fast on the Interstate without lights.

A feeling washed over him that was akin to pulling out of a dive; like when he was in Nam and he flew down close to the foliage to deliver flaming death, then at the last moment he would lift his chopper skyward and leave the earth behind him in a burst of red-yellow flame. Then, cruising the Vietnamese skies, he could only feel relief that his hands had responded and he had not been peppered and salted all over Nam.

Tramp turned off the stereo and considered. A bead of sweat balled on his upper lip. *Perhaps he had just seen the Black Bird.*

". . . ought to be safe in a convoy this size . . ." the words filtered out of Tramp's CB. He had been so lost in thought, he had missed the first part of the transmission. He turned it up. The chatter was furious. It was a convoy and its members were exchanging thoughts, stories, and good time rattle like a bunch of kids swapping baseball cards.

The twangy, scratchy voices were suddenly very comfort-able; forced memories of Nam back deep in his head, kept that black memory-bat from fluttering.

He thought again of what he might have seen. But now he had passed beneath the underpass and there was nothing. No car. No shape in the night. Nothing.

Imagination, he told himself. He drove on, listening to the CB.

The bead of sweat rolled cold across his lips and down his chin.

*   *   *

Tramp wasn't the only one who had seen something in the shadows, something like a car without lights. Sloppy Joe, the convoy's back door, had glimpsed an odd shape in his sideview mirror, something coming out of the glare of the overpass lights, something as sleek and deadly-looking as a hungry barracuda.

"Breaker 1-9, this is Sloppy Joe, your back door."

"Ah, come ahead, back door, this is Pistol Pete, your front door. Join the conversation."

"Think I might have something here. Not sure. Thought I saw something in the sideview, passing under those overpass lights."

Moment of silence.

"You say, think you saw? Come back."

"Not sure. If I did, it was running without lights."

"Smokey?" another trucker asked.

"Don't think so . . . Now wait a minute. I see something now. A pair of dim, red lights."

"Uh oh, cop cherries," a new trucker's voice added.

"No. Not like that."

Another moment of silence.

Sloppy Joe again: "Looks a little like a truck using nothing but its running lights . . . but they're hung too far down for that . . . and they're shaped like eyes."

"Eyes! This is Pistol Pete, come back."

"Infrared lights, Pistol Pete, that's what I'm seeing."

"Have . . . have we got the Black Bird here?"

Tramp, listening to the CB, felt that pulling out of a dive sensation again. He started to reach for his mike, tell them he was their back door, but he clenched the wheel harder instead. No. He was going to stay clear of this. What could a lone car—if in fact it was a car—do to a convoy of big trucks anyway?

The CB chattered.

"This is Sloppy Joe. Those lights are moving up fast."

"The Black Bird?" asked Pistol Pete.

"Believe we got a big positive on that."

"What can he do to a convoy of trucks anyway," said another trucker.

My sentiments exactly, thought Tramp.

"Pick you off one by one," came a voice made of smoke and hot gravel.

"What, back door?"

"Not me, Pistol Pete."

"Who? Bear Britches? Slipped Disk? Merry—"

"None of them. It's me, the Black Bird."

"This is Sloppy Joe. It's the Black Bird, all right. Closing on my tail, pulling alongside."

"Watchyerself!"

"I can see it now . . . running alongside . . . I can make out some slash marks—"

"Confirmed kills," said the Pilot. *"If I were an artist, I'd paint little trucks."*

"Back door, back door! This is Pistol Pete. Come in."

"Sloppy Joe here . . . There's a man with a gun in the sunroof."

"Run him off the road, Sloppy Joe! Ram him!"

Tramp, his window down, cool breeze blowing against his face, heard three quick, flat snaps. Over the whine of the wind and the roar of the engine, they sounded not unlike the rifle fire he had heard over the wind and the rotor blades of his copter in Nam. And he thought he had seen the muzzle blast of at least one of those shots. Certainly he had seen something light up the night.

"I'm hit! Hit!" Sloppy Joe said.

"What's happening? Come back, Sloppy Joe. This is Pistol Pete. What's happening?"

"Hit . . . can't keep on the road."

"Shut down!"

Tramp saw an arc of flame fly high and wide from the dark T-bird—which looked like little more than an elongated shadow racing along the highway—and strike Sloppy Joe's truck. The fire boomed suddenly, licked the length of the truck, blossomed in the wind. A molotov, thought Tramp.

Tramp pulled over, tried to gear down. Cold sweat popped
on his face like measles, his hands shook on the wheel.

Sloppy Joe's Mack had become a quivering, red flower of
flame. It whipped its tail, jackknifed, and flipped, rolled
like a toy truck across the concrete highway divider. When
it stopped rolling, it was wrapped in fire and black smoke,
had transformed from glass and metal to heat and wreckage.

The Bird moved on, slicing through the smoke, avoiding
debris, blending with the night like a dark ghost.

As Tramp passed the wrecked truck he glimpsed something moving in the cab, a blackened, writhing thing that
had once been human. But it moved only for an instant and
was still.

Almost in a whisper, came: "This is Bear Britches. I'm
the back door now. Sloppy Joe's in flames . . . Gone . . ."

Those flames, that burnt-to-a-crisp body, sent Tramp back
in time, back to Davy Cluey that hot-as-hell afternoon in
Nam. Back to when God gave Tramp his personal demon.

They had been returning from a routine support mission,
staying high enough to avoid small arms fire. Their rockets
and most of their M-60 ammo were used up. The two chop-
pers were scurrying back to base when they picked up the
urgent call. The battered remains of a platoon were pinned
down on a small hill off Highway One. If the stragglers
didn't get a dust-off in a hurry, the Cong were going to dust
them off for good.

He and Davy had turned back to aid the platoon, and
soon they were twisting and turning in the air like great
dragonflies performing a sky ballet. The Cong's fire buzzed
around them.

Davy sat down first and the stranded Marines rushed the
copter. That's when the Cong hit.

Why they hadn't waited until he too was on the ground
he'd never know. Perhaps the sight of all those Marines—
far too many to cram into the already heavily manned
copter—was just too tempting for patience. The Cong sent a
stream of liquid fire rolling lazily out of the jungle, and it

had entered Davy's whirling rotors. When it hit the blades it suddenly transformed into a spinning parasol of flames.

That was his last sight of the copter and Davy. He had lifted upward and flown away. To this day, the image of that machine being showered by flames came back to him in vivid detail. Sometimes it seemed he was no longer driving on the highway, but flying in Nam. The rhythmic beat of the tires rolling over tar strips in the highway would pick up tempo until they became the twisting chopper blades, and soon, out beyond the windshield, the highway would fade and the cement would become the lush jungles of Nam.

Sometimes, the feeling was so intense he'd have to pull over until it passed.

A CB voice tossed Nam out of Tramp's head.

"This is Bear Britches. The Bird is moving in on me."

"Pistol Pete here. Get away, get away."

"He's alongside me now. Can't shake him. Something sticking out of a hole in the trunk—a rifle barrel!"

A shot could be heard clearly over the open airways, then the communications button was released and there was silence. Ahead of him Tramp could see the convoy and he could see the eighteen-wheeler that was its back door. The truck suddenly swerved, as if to ram the Black Bird, but Tramp saw a red burst leap from the Bird's trunk, and instantly the eighteen-wheeler was swerving back, losing control. It crossed the meridian, whipping its rear end like a crocodile's tail, plowed through a barbed-wire fence, and smacked a row of pine trees with a sound like a thunderclap. The cab smashed up flat as a pancake. Tramp knew no one could have lived through that.

And now ahead of him, Tramp saw another molotov flipping through the air, and in an instant, another truck was out of commission, wearing flames and flipping in a frenzy along the side of the road. Tramp's last memory of the blazing truck was its tires, burning brightly, spinning wildly around and around like little inflamed ferris wheels.

"Closing on me," came a trucker's voice. "The sonofabitch is closing on me. Help me! God, someone help me here."

Tramp remembered a similar communication from Davy that day in Nam; the day he had lifted up to the sky and flown his bird away and left Davy there beneath that parasol of fire.

Excited chatter sounded over the air waves as the truckers tried to summon up the highway boys, tried to call for help.

Tramp saw a sign for a farmroad exit, half a mile away. The stones settled in his gut again, his hands filmed with sweat. It was like that day in Nam, when he had the choice to turn back and help or run like hell.

No trucks took the exit. Perhaps their speed was up too much to attempt it. But he was well back of them and the Bird. What reason did he have to close in on the Bird? What could he do? As it was, the Bird could see his lights now and they might pop a shot at him any second.

Tramp swallowed. It was him or them.

He slowed, took the exit at fifty, which was almost too fast, and the relief that first washed over him turned sour less than a second later. He felt just like he had that day in Nam when he had lifted up and away, saved himself from Death at the expense of Davy.

"Report!" said the Pilot.

Through the headphones came Micky's guttural whine. "Tail gunner reporting, sir. Three of the enemy rubbed out, sir."

"Confirmed," came the voice of the turret gunner. "I have visual confirmation on rear gunners report. Enemy formation affecting evasive maneuvers. Have sighted two more sets of enemy lights approaching on the port quarter. Request permission to break off engagement with forward enemy formation and execute strafing attack on approaching formation."

"Permission granted," said the Pilot. "Sparks! Report State Escort wherebouts."

"Catching signals of approaching State Escorts, sir. ETA three minutes."

"Number of Escorts?"

"Large squadron, sir."

"Pilot to flight crew. Change in orders. Strafe forward formation, to prepare to peel off at next exit."

The Bird swooped down on the forward truck, the turret gun slamming blast after blast into the semi's tires. The truck was suddenly riding on the rims. Steel hit concrete and sparks popped skyward like overheated fireflys.

The Bird moved around the truck just as it lost control and went through a low guardrail fence and down into a deep ditch.

Black smoke boiled up from the Black Bird's tires, mixed with the night. A moment later the sleek car was running alongside another truck. The turret gunner's weapon barked like a nervous dog, kept barking as it sped past the trucks and made its way to the lead semi. The turret gunner barked a few more shots as they whipped in front of the truck, and the tail gunner put twenty fast rounds through the windshield. Even as the driver slumped over the semi's wheel and the truck went barreling driverless down the highway, the Bird lost sight of it and took a right exit, and like a missile, was gone.

Black against black, the Bird soared, and inside the death machine the Pilot, with the internal vision of his brain, turned the concrete before him into a memory:

Once he had been whole, a tall young man with a firm body and a head full of technicolor dreams. The same had been true of his comrades. There had been a time when these dreams had been guiding lights. They had wanted to fly, had been like birds in the nest longing for the time when they would try their wings; thinking of that time, living for that time when they would soar in silver arrows against a fine blue sky, or climb high up to the face of the moon.

Each of them had been in the Civil Air Patrol. Each of them had hours of air time, and each of them had plans for the Air Force. And these plans had carried them through many a day and through many a hard exam and they had talked these plans until they felt they were merely reciting facts from a future they had visited.

But then there was the semi and that very dark night.

The four of them had been returning from Barksdale Air Force Base. They had made a deal with the recruiter to keep them together throughout training, and their spirits were high.

And the driver who came out of the darkness, away from the honky-tonk row known as Hell's Half Mile, had been full of spirits too.

There had been no lights, just a sudden looming darkness that turned into a White Freight Liner crossing the middle of the highway; a stupid, metallic whale slapdash in the center of their path.

The night screamed with an explosion of flesh, metal, glass, and chrome. Black tire smoke boiled to the heavens and down from the heavens came a rain of sharp, hot things that engulfed the four; and he, the one now called the Pilot, awoke to whiteness. White everywhere, and it did not remind him of cleanliness, this whiteness. No. It was empty, this whiteness, empty like the ever-hungry belly of time; the people floated by him in white, not angel-white, but wraith-white; and the pain came to live with him and it called his body home.

When enough of the pain had passed and he was fully aware, he found a monster one morning in the mirror. A one-legged thing with a face and body like melted plastic. But the eyes. Those sharp hawk eyes that had anticipated seeing the world from the clouds, were as fine as ever; little green gems that gleamed from an overcooked meat rind.

And the others:

Sparks had lost his left arm and half his head was metal. He had been castrated by jagged steel. Made sad jokes about being the only man who could keep his balls in a plastic bag beside his bed.

Ted had metal clamps on his legs and a metal jaw. His scalp had been peeled back like an orange. Skin grafts hadn't worked. Too burned. From now on, across his head—

like some sort of toothless mouth—would be a constantly open wound behind which a smooth, white skull would gleam.

Micky was the worst. Legs fried off. One eye cooked to boiled egg consistency—a six-minute egg. Face like an exploding sore. Throat and vocal cords nearly gone. His best sound was a high, piercing whine.

Alone they were fragments of humanity. Puzzle parts of a horrid whole.

Out of this vengeance grew.

They took an old abandoned silo on Spark's farm—inherited years back when his father had died—fixed it up to suit their needs; had the work done and used Spark's money.

They also pooled their accounts, and with the proper help, they had elevators built into the old gutted silo. Had telescopes installed. Radios. And later they bought maps and guns. Lots of guns. They bought explosives and made super molotovs of fuel and plastic explosives. Bad business.

And the peculiar talents that had been theirs individually, became a singular thing that built gadgets and got things done. So before long, the Pilot, stomping around on his metallic leg, looking like a run-through-the-wringer Ahab, became their boss. They cut Micky's T-bird down and rerigged it, rebuilt it as a war machine. And they began to kill. Trucks died on the highway, became skeletons, black charred frames. And the marks on the sides of the Black Bird grew and grew as they went about their stalks . . .

Highway now. Thoughts tucked away. Cruising easily along the concrete sky. Pilot and crew.

Tramp felt safe, but he also felt low, real low. He kept wondering about Nam, about the trucks, about that turnoff he'd taken a few miles and long minutes back, but his considerations were cut short when fate took a hand.

To his left he saw eyes, red eyes, wheeling out of a dark connecting road, and the eyes went from dim to sudden-bright (fuck this sneaking around), and as Tramp passed that road, the eyes followed and in the next instant they were looking up his tailpipe, and Tramp knew damn good and well whose eyes they were, and he was scared.

Cursing providence, Tramp put the pedal to the metal and glanced into his sideview mirror and saw the eyes were very close. Then he looked forward and saw that the grade was climbing. He could feel the truck losing momentum. The Bird was winging around on the left side.

The hill was in front of him now, and though he had the gas pedal to the floor, things were Slow-City, and the truck was chugging, and behind him, coming ass-over-tires, was the Black Bird.

Tramp trembled, thought: This is redemption. The thought hung in his head like a shoe on a peg. It was another chance for him to deal the cards and deal them right.

Time started up for Tramp again, and he glanced into the sideview mirror at the Bird, whipped his truck hard left in a wild move that nearly sent the White Freight Liner side-over-side. He hit the Bird a solid bump and drove it off the road, almost into a line of trees. The Bird's tires spat dirt and grass in dark gouts. The Bird slowed, fell back.

Tramp cheered, tooted his horn like a madman, and made that hill; two toots at the top and he dipped over the rise and gave two toots at the bottom.

The Black Bird made the road again and the Pilot gave the car full throttle. In a moment the Bird found its spot on Tramp's ass.

Tramp's moment of triumph passed. That old Boogy Man sat down on his soul again. Sweat dripped down his face and hung on his nose like a dingleberry on an ass hair, finally fell with a plop on the plastic seat cover between Tramp's legs, and in the fearful silence of the cab the sound was like a boulder dropping on hard ground.

Tramp's left side window popped and became a close-weave net of cracks and clusters. A lead wasp jumped around the cab and died somewhere along the floorboard. It was a full five seconds before Tramp realized he'd been grazed across the neck, just under his right ear. The glass from the window began to fall out like slow, heavy rain.

Tramp glanced left and saw the Bird was on him again, and he tried to whip in that direction, tried to nail the bastard again. But the Bird wasn't having any. It moved forward and away, surged around in front of Tramp.

The Bird, now directly in front of him, farted a red burst from its trunk. The front window of the truck became a spiraling web and the collar of Tramp's shift lifted as if plucked by an unseen hand. The bullet slammed into the seat and finally into the back wall of the truck.

The glass was impossible to see out of. Tramp bent forward and tried to look out of a small area of undamaged windshield. The Bird's gun farted again, and Tramp nearly lost control as fragments flew in on him like shattered moonlight. Something hot and sharp went to live in his right shoulder, down deep next to the bone. Tramp let out a scream and went momentarily black, nearly lost the truck.

Carving knives of wind cut through the windshield and woke him, watered his eyes, and made the wound ache like a bad tooth. He thought: The next pop that comes I won't hear, because that will be the one that takes my skull apart, and they say the one that gets you is the one you don't hear.

But suddenly the two asslights of the Bird fell away and dipped out of sight.

The road fell down suddenly into a dip, and though it was not enormous, he had not expected it and his speed was up full tilt. The truck cab lifted into the air and shot forward and dragged the whipping cargo trailer behind it. As the cab came down, Tramp fully expected the trailer to keep whipping and jackknife him off the road, but instead it came down and fell in line behind the cab and Tramp kept going.

Ahead a narrow bridge appeared, its suicide rails painted phosphorescent white. The bridge appeared just wide enough to keep the guardrail post from slicing the door handles off a big truck.

Tramp's hand flew to the gear shift. He shifted and gassed and thought: This is it, the moment of truth, the big casino,

die dog or eat the hatchet; my big shot to repay the big
fuckup. Tramp shifted again and gave the White Freight
Liner all it had.

The White Freight Liner was breathing up the tailpipe of
the Black Bird and the Pilot was amazed at how much speed
the driver was getting out of that rig; a part of him appreciated the skill involved in that. No denying, that sonofabitch
could drive.

Then the Pilot caught a scream in his ruptured throat.
They were coming up on the bridge, and there were no lefts
or rights to take them away from that. The bridge was
narrow. Tight. Room for one, and the Pilot knew what the
truck driver had in mind. The truck was hauling ass, pushing
to pass, trying to run alongside the Bird, planning to push it
through the rails and down twenty feet into a wet finale of
fast-racing creek. The senseless bastard was going to try and
get the Bird if he had to go with it.

The Pilot smiled. He could understand that. He smelled
death, and it had the odor of gasoline fumes, burning rubber, and flying shit.

Behind the Bird, like a leviathan of the concrete seas,
came the White Freight Liner. It bumped the Bird's rear
and knocked the car to the right, and in that moment, the
big truck, moving as easily as if it were a compact car, came
around on the Bird's left.

The semi began to bear right, pushing at the Bird. The
Pilot knew his machine was fated to kiss the guardrail post.

"Take the wheel!" the Pilot screamed to Sparks, and he
rose up to poke his head through the sunroof, pull on
through, and crawl along top. He grabbed the semi's left
sideview mirror and allowed the truck's momentum to pull
him away from the car, keeping his good and his ruined leg
high to keep from being pinched in half between the two
machines.

Sparks leaped for the steering wheel, got a precious grip
on it even as the Pilot was dangling on top of the car,

reaching for the truck's mirror frame. But Sparks saw immediately that his grabbing the wheel meant nothing. He and the others were goners; he couldn't get the Bird ahead of the truck and there just wasn't room for two, they were scraping the guardrail post as it was, and now he felt the Bird going to the right and it hit the first post with a *kaplodata* sound, then the car gathered in three more posts, and just for an instant, Sparks thought he might be able to keep the Bird on the bridge, get ahead of the semi. But it was a fleeting fancy. The Bird's right wheels were out in the air with nothing to grab, and the Bird smashed two more posts, one of which went through the window, then hurtled off the bridge. In dim chorus the crew of the Bird screamed all the way down to where the car struck the water and went nose first into the creek bed. Then the car's rear end came down and the car settled under the water, except for a long strip of roof.

No one swam out.

The Pilot saw the car go over out of the corner of his eye, heard the screams, but so be it. He had tasted doom before. It was his job to kill trucks.

Tramp jerked his head to the right, saw the maimed face of the Pilot, and for one brief moment, he felt as if he were looking not at a face but into the cold, dark depths of his very own soul.

The Pilot smashed the window with the hilt of a knife he pulled from a scabbard on his metal leg, and started scuttling through the window.

Tramp lifted his foot off the gas and kicked out at the door handle, and the door swung open and carried the Pilot with it. The Pilot and the door hit a guardrail post and sparks flew up from the Pilot's metal leg as it touched concrete.

The door swung back in, the Pilot still holding on, and Tramp kicked again, and out went the door, and another post hit the Pilot and carried him and the door away, down into the water below.

And in the same moment, having stretched too far to kick
the door, and having pulled the wheel too far right, the
White Freight Liner went over the bridge and smashed half
in the water and half out.

Crawling through the glassless front of the truck, Tramp
rolled out onto the hood and off, landed on the wet ground
next to the creek.

Rising up on his knees and elbows. Tramp looked out at
the creek and saw the Pilot shoot up like a porpoise, splash
back down, and thrash wildly in the water, thrashing in a
way that let Tramp know that the Pilot's body was little
more than shattered bones and ruptured muscles held together by skin and clothes.

The Pilot looked at him, and Tramp thought he saw the
Pilot nod, though he could not be sure. And just before the
Pilot went under as if diving, the tip of his metal leg winking
up and then falling beneath the water, Tramp lifted his hand
and shot the Pilot the finger.

"Jump up on that and spin around," Tramp said.

The Pilot did not come back up.

Tramp eased onto his back and felt the throbbing of the
bullet wound and thought about the night and what he had
done. In the distance, but distinct, he could hear the highway whine of truck tires on the Interstate.

Tramp smiled at that. Somehow it struck him as amusing.
He closed his eyes, and just before he drifted into an exhausted sleep, he said aloud, "How about that, Davy? How
about that?"

STALKER

Ed Gorman

1

Eleven years, two months, and five days later, we caught him. In an apartment house on the west edge of Des Moines. The man who had raped and murdered my daughter.

Inside the rental Pontiac, Slocum said, "I can fix it so we have to kill him." The dramatic effect of his words was lost somewhat when he waggled a bag of Dunkin' Donuts at me.

I shook my head: "No."

"No to the donuts. Or no to killing him?"

"Both."

"You're the boss."

I suppose I should tell you about Slocum. At least two hundred pounds overweight, given to western clothes too large for even his bulk (trying to hide that slope of belly, I suppose), Slocum is thirty-nine, wears a beard the angriest of Old Testament prophets would have envied, and carries at all times in his shoulder holster a Colt King Cobra, one of the most repellent-looking weapons I've ever seen. I don't suppose someone like me—former economics professor at the state university and antigun activist of the first form— ever quite gets used to the look and feel and smell of such weapons. Never quite.

I had been riding shotgun in an endless caravan of rented cars, charter airplanes, Greyhound buses, Amtrak passenger cars, and even a few motorboats for the past seven

months, ever since that day in Chicago when I turned my
life over to Slocum the way others turned their lives over to
Jesus or Republicanism.

I entered his office, put twenty-five thousand dollars in
cash on his desk, and said, "Everybody tells me you're the
best. I hope that's true, Mr. Slocum."

He grinned at me with teeth that Red Man had turned the
color of peach wine. "Fortunately for you, it is true. Now
what is it you'd like me to do?" He turned down the Hank
Williams, Jr. tape he'd been listening to and waved to me,
with a massive beefy hand bearing two faded blue tattos, to
start talking.

I had worked with innumerable police departments, innumerable private investigators, two soldiers of fortune, and a
psychic over the past eleven years in an effort to find the
man who had killed my daughter.

That cold, bright January day seven months ago, and as
something of a last resort, I had turned to a man whose
occupation sounded far too romantic to be any good to me:
Slocum was a bounty hunter.

"Maybe you should wait here."

"Why?" I said.

"You know why."

"Because I don't like guns? Because I don't want to
arrange it so we have to kill him?"

"It could be dangerous."

"You really think I care about that?"

He studied my face. "No, I guess you don't."

"I just want to see him when he gets caught. I just want
to see his expression when he realizes he's going to go to
prison for the rest of his life."

He grinned at me with his stained teeth. "I'd rather see
him when he's been gut-shot. Still afraid to die but at the
same time wanting to. You know? I gut-shot a gook in Nam
once and watched him the whole time. It took him an hour.
It was one long hour, believe me."

Staring at the three-story apartment house, I sighed.
"Eleven years."

"I'm sorry for all you've gone through."

"I know you are, Slocum. That's one of the things a good liberal like me can't figure out about a man like you."

"What's that?"

"How can you enjoy killing people and still feel so much compassion for the human race in general."

He shrugged. "I'm not killing humanity in general, Robert. I'm killing animals." He took out the Cobra, grim gray metal almost glowing in the late June sunlight, checked it, and put it back. His eyes scanned the upper part of the red brick apartment house. Many of the screens were torn and a few shattered windows had been taped up. The lawn needed mowing and a tiny black baby walked around wearing a filthy and too-small T-shirt and nothing else. Twenty years ago this had probably been a very nice middle-class place. Now it had the feel of an inner-city housing project.

"One thing," he said, as I started to open the door. He put a meaty hand on my shoulder for emphasis.

"Yes?"

"When this is all over—however it turns out—you're going to feel let down."

"You maybe; not me. All I've wanted for the past eleven years was finding Dexter. Now we have found him. Now I can start my life again."

"That's the thing," he said. "That's what you don't understand."

"What don't I understand?"

"This has changed you, Robert. You start hunting people—even when you've got a personal stake in it—and it changes you."

I laughed. "Right. I think this afternoon I'll go down to my friendly neighborhood recruiting office and sign up for Green Beret school."

Occasionally, he got irritated with me. Now seemed to be one of those times. "I'm just some big dumb redneck, right, Robert? What would I know about the subtleties of human psychology, right?"

"Look, Slocum, I'm sorry if—"
He patted his Cobra. "Let's go."

2

They found her in a grave that was really more of a wide
hole up in High Ridge forest where the scrub pines run
heavy down to the river. My daughter Debbie. The coroner
estimated she had been there at least thirty days. At the
time of her death she'd been seventeen.

This is the way the official version ran: Debbie, leaving
her job at the Baskin-Robbins, was dragged into a car,
taken into the forest, raped, and killed. Only when I pressed
him on the subject did the coroner tell me the extent to
which she had been mutilated, the mutilation coming, so far
as could be determined, after she had died. At the funeral
the coffin was closed.

At the time I had a wife—small, tanned, intelligent in a
hard sensible way I often envied, quick to laugh, equally
quick to cry—and a son. Jeff was twelve the year his sister
died. He was seventeen when he died five years later.

When you're sitting home watching the sullen parade
of faceless murders flicker and die on your screen—the
weeping mother of the victim, the carefully spoken detective in charge, the sexless doll-like face of the reporter
signing off on the story—you don't take into account the
impact that the violent death of a loved one has on a
family. I do; after Debbie's death, I made a study of the
subject. Like so many things I've studied in my life, I
ended up with facts that neither enlightened nor comforted.
They were just facts.

My family's loss was measured in two ways—my wife's
depression (she came from a family that suffered mental
illness the way some families suffered freckles) and my son's
wildness.

Not that I was aware of either of these problems as they
began to play out. When it became apparent to me that the

local police were never going to solve the murder—their
entire investigation centered on an elusive 1986 red Chev-
rolet—I virtually left home. Using a generous inheritance
left to me by an uncle, I began—in tandem with the private
eyes and soldiers of fortune and psychics I've already
mentioned—to pursue my daughter's killer. I have no doubt
that my pursuit was obsessive, and clinically so. Nights I
would lie on the strange, cold, lonely bed of a strange, cold,
lonely motel room thinking of tomorrow, always tomorrow,
and how we were only hours away from a man we now
knew to be one William K. Dexter, age thirty-seven, twice
incarcerated for violent crimes, unduly attached to a very
aged mother, perhaps guilty of two similar killings in two
other midwestern states. I thought of nothing else—so much
so that sometimes, lying there in the motel room, I wanted
to take a butcher knife and cut into my brain until I found
the place where memory dwelt—and cut it away. William K.
Dexter was my only thought.

During this time, me gone, my wife began a series of
affairs (I learned all this later) that only served to increase
the senseless rage she felt (she seemed to resent the men
because they could not give her peace)—she still woke up
screaming Debbie's name. Her drinking increased also and
she began shopping around for new shrinks the way you
might shop around for a new car. A few times during her
last two months we made love when I came home on the
weekend from pursuing Dexter in one fashion or another—
but afterward it was always the same. "You weren't a good
father to her, Robert." "I know." "And I wasn't a good
mother. We're such goddamned selfish people." And then
the sobbing, sobbing to the point of vomiting, vomiting to
the point of passing out (always drunk of course) in a
little-girl pile in the bathroom or the center of the hardwood
bedroom floor.

Jeff found her. Just home from school, calling her name,
not really expecting her to be there, he went upstairs to the
TV room for the afternoon ritual of a dance show and there
he found her. The last images of a soap opera flickering on
the screen. A drink of bourbon in the Smurf glass she

always found so inexplicably amusing. A cigarette guttering
out in the ashtray. Dressed in one of Jeff's T-shirts with the
rock-and-roll slogan on its front and a pair of designer jeans
that pointed up the teenaged sleekness of her body. Dead.
Heart attack.

On the day of the funeral, up in the TV room where she'd
died, I was having drinks of my own, wishing I had some
facts to tell me what I should be feeling now . . . when Jeff
came in and sat down next to me and put his arm around my
neck the way he used to when he was three or four. "You
can't cry, can you, Dad?" All I could do was sigh. He'd
been watching me. "You should cry, Dad. You really should.
You didn't even cry when Debbie was killed. Mom told
me." He said all this in the young man's voice I still couldn't
quite get used to—the voice he used so successfully with
ninth-grade girls on the phone. He wasn't quite a man yet
but he wasn't a kid, either. In a moment of panic I felt he
was an imposter, that this was a joke; where was my little
boy? "That's all I do, Dad. Is cry, I mean. I think it helps
me. I really do."

So I'd tried, first there with Jeff in the TV room,
later alone in my bedroom. But there were just dry
choking sounds and no tears at all. At all. I would think
of Debbie, her sweet soft radiance; and of my wife, the
years when it had been good for us, her so tender and
kind in the shadows of our hours together; and I wanted
to cry for the loss I felt. But all I could see was the
face of William K. Dexter. In some way, he had become
more important to me even than the two people he'd taken
from me.

Jeff died three years later, wrapped around a light pole on
the edge of a county park, drugs and vodka found in the
front seat of the car I'd bought him six months earlier.

Left alone at the wake, kneeling before his waxen corpse,
an Our Father faint on my lips, I'd felt certain I could cry. It
would be a tribute to Jeff; one he'd understand; some part
of the process by which he'd forgive me for being gone so

much, for pursuing William K. Dexter while Jeff was discovering drugs and alcohol and girls too young to know about nurturing. I put out my hand and touched his cheek, his cold waxen cheek, and I felt something die in me. It was the opposite of crying, of bursting forth with poisons that needed to be purged. Something was dead in me and would never be reborn.

It was not long after this that I met Frank Slocum and it was not long after Slocum took the case that we began to close inexorably in on William K. Dexter.

And soon enough we were here, at the apartment house just outside Des Moines.

Eleven years, two months, and five days later.

3

The name on the hallway mailbox said Severn, George Severn. We knew better, of course.

Up carpeted stairs threadbare and stained, down a hallway thick with dusty sunlight, to a door marked 4-A.

"Behind me," Slocum whispered, waving me to the wall.

For a moment, the only noises belonged to the apartment building; the thrum of electricity snaking through the walls; the creak of roof in summer wind; a toilet exploding somewhere on the floor below us.

Slocum put a hefty finger to his thick mouth, stabbing through thistle of beard to do so. Sssh.

Slocum stood back from the door himself. His Cobra was in his hand, ready. He reached around the long way and set big knuckles against the cheap faded pine of the door.

On the other side of the door, I heard chair legs scrape against tile.

Somebody in there.

William K. Dexter.

Chair legs scraped again; footsteps. They did not come

all the way to the door, however, rather stopped at what I imagined was probably the center of the living room.

"Yeah?"

Slocum put his finger to his lips again. Reached around once more and knocked.

"I said 'Yeah.' Who the hell is it?"

He was curious about who was in the hall, this George Severn was, but not curious enough to open the door and find out.

One more knock. Quick rap really; nothing more.

Inside, you could sense Severn's aggravation.

"Goddammit," he said and took a few loud steps toward the door but then stopped.

Creak of floor; flutter of robin wings as bird settled on hallway window; creak of floor again from inside the apartment.

Slocum held up a halting hand. Then he pantomined Don't Move with his lips. He waited for my reaction. I nodded.

He looked funny, a man as big as he was, doing a very broad, cartoon version of a man walking away. Huge noisy steps so that it sounded as if he were very quickly retreating. But he did all this in place. He did it for thirty seconds and then he eased himself flat back against the wall. He took his Cobra and put it man-high on the edge of the door frame.

Severn didn't come out in thirty seconds but he did come out in about a minute.

For eleven years I'd wondered what he'd look like. Photos deceive. I always pictured him as formidable. He would have to be, I'd reasoned; the savage way he'd mutilated her . . . He was a skinny fortyish man in a stained white T-shirt and Levis that looked a little too big. He wore the wide sideburns of a hillbilly trucker and the scowl of a mean drunk. He stank of sleep and whiskey. He carried a butcher knife that appeared to be new. It still had the lime-green price sticker on the black handle.

When he came out of his apartment, he made the mistake of looking straight ahead.

Slocum did two things at the same time: slammed the Cobra's nose hard against Severn's temple and yanked a handful of hair so hard, Severn's knees buckled. "You're dead, man, in case you haven't figured it out already." Slocum said. He seemed enraged; he was a little frightening to watch.

He grabbed some more hair and then he pushed Severn all the way back into his apartment.

4

Slocum got him on a straight-backed chair, hit him so hard in the mouth that you could hear teeth go, and then handcuffed him, still in the chair, to the aged formica dining-room table.

Slocum then cocked his foot back and kicked Severn clean and hard in the ribs. Almost immediately, Severn's mouth started boiling with red mucus that didn't seem quite thick enough to be blood.

Slocum next went over to Severn and ripped his T-shirt away from his shoulder. Without a word, Slocum motioned me over.

With his Cobra, Slocum pointed to a faded tattoo on Severn's right shoulder. It read: *Mindy* with a rose next to it. Not many men had such a tattoo on their right shoulder. It was identical to the one listed in all of Severn's police records.

Slocum slapped him with stunning ferocity directly across the mouth, so hard that both Severn and his chair were lifted from the floor.

For the first time, I moved. Not to hit Severn myself but to put a halting hand on Slocum's arm. "That's enough."

"We've got the right guy!" It was easy to see he was crazed in some profound animal way I'd never seen in anybody before.

"I know we do."

"The guy who killed your daughter!"

"I know," I said, "but—"

"But what?"

I sighed. "But I don't want to be like him and if we sat here and beat him, that's exactly what we'd be. Animals—just like him."

Slocum's expression was a mixture of contempt and disbelief. I could see that whatever respect he'd had for me—or perhaps it had been nothing more than mere pity—was gone now. He looked at me the same way I looked at him—as some alien species.

"Please, Slocum," I said.

He got one more in, a good solid right hand to the left side of Severn's head. Severn's eyes rolled and he went out. From the smell, you could tell he'd wet his pants.

I kept calling him Severn. But of course he wasn't Severn. He was William K. Dexter.

Slocum went over to the ancient Kelvinator, took out a can of Hamms and opened it with a great deal of violence, and then slammed the refrigerator door.

"You think he's all right?" I said.

"What the hell's that supposed to mean?"

"It means did you kill him?"

"Kill him?" He laughed. The contempt was back in his voice. "Kill him? No, but I should have. I keep thinking of your daughter, man. All the things you've told me about her. Not a perfect kid—no kid is—but a real gentle little girl. A girl you supposedly loved. Your frigging daughter, man. Your frigging daughter." He sloshed his beer in the general direction of Dexter. "I should get out my hunting knife and cut his balls off. That's what I should do. And that's just for openers. Just for openers."

He started pacing around, then, Slocum did, and I could gauge his rage. I suppose at that moment he wanted to kill us both—Dexter for being an animal, me for being a weakling—neither of us the type of person Slocum wanted in his universe.

The apartment was small and crammed with threadbare and wobbly furniture. Everything had been burned with cigarettes and disfigured with beer-can rings. The sour smell of bad cooking lay on the air; sunlight poured through filthy windows; and even from here you could smell the rancid odors of the bathroom. On a bureau lay two photographs, one of a plump woman in a shabby housedress standing with her arm around Dexter, obviously his mother; and a much younger Dexter squinting into the sun outside a gray metal barracks where he had served briefly as an army private before being pushed out on a mental.

Peeking into the bedroom, I found the centerfolds he'd pinned up. They weren't the centerfolds of the quality men's magazines where the women were beautiful to begin with and made even more so with careful lighting and gauzy effects; no, these were the women of the street, hard-eyed, flabby-bodied, some even tattooed like Dexter himself. They covered the walls on either side of his sad little cot where he slept in a room littered with empty beer cans and hard-crusted pizza boxes. Many of the centerfolds he'd defaced, drawing penises in black ballpoint aimed at their vaginas or their mouths, or putting huge blood-dripping knives into their breasts or eyes or even their vaginas. All I could think of was Debbie and what he'd done to her that long ago night . . .

A terrible, oppressive nausea filled me as I backed out of the bedroom and groped for the couch so I could sit down.

"What's the matter?" Slocum said.

"Shut up."

"What?"

"Shut the fuck up!"

I sank to the couch—the sunlight through the greasy window making me ever warmer—and cupped my hands in my face and swallowed again and again until I felt the vomit in my throat and esophagus and stomach recede.

I was shaking, chilled now with sweat.

"Can you wake him up?"

"What?"

"Can you wake him up?"

"Sure," Slocum said. "Why?"

"Because I want to talk to him."

Slocum gulped the last of the beer, tossed the can into a garbage sack overflowing with coffee grounds and tomato rinds, and then went over to the sink. He took down a big glass with the Flintstones on it and filled it with water, then took the glass over to where he had Dexter handcuffed. With a certain degree of obvious pleasure, he threw the water across Dexter's head. He threw the glass—as if it were now contaminated—into the corner where it shattered into three large jagged pieces.

He grabbed Dexter by the hair and jerked his head back. Groaning, Dexter came awake.

"Now what?" Slocum said, turning to me.

"Now I want to talk to him."

"Talk to him," Slocum said. "Right."

He pointed a large hand at Dexter as if he were a master of ceremonies introducing the next act.

It wasn't easy, getting up off that couch and going over to him. In a curious way, I was terrified of him. If I pushed him hard enough, he would tell me the exact truth about the night. The truth in detail. What she had looked like and sounded like—her screams as he raped her; her screams as she died—and then I would have my facts . . . but facts so horrible I would not be able to live with them. How many times—despite myself—I had tried to recreate that night. But there would be no solace in this particular truth; no solace at all.

I stood over him. "Have you figured out who I am yet?"

He stared up at me. He started crying. "Hey, man, I never did nothing to you."

"You raped and killed a girl named Debbie eleven years ago."

"I don't know what you're talking about, man. Honest.
You got the wrong guy."

"Couldn't you have just raped her and let her go? Wouldn't
that have been enough?"

I knew that by the way I studied his face—every piece of
beard stubble, the green matter collected in the corners
of his eyes, the dandruff flaked off at the front of his
receding hairline—that I was trying to learn something about
him, something that would grant me peace after all these
years.

A madman, this Dexter, and so not quite responsible for
what he'd done and perhaps even deserving of pity in my
good gray liberal soul.

But he didn't seem insane, at least not insane enough to
move me in any way. He was just a cheap trapped frightened animal.

"Wouldn't that have been enough?" I said. "Just to rape
her?"

"Really, man; really, I don't know what the hell you're
talking about."

"If you'd just raped her, I wouldn't have tracked you
down all those years. I wouldn't be here today."

"Jesus, man; listen—"

"You're going to hate prison, Dexter. Or maybe they'll
even execute you. Did you ever read anything about the
injections they give? They make it sound so humane but it's
the waiting, Dexter. It's the waiting—"

"Please," he said, "please," and he writhed against
his handcuffs, scraping the table across the floor in the
process.

"You could have just raped her and let it go at that,
Dexter."

I could hear my voice, what was happening to it—all my
feelings about Dexter were merging into my memories of
those defaced centerfolds in his bedroom—and Slocum must
have known it too, with his animal wisdom, known at just
what moment I would be right for it

because just then and just so
the Cobra came into my hands and I
shot Dexter once in the face and once in the
chest and I

5

Slocum explained to me—though I really wasn't listening—
that they were called by various names (toss guns or throw
guns) but they were carried by police officers in case they
wanted to show that the person they'd just killed had been
armed.

From a holster strapped to his ankle, Slocum took a .38,
wiped it clean of prints, and set it next to Dexter's hand.

Below and to the side of us the apartment house was a
frenzy of shouts and cries—fear and panic—and already in
the distance sirens exploded red on the soft blue air of the
summer day.

6

That evening I cried.

I sat in a good room in a good hotel with the air conditioning going strong, a fine dinner and many fine drinks in
my belly, and I cried.

Wept, really.

Whatever had kept me from crying for my daughter and
then my wife and then my son was gone now and so I could
love and mourn them in a way I'd never been able to. I
thought of each of them—their particular ways of laughing,
their particular set of pleasures and dreams, their particular
fears and apprehensions—and it was as if they joined me
there in that chill antiseptic hotel room, Debbie in her blue
sweater and jeans, my wife in her white linen sheath, Jeff in
his Kiss T-shirt and chinos—came round in the way the

medieval church taught that angels gathered around the bed of a dying person . . . only I wasn't dying.

My family was there to tell me that I was to live again. To seek some sort of peace and normalcy after the forced march of these past eleven years.

"I love you so much," I said aloud to each of them, and wept all the more; "I love you so much."

And then I slept.

7

"I talked to the district attorney," Slocum said in the coffee shop the following morning. "He says it's very unlikely there will be any charges."

"He really thought Dexter was armed?"

"Wouldn't you? A piece of trash like Dexter?"

I stared at him. "You know something terrible?"

"What?"

"I don't feel guilty."

He let go with one of those cigarette-raspy laughs of his. "Good."

Then it was his turn to stare at me, there in the hubbub of clattering dishes and good sweet coffee smells and bacon sizzling on the grill. "So what now?"

"See if I can get my job back."

"At the university?"

"Umm-hmm."

He kept staring. "You don't feel any guilt, do you?"

"No. I mean, I know I should. Whatever else, he was a human being. But—"

He smiled his hard Old Testament smile. "Now don't go giving me any of those mousy little liberal 'buts,' all right?"

"All right."

"You just go back and live your life and make it a good one."

"I owe you one hell of a lot, Slocum."

He put forth a slab of a hand and a genuine look of

affection in his eyes. "Just make it a good one," he said. "Promise?"

"Promise."

"And no guilt?"

"No guilt."

He grinned. "I knew I could make a man out you."

8

Her name was Anne Stevens and she was to dominate my first year back at the university. Having met at the faculty picnic—hot August giving way to the fierce melancholy of Indian summer—we began what we both hoped (her divorced; me not quite human yet) would be a pleasant but slow-moving relationship. We were careful to not introduce real passion, for instance, until we both felt certain we could handle it, about the time the first of the Christmas decorations blew in the gray wind of Harcourt Square.

School itself took some adjusting. First, there was my duty to the hours themselves—not so much rising early; I'd spent eleven years of rising early, moving to find William K. Dexter. And there was the fact that the students seemed less bright and inquisitive, more deadingly conservative than the students I remembered. The faculty had some doubts about me, too; given my experiences over the past eleven years, they wondered how I would fit into a setting whose goals were at best abstract. I wondered, too.

After the first time we made love—her place, unplanned, satisfying if slightly embarrassed—I went home and stared at the photograph of my wife I keep on my bureau. In whispers, I apologized for what I'd done. If I'd been a better husband I would have no guilt now. But I had not, alas, been a better husband at all . . .

In the spring, a magazine took a piece on inflation I wrote and the academic dean made a considerable fuss over this fact. Also in the spring Anne and I told each other that we loved each other in a variety of ways, emotionally, sexually, spiritually. We set June 23 as our wedding day.

It was on May 5 that I saw the item in the state newspaper. For the following three weeks I did my best to forget it, troubling as it was. Anne began to notice a difference in my behavior, and to talk about it. Several times I tried to explain but I could not. I just kept thinking of the newspaper item and of something Slocum had said that day when I killed Dexter.

In the middle of a May night—the breeze sweet with the newly blooming world—I typed out a six-page letter to Anne, packed two bags, stopped by a 7-11 and filled the Volvo and dropped Anne's letter in a mailbox, and then set out on the Interstate.

Two mornings later, I walked up a dusty flight of stairs inside an apartment house. A Hank Williams, Jr. record filled the air.

To be heard above the music, I had to pound.

I half-expected what would happen, that when the door finally opened a gun would be shoved in my face.

A Cobra.

I didn't say anything. I just handed him the news clipping.

He waved me in—he lived in a place not dissimilar from the one Dexter had lived in—read the clipping as he opened an 8:48 A.M. beer.

Finished reading it, he let it glide to the coffee table that was covered with gun magazines.

"So?"

"So I want to help him. I don't want him to go through what I did."

"You know him or something?"

"No."

"Just some guy whose daughter was raped and killed and the suspect hasn't been apprehended."

"Right."

"And you want what?"

"I've got money and I've got time. I quit my job."

"But what do you want?"

"I want us to go after him. Remember how you said that I'd changed and that I didn't even know it?"

"Yeah, I remember."

"Well, you were right. I have changed."

He stood up and started laughing, his considerable belly shaking beneath his Valvoline T-shirt. "Well, I'll be goddamned, Robert. I'll be goddamned. I did make a man out of you, after all. So how about having a beer with me?"

At first—it not being nine A.M. yet—I hesitated. But then I nodded my head and said, "Yeah, Slocum. That sounds good. That really sounds good."

Rick Hautala may well be one of the next few horror writers to become a Brand Name, his *Winter Wakes* (Warner) selling extremely well and receiving some exceptional notices. Only recently has he turned to shorter fiction and, as you'll see here, he's done quite well by the form.

GETTING THE JOB DONE

Rick Hautala

1

"I'm the perfect man to get the job done!" Phil SanSouci said. "I can't believe you're not letting me run with this."

He was standing in front of Captain Richards' desk, both fists clenched, supporting himself as he leaned forward. He was telling himself to stay calm, that any agitation he displayed would only strengthen Richard's contention that someone else should take over the case he and McCammon, his partner, had been working on for the last few months.

A good cop learns to read upside down so he can see whatever's on someone's desk—you never knew when it would give you a lead—but Phil didn't need to read a word of the file Richards had spread out in front of him; it was *everything* they had gotten to date on the man the local press had dubbed "The Alley Cat." He was suspected of at least six separate attacks on young women in the past seven months—six attacks that had left five women dead, all of them found with their throats slit from ear to ear. The sixth had—fortunately—made it to her car, locked the door, and gotten away with her life and a broken side window.

"You *have* run with it," Richards said as mildly as was

possible for him. A throat wound from Viet Nam had turned his voice into a rumbling growl even when he whispered, which wasn't often.

"You've run *too* far with it, and I'm turning it over to someone else. You're too close to it, Phil, and that's when cops make mistakes . . . sometimes *fatal* mistakes."

Phil had to take a deep breath and hold it in tightly before he said something he might regret. The heels of his hands were tingling from lack of blood, and he found himself wishing, just this once, that Richards *wasn't* his superior; he'd like nothing better than to haul off and slug him.

"Goddamnit! I'm the perfect man to get the job done," Phil said, straining to keep his voice steady. "I've got the motivation to run this bastard down and get him."

Richards heaved a deep sigh and began drumming his felt-tipped pen on his ink blotter. Phil knew the signal— *That's all! End of discussion!*—but he couldn't let it drop . . . not yet . . . not when Annie was involved.

"Detective work is not revenge," Richards said. His voice was calm, but the edges of his mouth twitched, showing his growing impatience. "You should just thank your lucky stars that it was Annie who got away from this—this Alley Cat. Think about the five women who didn't."

"I do—all the time," Phil said, stepping back from the desk and trying like hell to loosen his fists. "I think about them every day we're out there looking for this creep."

"Well, you won't have to any more," Richards said. He slammed the file folder shut with his beefy hand and slid it to the side of his desk. "As of right now, Piper and Scott have the case. That's final. Check with McCammon. I've already assigned him something else."

For the count of three heartbeats—Phil counted them, hammering like velvet drums in his ears—he stayed in front of the captain's desk. Then, turning sharply on his heel, he snapped, "Yes, sir," and strode out of the office. Just before he rounded the corner, he glanced back to see if Richards was watching, but the chief was looking down at his desk, reading something.

Probably working through the junior crossword puzzle, Phil thought. He stormed into the office he shared with McCammon and grabbed his coat. Without a word, they both went out to the car in the parking lot.

2

That's the whole goddamned trouble with the whole goddamned press," McCammon said as he hunched over his coffee and blueberry pie in Bryant's, where he and Phil had lunch just about every day. "They take someone like this Alley Cat guy and blow him up until he's larger than life. They make heroes outta these guys, going all the way back to Jesse James . . . even earlier—like, Robin Hood."

Phil looked at his half-eaten tuna sandwich and slid it to the side. He wiped his mouth with a napkin, then crumpled it and tossed it on top of the sandwich.

"I think there's a slight difference between Robin Hood and someone who goes around town slicing women's throats," Phil said. He tipped his coffee cup and looked inside and, scowling, pushed it over next to the sandwich plate.

"Yeah, sure . . . maybe," McCammon said. "I was just making the point that it's the goddamned press that causes half the trouble. They give this guy the attention he's looking for. They turn him into a media star, so what's he gonna do? He's gonna go right on doing what he's doing so he can see his name in the papers and on TV. What the hell! Let it drop. Maybe Piper and Scott will crack it."

"Piper and Scott couldn't find their asses without a road map," Phil said as he rubbed his eyes vigorously with both hands and sighed.

"Oh, I don't know about that. I think they could," McCammon said, a half smile twitching at the corner of his mouth. "But I don't think they'll find the Alley Cat."

"Yeah—well . . . I dunno," Phil said, shaking his head with disgust. "I just think it would have been nice if the frigging press had kept Annie's name out of it."

"What, is she still spooked?"

"Who wouldn't be?" Phil snapped. For such a sharp detective, McCammon sure had a way of sounding stone stupid sometimes. Maybe that was how he got results, Phil thought; like the TV detective Columbo, he'd make them think he didn't know what the hell was going on and then—*wham-o!*—*gotcha!*

McCammon shrugged. "I told yah before—I don't think she's got anything to worry about. His M.O. doesn't strike me as revenge-orientated."

"That's *oriented*," Phil said. "Not *orientated*."

"Whatever! All I'm saying is, I think—yeah, sure, I don't blame Annie for being upset by what happened, but that was a good two weeks ago. If this guy's gonna do something, I think he would've tried it by now."

Phil shook his head and spun around off the stool. He started digging into his hip pocket for his wallet, but McCammon stopped him. "I got it," he said as he took a ten-dollar bill from his pants pocket and slid it under his clean-as-a-whistle plate. They nodded greetings to a few of the regulars and left.

3

The night was alive with the song of crickets, and a fingernail sliver of moon was riding low in the sky as Phil took a left turn onto Maple Street. Driving slowly, he cruised past Annie's house. This was the third pass this hour, he noted, glancing at the green digital clock on his dashboard. It was almost one o'clock in the morning. If anything was going to happen, it would have happened by now, he thought. Call it a day—a double shift day at that: one "official" and one "personal." Time to head home and get some rest.

With each pass by his girlfriend's house, Phil had noticed all the subtle changes. A light that had been on downstairs would be out; another would be on upstairs. The gate to the back yard was closed, as was the garage door. On his last pass down the street, he had seen two people—a man and a woman—walking down the street holding hands. That was it. Nothing else broke the quiet calm of the night. It never failed to amaze him how quiet Annie's neighborhood was, and only two blocks from downtown.

He had gone through a whole thermos of coffee during the night, and his bladder was feeling the pressure. He considered stopping in at Annie's, but she had just turned out the light upstairs. He didn't think a knock on the door at one A.M. was such a hot idea. At the end of Maple Street, he put the car into park and—leaving it running—got out, deciding it was better to water the neighbor's hedge than have to hold it all the way home, across town.

After he was done, as he was walking back to his car, he saw—*thought* he saw—a shadow shift beside the garage on the opposite side of the street, the house directly across from Annie's! He didn't break his stride, though, as he shifted his gaze to try to see what was there. Were the shadows there shifting, or was it just a trick of the eye? He couldn't resist a shiver as he paused by the car door; then he swung the door open, got in, shifted into gear, and pulled away from the curb. A hundred feet down the street, he spun the wheel and took the right-hand turn onto Middle Street.

"Let's just check you out, sucker," he muttered as he drove slowly up Middle and turned onto Union Street. He was hoping that *if* there had been someone creeping around, and *if* they had noticed him, they wouldn't immediately recognize his car as it made another pass down Maple Street.

He rolled down the window on the passenger's side and listened intensely as he got closer to Annie's house. If the moon had been fuller, it would have helped, he thought, looking longingly at the portable spotlight on the seat beside him.

The lights were still off in Annie's house—at least *she* hadn't heard anything outside. Everything looked like it had on the last pass. *If* someone had been out there, either he wasn't there anymore—or he was hiding. Phil wondered why, right after the first attack, Annie hadn't taken his advice and gotten a dog. They may be sloppy and drooly, and they may shed all over the rugs and furniture, but you can't beat them for an advance warning system.

Phil was pretty sure—if it had been anything at all across the street—he had probably seen a cat, or maybe a raccoon from the woods nearby, making a midnight raid on someone's trashcans. The night was as silent and peaceful as always. In the back of his mind, *something* nagged him—a vague uneasiness that not quite everything was as it had been, but as his car crept past Annie's, he just couldn't quite pin it down. He shook his head, feeling a sudden heaviness on his eyelids, and stepped on the accelerator. "You're worn out," he told himself as he slowed for the stop sign. "Time to drag your ass to bed."

4

Annie had been nervous all evening, as she had been every evening since that night over two weeks ago. She had become compulsive about the doors and windows, and every fifteen or twenty minutes throughout the evening, she had made a run through the house, double checking that everything was locked. Even on a hot night like this, there was no way she was going to leave a window open, not even a crack.

She had listened tensely every time a car passed the house, going either up or down the street. One car in particular seemed to be driving past the house several times—she could tell by the sound of the engine—but she didn't dare look out. Her mind filled with the image of her pulling back the curtain and seeing a horribly, twisted face, scarred and laced with pockmarks, grinning in at her with wild, manical eyes. Instead, she just sat there, wishing she had taken Phil's advice and gotten a dog—or at least a gun.

Finally, after Johnny Carson, she switched off the TV and went upstairs to bed. She knew sleep would be a long time coming, and she worried that her recent lack of sleep might be affecting her performance at the bank. Hell, there was no doubt about it; it *was*, but she had other, deeper worries.

She had barely settled into bed when she heard a sound. It seemed to come from the back yard, she thought. Freezing into position, not even daring to turn on the light, she lay on her back, staring up at the ceiling. She held her breath until it hurt, and she waited . . . waited for the sound to be repeated.

But it never came again.

The silence twisted her nerves like they were strands of rope. She hardly breathed in the darkness, waiting for that sound—or *any* sound—to disturb the night. After a while—she didn't dare guess how long—she heard another . . . *or was it the same?* . . . car drive down the street. As the car rounded the corner and the sound gradually faded, she had just started to release her tension when she heard glass breaking downstairs.

In the dark, she fumbled blindly for the telephone when she heard a window slide up followed by the heavy grunt of someone clambering into the house. It sounded like he was coming in through the living room window. She wanted to scream but couldn't find enough air in her lungs when she heard the heavy tread of footsteps, starting up the stairs.

5

Phil was just pulling out into the intersection, past the house where he had watered the shrubbery, when that *something* in the back of his mind clicked up to the front.

The back yard gate . . . It had been open! he thought, and a ripple of chills danced up his spine between his shoulders. *It had been closed tight earlier, but this last time it had been partway open!*

He had two options; either drive around the block again, trying not to draw attention from the neighbors, or do a U-turn here and lose the element of surprise if it *was* the Alley Cat.

No sense taking chances this time, he decided.

He jammed the car into reverse and, looking back over his shoulder, stepped down hard on the accelerator. The wheels left streaks of rubber on the road as the car swerved from side to side, heading back toward Annie's. All the while, he was picturing in his mind the open gate, like the black gap of a missing tooth in a smile. While he squealed to a stop in Annie's driveway and looked at the gate door—definitely open *now,* if it hadn't been before—he saw a light come on inside the house and, a second later, a wailing scream filled the night.

As soon as he heard the scream, Phil snagged his radio microphone and punched the button. He had his car door open, and one foot was already out on the asphalt.

"Officer needs assistance," he shouted when the night dispatcher came on. "Seventy-two Maple Street. In pursuit on foot. Send backup."

He cut the transmission, got out of the car, and, service revolver in hand, ran up the driveway to the door. His heart was thumping heavily in his ears, so he wasn't sure whether or not he had heard something break—it had sounded like glass. He took the porch steps two at a time and hammered the door with his fist.

"Annie! Annie! Open up! It's me, Phil!" he shouted.

He rained heavy blows on the door, heavy enough to pound the door to splinters, he thought, as he strained to hear any sound from inside the house. He *had* to know that Annie was all right! When his knocking didn't get an answer, he jumped off the porch into the driveway and looked up at what he knew was Annie's bedroom window.

Cupping his hands to his mouth, he yelled, "Annie! For God's sake! It's me! Is everything all right?"

A dash of chills gripped him when he saw the bedroom window slide up and Annie, her eyes wide with fright, stuck her head out the window.

"Phil! Jesus Christ, help! He's here! There's someone in the house!" she shouted. Then her head ducked back inside.

"Get out! Use the back stairs!" Phil yelled. He leapt up

onto the porch and rammed into the door as hard as he could with his shoulder. The door reverberated, but it didn't give. He shook his head, pulled back, and rammed it again and again. On the fourth try, the bolt gave way. Clawing blinding at the darkness to keep his balance, he fell forward into the entryway.

Not exactly correct procedure, he thought as he stumbled into the kitchen, fishing for the light switch. Richards' words came back to him, ringing in his memory as clearly as if he had been standing there beside him:

—You're too close to it!

After a frantic second of searching for the light, he decided to hell with it; the Alley Cat would be just as blind as he was . . . unless, like a real cat, he could see in the dark.

With his revolver held at ready, he charged through the living room to the stairway. He was just turning the corner when something—something fast and solid—shot out of the darkness and caught him squarely in the gut. An explosion of pain reached from his throat to his knees, making him double over. He was only barely aware of hitting the floor.

—That's when cops make mistakes . . .

6

Still numb with pain, Phil came to—he didn't dare think how much later. Grunting and shaking his head, he sat up. Spinning yellow lights continued to weave and dance across his vision as he hoisted himself to his feet. Purely by luck, he found the wall switch for the stair light and snapped it on. He saw his revolver lying on the floor where he had dropped it and, scooping it up, ran up the stairs, taking them three at a time.

"Annie!" he shouted as he burst through her bedroom door, fully expecting to see her sprawled on her bed, staring blankly up at the ceiling as a pool of blood slowly widened on her pillow . . . a gaping red slice under her chin.

But the room was empty. Maybe she got away, he thought, not wanting to hope too much . . . just maybe . . .

The doorway to the back stairway was wide open, and this further raised his hopes. If she had made it down as soon as he had yelled to her, and if the Alley Cat—*It's gotta be him!*—had come down and, after nailing him, had had to run all the way around to get out back, then she just might have made it.

But how long ago? he wondered. He glanced at the clock on Annie's bedstand. It was just a few minutes after one. So he hadn't been out *that* long.

He raced recklessly down the back stairway. Every breath burned like acid in his lungs, but he doubled his speed once he vaulted the back porch railing. There was no sign to indicate which way Annie and the Alley Cat might have run, but he figured she would have tried through the neighbor's yard and onto Middle Street. As he leaped over the split-rail fence behind Annie's house, the scream that suddenly shattered the quiet calm of the night told him he had chosen correctly. His arms pumping madly, his breath puffing like a runaway train, he crossed the lawn and ran into the street.

Again, he didn't know which way to run. Each end of the street glowed with the mellow light of the street lamps. Overhanging leaves ruffled gently in the breeze, casting thin shadows on the road. The echo of the scream had long since faded. But then, about a hundred yards up the street, he saw another shadow, this one *not* cast by the trees. There was the stooped-over figure of a man, sticking up out of the waist-high weeds growing in a vacant lot. He was obviously leaning over something—or some*one!*

It's the Alley Cat! . . . He's got her pinned!

In the instant that Phil hesitated, registering the silhouette, he saw the man lift his arm up slowly into the air. The streetlight caught the edge of the knife blade and glinted on it like wild sparks. Slowly . . . slowly, the arm went up higher . . .

"No . . . *No!*" Phil shouted as he ran toward the figure in a burst of speed. He felt the weight of his revolver in his hand, and he wanted to aim and fire, but the Alley Cat was on top of Annie. If he missed him, he might hit her. He couldn't take that chance.

As the knife reached its apex, Phil felt an adrenaline jolt that almost made him scream aloud. Barely knowing what he was doing, he crouched in his run and, imagining his days in college football, hit the dark figure with everything he had just as the hand started to descend.

There was an explosive grunt upon impact; Phil wasn't even sure if it came from him or the Alley Cat. He did know that he lost the grip on his revolver, and it spun to the ground, lost somewhere in the darkness.

The man collapsed beneath him, rolling off Annie as they both sank into the weeds, scrambling to get in either a good hold or a solid punch. Phil had the advantage in weight, but he could tell right away that this man underneath him was tough. If he didn't finish him fast, he was going to be in trouble.

Both of them struck out blindly, swinging wild haymakers. The only sounds were their labored breathing—hot, animal grunts.

—You're too close to it.

The words echoed in Phil's mind as he scrambled to keep the advantage on the Alley Cat.

That's when cops make mistakes.

Suddenly, out of nowhere, a rock-solid fist connected with his chin and snapped his head back. He was vaguely aware of the coppery taste of blood filling his mouth. The man's other hand followed, predictably, from the other side. The knife whickered in the night air as it slashed out at him like a snake, but even though he was dazed from the punch, Phil responded quickly. He knocked the knife hand aside with a quick upper block.

As he dove forward, trying to pin the man beneath him, Phil saw with hallucinatory intensity the knife in the Alley Cat's hand. It was a switchblade, with a six-inch blade, honed narrow and sharp—just what the coroner for the

Alley Cat's first five victims had said to look for. The blade was glowing with an eerie blue light.

Phil drove all of his weight down on the man's shoulder, hoping at least to pin him on that side. If he could disarm him first, then he could take his time and finish him.

But the man, small though he was, was wiry; he kicked and scrambled beneath Phil like a frantic bronco. His heels and elbows dug into the ground, trying for enough purchase to toss Phil free of him. His throat was making deep growling sounds as he struggled, and his heated breath washed over Phil's face.

From behind him, Phil had been expecting to hear Annie yell something—*anything* to indicate that she was all right. Maybe her silence was because she was too frightened to speak . . . or maybe it was because the slash Phil had stopped hadn't been the first! Maybe, he thought with a sudden flood of panic that made him redouble his efforts, she's already dead!

That idea drove him into a rage. He cocked back his fist and drove it straight into the Alley Cat's stomach. The impact made a squishy sound, and Phil felt immense satisfaction when he heard the man's breath explode out of him. But it didn't stop him, as Phil had expected.

What is this guy, inhuman? You can't take a punch like that and keep going, he thought.

The Alley Cat still struggled to bring his knife hand around; if he did that, Phil knew it would be all over—for him *and* for Annie.

As the man shifted his weight upward, Phil suddenly grabbed him by the shoulder and pulled him close to him, adding to, rather than resisting, the man's momentum. Looking more like one body than two, they rolled over twice in the weeds, so close neither one of them could get the advantage.

At the end of the second roll, Phil ended up on top. The streetlight was shining over his left shoulder, and what he saw sent a mindnumbing wave crashing through his brain.

"Holy Mother . . . *Richards*! What the—?"

He couldn't say anything else because Richards' hand shot up from the ground and caught him under the chin. Phil flew backwards, his arms and legs kicked as if someone had grabbed him by the scruff of the neck and lifted. The wind got slammed out of him when his back hit the ground, and before he could register much of anything else, Richards was up and coming for him.

"I suppose you had to find out eventually," Richards said, his voice a rumbling growl. He was grinning as he approached slowly, the knife held out in front of him. Both his teeth and the blade gleamed like cold bone in the glare of the streetlight.

"For Christ's sake—" Phil gasped.

—Sometimes fatal mistakes!

Phil was reorienting himself as quickly as he could. Past Richards on the ground, he could see Annie's slumped shape; and as he watched, he saw her move.

"Not so confusing why I took you off the case, now, is it?" Richards said softly. "I told you you were getting too close to it." He chuckled, low and hollow. "Now it's *your* turn!"

"You son-of-a—"

Face-down on the ground, Annie was struggling to get up. Her low moaning drew both men's attention.

She's not dead! Phil's mind yelled. Hurt, maybe, but not dead!

That thought alone gave him everything he needed to fight back. He was crab-walking backwards, coiling himself to be ready for Richards when he made his move, but then he almost burst out laughing when his hand hit something on the ground—something metal. His revolver! He couldn't believe his luck as his fingers closed around the handgrip.

In the same instant, Richards leapt for him, and he brought the revolver up. There were three ear-shattering explosions and bright flashes of light, followed by a high-pitched wailing as three bullets tore through Richards's chest. He threw his hands up over his head and flipped backwards, falling to the ground in a twisted heap.

"Annie!"

That single word tore from Phil's throat, feeling like it took a layer or two of skin with it.

He practically dove forward and then leaned over her still form. His hands were trembling as he rolled her over and tried to see how badly she was hurt. The weeds cast thick shadows, blocking his sight, but as leaned close to her, whispering her name, she stirred. Her eyes flickered open and she looked up at him, breathing heavily.

". . . Phil," she said, her voice a watery gasp. "I . . . my side . . . hurts." She coughed, and something dark, darker than saliva, bubbled out of her mouth.

"You're gonna be all right," Phil said, gently caressing her face. The night was suddenly pierced by the distant sound of a siren. "There's someone coming now. You just stay still. We'll take care of you."

He sat back on his heels and looked from Annie to the silent form of the dead police chief . . . the Alley Cat! Even in death, he was clutching the knife he had used to kill five women . . . and had tried to increase the count to six tonight. Rage—at Richards and at himself for never even *suspecting* the truth—boiled like lava in his gut. He shifted over to Richards, fighting the urge to spit in the dead man's face, to haul back and kick him until he was pulp.

"You lousy, rotten mother-humper," he said, sneering as he reached out and took hold of the knife. The man's fingers were already stiffening, and it took some effort to get the knife free.

As soon as he held the knife in his hand, Phil's eyes widened. He held the knife up and turned it back and forth, watching as the light from the streetlight played over the edge of the blade. He remembered how, during the struggle with Richards, the blade had seemed to glow, and he saw now that he hadn't been imagining things. Reflecting off the metal, the light danced like blue fire, tiny streaks of lightning that wound snakelike from the tip to the hilt. They shifted downward, encircling his hand and wrist. Phil turned the knife over and over, amazed by the feel of it, the heft of it, the energy he felt throbbing through the blade and into his hand, into his arm.

It was like . . . like suddenly his hand had been *filled*, had been *completed*! He was holding something that had been missing all his life, without his even knowing it . . . until now.

The wailing siren was drawing closer; and looking up, he could see the flashing blue lights of the cruiser as it rounded the corner onto Union Street. With just one glance from the knife blade—glowing as if it had its own electric generator—to Annie, he suddenly understood.

Leaning forward and leering, he looked down at his girlfriend. Her eyes were glazed with pain as she stared up at him, but the thought that she might be beyond feeling any more pain never crossed his mind. All he could think was, *he had to get the job done!*

With one quick slash, the blade laid her throat open from ear to ear. She made one brief gurgling noise, then her legs and arms twitched. It was as if a jolting current of electricity slammed through her. Then she lay still as her slowing heart pumped her blood from her neck onto the ground.

Phil sat back on his heels, looking from his hand to Annie and then back to his hand. The knife no longer glowed with blue light; it was just a knife again—a switchblade with a six-inch, honed blade.

Satisfied now, Phil wedged the knife handle into Richards' cold, clenched fist, then wiped the blood from his hands onto the grass. He stood up and walked out to the road just as the cruiser came to a skidding stop by the vacant lot. Two patrolmen got out of the car, their guns held at ready.

"Jesus Christ!" Phil said. His voice trembled and almost broke as he started toward the approaching policemen with stiff-legged, lurching steps.

"I got him . . . I nailed the Alley Cat," he said, grasping for air. "But—but not soon enough." He took a deep breath, and his throat made a loud, roaring sound. "They're both—over there." He hitched his thumb toward the weed-choked lot. "They're both dead . . . Dear God, he killed her! She's *dead*! . . . Annie's dead!"

Al Sarrantonio has been an editor and short-story writer and is presently a novelist and househusband. He has a deceptively resonant style, the sort that stays with you long after the tale itself is finished. While he's published several novels of note, his most adamant fans argue that his private eye novel *Cold Night* is thus far the most impressive.

———————— �☩ ————————

CHILDREN OF CAIN

Al Sarrantonio

Tonight I killed my mother in her bed.
Because:

Hank and I hit it off right away when he started school. It was late in the second semester, but they let him into the sixth grade anyway. He was a foster kid. I'd never met anyone like him before—he was always smiling and he always had good ideas for things to do. After classes we'd play wiffle ball, or check out the magazines at the drug store, or sit under the drooping umbrella of the weeping willow in my backyard and make believe we were trapped in a force field. We did everything together. He said I was like a brother to him.

"I've always wanted a brother," he smiled.

"You've got one," I smiled back.

One day near the end of April, a kid named Porky Kolhausen brought a one-pound bullfrog into school in his lunchbox and shoved it so far into our faces that we had to all but eat it. "Got it out of Cooper's Pond," he bragged, knowing we'd be impressed with the feat. "Bet you guys couldn't do that."

I said, "Bet there's bigger frogs than that in Cooper's Pond."

"Bet we could catch one of 'em," Hank quickly added.

"Bet you couldn't," Porky challenged, and that same afternoon after school found Hank and I outside the Cooper property.

We found the hole in Cooper's fence, and crawled along the concrete foundation of his tool shed. We stopped at the edge. Forty yards away was the pond, a cool oval of blue reflective water dotted with lilypads, waterflowers, banked by moss and close-cut grass. There was supposed to be bass in that pond, and Porky had bragged he had caught a bluegill but had no evidence since he claimed Cooper had started yelling at him from the house and he'd had to drop his net and run. That one we were allowed to doubt.

"Think we can make it?" Hank smiled.

I was more nervous. "I don't know—"

"Come on." And then he was gone ahead of me, crouched like a commando, moving past a green enameled metal table and chairs and into the open.

I followed, and swore I heard Cooper yell after us. But I looked back to see the flat white face of the back of his house, and no one in sight. The screened porch was empty. A hammock blew lazily between the two elms shading the porch.

"Come on!"

I hurried to catch up. Hank was already nearing the edge of the pond, squatting on a rock speckled with duck crap that jutted out boldly into the water.

"The old man's going to catch us, I know it."

"Don't worry about it," Hank said, stretching out to look into the water. The calmness in his face was reflected back at us.

There was nothing to see, just water and weeds, and drift of silt and last autumn's caught leaves at the bottom of the pond—and then I saw vague movement. "There," Hank

said, pointing to a spot a yard out to our right. I saw
nothing, then Hank added, "Keep watching." Something
separated itself from the drift of pure water: a lashing tail,
the lazy wave of tiny fins.

"A bluegill!" I said.

"It's a small bass," Hank corrected. His eyes were wide
with concentrated pleasure. I saw him lower his hand like a
snake charmer toward the water, then suddenly his arm
dived in and he came up with the fish. It tried to slide out of
his grip, throwing its small head from side to side, but Hank
quickly backed off the rock and laid the fish out on the
mossy lawn. It began to flop toward the water, drawn like a
magnet. Hank dug the toe of his sneaker under it and
flipped it away from the water another yard.

"Great. Let's see what else we've got."

I eyed the bass, which curled tentatively and then lay still,
and followed Hank around the bank toward the treed side
of the pond.

"Where you going?" I asked anxiously, my mind still on
the house and Cooper.

"This is where the bullfrogs would be."

He dipped into the deep shade, back away from the
water. For a moment I lost sight of him.

"Here."

He had reemerged in a tiny clearing surrounded by tightly
wound branches close to the lapping shore. There seemed
barely enough room for two. I kneeled close by.

My hand fell on something long and machined and I
pulled it up from the tangle of weeds.

"Hey, Hank, it's Porky's net!"

Hank stood staring at the water. "We don't need it."

"But—"

"Be quiet," he whispered.

This time his hand shot sideways, on the bank, and he
brought up something green and fat with long legs. I hadn't
even seen it.

Hank smiled. "They hide in with the grass and water
weeds," he explained. "He was there all the time, watching

us." He lowered the frog into Porky's net and took the handle from me. "Let's go back."

He turned into the woods and wound around toward the spot where we had left the bass. "Happy?" he smiled, and I nodded. He presented me with the fish, which seemed to pant in my hand and tried once to flip away from my grasp. Soon we were back at the hole in Cooper's fence and making our way to the back of the rubbled lot next door.

"Now comes the fun part," Hank said.

"Aren't we going to take them home?"

Hank smiled at me, his head tilted a little sideways. "Nah."

"But we've got Porky's net for evidence—"

"Screw Porky," Hank said, continuing to look at me that way. I had never seen him look like that before.

I was going to argue, but he turned away from me to the tall concrete wall at the back of the lot. The wall was topped by a ragged stretch of rusted barbed wire; behind it was a junked-car lot and the barbed wire kept nobody out because there was a hole in the concrete wall, a chipped circle two foot high gouged out over many years by kids with crowbars and screwdrivers and old hammers.

"Come on."

Hank wormed through the hole and waited for me. On the other side, surrounded by the cool shadows cast by rusted semis, he took the frog out of the webbing and tossed the net back among the truck parts.

"Hey."

"Never mind the net. Watch this," he said.

I watched the bullfrog. It had been quiet till now, quiescent in its captivity. Hank held it before him with both hands, like a barbarian holding a sword, and felt down with his fingers to a place on the frog's belly. "Now." He squeezed, and the frog began to croak, a low, belching sound. I laughed.

"Now keep watching," Hank said.

He pressed harder on the frog's belly. It emitted another croak, lower and huskier than the first, and then its mouth opened wide and its eyes widened and its tongue drew out as if it had been blown up like a tiny balloon.

Hank kept pressing as he turreted toward the concrete wall. The entire front of the frog now looked like a constricted balloon.

"What—" I started to say but Hank shrugged me off with a laugh as his hands closed suddenly around the frog's middle. There was a squishing sound and the frog's eyes exploded outward and its head split wide. Its tongue, along with much of its gut, flew out of its mouth and hit the wall like a projectile.

"Jesus!" I said and turned away from the red raw splotch of frog guts on the wall. "How could you do that?"

I looked at Hank. I thought he would have a retching look on his face, or would start laughing like some kids do when they see gross stuff, but his face was flushed red. When he dropped the remains of the frog he looked perfectly happy.

"Now you," he said.

"Are you crazy?"

I looked at the bass in my hand. It was nearly dead; already I could feel the scales around its middle where I'd been holding it beginning to dry out and peel away. Even if I had rushed it back to the pond or to other fresh water it would die. But that wasn't the point.

"I don't want to do that," I said.

Hank didn't do what I thought he would. He didn't say, "Are you chicken?" or laugh the whole thing off. He just kept staring at me expectantly.

"I don't want to," I repeated.

And then I did. Convulsively, I turned to the wall and choked the bass just behind the head, feeling its brain and upper guts fly out like a squeezed pimple. The head split off from the body and hit the cement wall whole, falling to the ground.

I stood watching it, and then I dropped the rest of the bass and ran, shimmying through the hole in the wall and running through the empty lot to the street. My legs pumped and tears filled my eyes as I jumped the curb and crossed the lawn of my house and ran into the garage and up to my room. I closed the door behind me and blocked it with a chair.

I threw myself on my bed and cried. When my mother came to call me for dinner I was still crying because I knew that I had killed that bass because I wanted to.

I didn't see Hank for a while after that. There were a hundred excuses, but he didn't push me. We were in the same home room, and the same math class, but I managed to not even pass him in the hallway. Once when we did bump into each other I looked at his face but didn't look into his eyes.

I spent a lot of time in my room. My mom began to ask me if I was all right, so I had to fake her out, tell her I was going to the library, then go out to the garage to be by myself, or tell her I was going to play ball in the park and then sit behind the grandstand with my knees up and my head down.

I kept seeing Hank's expectant smile. It was as if he'd known I would do what I did to that fish, as if he'd known that, suddenly, a door had opened in my mind that had nothing to do with fish or frogs but something much more horrible. All the frogs and fish that had ever died were just the first grains at the beginning of a beach leading to the largest ocean in the world.

I *hadn't* wanted to kill that fish.

I *had*.

I was afraid of Hank, and of myself.

It was four weeks after the day at Cooper's Pond that Hank came for me again. I had begun to think that he had forgotten about me, that maybe he had found someone else to hang around with, or perhaps had decided to leave me alone. I had dreamed about some of the things that Hank might do, and always the dreams ended with Hank's smile, his happy, knowing smile, hovering over me, detached, like a scythe.

But after a month even the dreams had started to go

away. It was the end of spring, the beginning of summer, and soon school would be over. I would be going away to camp, I had projects to finish before classes ended, and I had begun to forget, at least as much as I would, that day and what Hank and I had done.

I was up in my room. I remember the late spring breeze blowing in the curtains, bringing into the room the particular odor that late spring flowers have, a heavy pollen scent that smells like living things themselves. I was putting the last of my British Museum dinosaur models into a diorama I was building for the Science Fair at school, lowering a stegosaurus into its spot in the midst of HO model vegetation at the base of a papier-maché volcano, and when I heard the doorbell downstairs ring and then heard my mother call up to me I knew that it was Hank.

I dropped the model. I wanted to cry all of a sudden. I sat rocking myself, my eyes blurring with tears, my face growing hot, and then I clutched my hands into fists and buried my face in my lap and began to hit myself on the sides of the legs hard.

"No! No!" I sobbed, muffling my angry voice so my mother wouldn't hear.

"Rudy, you hear me?" my mother called. "I said Hank is here. Should I send him up?"

I must have made a noise in answer, because a moment later I heard a shuffle on the stairs and the door to my room opened and he was there.

"Hi, Rudy." The smile hadn't changed. Nothing about him had. He was still the same Hank I had known for two months, hit fungoes to, flipped baseball cards with, hunted for frogs—

"Whatcha doing?" he asked. It was as if he had seen me yesterday. He put his hands in his pockets and bent down to look at the diorama. "Neat." He uprighted the stegosaurus, set it down exactly where I would have, brushed some HO lichen from the spiked tail. He bent lower, bringing his eyes in line with the front view, sweeping them across the Jurassic landscape, up the slope of the volcano to the lava-rimmed crater. "Good stuff."

He stood up, tucked his hands deeper into his pockets, smiled. "So watcha been doing?"

"Not much," I answered, looking at the floor. "Been real busy."

"I bet." His eyes roamed away from me, around the room, over the baseball trophies, the autographed Mets baseball, the posters. "Oh, *neat!*" he said, going to a new model I had finished the week before, a red '56 Chevy convertible. "Where'd you get it?"

"My mother bought it for me," I answered quietly. "Good report card."

"Want to go somewhere?" he said suddenly, turning to look at me.

"No."

"You sure? Be a lot of fun."

"I've got too much to do. Got to finish this project."

"It's *Saturday*, for Pete's sake. You can do it tomorrow. Want me to ask your mom if it's all right?" He made as if to go out into the hallway.

"No. Don't. I . . . don't want to go with you."

I looked at him then, expecting to see feigned surprise, or hurt, on his face, but instead there was only his smile.

"Come on," he said.

"Jesus, Hank, I don't want to!"

We looked at each other for a few moments, and then my mother called up, "You boys behave, or I'll make you go outside!"

Hank's smile didn't waver. His eyes held the smile and expanded it, expanding it like the ocean that leads to the horizon that never finds land—

"Sure," I said, my voice barely a whisper. "Okay."

"Aw*right!*" Hank said, taking two long steps toward me, hugging his arm around me like a brother.

We avoided my mother, going out through the garage. "Need your bike," Hank said. I pulled my ten-speed from the wall and mounted it, riding out the open garage door into the full spring afternoon, waiting while Hank trotted up to the front porch to get his ten-speed and gear down beside me.

The day outside was like that breath of flower-life had been in my room. The world was burst open with flowers, green lawns and leaves—the trees so laden they looked wet. I breathed it in, feeling the lushness fill my lungs, breathing out the scent of chlorophyll and freshly spread fertilizer and mowed lawn. I wanted to feel life around me, forget the ocean that rolled and swelled in my head.

"Nice day," Hank said.

I just looked at him.

I followed him in low gear up the hill away from my house, then coasted down the long hill into town. We timed the lights so that we didn't have to brake. Hank took his hand from the handlebars and sat up, letting the wind blow across his face. We went straight through town and out, toward the farmstands and woods.

"Where are we going?" I asked.

"Follow, Bwana," he said, grinning.

I knew then where we were going. When Hank had first moved in I had showed him a special place—a hollow of woods at the end of a trail in an old Boy Scout camp which had been abandoned twenty years before after a forest fire. What had grown back was small and stunted between the burnout. I had cleared out the hollow with a couple of other kids the summer before. We had made plans to sleep out overnight when our parents gave us permission. My mother never had.

I had taken Hank there once, making plans to camp out with him the coming summer. The place had been overgrown with a year's worth of weeds then, but as we rounded off the road into the woods I saw that the trail had been cleared, the bushes pushed back, even cut in some spots where they were thick outcroppings. We passed the burned-out jamboree hall, a charred square of water-rotted timbers, and veered back into the forest.

"Almost there!" Hank called back, and the same sob that had assaulted me back in my room rose once again to my throat and threatened to break out.

We skirted a huddle of moss-grown picnic benches, then abruptly shot out into the mottled sunshine of the hollow.

The dale had been brushed clean. It looked as if an overnight Boy Scout campout had taken place, followed by a good cleanup, grass raked almost to the dirt, old leaves, branches, and twigs swept away.

"Like it?" Hank said, dismounting his bike, leaning it in a smooth motion against the thick trunk of an oak. "Been working like a dog out here."

I got off my bike slowly and mounted it on its kickstand.

He looked at me and laughed. "What's the matter? You look like you've seen the boogeyman."

I lowered myself to the ground, holding my stomach. I suddenly wanted to vomit. I closed my eyes, the ocean appearing before me, an ocean of thick red, thin clusters of veins, the bob of a gray organ in the swell, a hand reaching up out of the sickly-sweet-smelling sea to turn over and fall, disattached—

"Whoa, buster," I heard close-by. I looked up to see Hank standing over me. His face was blank. I smelled vomit, looked down to see my pants covered, my sneakers, my hands.

"You okay, pard?" Hank said.

"No."

"Take a minute. Clean yourself up." He stepped back away from me, from the smell. He'd left a handkerchief at my feet. I mopped myself, feeling my stomach turn over again, then keel to steadiness.

"Feel better?" he asked.

"A little."

"Good."

He began to whistle, thinly, through his teeth, as he worked something away from the backpack at the rear of his bicycle seat. It was a crinkled paper bag. Inside was a sandwich. He sat down Indian fashion next to his bicycle and began to eat. The vague smell of bologna and mustard came to me.

"Didn't get to eat lunch," he said. "Let me know when you're ready, bub."

He ate one half of the sandwich and then the other, watching the trees around us. Dappled sunlight brushed his face, making him squint. Suddenly he pointed excitedly into the underbrush, his words muffled by food. "Look, a fox!"

My stomach tightened. I wanted for him to jump up and chase after it, draw a knife from his belt and hack at the fox's face until all resemblance with nature was gone. But Hank didn't move. The fox was there, a red flash of tail with a white tip, and then it was gone.

"Neat-o!"

My stomach churned again, steadied.

"Tummy okay?" Hank said, giving his attention to me again.

I nodded weakly.

He put the remaining crust of his sandwich into the paper bag, crumpled it up, stood, dusted crumbs from his pants, and put the paper bag into his bike's knapsack. "Good," he said. "Then let's get to it."

To the right of his bicycle was a thin trail, and Hank abruptly slipped into it. I heard him thrashing around in the bushes. I heard his voice, low. At first I thought he was talking to himself, but with repetition his words became audible. "Here, fellas," he coaxed, over and over.

Movement stopped in the underbrush, and Hank stopped talking. Then I heard him say, *"Shit! Oh, shit!"* He moved through the woods again, reappearing with a large, high cardboard box in his arms, his face reddened with anger.

He set the box down in the middle of the clearing. "I thought it was high enough," he said, anger receding to embarrassment. "But one of them got out. Sorry." He looked at me with genuine contrition spread across his features.

I said nothing.

"Well," he expanded, "we'll just have to wing it."

He turned his attention to the box, lifting back the flaps.

His features lit up. "Hey, boy!" he said brightly to something down inside. He put his hands down into the depth of the box and brought something small, soft, and brown up.

A puppy. A mutt, mostly cocker spaniel, with ears hung flat down and huge brown eyes. Its paws were overlarge. Its tongue panted out expectantly, its attention riveted to Hank.

Hank laughed. "All right, boy, okay." He cradled the dog tightly with one hand, reaching into his jacket pocket to dig out a dog biscuit. The puppy snapped at it, taking it into its mouth with a grunt of pleasure, holding it with its paws and working it over with its teeth.

"Good fella," Hank said, putting the dog down and spreading a few more biscuits at its feet. "You won't run away, huh? Nah, you'll stay, right?"

The dog looked up at him adoringly. Hank laughed again. "Good boy."

Hank looked at me. "There were two," he said, "the other was bigger. He must have got his paws over the top of the box."

We both looked at the brown puppy, whose tail wagged happily as he growled away at the dog biscuits.

Hank suddenly rubbed his hands together and said, "It's showtime."

With a short laugh at the dog, he scooped it up and handed it to me.

My hands felt heavy as stones. The dog must have sensed my feelings, because it began to whine, trying to squirm its way out of my loose grip. Hank put his hands on top of it and held it down. "Whoa, boy, whoa, take it easy." He dipped back into his pocket and came up with a biscuit that had broken in half. He gave the half to the dog and rubbed its head down as it took it. The dog whined, then began to pant and growl playfully, working at the food.

"You can't freak 'em out," Hank said to me. He grinned down at the dog, rubbed the slick fur on its head. "Right, fella?"

The dog whined excitedly, looking for another biscuit.

"Sorry, no more food," Hank said, and then he took his hands away from the dog, leaving it in my grip.

"Go ahead," he said, turning his smile to me.

"I can't," I got out. I held the dog close to my body; it had warmed my hands, but my fingers trembled and threatened to pull apart, throwing the dog into the woods to join its escaped sibling.

"Wish that other sucker hadn't gotten away," Hank said ruefully. "It would have made things a lot easier." He rubbed the puppy's head then stepped back. "Sorry, but you have to do it by yourself."

"But I *can't.*"

"No?"

And then I did it. I turned the dog in my hands, belly up, cupping it so that I could see its face. I took its tiny head between my palms, its huge brown eyes looking up at me, and I squeezed, letting my mind be a vise that spread down my arms and into my hands. The puppy gasped once and then opened its mouth wide, trying to turn and bite me, but my grip was too tight. Its eyes grew wider, staring into my eyes, and then a bright light, the end of life, filled the eyes and then they blinked out as if a shade had been drawn down them as the dog's head imploded in my hands. My palms nearly met, and the dog's head spread out away from my hands, colors of red mingling with brown fur and bone. I kept squeezing. My hands nearly met. I wanted to feel my own live flesh against itself.

I heard a buzzing sound from far off that grew like a swarm of hornets and threatened to overwhelm me. Then I realized that it was my own mouth, screaming. I screamed and screamed and then someone's hands were upon me. A voice was trying to cut through the screams. The hands shook me and I let go of the dog, my arms flying wide, my eyes burning like hot coals. I threw the hands that held me away and screamed. The hands took hold of me again. My burning eyes saw Hank looking at me, smiling happily, and I reached out to take his face in my hands, but instead I put my hands to my own head, screaming, *"I don't want* to! I don't want to!" and then I sank to the ground and the hornets went away and I cried and cried and finally slept. . . .

When I woke up the sun was going down. Hank was gone. He'd taken his bike, but not before he had cleaned up. The hollow was as antiseptically brushed and raked as it had been when we arrived.

I sat up. I looked at my hands. Only when I looked under the nails could I see dried blood. Hank had cleaned me, too. My pants and shirt had been rubbed with soil. Most of the stains were gone. Those that remained were pale and undistinguished.

I crawled to a tree and sat with my back against it for a few minutes. Then I got up and rode my bike slowly out of the camp, through town and back to my house. When I got home it was suppertime. My mother didn't say anything to me about where I'd been. I ate dinner and then I went up to my room and closed the door. I put on my pajamas and got into bed, and slept.

I dreamed about the extinguishing light in the puppy's eyes, and about Hank's expectant, happy smile.

All night I dreamed.

The next day I woke up and didn't get out of bed, and my mother didn't notice because it was Sunday and she got up late. When it was time for breakfast she came to my room, and I told her I didn't feel well and stayed in bed. I stayed in bed all day. The next day my science project was due, but I stayed in bed the whole day, the dinosaur diorama passing through morning light and afternoon shadow to night again. At suppertime my mother came in with her worried look on.

"I don't like the way you look," she said. "Are you sure it's just a cold?"

I nodded; I'd been warming the thermometer up to 102° all day with a match and drinking all the orange juice and chicken broth she'd brought. The Panadol she'd given me I'd flushed down the toilet.

She continued to study me. "If you don't get better by tomorrow I'm calling the doctor. There's a lot of mononucleosis around. If you've got that you could miss the last month of school. And you wouldn't be able to see Hank for weeks. You don't want that, do you?"

I shook my head.

She produced another glass of orange juice. "Try to rest now. I'll be back in later to see if you need anything."

I drank the juice, and feigned rest, and thought about mononucleosis, and when she came in later to check on me I feigned sleep. After she was gone I stared at the ceiling as long as I could keep sleep away, and when it finally came the dreams came with it and hounded me till morning.

The next day I didn't use the match, lowering my temperature to normal. My mother pronounced me cured. As she bore away the last of my orange juice she stopped in the doorway. "I forgot to tell you, Rudy. Your friend Hank called. He said he'll either see you in school tomorrow, or come by in the afternoon. He said he had something 'neat-o,' as he put it, to show you." She looked at me, shaking her head as she closed the door behind her. "Still don't like the way you look . . ."

The rest of that day and all night, the dreams came with my eyes open.

The next day I went to school. Hank was late for home room, but he passed me a note during math class that read, 'See you after school?' I wrote back, 'Yes.' He didn't try to talk to me after class, and I didn't see him the rest of the school day.

After the last bell he appeared, falling into step beside me as I headed for home. "Can you come now?" he asked.

"I don't have my bike."

His grin widened. "You don't need it."

"I should tell my mom."

"Are you kidding?" he laughed. "Come on."

We walked two blocks to the county bus depot. Hank motioned me onto a bench while he went to the window. I saw him pull a wad of bills from his pocket and count them out, sliding them under the glass cutout. He came back with two tickets, handing me one. "Here," he said, "it's a round trip."

I looked on the ticket, and it had the name of a town forty miles away on it. "What the—"

"Trust me," he grinned. He pointed to an open garbage bin next to the bench. "Throw your schoolbooks in there," he said. "You won't need them anymore."

I did as he said, and then we boarded our bus. The doors hissed closed, and the bus groaned away from the station.

From our seats behind the driver we watched the scenery. It was quickly dominated by farmland. We passed through a few small towns, the bus braking to a halt in front of a dusty station before pulling out onto the road again. Soon it was all farmland we watched.

In an hour and fifteen minutes we had reached our stop, a mere sign on the highway. Hank urged me off the bus ahead of him. As he stepped off, he turned to the driver. "Last bus through at eight?" he asked. The driver nodded with boredom. Hank jumped off beside me.

We walked for two miles. It was a warm afternoon, the kind we would have played baseball on, but today we walked through a rutted farm field, ranked with cut feed-corn stalks, toward a near line of hills. "My foster parents built a summer house up there," Hank explained. "There's a cabin, a lake nearby." Smiling, he added, "No fish or frogs."

We climbed, the hill quickly shading itself with pins and spruce. There was no trail, but Hank used the sun, and soon we broke out onto a dirt road.

"Won't be long," Hank announced.

In another fifteen minutes we stood before the summer cabin, an A-frame with a wrap-around deck. It looked brand new. In confirmation, Hank said, "They finished it a month ago. My foster parents said we'd spend all of August up here."

He bounded up the steps onto the deck. He produced a key from his pocket and opened the front door. He held it open for me like a bellhop, letting me pass through first.

I entered a sparcely furnished room with sawdust still wedged in the corners, sunlight streaming through the glass-walled A of the front. The back of the A was high stone with an unused fireplace cut into the bottom.

"Neat, eh?"

I looked around at Hank.

He had settled into one of two bean-bag chairs in the center of the room. He crossed his outstretched legs at the ankles. "Hungry?" he asked. "I brought up some stuff yesterday, bologna and mustard and bread; some devil dogs, too."

"I'm not hungry."

He shrugged, settling his hands behind his head. "Suit yourself."

"Why are we here?"

I had begun to get that nauseous feeling again, a fever-like roiling that burned up from my stomach into the back of my eyes.

"Sit down," Hank suggested.

"I don't want to."

"Are you sure?"

My stomach was boiling, pushing bile into the back of my throat. I swallowed it down. I did want to sit down all of a sudden, and dropped into the second bean-bag chair across from Hank.

"Tell me why we're here, Hank."

"Soon." I looked at him through the blur of my sickened stomach and hot vision, and he smiled at me broadly.

"I don't want to be here," I said.

He bounded suddenly out of his chair. "Think I'll make a sandwich."

"Don't . . ."

I had trouble speaking. The ocean in my mind rolled me like a ship in a gale. I knew what the ocean was and wanted it to go away; wanted the limbs in the sea of blood to stop cresting the waves, reaching out to me, then sinking again to mingle with the screaming, dying fish below.

He stopped his retreat to the kitchen, walked slowly back to his chair, sat down.

"You okay?" he asked.

"No."

"There's nothing I can do for you," he said.

His smile was gone. In its place was not the dropped mask I had anticipated, the long-fanged, crazy, lustful visage of a murderer. He looked suddenly tired, and old.

"I can't help you, Rudy," he said, and, briefly, he touched my knee with his hand.

I must have screamed, then. I saw him lean toward me, and then fire filled my eyes, boiling back into my head. The sea not only was inside me but was everywhere. I was the sea, I was an ocean of blood myself, the limbs were my limbs and I possessed all of death, possessed it because it was me. I was death itself and my own screams were the screams of all the dead, swimming in and through me.

What have you done to me!" I screamed, and I forced my flaming eyes to see through their fire and found Hank kneeling close to me, peering into me as if I was a mirror. "WHAT HAVE YOU DONE!"

"I'm sorry," I heard him say. His face was so close I could feel his breath, and then he tilted his head back, giving me his throat.

Fire and blood filled me, was me, and I took his throat in my teeth and screamed. The world became red. There was another scream in my ocean of blood which was not my own, and at the end of the scream, as it became a wave of blood in my sea, I heard Hank say, in crying relief, *"Thank you . . ."*

I awoke in twilight. The sun burned weakly into my eyes through the huge A of the front window, a dying ember about to fall into the night.

I arose from the floor. There was a lamp silhouetted in the twilight, and I stumbled to it and turned it on.

Its weak wattage subsumed the sun and made weak day for me in the room.

Where I had been there was blood. Hank lay with his throat torn wide open. His face was disfigured, his severed limbs scattered about, chest and bowels ripped open, pulled from the body like stuffing from a mattress.

Near his shredded trousers, I saw the receipt half of the one-way ticket he had bought at the bus depot.

There was wood next to the fireplace, neatly stacked. I added kindling from a filled brass bucket and started a fire.

When I had the fire stoked to big hot logs, I put the pieces of Hank into it, feeding him to the flames as if he was wood himself. It took time, but the fire was hot enough and in the end there was just ash left. The blood I cleaned up. Then I showered, scrubbing my hands and face until they were clean as a baby. Under my fingernails was blood, and I could do nothing about that.

In the bedroom I found the change of clothes Hank had left for me. There was even a golf jacket in my size. He had known it would be chilly when I left the summer house.

I had a sandwich, bologna with mustard, and a devil dog, and then I turned off the light and left. I hiked back down the hill and across the fallow field to the bus stop. It was almost eight o'clock when I arrived. The bus found me ten minutes later.

When I got home my mother was waiting frantically for me. "Oh, God, Rudy, I've been so worried about you! Have you been with Hank today?"

I told her no; that I was off hunting Indian arrow heads by myself and had forgotten what time it was.

"Thank God! It's so awful—the police found Hank's foster parents in their house today, murdered. They're sure Hank had something to do with it." She looked at me as if she was afraid of hurting me, as if I was made of porcelain. "Oh, poor Rudy! They say he murdered his best friend and his real parents in Maine two months ago, and has been killing people ever since." She held me close. "Oh, God! You don't know where he is, do you?"

"No."

She continued to embrace me. "I want you to have some dinner and then go to bed."

"I'm not hungry."

"Poor baby."

I went to bed, and I lay staring at the ceiling, practicing my smile, and the dreams were real and they wouldn't go away.

I heard my mother go to bed, and I went into her bedroom and killed her. Then I packed a bag and left the house.

I'll wander until I find my brother.

A MATTER OF PRINCIPLE

Max Allan Collins

It had been a long time since I'd had any trouble sleeping. Probably Vietnam, and that was gunfire that kept me awake. I've never been an insomniac. You might think killing people for a living would give you restless nights. Truth is, those that go into that business simply aren't the kind who are bothered by it much.

I was no exception. I hadn't gone into retirement because my conscience was bothering me. I retired because the man I got my contracts through got killed—well, actually I killed him, but that's another story—and I had enough money put away to live comfortably without working, so I did.

The A-frame cottage on Paradise Lake was secluded enough for privacy, but close enough to nearby Lake Geneva to put me in contact with human beings, if I was so inclined, which I rarely was, with the exception of getting laid now and then. I'm human.

There was also a restaurant nearby, called Wilma's Welcome Inn, a rambling two-story affair that included a gas station, modest hotel accommodations, and a convenience store. I'd been toying with the idea of buying the place, which had been slipping since the death of Wilma; I'd been getting a little bored lately and needed something to do. Before I started putting people to sleep, I worked in a garage as a mechanic, so the gas station angle appealed to me.

Anyway, boredom had started to itch at me, and for the past few nights I'd had trouble sleeping. I sat up all night watching satellite TV and reading paperback westerns; then I'd drag around the next day, maybe drifting to sleep in the afternoon just long enough to fuck up my sleep cycle again that night.

It was getting irritating.

At about three-thirty in the morning on the fourth night of this shit, I decided eating might do the trick. Fill my gut with junk food and the blood could rush down from my head and warm my belly and I'd get the fuck sleepy, finally. I hadn't tried this before because I'd been getting a trifle paunchy since I quit working and since winter kicked in.

In the summer I'd swim in the lake every day and get exercise and keep the spare tire off. But in the winter I'd just let my beard go and belt size, too. Winters made me fat and lazy and, now, fucking sleepless.

The cupboard was bare so I threw on my thermal jacket and headed over to the Welcome Inn. At this time of night the convenience store was the only thing open, that and one self-serve gas pump.

The clerk was a heavyset brunette named Cindy from nearby Twin Lakes. She was maybe twenty years old and a little surly, but she worked all night, so who could blame her.

"Mr. Ryan," she said, flatly, as I came in, the bell over the door jingling.

"Cindy," I said, with a nod, and began prowling the place, three narrow aisles parallel to the front of the building. None of the snacks appealed to me—chips and crackers and Twinkies and other preservative-packed delights—and the frozen food case ran mostly to ice-cream sandwiches and popsickles. In this weather, that was a joke.

I was giving a box of Chef Boyardee lasagna an intent once-over, like it was a car I was considering buying, when the bell over the door jingled again. I glanced up and saw a heavyset man—heavyset enough to make Cindy look svelte—with a pockmarked face and black-rimmed glasses that fogged up as he stepped in.

He wore an expensive topcoat—tan, a camel's-hair number you could make payments on for a year and still owe—and his shoes had a bright black city shine, barely flecked with ice and snow. His name was Harry something, and he was from Chicago. I knew him, in another life.

I turned my back. If he saw me, I'd have to kill him, and I was bored, but not that bored.

Predictably, Harry Something went straight for the potato chips; he also rustled around the area where cookies were shelved. I risked a glimpse and saw him, not two minutes after he entered, with his arms full of junk food, heading for the front counter.

"Excuse me, miss," Harry Something said, depositing his groceries before Cindy. His voice was nasal and high-pitched, a funny, childish voice for a man his size. "Could you direct me to the sanitary napkins?"

"You mean Kotex?"

"Whatever."

"The toiletries is just over there."

Now this was curious, and I'll tell you why. I had met Harry Something around ten years before, when I was doing a job for the Outfit boys. I was never a mob guy, mind you, strictly a freelancer, but their money was as good as anybody's. What that job was isn't important, but Harry and his partner Louis were the locals who had fucked up, making my outsider's presence necessary. Harry and Louis had not been friendly toward me. They had threatened me, in fact.

They had beaten the hell out of me in my hotel room, when the job was over, for making them look bad.

I had never taken any sort of revenge out on them. I occasionally do take revenge, but at my convenience, and when a score strikes me as worth settling. Harry and Louis had really just pushed me around a little, bloodied my nose, tried to earn back a little self-respect. So I didn't hold a grudge. Not a major grudge. Fuck it.

As to why Harry Something purchasing Kotex in the middle of the night at some backwoods convenience store was curious, well, Harry and Louis were gay. They were queens of crime. Mob muscle who worked as a pair, and played as a pair.

I don't mean to be critical. To each his own. I'd rather cut off my dick than insert it in any orifice of a repulsive fat slob like Harry Something. But that's just me.

And me, I'm naturally curious. I'm not nosy, not even inquisitive. But when a faggot buys Kotex, I have to wonder why.

"Excuse me," Harry Something said, brushing by me.

He hadn't seen my face—he might not recognize me, in any case. Ten years and a beard and twenty pounds later, I wasn't as easy to peg as Harry was, who had changed goddamn little.

Harry, having stocked up on cookies and chips and Kotex, was not buying milk and packaged macaroni and cheese and provisions in general. He was shopping. Stocking up.

And now I knew what he was up to.

I nodded to surly Cindy, who bid me goodbye by flickering her eyelids in casual contempt, and went out to my car, a blue sporty Mazda I'd purchased recently. I wished I'd had the four-wheel-drive, or anything less conspicuous, but I didn't. I sat in the car, scooched down low; I did not turn on the engine. I just sat in the cold car in the cold night and waited.

Harry Something came out with two armloads of groceries —Kotex included, I presumed—and he put them in the front seat of the brown rental Ford. Louis was not waiting for him. Harry was alone.

Which further confirmed my suspicions.

I waited for him to pull out onto the road, waited for him to take the road's curve, then started up my Mazda and glided out after him. He had turned left, toward Twin Lakes and Lake Geneva. That made sense, only I figured he wouldn't wind up either place. I figured he'd be out in the boonies somewhere.

I knew what Harry was up to. I knew he wasn't exactly here to ski. That lardass couldn't stand up on a pair of skis. And he wasn't here to go ice-fishing, either. A city boy like Harry Something had no business in a touristy area like this, in the off-season—unless Harry was hiding out, holing up somewhere.

This would be the perfect area for that.

Only Harry didn't use Kotex.

He turned off on a side road, into a heavily wooded area that wound back toward Paradise Lake. Good. That was very good.

I went on by. I drove a mile, turned into a farmhouse gravel drive and headed back without lights. I slowed as I reached the mouth of the side road, and could see Harry's tail lights wink off.

I knew the cabin at the end of that road. There was only one, and its owner only used it during the summer; Harry was either a renter, or a squatter.

I glided on by and went back home. I left the Mazda next to the deck and walked up the steps and into my A-frame. The nine-millimeter was in the nightstand drawer. The gun hadn't been shot in months—Christ, maybe over a year. But I cleaned and oiled it regularly. It would do fine.

So would my black turtleneck, black jeans, black leather bomber jacket, and this black moonless night. I slipped a .38 revolver in the bomber jacket right side pocket, and clipped a hunting knife to my belt. The knife was razor sharp with a sword point; I sent for it out of the back of one of those dumb-ass ninja magazines—which are worthless except for mail-ordering weapons.

I walked along the edge of the lake, my running shoes crunching the brittle ground, layered as it was with snow and ice and leaves. The only light came from a gentle scattering of stars, a handful of diamonds flung on black velvet; the frozen lake was a dark presence that you could sense but not really see. The surrounding trees were even darker. The occasional cabin or cottage or house I passed was empty. I was one of only a handful of residents on Paradise Lake who lived year-round.

But the lights were on in one cabin. Not many lights, but lights. And its chimney was trailing smoke.

The cabin was small, a traditional log cabin like Abe Lincoln and syrup, only with a satellite dish. Probably two bedrooms, a living room, kitchenette, and a can or two. Only one car—the brown rental Ford.

My footsteps were lighter now; I was staying on the balls of my feet and the crunching under them was faint. I approached with caution and gun in hand and peeked in a window on the right front side.

Harry Something was sitting on the couch, eating barbecue potato chips, giving himself an orange mustache in the process. His feet were up on a coffee table. More food and a sawed-off double-barrel shotgun were on the couch next to him. He wore a colorful Hawaiian shirt; he looked like Don Ho puked on him, actually.

Hovering nervously nearby was Louis, a small, skinny, bald ferret of a man, who wore jeans and a black shirt and a white tie. I couldn't tell whether he was trying for trendy or gangster, and frankly didn't give a shit, either way.

Physically, all the two men had in common was pockmarks and a desire for the other's ugly body.

And neither one of them seemed to need a sanitary napkin, though a towelette would've come in handy for Harry Something. Jesus.

I huddled beneath the window, wondering what I was

doing here. Boredom. Curiosity. I shrugged. Time to look in another window or two.

Because they clearly had a captive. That's what they were doing in the boonies. That's why they were stocking up on supplies at a convenience store in the middle of night and nowhere. That's why there were in the market for Kotex. That's what I'd instinctively, immediately known back at the Welcome Inn.

And in a back window, I saw her. She was naked on a bed in the rustic room, naked but for white panties. She was sitting on the edge of the bed and she was crying, a black-haired, creamy-fleshed beauty in her early twenties.

Obviously, Harry and Louis had nothing sexual in mind for this girl; the reason for her nudity was to help prevent her fleeing. The bed was heavy with blankets, and she'd obviously been keeping under the covers, but right now she was sitting and crying. That time of the month.

I stood in the dark in my dark clothes with a gun in my hand and my back to the log cabin and smiled. When I'd come out into the night, armed like this, it wasn't to effect a rescue. Whatever else they were, Harry and Louis were dangerous men. If I was going to spend my sleepless nights satisfying my curiosity and assuaging my boredom by poking into their business, I had to be ready to pay for my thrills.

But the thing was, I recognized this young woman. Like Harry, I spent a lot of hours during cold nights like this with my eyes frozen to a TV screen. And that's where I'd seen her: on the tube.

Not an actress, no—an heiress. The daughter of a Chicago media magnate whose name you'd recognize, a guy who inherited and wheeled-and-dealed his way into more, including one of the satellite superstations I'd been wasting my eyes on lately. The Windy City's answer to Ted Turner, right down to boating and womanizing.

His daughter was a little wild—seen in the company of rock stars (she had a tattoo of a star—not Mick Jagger, a five-pointed *star* star—on her white left breast, which I could see from the window) and was a Betty Ford clinic dropout. Nonetheless, she was said to be the apple of her daddy's eye, even if that apple was a tad wormy.

So Harry and Louis had put the snatch on the snatch; fair enough. Question was, was it their own idea, or something the Outfit put them up to?

I sat in the cold and dark and decided, finally, that it just didn't matter who or what was behind it. My options were to go home, and forget about it, and try (probably without any luck) to get some sleep; or to rescue this somewhat soiled damsel in distress.

What the hell. I had nothing better to do.

I went to the front door and knocked.

No answer.

Shit, I knew somebody was home, so I knocked again.

Louis cracked open the door and peered out and said, "What is it?" and I shot him in the eye.

There was the harsh, shrill sound of a scream—not Louis, who hadn't had time for that, but the girl in the next room, scared shitless at hearing a gunshot, one would suppose.

I paid no attention to her and pushed the door open—there was no night latch or anything—and stepped over Louis, and pointed the nine-millimeter at Harry, whose orange-ringed mouth was frozen open and whose bag of barbecue potato chips dropped to the floor, much as Louis had.

"Don't, Harry," I said.

I could see in Harry's tiny dark eyes behind his thick black-rimmed glasses that he was thinking about the sawed-off shotgun on the couch next to him.

"Who the fuck . . ."

I walked slowly across the rustic living room toward the couch; in the background, an old colorized movie was playing on their captive's daddy's superstation. I plucked the shotgun off the couch with my left hand and tucked it under my arm.

"Hi, Harry," I said. "Been a while."

His orange-ringed mouth slowly began to work and his eyes began to blink and he said, "Quarry?"

That was the name he'd known me by.

"Taking the girl your idea, or are you still working for the boys?"

"We . . . we retired, couple years ago. God. You killed Louis. Louis. You killed Louis . . ."

"Right. What were you going to put the girl's body in?"

"Huh?"

"She's obviously seen you. You were obviously going to kill her, once you got the money. So. What was the plan?"

Harry wiped off his orange barbecue ring. "Got a roll of plastic in the closet. Gonna roll her up in it and dump her in one of the gravel pits around here."

"I see. Do that number with the plastic right now, for Louis, why don't you? Okay?"

Tears were rolling down Harry's stubbly pockmarked cheeks. I didn't know whether he was crying for Louis or himself or the pair of them, and I wasn't interested enough to ask.

"Okay," he said thickly.

I watched him roll his partner up in the sheet of plastic, using duct tape to secure the package; he sobbed as he did it, but he did it. He got blood on his Hawaiian shirt; it didn't particularly show, though.

"Now I want you to clean up the mess. Go on. You'll find what you need in the kitchen."

Dutifully, Harry shuffled over, got a pan of warm water and some rags, and got on his knees and cleaned up the brains and blood. He wasn't crying anymore. He moved slow but steady, a fat zombie in a colorful shirt.

"Stick the rags in the end of Louis' plastic home, would you? Thank you."

Harry did that, then the big man lumbered to his feet, hands in the air, and said, "Now me, huh?"

"I might let you go, Harry. I got nothing against you."

"Not . . . not how I remember it."

I laughed. "You girls leaned on me once. You think I'd kill a person over something that trivial? What kind of guy do you think I am, Harry?"

Harry had sense enough not to answer.

"Come with me," I said, and with the nine-millimeter's nose to Harry's temple, I walked him to the door of the bedroom.

"Open it," I said.

He did.

We went in, Harry first.

The girl was under the covers, holding the blankets and sheets up around her in a combination of illogical modesty and legitimate fear.

Her expression melted into one of confusion mingled with the beginnings of hope and relief, when she saw me.

"I've already taken care of the skinny one," I said. "Now Harry and me are going for a walk. You stay here. I'm going to get you back to your father."

Her confusion didn't leave, but she began to smile, wide, like a kid Christmas morning seeing her gifts. Her gift to me was dropping the blankets and sheets to her waist.

"Remember," I said. "Stay right there."

I walked Harry out, pulling the bedroom door shut behind me.

"Where are her clothes?"

He nodded to a closet. Same one he'd gotten the plastic out of.

"Good," I said. "Now let's go for a walk. Just you and me and Louis."

"Loo . . . Louis?"

"Better give Louis a hand, Harry."

Harry held the plastic-wrapped corpse in his arms like a B-movie monster carrying a starlet. The plastic was spattered with blood, but on the inside. Harry looked like he was going to cry again.

I still had the sawed-off shotgun under my arm, so it was awkward, getting the front door open, but I managed.

"Out on the lake," I said.

Harry looked at me, his eyes behind the glasses wary, glancing from me to his plastic-wrapped burden and back again.

"We're going to bury Louis at sea," I said.

"Huh?"

"Just walk, Harry. Okay? Just walk."

He walked. I followed behind, nine-millimeter in one hand, sawed-off in the other. Harry in his Hawaiian shirt was an oddly comic sight, but I was too busy to be amused. Our feet crunched slightly on the ice. No danger of falling in. Frozen solid. Kids ice-skated out here. But not right now.

We walked a long way. We said not a word, until I halted him about midway. The black starry sky was our only witness.

"Put him down, Harry," I said. The nine-millimeter was in my waistband; the shotgun was pointed right at him.

He set his cargo gently down. He stood looking gloomily down at the plastic shroud, like a bear contemplating its own foot caught in a trap.

I blasted both barrels of the shotgun; they blew the quiet night apart and echoed across the frozen lake and rattled the world.

Harry looked at me, stunned.

"What the fuck . . . ?"

"Now unroll Louis and toss him in." I said, standing near the gaping hole in the ice. "I'm afraid that plastic might float."

Horrified, the big man did as he was told. Louis slipped down the hole in the ice and into watery nothingness like a turd down the crapper.

"Slick," I said, admiringly.

"Oh Jesus," he said.

"Now you," I said.

"What?"

I had the mine-millimeter out again.

"Jump in," I said. "Water's fine."

"Fuck you!"

I went over quickly and pushed the big son of a bitch in. He was flailing, splashing icy water up on me, as I put six bullets in his head, which came apart in pieces, like a rotten melon.

And then he was gone.

Nothing left but the hole in the ice, the water within it making some frothy reddish waves that would die down soon enough.

I gathered the weapons and the plastic and, folding the plastic sheet as I walked, went back to the cabin.

This was reckless, I knew. I shouldn't be killing people who lived on the same goddamn lake I did. But it was winter, and the bodies wouldn't turn up for a long time, if ever, and the Outfit had used this part of the world to dump its corpses since Capone was just a mean street kid. Very little chance any of this would come back at me.

Nonetheless, I had taken a risk or two. I ought to get something out of it, other than killing a sleepless night.

I got the girl's clothes and went in and gave them to her. A heavy-metal T-shirt and designer jeans and Reeboks.

"Did you kill those men?" she said, breathlessly, her eyes dark and glittering. She had her clothes in her lap.

"That's not important. Get dressed."

"You're wonderful. You're goddamn fucking wonderful."

"I know," I said. "Everybody says the same thing. Get dressed."

She got dressed. I watched her. She was a beautiful piece of ass, no question. The way she was looking at me made it clear she was grateful.

"What can I do for you?" she said, hands on her hips.

"Nothing," I said. "You're on the rag."

That made her laugh. "Other ports in a storm."

"Maybe later," I said, and smiled. She looked like AIDS-bait to me. I could be reckless, but not that reckless.

I put her in my car. I hadn't decided yet whether or not to dump the brown rental Ford. Probably would. I could worry about that later. Right now, I needed to get her to a motel.

She slept in the car. I envied her, and nudged her awake when we reached the motel just inside the Illinois state line.

I'd already checked in. I ushered her in to the shabby little room, its floor space all but taken up by two twin beds, and she sat on the bed and yawned.

"What now?" she said. "You want your reward?"

"Actually, yes," I said, sitting next to her. "What's your father's number?"

"Hey, there's time for that later . . ."

"First things first," I said, and she wrote the number out on the pad by the phone.

I heard the ring, and a male voice said, "Hello?"

I gave her the receiver. "Make sure it's your father, and tell him you're all right."

"Daddy?" she said. She smiled, then she made a face. "I'm fine, I'm fine . . . the man you sent . . . what?"

She covered the receiver, eyes confused again. "He says he didn't send anybody."

I took the phone. "Good evening, sir. I have your daughter. As you can hear, she's just fine. Get together one-hundred-thousand dollars in unmarked, nonsequential tens, twenties, and fifties, and wait for the next call."

I hung up.

She looked at me with wide eyes and wide-open mouth.

"I'm not going to kill you," I said. "I'm just turning a buck."

"You bastard!"

I put the duct tape over her mouth, taped her wrists behind her, and taped her ankles too, and went over and curled up on the other bed, nine-millimeter in my waistband.

And slept like a baby.

Rex Miller used to be a big-city disk jocky (or "radio personality," as they say on job résumés) and you can tell that because on the phone he's as slick as an Amway recruiter. Rex is also a soon-to-be-major talent. His style can only be called grand operatic. His tactics are the literary equivalent of "Smokin' Joe" Frazier's boxing skills—he means to kill you with every punch. His messages seem to be as bleak and stark as a glimpse of a ghetto on an overcast February afternoon. Near early dark. He's learning, he's refining his talents, and while nobody can predict what type of book he'll ultimately settle on writing, you can bet that it will be a type of book all his own.

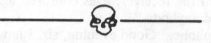

MISS DECEMBER

(A Jack Eichord Vignette)
Rex Miller

Eichord felt a spasm of pain from the crick in his neck and took the killer phone from his ear, moving his head slowly, back and forth, hearing a grinding noise, then a pop, and listening again, but with his head tilted dangerously to the right. It appeared to be an ordinary communication device, but this electronic, plastic pound of horrors that sat on his desk was Alex Bell's death ray. He was convinced that AT&T was using the instrument to bring about his agonizing demise. He had a killer phone and a killer hangover.

"Hello." Into his left ear, sharply.

"Hello. Chief Kuehl?"

"Yeah."

"Chief, this is Jack Eichord in Buckhead. We don't know

one another but I'm a Special Agent with the Major Crimes Task Force." Eichord paused.

"Yeah," the man said, curtly, as if to say—who gives a flying fuck.

"I just finished speaking with Diane Hames in the State's Attorney's office, and she told me you'd be the person to talk to on the McLaughlin case."

"Your name is what, now? I didn't catch your name."

"Jack Eichord."

"And you're with MacTuff out of D.C.?" He at least knew the task force acronym.

"Uh-no, sir. I work for the task force but I work out of the Homicide Squad in Buckhead Station."

The gruff voice on the other end of the phone showed a degree of animation for the first time.

"You the one got what's his name in Chicago? The Lonely Hearts case?"

"Yeah," Eichord said, "that's right."

"I didn't know how to say your name. I-cord. I was just reading about you." There was a smile in the voice.

"Oh?" Eichord said with a little self-deprecating chuckle.

"LAW ENFORCEMENT. Hell, Mr. Eichord, you're *famous.*"

"You know how the press is when they sink their teeth into something." He cringed. The magazine was in his brief-case. He'd winced a couple of times reading "STOPPING THE DEATH RHINO," a sensationalized and rather inac-curate story of Eichord's part in one of the most infamous mass murder cases in history. "They—"

"Yeah. In Chicago they think you can walk on water the way I hear tell."

"Hey—uh, you know—you get involved in a case like that and it gets a lot of ink and so on, first thing you know everything is all blown up way out of proportion." He never knew what to say about it. He called it 'putting on his television hat.'

"You know, that guy was through here. He had just killed a fella in Mount Vernon and stole his car, and—"

with that the chief was off on a rehash of an old chase story involving an investigation that was ancient history to Eichord. But he knew better than to interrupt the man. The hangover and the killer plastique against his ear made his head feel like it was caught in a vise, as the droning, harsh, metallic voice of a small-town Illinois police chief powered in through his left ear. Chief Kuehl had a voice by Black and Decker. Eichord held the receiver away a few inches after an appropriate "um hmm," and tried to exercise the crick. Exorcize the crap. Finally the man had to pause, and Jack said,

"You know I could really use your help on a case right now."

"How's that?" I thought you'd never ask.

"Diane Haines told me they filed charges on this guy Brad McLaughlin, luring kids into his car and so on. Could you fill me in on that?"

"You're a homicide guy. What you want to know on him? He didn't try to kill 'em."

"I understand. But I'm working on an investigation that has a possible parallel M.O., so anything you can tell me about the way the man operated might help."

"I'm surprised you even heard about it down there. Just a real routine deal."

"Well, whatever you can tell me I'd appreciate."

"We got him on four counts of attempted child abduction. Two-seven-year-olds and an eight- and nine-year-old. Little girls. Caucasian male. Thirty-three. Married. They have a little boy, two years old. Ordinary-looking guy. Salesman. He had to come through on business about every two weeks and he'd try to get the kids to get in his car. The fourth time at bat we nailed him."

The ex–Cook County cop, now a downstate police chief, proceeded to regale Eichord with chapter and verse of the thirty-three-year-old would-be child molster. Four failed attempts at abduction. Drug salesman with a failed marriage and a disintegrating career, his masculinity threatened by a world he saw as increasingly competitive, and he had withdrawn from it. Celibate now in the marriage, and with a bad case of incipient short eyes for the kiddies. But no experience or talent for it, fortunately. The little girls had more sense than he did and none of them reached for the fistful of money he offered like candy.

"He's being held on a hundred thousand dollars bond right now," the man told him. "No priors. I dunno much more to tell you. We checked at his job, places he might have traveled to. That's the package."

They talked some more and Jack extricated himself from the conversation with thanks. He drew a line through ILLINOIS ABDUCTIONS? on a legal-size yellow pad, and started to write something when all the light in the small cubbyhole was suddenly dim as if a heavy cloud had passed in front of the sun. The heavy object spoke.

"Wanna get something to eat?"

"Thanks," he told Dana Tuny, the fat half of the detective partnership known as Chink and Chunk, shaking his head no and smiling.

"Thass too bad," the massive, corpulent homicide cop said, unfolding the centerfold of a magazine he was carrying, showing the picture to Eichord. Airbrushed or not . . . she was incredible.

"Lordy," Eichord said, with reverence.

"Makes your tongue hard, don't it," the man said.

"Speaking of making something hard, what happened to our friend Lorraine?"

"Bitch pleaded guilty to second degree and you ain't gonna fucking believe what that no good, no dick, dumb putz of a judge gave her." He moved a little and a stab of fluorescent light speared Eichord in his hangover.

"Who was it—Hornsbeck?"

"None other." Tuny had just come from testifying in Buckhead Circuit Court. "The Late Judge Horny Hornsbeck, his eminent horseshit, presiding. He waltzes in an hour and ten minutes late of course. Then him and Jonesy and the defense attorney, some schlub bagel beak named Jewstein or Blustein, they go back in the back and decide if she'd go guilty to second degree, Jonesy'd plead it down, and Horny'd let the bitch cop do self-defense. They mumble around awhile. Then they come out and waste my whole fuckin morning in there while the fag sits up there making jokes and jerking himself off under his robes. If they were gonna let the bitch walk," he whined, "why didn't they just get it over in ten minutes? I mean I fucking testified for *NOTHIN*, man."

"What else is new? How come Jonesy went for the reduction?"

"Hey. Like I would fuckin know? Ask him, man. She gets NO goddamn time. Probation and five hundred hours of community service. That'll be flat on her back for Hornsbeck." He shook his huge head. "Another gallon of bullshit." He stuck the magazine in Eichord's face. "I'm goin to the john now and get some fist." He unblocked the doorway.

"Well, leave Miss December taped to the wall." He called after the man.

Somebody had decided the coppers in Buckhead would be more efficient if they had little private cubbyholes instead of just regular desks scattered around the squad bay, which was roughly the size of a small newspaper's city room. The administrative genius had puchased some little rinky-dink room separators made out of sturdy imitation fiberboard or something, and now each man or woman was squeezed into their own little semi-pseudo-quasi-private rectangle of space.

The partition butted up against the front of Eichord's desk, which was also the back partition of Mary Peletier's lavish accommodations, was covered in Scotch-taped notes, memos, and photographs.

ILLINOIS ABDUCTIONS was just one of a litany of horrors he'd been reciting to himself the last couple of days, working on the massive Datafax file already building in an investigation unlike any he'd ever touched. Then there were the photographs. Maybe sixty shots of abducted females taken throughout the country over the last couple of years. Hundreds fit the general M.O., but Eichord had reached out for specifics to minimize the wheel-spinning he'd face tracking down leads that dead-ended, missing persons with open files, runaways, sex offenders, the whole taco. He'd eliminated it to maybe five dozen individuals, and now he removed the photos of four lucky children from his gallery wall. Dark hair had been their shared trait with the investigation before him.

He opened a dossier marked X-RAYS/PRICE HILL SLASHER and began to study the conclusions of a forensic radiologist, a forensic dentist, and a pathologist. Three women dead in Ohio. What an unlikely case to come snaking out for him, coming down to him from the task force hierarchy, into which its darkest tentacle had covertly reached. Tonight, he would nurse his hangover. Tomorrow, he would fly into the heart of this disturbing series of homicides.

The dawn sky looked like wet concrete, the color of a tombstone. A few home fires were burning in wood stoves of Cincinnati's early risers and wispy tendrils mingled with the heat rising from the rooftops. This is MY town, he thought, the power surging through him. Smoke spiraled from chimneys here and there, and it gave the vista a steadfast look of working-class respectability.

He always left early. He liked to do all his paper work before the place got too busy and clear his decks for the day. That's the way he always phrased it—he went in early to clear the decks. He also left early because he had nothing outside of his job. There were no women anymore. His vicious, predatory bitch of a mother and that castrating shrew of a first wife, and that second worthless cunt tramp he'd married, they'd all taken care of that. He felt the hard, long, sleek thing in its leather sheath. That's my hard-on, now, he told himself.

The man pulled into his hunting ground three hours later. Hot to do it but cautious and circumspect. He had the power. It was so easy. If he was careful they would never catch him. He saw one he liked but when he called her over there was something too jarring in the voice and he decided he'd cut her loose, and he faked asking for directions and let her be.

About 9:45 A.M. he spotted one walking along an old residential street that felt about right and he nailed her. Did his thing and had her in the front seat and was moving, running his standard line of shit on her, the radio going just loud enough in the background, everything real cool. Got off on a little side street, nobody looking, leaned her over gently, and started fastening her to the thing.

"Hey!" she said, in a loud, grating voice, "what the hell do you think you're doing?" He didn't like to gag them. He just turned the noise up a little and finished securing her. So fucking easy. Nice and easy. He'd welded this pair of steel U-shaped retainers under the dashboard and you could take a stout, wide canvas strap and run it through there, come back around each wrist, go around again and between the wrists, cinch it up real tight. No worries. Nice 'n' slick.

"HELLLLLLLLP! SOMEBODY HELP ME!"

"Don't, angel buns, you're giving me a splitting head-ache. Be cool." Letting her have a little tap on the skull to get her attention. Not enough to do anything. He wanted her bright-eyed and bushy-tailed when the thing went in the first time.

He wanted her screaming like she had a pair when that big steel hard-on of his penetrated her smug bitch cunt world.

"You really think you're some special piece of poontang, don't you?"

"Go to HELL. Let me *LOOSE,* YOU DIRTY BAS-TARD."

"Just stay down there on the floorboard with the rest of the filth, you scummy twat."

"What are you doing this for?"

"What are you DOING this ferrrrrr?" he mimicked.

"Please. Let me loose."

"Let me loose, let me loose, Mother Goose, Mother Goose," he sang to her. His voice well modulated and pleasant.

She let a few seconds go by and screamed HELP again at the top of her lungs and it broke him up.

"I love it," he told her, laughing.

"You're CRAZY, mister," she told him, very solemnly, and that broke him up even more.

"You slay me," he said, calmly. "You really do." He pulled over again after a bit and secured her legs with some of the same canvas material he'd used to bind her wrists. No way could she maneuver around to kick at him the way he had her trussed up, but this was for when he got to the place where he cut them. He was a large, muscular man, and he knew how to handle himself. Just the same he was real careful until they were trussed up good. From the moment when he took them loose from the dashboard retainers until he had them inside—that was the most vulnerable time. He watched them so they couldn't bite him or head-butt him.

"I'm going to enjoy—" he started to tell this one, but decided to opt for discretion. No point in showing his hole card. Make them think it was hopeless and they'd fight a lot harder.

"PLEASE, mister. Let me go. I won't say anything. You haven't done anything. You haven't touched me yet. You haven't even broken the law. I won't tell anybody I swear. And I prom—"

"Listen. Darling. Hold it. Whoa. Hold on, there, sweet cheeks. Lookee here now, you think I wanna RAPE you or something? Forget it. I mean—you don't look all that GOOD to me, Wanda. Hey." He laughed. "I wouldn't touch you with somebody else's dick. I just want to TALK to you about something. That's all. Ask you a few questions where nobody will interrupt us. And if I like the way you answer, I'll cut you loose, Mother Goose." I'll cut you all right, he thought, smiling.

"I haven't done anything to you," she said, and started crying. He loved it when they started bawling, the fucking cunts.

He came to the spur about twenty minutes out of Glenway. He pulled the vehicle off the road and eased down some gravel that turned to a mud road. He went very slowly, cruising past the building, eyes scanning for signs of humanity. It looked okay. He stopped the car and backed up, pulling up the little slope and backing around the building. He stopped about a yard short of the opening in the back wall.

It was all that was left of an old concrete block house. He liked to back right up to it because it made 'em so much easier to load when he was finished.

He got out in high weeds and looked around a bit before he walked around and unlocked the passenger side. The girl was whimpering in fear.

"Hey, honeybuns, it's cool. Take it easy. We'll go inside and have our talk. You'll tell me what I want to know, and I'll cut you . . . loose. Okay?" He was grinning now. Enjoying the hell out of himself. "You'll be fine as long as a big old snake doesn't slither up and bite you on the snatch," he patted her leg paternally as he turned her head away from him so she couldn't see the blade.

It was honed razor sharp and he held the right wrist in place and slashed the canvas right by the knot, holding the big knife in his left hand. It was more awkward but this was the time he had to be extremely careful with them.

He was steady as a rock. No grab-ass now. Slipping the blade back in its oiled sheath before she could see it. Then it was a simple matter to keep that right hand pinned, while you took hold of the loose end of the canvas and worked her arms back behind her, securing the wrists behind her before he brought her out of the car.

This one was heavy and he took his time getting her erect and upright, keeping her facing away from him all the time. Moving her with the arms, horsing her out, the young woman not giving him any help with her legs bound and he dropped her in the tall weeds and looked around again.

"Whew. Angel, you're gonna have to give up those jelly donuts. Damn." He caught his breath. "Hey. Two ways we can do this. I can drag you in, or you can help. Now stand up and start walking backwards or I'll pull you in by your hair." She let him help her to her feet and started moving in little hobbled steps, then suddenly screamed out a piercing yell,

"*H H H H H E E E E E E E E E E E E E E L L L L L L L L L L L L L L L L L L L P P P P P P P P!* SOMEBODY HELP ME! HELP! POLICE!" He laughed so hard he had to stop again, laughing and leaning on her for a second, one hand on her bound wrist, the other gently on the back of her neck.

"You're a comedian, you know that. You're a scream." He chuckled good-naturedly and they kept moving into the shadows of the blockhouse.

"Needless to say, nobody's around to hear you but little old me. And I ain't impressed so far. I suggest you speak only when spoken to from now on." Without further ceremony he looped a length of something he had in his pocket through her wrists and bound her to a massive, rust-covered iron girder.

He was wearing one of those cheap, transparent plastic raincoats, and she was suddenly aware of the fact he was wearing rubber boots. The young woman began sobbing again and sank to the cold ground.

"Please . . . oh, please . . . I . . ." she started begging him between sobs and he gave her a pair of stinging slaps on the cheek.

"Get hold of yourself you vile, worthless CUNT. You shut that hole and listen to me. I am GOD now, do you read me? If you tell me what I want to know, you go free. It's just that simple. But if you DON'T tell me what I want to know," he produced the knife and held it close to her. She caught her breath and her tear-filled eyes were suddenly as big as half-dollars. "Well . . . I'll have to cut THESE." He slashed across her breasts and, mercifully, she fainted even before she bled. The blade cut through the thin coat like it wasn't there.

"No more for now, muffin buns," he told the girl in a soft voice. "Got to bring you around for the fun and games."

The man went back and unlocked the trunk. He took out the body bag, unzipped it, and tossed it into the weeds beside him. He removed a couple of the water jugs and moved them over beside the girder to which the inert girl was bound. Got a sack out for the boots and various discards such as the rags he would use to clean up, studied his mental checklist for a moment, and took one last look out the back, and around the side of the old ruins.

"I love the boonies," he told her, and went over and poured some water on her face. "Not too much now, don't want to DROWN your ass." And he took the blade and made his next point.

It took him longer to clean up than it did to finish with her. He cleaned some off the girl by simply pouring water on her, and dragging her over by the body bag. By the time he got her zipped into the bag it was a mess and he rinsed it off real thoroughly, first with poured water, then the little tissues he used. When the bag was clean he worked on himself, and then took the plastic raincoat off and put it in the discard bag. He washed off the rubber boots and changed into other shoes, then proceeded to load the bag.

Next he cleaned the knife and put it away, and took a small spade out and began cleaning up the dirt floor of the blockhouse. He did a little more washing with the water jugs, and the rags, gloves, and empty jugs all went into the trunk with the bag. He would wear another disposable plastic coat and gloves when he unloaded her across town. Then the disposables went into the empty body bag, and that went into the fire. Nice 'n' easy. Pays to work neat.

Eichord didn't like any of it. He'd been in Ohio for—shit, what time was it now?—three days. THREE FUCKING DAYS. That was one thing. He decided he'd list everything that was wrong. He took out a black felt-tipped pen and uncapped it and printed:

1. I am in Cincinnati.
2. I do not feel well
3. Everything

He crumpled the paper into a ball and, through force of habit, put it in his case. After catching a woman sorting through his waste basket once he'd started taking his doodles home. His wife had given him an "executive shredder" for a present recently. It was some world.

This one wouldn't go in the shredder, he thought. It was the skinny from WOUND ANALYSIS and he read again the stuff about the findings on the three homicides, then picked up the memo that dealt with the weapon.

V-grind this. Cannel-edge that. Ricasso something. Such-and-such a choil, with a modified Wharncliffe. All broken down by tip, false edge, shoulder, spine—finally you began to understand they were talking about a knife, fer crissakes. Say KNIFE. Will it kill you to say it in English? He had no patience this morning.

"The blade has a clipped point and a wide central fuller or blood groove placement. Penetration ranges from 5 to 6 and ⅞ inches." He was always pleased when they translated from metric system. "Configuration matches that of so-called military fighting knives' such as the copies and modifications of the U.S. Navy Mark 2 or 'frogman' knife, U.S. Marine Corps 'Ka-Bar' knives or—" Or any of ten grillion zillion knives. Thanks a humongous fucking lot por nada. De nada, señor.

The wound and weapon stuff went into the dossier marked INTERVIEWS. Only Eichord understood his shorthand and the way he liked to free-associate. Day 3. Three Victims. He pondered the mystical significance of the numeral. For three seconds.

He was at a borrowed desk, sitting on a borrowed chair, with a borrowed telephone at his disposal. His headache was not borrowed, however, it was very much his own. Eichord had reached that stage of drinking where it was soon going to be fish or cut bait. He was going to have to start drinking earlier in the day or give it up entirely. The mornings were just too rough to hack. The thought made him smile. Clearly, the only option was to begin earlier.

"Doin' okay," the local honcho asked him over his shoulder. Not a question.

"Just fine. Thanks." Eichord's mouth felt cottony.

"Perry Crouch's in. Wanna—?" he left it unfinished vocally, finishing it with a movement of his head.

"Sure," Eichord said, unconvincingly, hauling himself to his feet and following the man down the hall and into a nearby office.

"Perry, Jack Eichord," the man said, introducing them.

"Hi," Eichord said, extending his hand.

"Well, well," the one called Perry said, shaking hands hard, giving Jack an early-morning bone crusher. Saying it in a wise ass tone like he was saying hot shit instead of well, well.

" 's Perry Crouch, Jack," the honcho said unnecessarily. "He's been with the Price Hill Slasher all the way, so he can give you whatever you need. I'm going to let you guys get at it." Eichord smiled politely. "Let me know whatever you need, Jack."

"Thanks," Eichord said to the head of Cincinnati Homicide, who clearly couldn't wait to be shed of him.

"Major Crimes Task Force," the detective said in his smart, sneering voice.

"Yeah," Jack said with a little fake chuckle, trying to deflate the man's antagonism. Perry Crouch was late twenties, early thirties, white bread, tall, athletic, trim, spent a lot of money on hair styling and wardrobe, and he reeked of too much cologne and hostile vibes.

"We'll get to the bottom of this shit now," the man said. Both of them smiling.

"Give me a break," Jack said. Throwing it away. Still smiling. Thinking to himself, don't ask me to have a seat or anything, you goofy asshole.

"Yep. I can go on vacation now. The Task Force is on the jay oh bee. MacTuff is on the job." Arrogant, loopy voice. One of those flakes who thinks in put-ons and put-downs. Eichord had been in the 513 area code for three days and so far he hadn't met anything but extraterrestrial, other-worldly assholes of one kind or another. He was beginning to wonder if Cincinnati was populated by anything or anyone other than these strangely alien rectums.

"Yeah," Jack's smile was starting to ache a bit, "take the rest of the day off. Give yourself a raise."

"Sounds good," the man said in his hale, hearty, hard-on voice. "Particularly the part about the raise. Of course Cincy Homicide doesn't pay in the big bucks you're used to." Eichord laughed his heh-heh-heh laugh.

"Right. Big bucks. That's me."

"Well," Crouch said brightly, "where do ya want to start?"

"Aw, hell," Eichord said, equally brightly, "I dunno. How's about Price Hill?"

"Whatever makes ya happy." The detective slammed a sheaf of papers into an open drawer and stood up, stretching noisily. What was he so pissed about, Eichord wondered vaguely, realizing even as he did so that this was just one of those people who go around with an attitude.

Eichord had one himself this morning. He'd come in three days ago on Piece of Shit Airlines, a horrible and long trip, and he'd let himself get about half schnockered on the plane. A cabbie had ripped him off, which he didn't mind as much as he had the long and unpleasant drive to the hotel, while he'd listened to some Neanderthal recount of woes and complaints, only because Eichord was too tired and too plotzed to tell him to shut his yap. He'd bought a pint at the hotel, another mistake, and he'd gone to sleep whacked, waking up to the switchboard call at 6:30 with the television on and a headache pounding like a jackhammer in tempo with the hot water in the hotel plumbing. Two days of "INTERVIEWS" had yielded absolutely zero.

So far everyone he'd met in this shit town had been a jerk, and the feeling was obviously mutual. He felt hung over, tired, old, and he hated fucking "Cincy."

It took them forever to get out to the vehicle. Perry Crouch's bit was to stop everybody he knew and introduce them to Jack Eichord "the famous G-Man," a phrase that made Eichord think of Melvin Purvis shields, a lost catch phrase from the era when Hoover was still a hero and the Dead End Kids were at the Rialto. He'd known a zillion schmucks like Crouch. Dead-end kids in dead-end jobs.

"Lookee who's here in the Big C," he called out, "the Man himself." Jack had known him for five minutes and he was already starting to be a pain in the ass. Jack smiled at the way his pals back in Buckhead Station would have eaten this guy's lunch. He could see fat Dana Tuny throwing him up against a wall and breathing his burrito breath into the dude's wise-ass mustache. Telling him how it was going to be. "Jack Eichord, the serial murder expert." Saying it nice enough you couldn't call him on it. Letting you know he fancied himself a real ironist.

Eichord just kept satchin and they made their way to the car. Once Crouch got the car moving he was a little better. Getting him out of the building was a step in the right direction. He was the type you could flatter and he'd take the ball and run with it until he hit a wall. Motor mouth. Jack asked him some questions he already knew the answers to and tuned out as the car headed through traffice to Price Hill.

It was a completely different town than Eichord recalled from the old days. Everything seemed to radiate out from the stadium in geocentric circles. Urban Renewal, high-rises, rehabs, a whole new look, circles of commerce and industry pushing the town out farther away from the river.

Used to be you could drive down River Road and you'd think you'd fallen off the edge of North America. It looked like some dirty little river burg in West Germany. Right off the end of the world. Even the people gave you that foreign feeling you would get in some isolated ethnic clusters—one or two places in southern New England, Pennsylvania, off the coastline of the southern states. Eichord remembered a Moravian/Serbo-Croation community in Omaha that was less insular and alien than Cincy-nasty.

But be fair—he thought. Of COURSE you hate it. You've never been handed one quite like this little hot potato. The sun ain't over the yardarm yet. Of course you hate it.

The talking asshole was keeping up a running commentary of Eichord's press coverage. Eichord was seeing a map in his head, trying to sort out the western suburbs. Anderson Township? Delhi? Price Hill. Westwood or Western Hills—something. All older, a different Cincinnati. Predictably, Second was now Pete Rose Way or some damn thing. A whole 'nother smoke.

"—put you on the boob tube. First thing you got a book you're hypin', right? Then they're fightin' over rights to buy the Eichord Story and—" He listened with a fraction of his brain so he could give a little chuckling noise now and then. Letting asshole do his thing, fielding all the usual questions about Dr. Demented and the Lonely Hearts cases. Stuff he'd normally talk about when it was a law enforcement guy doing the asking, but he knew this jerk was just looking for a chain to pull, and Jack had his mind on more important matters.

After a few more minutes he felt a change in the talking anus's speech rhythms and he let his brain kick in.

"—of old residential-type abductions. So see, it doesn't even have anything to do with Price Hill. That's all newspaper bullshit, that Price Hill Slasher crap."

"I understand. Just familiarizing myself with the town." That wasn't what he was doing at all.

"Yeah. Well. There you go," he gestured at a nondescript older home up on a sloping bank. "That's where the Eastons live." Eichord thought they were on Purcell. He looked up at the house, but concentrated now on the words of the investigating officer. "Their kid had been away to school for a semester. No enemies." He made a face, screwing his mouth up into a real pretty snarl as Eichord turned back and looked at him.

"But she was home visiting for Christmas at the time of her abduction?"

"Yeah."

Eichord glanced at a sheaf of papers he was carrying.

"Art Education major. Eighteen years old and very pretty. Uh—you were on the original team at the dump site, right?"

"Yup."

"Says three stab wounds in the torso. Throat cut. No

witnesses. No clues. No trace of sexual assault." The detective said nothing, just sat there looking bored. "Why do you suppose . . . ? Girl like that. Smart, *good*-looking college girl. She's not going to go out for a short walk, visiting her folks, and let herself get picked up."

"You'd think not."

"Unless—"

"Eh. Maybe she knew the person."

"Yeah. Maybe. Or maybe a couple of college boys recognize her, let's say. Take her someplace. Drunk. Try to get her to put out for 'em. She's not having any. They stab her. Then cut her throat to make sure she doesn't talk?"

"Slashed that carotid artery. Zip. She's a memory."

"But no sexual assault on any of 'em so that's out—right?" The cop shrugged. It dawned on Eichord he'd worked an extradition case out of Hong Kong and Kowloon where the locals gave him more cooperation than he was getting now.

"See, that's why you get the big bucks," Crouch said to him in his wise-ass tone, and they pulled out for the location on Gurley. The word triggered an association in Jack's mind and he sat there looking at his mental gallery. The three pictures he'd christened Miss November, Miss January, and Miss December. Eichord's grisly pin-ups. Regina Easton. The pretty one. Then this poor kid on Gurley, Melissa Moore.

He started asking Perry Crouch about the girl from the January kill of thirteen months later. Why it had taken a bizarre stroke of luck to even tie the two together. He listened to the rhythms and cadences and patterns of his responses. Thinking about Melissa.

He saw her vividly taped to his office wall. A family snapshot made by a relative or friend of the family walking in and catching the woman with her eyes cast down, not looking, and stealing a shot of Melissa. She had not been a girl who wanted to pose for pictures.

Eichord visualized the pile of black hair on top and one of those haircuts that looked like a man's on the sides. Extremely overweight, Melissa was twenty-three years old in the dossier, but she could have been any age from seventeen to forty. Asexual, at least in the crime scene shots and the family Polaroids.

"Perry," Eichord said, familiarly, "again—no sexual assault. Sixteen stab wounds and the throat slashed. Turned her into a pincushion this time. Guy was getting off on his action. Hearing that nice solid thwock of the blade going into all the dead meat."

"Tell you what though, getting back to your scenario about the college boys. You may have hit on something. What if they got off on the power trip. They know what's her name, the Easton kid. They pick her up to give her a lift back home. Let's say they're gay. Thrill killers." He was starting to really sell the idea. It was the most animated he'd become. "A year or so later, they got to get another taste. Huh? It might play."

"Anything's possible."

"The gay college boys. They could be into pain and punishment. Satanic shit. You know, mutilation rites."

"Then we got Jane Doe."

"Yeah, right." Crouch started driving and then asked Eichord, "I assume you don't wanna look at the house?"

"No. That's fine. Let's go on over to the place they found the other one."

"No telling where she was from. See—that's another reason why it's bullshit talking about Price Hill killings. She could be from Cleveland for all we know."

"Sure. Two years and a month later he takes another one out." He almost said Miss December. "Miss Doe. Again—in the wintertime. She's maybe late twenties. No raving beauty. A ring could be a wedding ring. Fair skin. Dark hair. A new dump site. Wrists appear to have been tied when she was cut. Probably clothesline, is my guess. Okay, so far?"

"Great. Now tell us something we DON'T know."

"You must be confusing me with that guy in the movies. Inspector Clouseau."

"Come on, man. I got the MacTuff supersleuth here. Tell me something about Jane Doe. We had a wallet photo and everything. No ID. Was she a hooker? Maybe all these broads are part-timers, huh? Maybe fag college boys offered her fifty each to get in the car with them?"

"A hooker dressed like THAT?"

"Sure. You obviously haven't worked vice, man. They ain't all parading around in short shorts. Not in Cincy in the winter. Freeze that little beaver."

"Uh huh." Eichord let his voice harden a bit. "According to what I read, you guys didn't link up the first two kills. Not until the computer put 'em together with the December girl. The lab report got fucked up? Is that what it was?"

"Aw, they lost the goddamn lab work. That's why we never put 'em together—the Easton and Moore homicides. When the Jane Doe turned up, the computers matched the wound to Easton and—" Again Eichord concentrated on the pattern to defuse but still—at least the guy was finally talking business instead of all that bogus crap. Crouch took him to the third dump site, and then they went back to headquarters.

They went into the Homicide unit and the honcho was standing there with some of the other detectives. He called Eichord aside and whispered something to him and Perry Crouch felt his arms being pinned by one man, while one of the detectives reached in and took his weapon. One of them was I.A.D.

"What the fuck—?"

"Sorry, Perry," the boss said, reaching in and getting his ID and shield. The I.A.D. man was giving him a full frisk like he was some fucking hype.

"What in the fucking shit do you sons of bitches think you're doing?"

"You're under arrest, detective," the one from Internal Affairs told him, and began reading him Miranda.

"Hold it. HOLD IT, goddammit. Talk to me."

"We gotcha dead bang, ace," one of the detectives said.

"Is this some scam the hotshot here is running?" He looked at Eichord who stood quietly watching him.

"Eichord didn't have anything to do with nailing you,

Perry," the honcho told him. "It was Mark Troutt. Youngster in Metro. That's who nailed him—right, Jack?"

"Absolutely. The way it looks is he did Regina Easton and it was too easy and he had to have an encore. A year or so later he got the Moore Girl. It made sense it was something like a cop. Had to be somebody who was in authority. Make 'em get in with him. Melissa Moore, for example, the January kill, she'd *never* have left with anybody unless she was abducted. She was scared of her own shadow. Her mother and grandmother swore she would have never left those kids alone like that. You *made* her get in the car. Offed her. Then—maybe another we don't know about—maybe a couple more—but in December two years later you screwed the pooch."

"Jesus, you must be more tanked than I thought." The man laughed.

"Wish I was. It was perfect, you were your own investigation team. You could make it seamless. Why only wintertime kills? Nobody in the streets or the yards. Minimize the chance of a witness. Why did it take a lab tech to put the first and second kills together even though they had a near identical M.O.? The one guy who had the motive and the opportunity conveniently lost the paperwork. Why no sexual assault? All we can go by is your track record, Perry. It's all in your package about your childhood, and the bad marriages. Then, as I said, the December target is where you stepped in it."

"Go fuck yourself. This is bullshit. *BULLSHIT!*"

"When the investigators went to the Easton and Moore neighborhoods, they asked questions trying to find witnesses, but nobody even asked any questions in Price Hill about the third woman. Finally, a young divorcee called the cops. She'd been looking out the window and she'd seen a girl who looked like Jane Doe get into a police car. She hadn't wanted to get involved but the incident had stuck in her mind, and when they showed the photo of the woman in the paper and on TV, she decided she'd better get in touch with the authorities even though "it was none of her business."

"It was just luck she got a straight young copper who used his head. He went to the honcho with it quietly, and from there I.A.D. came in on it. That's how the Task Force came into the picture."

"This isn't even funny. Bunch of fucking jive NONSENSE, man. I don't know who you people think you're kidding—"

"We narrowed it down to three guys with unmarked cars and red balls. You were number three. I kept you occupied while the B & E boys hit your place. Got a—what was it?"

The honcho glanced at a piece of paper, "U.S. Navy Mark 2 sheath knife. Camillus Cutlery. Matches the weapon description, and my bet is the lab boys'll say BINGO!"

Perry Crouch looked daggers at Eichord.

"YOU'RE the one who's gonna have red balls before this is over, you goddamn looney SHIT. I could hardly stand it in the car with MacTuff here. He smelled like a distillery. Jeezus—any moron can buy a *red ball* and stick it on top of their car."

"Yeah, but who says the killer stuck it on *top* of his car?" one of the other detectives said, before he thought. Eichord let himself smile at that one a little.

"Where else is he gonna stick it, numb nuts, up his *ass*?" With that Crouch was hustled off to the lock-up.

There had been only three men who looked good. Where the times and places and dates all, as the jargon currently had it, interfaced. Crouch was looking for it from jump street, the most suspicious behavior of the three possible suspects, and a fucked-up personal history that could have sewn some evil seeds inside a potential killer.

But what you never did was let a perp see how much you were holding, and for three days their eyeball witness, the one who'd seen a cop run his game on Jane Doe in a side street off Anderson Ferry Road, she'd sat in the living room of strangers. Waiting across the street from where the November victim had been abducted; waiting for a look at her cop. Jack's "Interviews."

They thought she'd stand up when they put Perry in a

line-up, so they'd do it and keep that little goody for later. Give it to Crouch's lawyer in discovery.

"Outstanding," the honcho said, shaking Eichord's mitt for what he hoped would be the last time.

"Not really. If the lab doesn't make the blade, this'll fall apart like cheap toilet paper."

And before you can say "occupado" he was back on the vomit comet and heading for Buckhead or a long fall, whichever came first.

A young lady with legs along the lines of Theresa Russell's and a behind like a sack full of watermelons stopped with a tray of liquid refreshments. He was poised over a crossword; he needed a ten-letter word meaning "to peel off in scales" and he whispered it just as she looked at him.

"Desquamate?"

"We're all out of that, sir. Would you care for another Jack Daniel's?" Do bears potty in the woods?

"I guess the sun's over the yardarm," he said into his teeth.

"Here you go," she said. She smiled professionally, thinking boy, is he swacked, and pushed her mobile bar along the aisle to the next seats.

He sipped that liquid gold and let himself fill with the nice glow. The soft lights of the plane. The gentle bite of the Tennessee sippin' whiskey. Mother Theresa's world class thighs. She was really looking good. Definitely gatefold material. He wondered if she had any idea how easy it was now for a young lady to become Miss December.

John Maclay spent a few years as a small-press publisher (J. N. Williamson's first two *Masque* anthologies being high on his list of credits), then set that occupation aside to try the strange and terrifying world of full-time freelance fiction writing. Thus far, he's sold seventy-five stories to such markets as "Twilight Zone" and "Night City" and is presently finishing the first draft of a novel.

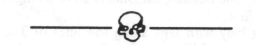

MATTER OF FIRING

John Maclay

He was a vice-president, one of many, of a bank in Manhattan. But since the bank was in New York, it was a giant, and Bill Ames, at fifty-five, with his distinguished gray hair and expensive suits, was in charge of a hundred people. And one of his duties was to hire . . . and fire.

The firings bothered him, of course. But when he left his corner office, went to the commuter train and evenings at his home in Stamford, Ames let his unease drain away. After all, he reasoned, he too was only a cog in a machine that had to run smoothly, and he couldn't be held responsible.

Yet the memory of a few dismissals stayed with him. The woman M.B.A. who'd shown such promise, but whose demanding husband had overwhelmed her. The balding veteran who just hadn't been able to make it to retirement age. And especially, the brilliant young man whose only fault was that he didn't fit in. So in spite of himself and his history of ulcers, Bill Ames kept tabs on these, liking to think he hadn't lost his sensitivity over the years.

His means of doing this was another veteran, an assistant

who would make it to retirement, if nothing else; an easygo-
ing fellow who belonged to all the professional groups. And
one rainy Friday, in the paneled executive dining room, Bill
was casually quizzing him.

"Whatever happened to . . . ?"

"Oh, her. Well, I heard she's at Citibank now, and doing
fine . . . without that husband."

"Glad to hear it. And . . . ?"

"I still play tennis with him. Used the settlement to buy a
fishing boat, and does okay on charters."

"Maybe you and I should be so lucky. And . . . ?"

But when he mentioned the name of the brilliant young
man, Ames saw his companion's expression change . . . and
received an answer his long training told him was, at the
least, evasive.

"Oh. Him. Well, I don't mean to trouble you . . . not
your fault at all . . . but you may have heard about the
rough time he had, with the bottle."

"No, I hadn't . . . I'm sorry." And though he didn't want
the story on his conscience, didn't really think it should be,
Bill's instinct for the bottom line made him pursue. "And
now . . . ?"

"Well . . . he did blame you. And people who mentioned
him later, said he was out of the game . . . 'only a ghost of
his former self.' "

Bill Ames shook his head; shook off what he'd heard. But
that night, on his walk to the train home, was the first time
he saw the shadow.

It was still raining, and being January, was cold and dark
at seven o'clock. Though the lower-echelon people had
thinned out, the Manhattan sidewalks were still crowded
with late-working executives like himself, topcoat collars
turned up and umbrellas raised. So it was only a flash that
Bill saw, between figures, in an alley between buildings, so
quick that it could have been imaginary.

But it wasn't, he knew. A shadowy form, again so fleeting
that it could have been wind-blown rain, or a reflection on a
wet stone wall. Dressed, he thought, in a tattered business

suit. One thin arm extended, menacing . . . holding something blunt, and metallic.

Wasn't imaginary, he knew. Because, despite the dozens of people on the sidewalk, it was facing, gesturing toward . . . him. And because, as he pressed on through the icy rain, looking over his shoulder in a way that must have seemed suspicious to the others . . . it emerged from the alley, and followed. Darting, momentarily appearing then vanishing, among the blank-faced crowd behind.

When he reached the apparent safety of the train, Bill Ames's heart was pounding. Probably one of the dopers, the crazies, who are part of New York today, he reasoned, tried to tell himself. Only yesterday, his secretary had told him about an old, well-dressed man, right out front, being clubbed to the ground and robbed by two of them. At least, he thanked God when he looked around the brightly lit coach, the figure was gone.

But what about the business suit? he wondered as he rode home to Stamford. A crazy would have been dressed in jacket and jeans. And why did it single out . . . me?

On Saturday the rain was gone, and Bill spent the weekend playing golf, and socializing with his wife and some friends. He successfully put the menacing figure out of his mind . . . until Sunday night, when, catching up on some work, he sat in the living room, briefcase on his knees.

It was then that he connected the shadowy form with the brilliant young man he'd fired.

And it was then, too, that some of his longstanding assumptions broke down . . . when he felt found out, naked; no longer a cog in a blank-faced machine, but a person, for whose actions he'd been held responsible by at least one man.

And when he went to bed, seeking comfort in sleep, he had a dream. An old, heart-racing nightmare, from childhood: about heavy feet, pounding inexorably forward from some far corner of the world . . . their eventual destination, himself.

But on Monday morning, Bill Ames was back in his

corner office as usual, doing his best to go on with his job. His only concession to his fear, his new guilt, was to be unusually nice to his people. That, and the fact he was supposed to fire someone today; he put it off. He knew he couldn't mention what he'd seen to anyone at the office, even his veteran assistant, or it would be thought he'd been working too hard. So at seven o'clock, he walked to the train alone.

The figure was on the sidewalk again . . . and following.

It wasn't raining tonight, so the form appeared more clearly defined, though still fleetingly as it darted in and out of alleys, through the thick crowd. For a moment, Bill wondered if only he could see it, if he had been under too much strain . . . but that didn't matter anyway, because there or not, it moved so swiftly that one had to be looking for it.

Looking for it, Ames thought: could he, in fact, out of a buried guilt, have somehow conjured up or attracted the menacing figure, which he was certain by now was that of the brilliant young man whose career he'd ended?

But that didn't matter either. Because, in his last clear glimpse before he entered the safety of the train, he determined that the blunt shape in the young man's hand was . . . a gun.

Monday night held no nightmares . . . but, though he did tell his wife the whole story and was reassured, it was sleepless.

And on Tuesday, when the seven o'clock walk to the train he'd looked forward to out of his fatigue, but dreaded because of his experiences, came around . . . the figure was there again.

So on Wednesday morning, his hand having hesitated above the phone for half an hour, Bill did something he thought was sensible: he called the police.

"Uh . . . I want to report being followed . . . stalked. By someone I know . . . knew."

After several switchings around, a gruff, older voice came on, and he gave the details.

"Well, Mr. Ames," came the eventual reply, "we can do two things. One, check if the guy has a criminal record. And two, find out where he lives now, so if you want to, you can come down and file a complaint." A pause. "Let me take your number, and call you back."

Bill drummed his fingers on his desk, unable to do any work. Then the return call came, the phone's ring making him jump surprisingly; he hadn't realized how tense this whole thing had made him.

"Uh, Mr. Ames?"

"Yes?"

"I checked in the computer, and there's no record of your young man."

"Well, I suppose he wouldn't have a criminal record . . . yet, but . . ."

"No, you don't understand. We tried all the current government files. And, uh, there's no record at all."

The rest of the short January day, Ames just sat in his office, door closed, even skipping lunch, going over his problem in his mind. And he found that it was a process in which, over the years, he'd become unaccustomed. Just as he'd never really felt guilty about his action of hiring and firing, so all of his decisions had been within a framework, a routine. But now all of that was crumbling; there were no tidy answers, for example, even in government records. For the first time in his life he was on the defensive . . . even physically, from this shadowy figure on the street.

And as it got dark outside his windows, and seven o'clock came, he felt an absolute, gut-wrenching terror. Make it . . . him . . . go away, he thought, appealing to some unseen comforter. But there was no help. So, near eight, he dragged his exhausted older body out of the building . . . and hailed a cab.

"Only a few blocks?" the forthright New York driver asked.

"Sore leg," Bill lied, wondering what in the world had happened to him.

"Yeah. Yeah."

In the safety of the train again, he got his pounding heart under control, breathed easier. Relaxed into the seat, even scanned the *Wall Street Journal.* Looked around . . .

And there was the shadow. Barely visible, between the other standees, at the back of the coach.

During the rest of the hour-long trip, which seemed like a whole new, unfamiliar lifetime, Bill sat frozen, not knowing what to do . . . except, possibly, pray for the peace of death. It wasn't only the threatening figure of the young man, he knew now, that was haunting him; it was also something deep inside. So when he reached his stop, it was even little comfort that, when he ventured a fearful look around, the shadow was gone.

And that night, when he finally got to sleep, he had the nightmare, the vision of the heavy, advancing feet, again. Only this time, they were much closer . . . practically on top of his tightened chest.

Thursday dawned sunny again. But to Bill Ames, as he dressed mechanically, exchanged halting talk with his worried wife, it seemed as rainy and dark as the previous Friday.

However, there was a difference. Because sometime in the middle of the night, while he lay clutching the sheets, a remnant of his business training had come back to him. That of needing to face problems squarely; not wanting to wait, but to act. And this was responsible for what, as he rode into the city, and now, as he sat again in his corner office, he carried in his pocket. Something he'd slipped out of the dresser drawer, without his wife noticing. That had been kept there for years, in case of burglars.

A gun of his own.

Ames spent a second day with his door closed, not working. But this time, he wasn't struggling to think; he was simply, coldly, waiting. Yet not uncomfortably . . . because his decision had been made.

And when seven o'clock came, he walked purposefully out into the dark street. Blended into the topcoated crowd, only looking to the side as he passed the deeper darkness of the openings of alleys. Until, in one of them and as he knew he would, he saw the lurking figure that had now become his life.

He dashed in, and confronted it. It didn't retreat. It just stood there, a yard away from him, in a soiled and tattered suit that had once been expensive and new. A guant, haunted look on its unshaven face. And its eyes . . . Bill shivered to his bones at the eyes . . . bloodshot and piercing, meeting his own with an intensity . . . a damned and damning, accusing intensity . . . he would never have believed.

And then, its foul, resinous breath tangible in his face, the shadow spoke.

"You said I didn't fit into your world," it wheezed. " 'Too brilliant,' you said . . . when you fired me. Or," it turned querulous, "maybe too . . . deep?"

"I'm sorry . . ." Bill Ames replied mechanically. But he knew it wasn't enough.

"Well, now," the figure of the once-young man pursued, its hand raising blunt metal, "I think we're about to find out . . . how you fit into mine!"

In spite of his fear, his still-present disbelief, Bill grabbed for what was in his own pocket, and fired first . . . again. Six shots, each echoing in the stony alley, and each dead on target.

But the form opposite him didn't fall. It only smiled . . . and leveled its gun at his heart.

It was then, as a seventh, real-enough shot sounded, and he fell backward into another kind of place, that Bill remembered the policeman's gruff voice on the phone: "No record at all." And what his veteran assistant had reported at lunch, of the young man, the week before.

"Only a ghost of his former self," he'd said.

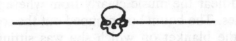

THE SACRED FIRE

Charles de Lint

No one lives forever,
and dead men rise up never,
and even the longest river
winds somewhere safe to sea.
>—from British forklore;
>collected by
>Stephen Gallagher

There were ten thousand maniacs on the radio—the band, not a bunch of lunatics; playing their latest single, Natalie Merchant's distinctive voice rising from the music like a soothing balm.

Trouble me . . .

Sharing your problems . . . sometimes talking a thing through was enough to ease the burden. You didn't need to be a shrink to know it could work. You just had to find someone to listen to you.

Nicky Straw had tried talking. He'd try anything if it

would work, but nothing did. There was only one way to deal with his problems and it took him a long time to accept that. But it was hard, because the job was never done. Every time he put one of them down, another of the freaks would come buzzing in his face like a fly on a corpse.

He was getting tired of fixing things. Tired of running. Tired of being on his own.

Trouble me . . .

He could hear the music clearly from where he crouched in the bushes. The boom box pumped out the song from one corner of the blanket on which she was sitting, reading a paperback edition of Christy Riddell's *How to Make the Wind Blow*. She even looked a little like Natalie Merchant. Same dark eyes, same dark hair; same slight build. Better taste in clothes, though. None of those thrift shop dresses and the like that made Merchant look like she was old before her time; just a nice white Butler U. T-shirt and a pair of bright yellow jogging shorts. White Reeboks with laces to match the shorts; a red headband.

The light was leaking from the sky. Be too dark to read soon. Maybe she'd get up and go.

Nicky sat back on his haunches. He shifted his weight from one leg to the other.

Maybe nothing would happen, but he didn't see things working out that way. Not with how his luck was running.

All bad.

Trouble me . . .

I did, he thought. I tried. But it didn't work out, did it?

So now he was back to fixing things the only way he knew how.

Her name was Luann. Luann Somerson.

She'd picked him up in the Tombs—about as far from the green harbor of Fitzhenry Park as you could get in Newford. It was the lost part of the city—a wilderness of urban decay stolen back from the neon and glitter. Block on block of decaying tenements and rundown buildings. The kind of place to which the homeless gravitated, looking for squats;

where the kids hung out to sneak beers and junkies made
their deals, hands twitching as they exchanged rumpled bills
for little packets of short-lived empyrean; where winos slept
in doorways that reeked of puke and urine and the cops
only went if they were on the take and meeting the money
man.

It was also the kind of place where the freaks hid out,
waiting for Lady Night to start her prowl. Waiting for dark.
The freaks liked her shadows and he did too, because he
could hide in them as well as they could. Maybe better. He
was still alive, wasn't he?

He was looking for the freaks to show when Luann approached him, sitting with his back against the wall, right on
the edge of the Tombs, watching the rush hour slow to a
trickle on Gracie Street. He had his legs splayed out on the
sidewalk in front of him, playing the drunk, the bum. Three-
days stubble, hair getting ragged, scruffy clothes, two dimes
in his pocket—it wasn't hard to look the part. Commuters
stepped over him or went around him, but nobody gave him
a second glance. Their gazes just touched him, then slid on
by. Until she showed up.

She stopped, then crouched down so that she wasn't standing over him. She looked too healthy and clean to be hanging around this part of town.

"You look like you could use a meal," she said.

"I suppose you're buying?"

She nodded.

Nicky just shook his head. "What? You like to live
dangerously or something, lady? I could be anybody."

She nodded again, a half smile playing on her lips.

"Sure," she said. "Anybody at all. Except you're Nicky
Straw. We used to take English 201 together, remember?"

He'd recognized her as well, just hoped she hadn't. The
guy she remembered didn't exist anymore.

"I know about being down on your luck," she added
when he didn't respond. "Believe me, I've been there."

You haven't been anywhere, he thought. You don't want
to know about the places I've been.

"You're Luann Somerson," he said finally.

Again the smile. "Let me buy you a meal, Nicky."

He'd wanted to avoid this kind of a thing, but he supposed he'd known all along that he couldn't. This was what happened when the hunt took you into your hometown. You didn't disappear into the background like all the other bums. Someone was always there to remember.

Hey, Nicky. How's it going? How's the wife and that kid of yours?

Like they cared. Maybe he should just tell the truth for a change. You know those things we used to think were hiding in the closet when we were too young to know any better? Well, surprise. One night one of those monsters came out of the closet and chewed off their faces . . .

"C'mon," Luann was saying.

She stood up, waiting for him. He gave it a heartbeat, then another. When he saw she wasn't going without him, he finally got to his feet.

"You do this a lot?" he asked.

She shook her head. "First time," she said.

All it took was one time . . .

"I'm like everyone else," she said. "I pretend there's no one there, lying half-starved in the gutter, you know? But when I recognized you, I couldn't just walk by."

You should have, he thought.

His silence was making her nervous and she began to chatter as they headed slowly down Yoors Street.

"Why don't we just go back to my place?" she said. "It'll give you a chance to clean up. Chad—that's my ex—left some clothes behind that might fit you . . ."

Her voice trailed off. She was embarrassed now, finally realizing how he must feel, having her see him like this.

"Uh . . ."

"That'd be great," he said, relenting.

He got that smile of hers as a reward. A man could get lost in its warmth, he thought. It'd feed a freak for a month.

"So this guy," he said. "Chad. He been gone long?"

The smile faltered.

"Three and a half weeks now," she said.

That explained a lot. Nothing made you forget your own troubles so much as running into someone who had them worse.

"Not too bright a guy, I guess," he said.

"That's . . . Thank you, Nicky. I guess I need to hear that kind of thing."

"Hey, I'm a bum. We've got nothing better to do than to think up nice things to say."

"You were never a bum, Nicky."

"Yeah. Well, things change."

She took the hint. As they walked on, she talked about the book she'd started reading last night instead.

It took them fifteen minutes or so to reach her apartment on McKennit, right in the heart of Lower Crowsea. It was a walk-up with its own stairwell—a narrow, winding affair that started on the pavement by the entrance of a small Lebanese groceteria and then deposited you on a balcony overlooking the street.

Inside, the apartment had the look of a recent split-up. There was an amplifier on a wooden orange crate by the front window, but no turntable or speakers. The bookcase to the right of the window had gaps where apparently random volumes had been removed. A pair of rattan chairs with bright slipcovers stood in the middle of the room, but there were no end tables to go with them, nor a coffee table. She was making do with another orange crate, this one cluttered with magazines, a couple of plates stacked on top each other, and what looked like every coffee mug she owned squeezed into the remaining space. A small portable black-and-white Zenith TV stood at the base of the book-case, alongside a portable cassette deck. There were a couple of rectangles on the wall where paintings had obviously been removed. A couple of weeks' worth of newspapers were in a pile on the floor by one of the chairs.

She started to apologize for the mess, then smiled and shrugged.

Nicky had to smile with her. Like he was going to complain about the place, looking like he did.

She showed him to the bathroom. By the time he came out again, showered and shaved, dressed in a pair of Chad's corduroys and a white linen shirt, both of which were at least a size too big, she had a salad on the tiny table in the kitchen, wineglasses out, the bottle waiting for him to open it, breaded pork chops and potatoes on the stove, still cooking.

Nicky's stomach grumbled at the rich smell that filled the air.

She talked a little about her failed marriage over dinner—sounding sad rather than bitter—but more about old times at the university. As she spoke, Nicky realized that the only thing they had shared back then had been that English class; still he let her ramble on about campus events he only half-remembered and people who'd meant nothing to him then and did even less now.

Because at least they hadn't been freaks.

He corrected himself. He hadn't been able to *recognize* the freaks among them back then.

"God, listen to me," Luann said suddenly.

They were finishing their meal and sitting in her living room having coffee. He'd been wrong; there were still two clean mugs in her cupboard.

"I am," he said.

She gave him that smile of hers again—this time it had a wistfulness about it.

"I know you are," she said. "It's just that all I've been talking about is myself. What about you, Nicky? What happened to you?"

"I . . ."

Where did he start? Which lie did he give her?

That was the one good thing about street people. They didn't ask questions. Whatever put you there, that was your business. But citizens always wanted whys and hows and wherefores.

As he hesitated, she seemed to realize her faux pas.

"I'm sorry," she said. "If you don't want to talk about it . . ."

"It's not that," Nicky told her. "It's just . . ."

"Hard to open up?"

Try impossible. But oddly enough, Nicky found himself wanting to talk to her about it. To explain. To ease the burden. Even to warn her, because she was just the kind of person the freaks went for.

The fire inside her shimmered off her skin like a high-voltage aura, sending shadows skittering. It was a bright shatter of light and a deep golden glow like honey, all at the same time. It sparked in her eyes, blazed when she smiled. Sooner or later it was going to draw a nest of the freaks to her, just as surely as a junkie could sniff out a fix.

"There's these . . . things," he said slowly. "They look enough like you or me to walk among us—especially at night—but they're . . . they're not human."

She got a puzzled look on her face which didn't surprise him in the least.

"They're freaks," he said. "I don't know what they are, or where they came from, but they're not natural. They feed on us, on our hopes and our dreams, on our vitality. They're like . . . I guess the best analogy would be that they're like vampires. Once they're on to you, you can't shake them. They'll keep after you until they've bled you dry."

Her puzzlement was turning to a mild alarm, but now that he'd started, Nicky was determined to tell it all through, right to the end.

"What," she began.

"What I do," he said, interrupting her, "is hunt them down."

The song of 10,000 Maniacs ended and the boom box's speakers offered up another to the fading day. Nicky couldn't name the band this time, but he was familiar with the song's punchy rhythm. The lead singer was talking about burning beds . . .

Beside the machine, Luann put down her book and stretched.

Do it, Nicky thought. Get out of here. Now. While you still can.

Instead, she lay down on the blanket, hands behind her head, and looked up into the darkening sky, listening to the music. Maybe she was looking for the first star of the night. Something to wish upon.

The fire burned in her brighter than any star. Flaring and ebbing to the pulse of her thoughts.

Calling to the freaks.

Nicky's fingers clenched into fists. He made himself look away. But even closing his eyes, he couldn't ignore the fire. Its heat sparked the distance between them as though he lay beside her on the blanket, skin pressed to skin. His pulse drummed, twinning her heartbeat.

This was how the freaks felt. This was what they wanted, what they hungered for, what they fed on. This was what he denied them.

The spark of life.

The sacred fire.

He couldn't look away any longer. He had to see her one more time, her fire burning, burning . . .

He opened his eyes to find that the twilight had finally found Fitzhenry Park. And Luann—she was blazing like a bonfire in its dusky shadows.

"What do you mean, you hunt them down?" she asked.

"I kill them," Nicky told her.

"But—"

"Understand, they're not human. They just *look* like us, but their faces don't fit quite right and they wear our kind of a body like they've put on an unfamiliar suit of loose clothing."

He touched her borrowed shirt as he spoke. She just stared at him—all trace of that earlier smile gone. Fear lived in her eyes now.

That's it, he told himself. You've done enough. Get out of here.

But once started, he didn't seem to be able to stop. All the lonely years of the endless hunt came spilling out of him.

"They're out there in the night," he said. "That's when they can get away with moving among us. When their shambling walk makes you think of drunks or some feeble old homeless baglady—not of monsters. They're freaks and they live on the fire that makes us human."

"The . . . the fire . . . ?"

He touched his chest.

"The one in here," he said. "They're drawn to the ones whose fires burn the brightest," he added. "Like yours does."

She edged her chair back from the table, ready to bolt. Then he saw her realize that there was no place to bolt to. The knowledge sat there in her eyes, fanning the fear into an ever-more debilitating panic. Where was she going to go that he couldn't get to her first?

"I know what you're thinking," he said. "If someone had come to me with this story before I . . . found out about them—"

("Momma! Daddy!" he could hear his daughter crying. "The monsters are coming for me!"

Soothing her. Showing her that the closet was empty. But never thinking about the window and the fire escape outside it. Never thinking for a minute that the freaks would come in through the window and take them both when he was at work.

But that was before he'd known about the freaks, wasn't it?)

He looked down at the table and cleared his throat. There was pain in his eyes when his gaze lifted to meet hers again—pain as intense as her fear.

"If someone had told me," he went on, "I'd have recommended him for the Zeb, too—just lock him up in a padded cell and throw away the key. But I don't think that way now. Because I can see them. I can recognize them. All it takes is one time and you'll never disbelieve again.

"And you'll never forget."

"You . . . you just kill these people . . . ?" she asked.

Her voice was tiny—no more than a whisper. Her mind was tape-looped around the one fact. She wasn't hearing anything else.

"I told you—they're not people," he began, then shook his head.

What was the point? What had he thought was going to happen? She'd go, yeah, right, and jump in to help him? Here, honey, let me hold the stake. Would you like another garlic clove in your lunch?

But they weren't vampires. He didn't know what they were, just that they were dangerous.

Freaks.

"They know about me," he said. "They've been hunting me for as long as I've been hunting them, but I move too fast for them. One day, though, I'll make a mistake and then they'll have me. It's that, or the cops'll pick me up and I wouldn't last the night in a cell. The freaks'd be on me so fast . . ."

He let his voice trail off. Her lower lip was trembling. Her eyes looked like those of some small panicked creature, caught in a trap, the hunter almost upon her.

"Maybe I should go," he said.

He rose from the table, pretending he didn't see the astonished relief in her eyes. He paused at the door that would let him out onto the balcony.

"I didn't mean to scare you," he said.

"I . . . you . . ."

He shook his head. "I should never have come."

"I . . ."

She still couldn't string two words together. Still didn't believe that she was getting out of this alive. He felt bad for unsettling her the way he had, but maybe it was for the best. Maybe she wouldn't bring any more strays home the way she had him. Maybe the freaks'd never get to her.

"Just think about this," he said, before he left. "What if I'm right?"

Then he stepped outside and closed the door behind him.

He could move fast when he had to—it was what had kept him alive through all these years. By the time she reached her living room window, he was down the stairs and across the street, looking back at her from the darkened mouth of an alleyway nestled between a yuppie restaurant and a bookstore, both of which were closed. He could see her, studying the street, looking for him.

But she couldn't see him.

And that was the way he'd keep it.

He came out of the bushes, the mask of his face shifting and unsettled in the poor light. Luann was sitting up, fiddling with the dial on her boom box, flipping through the channels. She didn't hear him until he was almost upon her. When she turned, her face drained of color. She sprawled backwards in her attempt to escape and then could only lie there and stare, mouth working, but no sound coming out. He lunged for her—

But then Nicky was there. The hunting knife that he carried in a sheath under his shirt was in his hand, cutting edge up. He grabbed the freak by the back of his collar and hauled him around. Before the freak could make a move, Nicky rammed the knife home in the freak's stomach and ripped it up. Blood sprayed, showering them both.

He could hear Luann screaming. He could feel the freak jerking in his grip as he died. He could taste the freak's blood on his lips. But his mind was years and miles away, falling back and back to a small apartment where his wife and daughter had fallen prey to the monsters his daughter told him were living in the closet . . .

The freak slipped from his grip and sprawled on the grass. The knife fell from Nicky's hand. He looked at Luann, finally focusing on her. She was on her knees, staring at him and the freak like they were both aliens.

"He . . . his face . . . he . . ."

She could barely speak.

"I can't do it anymore," he told her.

He was empty inside. Couldn't feel a thing. It was as

though all those years of hunting down the freaks had finally extinguished his own fire.

In the distance he could hear a siren. Someone must have seen what went down. Had to have been a citizen, because street people minded their own business, didn't matter what they saw.

"It ends here," he said.

He sat down beside the freak's corpse to wait for the police to arrive.

"For me, it ends here."

Late the following day, Luann was still in shock.

She'd finally escaped the endless barrage of questions from both the police and the press, only to find that being alone brought no relief. She kept seeing the face of the man who had attacked her. Had it really seemed to *shift* about like an ill-fitting mask, or had that just been something she'd seen as a result of the poor light and what Nicky had told her?

Their faces don't fit quite right . . .

She couldn't get it out of her mind. The face. The blood. The police dragging Nicky away. And all those things he'd told her last night.

They're freaks . . .

Crazy things.

They live on the fire that makes us human.

They seemed to well up out of some great pain he was carrying around inside him.

They're not human . . . they just look *like us . . .*

A thump on her balcony had her jumping nervously out of her chair until she realized that it was just the paperboy tossing up today's newspaper. She didn't want to look at what the *Daily Journal* had to say, but couldn't seem to stop herself from going out to get it. She took the paper back inside and spread it out on her lap.

Naturally enough, the story had made the front page. There was a picture, looking washed out and stunned. A shot of the corpse being taken away in a body bag. A head and shoulders shot of Nicky . . .

She stopped, her pulse doubling its tempo as the headline under Nicky's picture sank in.

"KILLER FOUND DEAD IN CELL—POLICE BAFFLED."

"No," she said.

They know about me.

She pushed the paper away from her until it fell to the floor. But Nicky's picture continued to look up at her from where the paper lay.

They've been hunting me.

None of what he'd told her could be true. It had just been the pitiful ravings of a very disturbed man.

I wouldn't last the night in a cell. The freaks'd be on me so fast . . .

But she'd known him once—a long time ago—and he'd been as normal as anybody then. Still, people changed . . .

She picked up the paper and quickly scanned the story, looking for a reasonable explanation to put to rest the irrational fears that were reawakening her panic. But the police knew nothing. Nobody knew a thing.

"I suppose that at this point, only Nicky Straw knows what really happened," the police spokesman was quoted as saying.

Nicky and you, a small worried voice said in the back of Luann's mind.

She shook her head, unwilling to accept it.

They're drawn to the ones whose fires burn the brightest.

She looked to her window. Beyond its smudged panes, the night was gathering. Soon it would be dark. Soon it would be night. Light showed a long way in the dark; a bright light would show farther.

The ones whose fires burn the brightest . . . like yours does.

"It . . . it wasn't true," she said, her voice ringing hollowly in the room. "None of it. Tell me it wasn't true, Nicky."

But Nicky was dead.

She let the paper fall again and rose to her feet, drifting across the room to the window like a ghost. She just didn't seem to feel connected to anything anymore.

It seemed oddly quiet on the street below. Less traffic than usual—both vehicular and pedestrian. There was a figure standing in front of the bookstore across the street, back to the window display, leaning against the glass. He seemed to be looking up at her window, but it was hard to tell because the brim of his hat cast a shadow on his face.

Once they're on to you, you can't shake them.

That man in the park. His face. Shifting. The skin seeming too loose.

They'll keep after you until they bleed you dry.

It wasn't real.

She turned from the window and shivered, hugging her arms around herself as she remembered what Nicky had said when he'd left the apartment last night.

What if I'm right?

She couldn't accept that. She looked back across the street, but the figure was gone. She listened for a footstep on the narrow, winding stairwell that led up to her balcony. Waited for the movement of a shadow across the window.

Edward D. Hoch is the pro's pro, the only living person in America to make his living from short fiction. He works in a variety of styles, to a variety of ends, and in a variety of forms. Here, he gives us a look at the curious life of Simon Ark, one of his most fascinating and engaging protagonists, all done up with great economy and style.

THE STALKER OF SOULS

Edward D. Hoch

There's an old horror story that I read once, by an author I've forgotten, about a man who kept hearing footsteps behind him. Whenever he turned to look, there was no one in sight. I thought of that story while I was talking on the telephone to Arno Blackmoor in Stockholm. I'd met Blackmoor the previous October at the Frankfurt Book Fair and we'd became fast friends, the way people sometimes do when thrown together far from home at a convention or trade show.

Blackmoor was thirty-eight, a native of Stockholm, and senior editor at a small publishing house that specialized in "new age" books, a term that has come to mean anything from reincarnation and the occult to flying saucers and pyramidology. We'd spent a few evenings together in Frankfurt over drinks, discussing the publishing problems of New York and Stockholm, and he'd phoned me once at Christmastime to impart season's greeting and casually inquire as to my opinion of a certain Manhattan literary agent.

Now, in February, he was on the phone again. When we'd disposed of the small talk he came to the point. "In one of our conversations at the Book Fair you mentioned a close friend, a man named Simon Ark. You pictured him as something of an exorcist."

I had to laugh at his choice of words. "Oh, Simon may be a seeker after the devil, but I'd hardly call him an exorcist."

"Nevertheless, I may be in need of his services. I'm having some very peculiar experiences."

It was not the sort of conversation I usually held with a business acquaintance nearly half a world away, but his voice was clear and the concern was evident. "What's the trouble?" I asked.

"I live in the Old Town section of the city, as I've told you. My wife and I have a quite modern home behind one of the medieval housefronts at Stortorget. I work downtown, near the Royal Opera, and it's only a brief walk across the bridge to Old Town. These nights, of course, darkness comes so early that it's night when I arrive home. Old Town can be an eerie place at night."

He paused, and I could only urge him to continue. I'd become caught up in those words coming to me from so far away. "Go on. What happened?"

"For the past three nights someone has followed me on the way home. I hear these sounds behind me, like hoofbeats on the cobblestones, but when I look there is no one in sight."

"I'll mention it to my friend," I promised, "but I don't really think he can be of much help. Perhaps you're hearing a dog or some other animal."

"Not an animal, no." His voice changed, as if someone had entered the office. "It's been good talking to you," he told me. "My thanks for the information. If you can handle this matter for me it would be greatly appreciated."

"I'll speak to my friend," I promised him.

At that time I had not seen Simon Ark in nearly a year, but we'd spoken a few times on the telephone and I knew he was in the city, pursuing some research of his own involving the unicorn tapestries. I had every intention of calling him about my Swedish friend, but as it happened my good intentions came to naught. Arno Blackmoor was dead within twenty-four hours.

It was a cablegram from his wife that brought me the sad news. *Arno died suddenly Thursday,* she informed me. *Memorial service on Tuesday.* The terse message seemed to take for granted the possibility that I would attend, though I had no real excuse to make the trip. The man had been a casual friend of a few nights and some subsequent telephone calls, a good deal younger than me and living in a different world.

"You're not thinking of going, are you?" my wife Shelly asked when I told her of the message that evening.

"I don't know. I think I should call Simon Ark."

Shelly sighed and went into the kitchen, and she may have feared then that I'd be making the journey.

When I reached Simon on the phone later that evening, he seemed pleased to hear my voice. "I hope I'm not interrupting your research."

"No, no, my friend. I was merely writing a brief paper on the age-old controversy about unicorns' hoofs—whether they are solid or cloven. The descriptions of early writers were split about evenly, you know. I visited the Metropolitan this afternoon to view *The Unicorn in Captivity,* which definitely shows the hoofs to be cloven."

"Like the devil's," I suggested, unable to resist a little dig at Simon Ark's main area of interest.

"Well, yes," he admitted. "But the unicorn has always been a symbol of good."

"Simon, I'm calling because a friend of mine in Stockholm has died. He called me earlier in the week and wanted me to get in touch with you. I didn't do it soon enough." I told him Blackmoor's story.

"His wife didn't tell you how he died?"

"No."

"I believe I saw a small item in the London *Times.* The New York papers didn't carry it. Ah, here it is, in this morning's edition. A shop near the university receives it by air every afternoon. *Swedish Editor Slain.*"

The fact of his murder didn't surprise me. "Does it give any details?"

"Only that he was killed on the way home from his office, shortly after six P.M. yesterday. That would have been shortly after noon New York time. The police suspect robbery was the motive."

"Is there any indication what sort of weapon was used?"

"No. It's a brief article. The second paragraph tells of his publishing career. There's to be a memorial service on Tuesday. Do you plan to attend?"

"It's a long journey all the way to Stockholm, and he wasn't that close a friend," I said, repeating the arguments I'd made to myself earlier.

"I would be willing to accompany you, my friend. The man thought I could help him. Perhaps I still can."

"But he's dead, Simon!"

"Nevertheless—"

I think Shelly had known I'd be going as soon as she heard Simon Ark was involved. In my younger days, when I saw more of him, he was often taking me off to some exotic locale, much to her dismay. This time I tried to reassure her. "We'll only be gone a few days. I'll bring you back some Swedish crystal."

"You'd better!"

The flight from New York to Stockholm was long and uneventful. When I wasn't dozing I listened to Simon's account of his activities during the past year. Much of it could be viewed as pseudoscientific hogwash, but occasionally he'd spark my interest with some bit of arcane knowledge. He was just launching into a discussion of Sanskrit grammar when the plane came in for a perfect landing at Arlanda Airport, some twenty-three miles north of the city. It was mid-morning on a sunny February weekend, though the air was brisk and the temperature near freezing. Here and there we could see patches of snow on the ground.

I had never met Greta Blackmoor, though I'd sent her a

cable advising her of our plans. We'd taken a large room at the Grand Hotel, overlooking the water and only a few steps from the bridge to the Old Town section, where the Blackmoors lived. I telephoned Greta to tell her we'd arrived, and she immediately invited us to her home that afternoon. Some of Arno's old friends would be stopping by later, she explained, and it would be an opportunity to meet them before the memorial service on Tuesday. I accepted, but told her we'd have Sunday dinner first at our hotel.

While we dined Simon was regretting his poor knowledge of the Swedish language. "You won't need it today," I assured him. "Mrs. Blackmoor speaks perfect English and I'm sure Blackmoor's friends do too. Swedish schoolchildren learn English from the age of nine, and have done so since shortly after World War II. Almost everyone under the age of fifty speaks it well. When I spent that time with Blackmoor at the Book Fair he told me Swedish bookstores all have an English-language section. They import a great many books from Britain and some from America."

We found the Blackmoor home with little difficulty, after only one false turn among the narrow medieval streets of *Gamla Stan,* or Old Town. It was a three-story building overlooking a small square where round wooden tubs obviously held flowers in the warm weather. Greta Blackmoor opened the big wooden door herself in response to our ring. "Come in," she said. "I am Greta." She was a pretty woman in her mid-thirties, wearing a black dress with white trim that went well with her golden hair and healthy complexion. "It's such a pleasure to meet you. My husband spoke of you often after meeting you in Frankfurt."

I shook her hand gently. "It was a pleasure knowing him. In New York we have a habit of forgetting that book publishing is carried on in other cities as well. And this is my old friend Simon Ark."

The smile faded for just an instant and then reappeared. "I only wish you could have come sooner. My husband believed you might have saved his life."

"Then his death was not merely a street crime?" Simon asked, shedding his topcoat.

"Someone had been following him for days, stalking him, he said. He could hear their steps behind him but he never saw who it was."

"He told me that on the telephone," I said.

She led us into the living room, and I saw now that the entire inside of the building had been gutted and rebuilt. The cathedral ceiling rose all the way to the building's roof, where skylights admitted the light of the day. Balconies on the second and third floors led to bedrooms and baths, Greta Blackmoor informed us, along with a room where Arno had worked when at home. She mentioned his name without emotion, seemingly resigned to what had happened.

As we sat around a large glass coffee table, I asked for details of his death. "He phoned me on Wednesday afternoon," I told her. "It would have been evening here and I suppose he was calling from home."

She confirmed that with a nod. "He was very upset about being followed for three straight nights and he remembered your mention of your friend Simon Ark."

Simon shifted his position on the leather-covered couch. "Why me? Had he been to the police?"

"He did not believe the police could help him."

"But wasn't it a robbery?" I asked.

"In a sense. My husband believed someone was trying to steal his soul. His body was—almost decapitated when they found it."

Simon Ark stared up at the skylight in silence, and for a moment nobody spoke.

It was the ringing of the doorbell that broke the spell, and Greta Blackmoor hurried to answer it. She returned with two men who reminded me vaguely of Arno. Both were in their thirties, blond, and with the appearance of successful businessmen. Mrs. Blackmoor introduced them as two of her late husband's oldest and dearest friends. The taller of the two was Bertil Millman, assistant director of the Museum of Antiquities at the Royal Palace. The other man, both shorter and stouter, was Carl Kiruna, a designer of computer chips.

"You've come all the way from New York?" Kiruna asked, finding this little short of amazing. "Did you know Arno well?"

"Not really," I admitted. "A few days at the Frankfurt Book Fair last October, and some telephone calls since then. But I spoke with him just a day before he was killed."

"A terrible crime," Bertil Millman said, seating himself next to me. "Simply terrible! To die like that—"

"The police have no clues?" Simon asked.

"Apparently not. They think it was a random thing." Millman took out a pipe and nervously began to fill it. "Just some madman on the prowl who happened upon poor Arno."

"He was followed for three nights," I pointed out. "He told me so on the phone. It was as if he was being stalked."

"Perhaps the killer was waiting for an opportunity." Carl Kiruna suggested.

Greta was growing impatient. "I didn't invite you here to discuss Arno's death, but his life. Bertil and Carl, would you both be willing to say a few words at the service on Tuesday?"

"Certainly."

"Of course." Millman lit his pipe and drew on it. "What about Wahlstrom? Will he be there?"

Greta Blackmoor hesitated. "I don't know. He was one of the original crowd at the university, wasn't he? The four of you—"

"Five," Kiruna corrected, "but of course Semlor is dead now."

"My God!" Greta put a hand to her mouth and I saw the color drain from her face. "I just remembered!"

"What is it?" Simon Ark asked.

"When Semlor died in that motorcycle accident last year. Arno told me he'd been decapitated in the crash. He died the same way as Arno. Did someone steal his soul too?"

* * *

Simon Ark stood against the mantel of the fireplace, looking like a commanding elder statesman in his black suit and tie. "I have heard enough about this stealer of souls. Will someone please tell me what it's all about?"

Millman and Kiruna exchanged glances. "Nothing serious," Kiruna replied finally. "Schoolboy foolishness."

"Arno told me about it once, shortly after we were married," Greta said, ignoring her late husband's friends. "It was when they were all at the university together, nearly twenty years ago. They had a foolish ceremony and sold their souls to the devil."

I let out my breath. "And that's why your husband wanted Simon Ark. That's why he spoke of an exorcist. He feared the devil was coming to collect."

"It's true, isn't it?" she challenged the others, but they remained guiltily silent.

"Why the head?" Simon asked softly. "Why would Satan cut off the head, if that is what you believe happened?"

"I don't know what to believe," she admitted. "There was a story by Poe in which a man bet the devil his head."

I smiled slightly. "Poe meant that story to be humorous, though perhaps something was lost in the translation to Swedish."

Finally Millman said it. "Go talk to Hans Wahlstrom if you need to. He'll tell you all about it. He even mentioned it once in a newspaper interview."

I could feel the tension in the room, and I knew Simon and I were partly the cause of it. When I suggested we leave, Greta Blackmoor seemed almost relieved. She went off for our coats and then saw us out. "I'll look for you at the service on Tuesday morning," she said. "It will be ten o'clock at St. Jacob's Church near your hotel."

"If we decide to visit Hans Wahlstrom, where can he be found?" Simon asked.

She hesitated, her hand on the big wooden door. "Wahlstrom was no friend of my husband's. They had a falling-out some years ago over a book he'd written. Arno refused to publish it and Wahlstrom barely spoke to him after that. He lives on Karlavagen. You can find the number in the phone book."

"Thank you," Simon Ark said. "We will do what we can."

As we strolled back to the hotel the late afternoon air seemed to chill our bodies. It was already growing dark and I increased the pace. "There aren't many people in this area of the city, especially when the shops are closed."

"Never fear, my friend. The devil does not want our heads."

"What would the head have to do with the soul, Simon?"

"Some cultures believe the soul exits the body through the mouth after death. I suppose some might feel that decapitation speeds up the process."

"That's insane."

"Let us visit Hans Wahlstrom tomorrow and see what he thinks of the matter."

"Those other two certainly didn't want to talk about it."

"Wahlstrom may be more willing."

I was awakened early in our hotel room by the sound of Monday morning commuters coming off the small ferry boats that docked regularly just outside our windows. I watched for a time as they came off in the near-darkness and hurried up the streets to their offices and shops. As the sky gradually brightened I saw there were a few flurries of snow in the morning air.

Simon Ark came out of the bathroom and began to dress. I hadn't even realized he was up. "What is the weather, my friend?"

"Some snow flurries. I don't think it'll amount to much."

After breakfast at the hotel I looked up Hans Wahlstrom's number and telephoned him. He agreed to see us at his home that afternoon. We were about to go off for some sightseeing when a tall, gaunt man in a topcoat and hat intercepted us in the lobby. He greeted us by name and then identified himself. "Superintendent Frowler of the Stockholm Police. I wonder if I might have a few words with you gentlemen."

We sat down in a lounge area of the lobby while I explained my casual friendship with Arno Blackmoor. He questioned Simon too, and seemed unconvinced by the answers he got. "You see, gentlemen, my department is investigating a very serious crime here. Arno Blackmoor was a highly respected citizen. To be killed like that on a dark street in Old Town, virtually decapitated by some madman, is more than we can tolerate. His widow told me you arrived yesterday, and she told me he spoke to you by telephone the day before his death."

"That's correct." I described the call as best I could remember it.

"He felt he was being stalked by someone or something?"

"He did."

"But he gave no hint of what it might be?"

I hesitated. "Well, he had the misapprehension that my friend Simon here was an exorcist. He wanted his help. I suppose that implies a fear of satanic possession."

"Come, now! Mr. Blackmoor was an intelligent, educated man. Why would be believe he was possessed of demons?"

"I have no idea. Perhaps his widow might know."

"I've spoken to her twice. She seems unable or unwilling to tell us more. That's why I was hoping you gentlemen might be of help."

"We may be," Simon Ark told him, "but not yet. Sometimes puzzles must await the proper moment for their solution."

"The proper moment? When there's another killing?"

"There may have been another killing already," Simon told him. "You might investigate the death of a man named Semlor in a motorcycle accident last year. I understand he was decapitated in the crash."

The detective frowned. Obviously this information was new to him and he made a note of the name. "How long will you be staying in our city?" he asked as he prepared to leave them.

"Through tomorrow, at least," I told him. "After the memorial service we'll see how long we're needed."

"I hope you won't leave without contacting me."

I promised we'd be in touch, but I had the distinct feeling there'd be little chance of our slipping away without his knowing about it.

It was early afternoon when we reached the address of Karlavagen where Hans Wahlstrom lived. It was an elaborate apartment building, no more than ten years old, with a uniformed doorman to announce our arrival. Wahlstrom was waiting to greet us when we stepped from the elevator. "Come in, gentlemen. I don't really know how I can help you, though. I have not been close to Arno Blackmoor in recent years."

He seated himself near the windows, with the light to his back. A large man with a middle-aged stomach, he hardly seemed like a classmate of the others we'd met. He brushed back the thinning hair from his deep brown eyes and asked, "First off, who told you about me?"

"A man named Bertil Millman, actually."

"Ah, Millman!"

"He said you'd tell us about some sort of pact with the devil you all made when you were at the university together."

"You want to know about *that*?" He leaned back and laughed.

"He said you mentioned it once in an interview."

"As a writer perhaps I viewed the whole episode with more humor than they did."

"You were a writer in your university days?" Simon asked.

"Short stories for our literary magazine."

"Did you ever write about this so-called pact with Satan?"

"No, no—I would never use friends in my fiction. That was one of the reasons for my falling-out with Arno. His firm had published two novels of mine with a fair degree of success. Then I submitted a third book and Arno himself rejected it. He claimed I had introduced real people into my fiction and he feared they could be identified. I told him that was foolish, but his mind was set. The book was finally

published by a rival firm after I'd shortened it a bit. But I've
wandered off the subject, as I often do. You asked about
the pact with Satan. I never wrote about it, but I mentioned
it last year in an interview in connection with this book.
Since it dealt with young people in their university days, the
interviewer asked if I'd ever done anything wild during my
own time at the university. I told him there were no sex
orgies, but some friends and I once sold our souls to the
devil."

He seemed to treat it as an enormous joke, and Simon
carefully entered into the spirit of it. "How did that happen
to come about?" he asked with a rare smile.

"Oh, there were five of us and we'd been drinking. Semlor
and Millman shared a room, as I remember it, and that's
where we were. I was a couple of years older than the other
four. Maybe that's why I didn't take it quite so seriously as
they did. We were sitting around on the floor finishing off a
bottle, probably passing around a joint, and talking about
the future. About our careers. This was in the early seventies, remember, when the country was full of Americans
fleeing the Viet Nam draft. Jobs weren't that easy to find.
Someone suggested we should make a pact with the devil,
selling our souls for success in our chosen fields."

"Who suggested it?" Simon wanted to know.

"I'm not certain. It could have been Arno."

"Go on."

"Someone drew a chalk pentagram on the wooden floor
and we took turns reading passages backwards out of the
Bible. There were candles burning and it was an eerie
setting, especially after a few drags of pot. Carl Kiruna
claimed he actually saw something, but no ne really believed
him."

"Was any time limit placed on this soul-selling?"

"No, I don't think so. We simply said we would sell our
souls to the devil in exchange for success in our chosen
careers. You know something? We all did succeed too—
Blackmoor as an editor, myself as a writer, Kiruna in computers, Millman at the museum, and Semlor as an actor.

None of us were huge sucesses yet, but we achieved a great deal while still under forty."

"Semlor was killed," I reminded him.

"I know." He turned serious for a moment. "It was Carl Kiruna who phoned to tell me about it last year. He even mentioned the pact with Satan, which I hadn't thought of in years. He wondered if the devil was starting to collect."

"His head—"

"It was a motorcycle accident, at dusk. He didn't see a steel construction cable stretched across the road at one point. There were warning signs, but he ignored them. He told me once that riding the motorcycle gave him a feeling of immortality."

"He was wrong," Simon said dryly. "What about the others?"

"I haven't seen any of them since my breakup with Arno over the book. Carl phoned me that one time, and Bertil Millman phoned, quite upset, after that interview appeared about the pact with Satan. No one took it seriously, though."

"And yet Arno Blackmoor is dead now too, and he also lost his head."

"A coincidence. This was murder, the first was an accident."

"Perhaps. Did anyone see Semlor's accident?"

"I—no, I suppose not. He was said to be alone at the time."

We left shortly after that, and Wahlstrom rode down in the elevator with us. Perhaps he was being a good host in seeing us to the outer door. Perhaps he just wanted to make certain we were really gone.

The following morning was sunny, but with a chill wind from the sea that had us turning up our coat collars as we walked the few blocks to the memorial service at the nearby church. It was an old building, dating from the seventeenth century, and so spacious that the mourners seemed lost among its columns and shadows. The brief memorial service was in Swedish, so Simon and I could understand little of it, but when it was over we gathered outside with the others.

"Please come back to the house with the others," Greta Blackmoor urged us. "I so appreciate you traveling all this distance."

As we walked across one of the other bridges to the Old Town section, further down from our hotel, Bertil Millman from the Museum of Antiquities fell into step with us. "You must visit my museum at the Royal Palace before you depart," he urged.

"There is so much to see here," I agreed. "What's that modern building to our right?"

"Stadshuset, our handsome city hall. It's where the Nobel Prize receptions are held each December."

As we left the bridge and entered the street of Old Town, Simon Ark said, "Blackmoor could have been beheaded with a sword. I imagine there are many such ceremonial weapons in your museum, Mr. Millman."

"Not so many as you'd think. The city contains several statues of St. George and the Dragon, but none in which the sword is easily removable. However, if the stalker of Arno Blackmoor's soul was a supernatural being, it would not have needed a sword from my museum or anywhere else."

"Surely you don't believe in this supernatural business!" I said, surprised by his words.

"I don't really know," he answered in all seriousness. "I too have heard recently the footsteps behind me."

"Tell us about it," Simon Ark urged, immediately interested.

"It was only that, a sound behind me that was not quite footsteps."

"More like hoofbeats?"

"Perhaps, or only the beating of my own heart."

"Distant, or close?"

"Close, and gaining on me. I turned to look, of course, but there was nothing in sight."

"When was this?"

"Sunday evening, on the way home from Greta's house, and again last night after I left work at the museum.

"Have you told the police?"

He shrugged. "What can they do? It may be all my imagination."

"You seem to be a sensible person, Mr. Millman. If you heard steps behind you, I doubt if they were your imagination."

"We saw Hans Wahlstrom yesterday," I told him.

"Oh?"

"He told us about the pact with the devil."

"Mere adolescent foolishness. It meant nothing and no one believed in it. I'd quite forgotten it until that fool Wahlstrom mentioned it in his interview."

"Yet two of the five who made the pact are now dead, and both were decapitated."

"There was nothing suspicious about Semlor's death. It was a motorcycle accident."

"Maybe he heard something behind him too," I suggested. "Maybe he was fleeing from something and didn't see the steel cable that killed him."

We had reached the Blackmoor home by that time and the conversation ceased as we entered. Greta took our coats off to another room and Carl Kiruna performed the introductions, leading us among small groups of relatives and friends. At one point I looked around for Millman, but he'd gone into one of the other rooms.

When Greta Blackmoor rejoined us, Simon asked, "Didn't Hans Wahlstrom attend the service?"

She shook her head. "I didn't invite him. He was no friend of Arno's."

"We saw him yesterday."

"Bertil already told me."

"Did he also tell you he has heard the sound of feet or hoofs behind him, as your husband did?"

She seemed startled by this. "When?"

"The last two nights."

"Arno heard them for three nights before he died."

"Do you believe—" Simon began, but was halted in midsentence by the expression on her face. She was looking over his shoulder and when I followed her line of sight I saw that Superintendent Frowler was standing at the door, just admitted by one of the neighbors, who'd apparently heard his knock. Greta moved away from us to greet him.

"Excuse me for coming at such a time," the police official told her. "We've found the murder weapon dropped down one of the sewers. I was wondering if you might step outside and tell us if you've ever seen it before."

The color had drained from her face at his request. "I'll go with you," I offered.

"Thank you," she said, accepting my arm. Simon Ark trailed along after us.

Frowler's official car was parked at the curb. He opened the trunk and showed us a carefully sealed plastic evidence packet. Inside was a long-handled ax, its blade dirty and stained. Greta Blackmoor gasped and looked away. "I've never seen it before," she managed to say.

"Your husband had no such tool?"

"No. We buy our firewood already cut. There is no use in the city for a woodsman's ax."

"It's a large weapon for someone to carry through the streets," I pointed out.

The superintendent shrugged. "But one easily concealed beneath a long winter coat."

Mrs. Blackmoor excused herself and went back inside. "A powerful man must have swung that ax," I suggested.

"Not necessarily. There were two or more blows. We believe the first one tore through the back of his coat and probably knocked him down. Then the killer stood over him and delivered the fatal blow or blows."

"And no one saw this?"

"These streets are narrow and some of them are not well lighted. Street crime is not common in Stockholm but it does happen. Our own prime minister was assassinated in the street a few years ago."

"They may not have seen him because he was invisible," Simon Ark suggested.

"Invisible?"

"Arno Blackmoor told my friend of the footsteps or hoof-

beats behind him, yet he saw nothing. I understand someone else had had the same experience."

"Who would that be?" the superintendent asked.

But Simon ignored the question. "It's chilly out here. We
must get back inside."

"When will you be going back to America?" he asked.

I answered for both of us. "Tomorrow, I think. Tomorrow, if we can get a flight."

From our room that evening Simon phoned Bertil Millman
at home. "Ah, Mr. Millman. I wanted to be certain you
arrived home safely and without incident. Good! Perhaps
the sounds you heard were merely a trick of the wind. Are
you in for the evening now? Oh, a meeting of the Antiquar-
ian Society. Where would that be—at the Museum? I see.
Well, good night, Mr. Millman."

"What was all that?" I asked.

"He heard no sounds this evening, but he must return to
the museum for an eight o'clock meeting."

"Do you really think he's in danger?"

"There was a gap of several months between the first two
deaths. It hardly seems likely that the stalker of souls would
be on the prowl so soon. And yet—"

"I know. You want to go out, just to be certain he's
safe."

"If I am wrong in my theory, it may truly be the devil
who pursues him, and who can say what sort of calendar the
devil uses?"

That night, as we crossed the bridge and prowled once
more through the narrow streets of Old Town, I felt the way
Simon Ark might have, if he'd really been pursuing Satan
for the past two thousand years. I felt like someone prowling these very streets seven hundred years ago, searching for
whatever evil might have lurked here then.

"It will happen on the way home, if it happens at all,"
Simon decided.

"Why is that?"

"The full moon is directly overhead now, bathing these

narrow streets in its glow. An hour from now, after the meeting, the shadows will once again reign here."

We watched a little of the meeting from the back row, but left before it was over. Simon didn't want Millman to know we were following him. But as we waited outside and the small crowd filed out, he grew increasingly nervous.

"Something is wrong, my friend." He stopped a stocky woman who'd been on the platform with Millman. "Pardon me, has the assitant director left yet?"

She was startled at being addressed in English but managed to reply, "Yes. He went out the back door."

"You take that street," Simon told me, really alarmed now. "I will go to the left. Hurry!"

I trotted about a half-block unti I became winded and slowed to a fast walk. The street ahead was in semi-darkness and I could see no one. I was alone.

Except that I could hear something very close behind me. It was like an echo of my own footsteps.

I whirled around quickly and saw—

Nothing.

I started walking again, and heard it again.

Were those the sounds of hoofs on the stone paving? Or were they the sounds of the stalker of souls prowling the night with his ax?

I started running.

At the next corner I turned left, hoping to encounter Simon Ark, but there was only another empty street. Far ahead I could see a well-lit square with people but I knew I would never reach it in time. The footsteps behind me seemed louder now.

And then I reached the next corner, and saw the three men locked in a deadly struggle not twenty feet away.

"Simon!"

I ran forward, forgetting my invisible pursuer, and threw myself on them, going for the man with the ax in his hand. Simon pulled Millman free and in a moment we had the assailant down in the street. I yanked the ax from his grip and then reached up to pull away the scarf that hid his features.

"It is Mr. Carl Kiruna, of course," Simon Ark said. "Our designer of computer chips. If you two will continue holding him, I will summon the police."

An hour later, Simon and I sat with Bertil Millman in Greta Blackmoor's living room, listening to Superintendent Frowler outline the case. He'd asked us to assemble there so he could take statements to wrap up the investigation. Millman told of the footsteps he'd heard, and Simon and I recounted our chase after him through the streets of Old Town.

"I was nearly to the corner when I heard the steps behind me again," Millman said. "I looked back, but of course no one was there. As I increased my pace a bit, this figure stepped suddenly from a doorway on my right. I saw him raise the ax, and then Mr. Ark shouted at him from down the block. The three of us tussled, and Mr. Ark's friend ran up to join in. When we got the assailant down on the ground, we saw that it was Carl—Carl Kiruna. I couldn't believe it."

"He's admitted killing your husband, Mrs. Blackmoor, but he'll say nothing about his motive." Frowler was reviewing his notes as he spoke. "He denies any part in the death of Mr. Semlor, however. I expect by tomorrow he may be willing to make a fuller statement."

Greta Blackmoor tried to pour us some coffee but her hand was shaking. I took the pot from her. "Was he carrying anything unusual in his coat pocket?" Simon asked.

"He was, now that you mention it." The superintendent unzipped his briefcase and removed a black plastic gadget somewhat larger than a pack of cigarettes. "Looks a bit like one of those devices that automatically opens your garage doors."

"I believe that's exactly what it is," Simon Ark told him, "though in this case it served a different purpose. As soon as I heard the description of these so-called hoofbeats or footsteps where there was no person or animal present, the thought occurred to me that they might be some sort of electronic sounds. Mr. Kiruna was introduced as a designer of computer chips and my interest immediately forcused on him. We've all seen greeting cards that play a simple tune when opened." He turned to me. "My friend—"

I knew what was coming and I handed over my coat, which I'd kept folded on my lap.

"Both Mr. Millman and my friend here heard the mysterious sounds tonight, shortly before Mr. Millman was attacked." He turned up the collar of my coat and cut a few threads in back, where the collar was sewn to the body of the coat. From inside the collar he extracted a tiny plastic disk about the size of a penny. He pressed the button on the black box Kiruna had been carrying, and the disk immediately began to emit electronic sounds exactly like footsteps. Simon Ark smiled. "When muffled by the fabric of the wearer's coat, they sounded just far enough away to be mistaken for a follower. Yet the street remained empty. Kiruna was watching from a distance, of course, and only activated the device when no one else was nearby. There's an identical one in Mr. Millman's coat collar. Tonight, when he turned it on, my friend on the next street was also within range and his device was activated accidentally."

"What was the purpose of it?" Millman wanted to know.

"To frighten the intended victim. He would speak of it to others, even phoning New York in the case of Arno Blackmoor, and when he was later killed the murder would take on a supernatural aspect. Decapitation with an ax was chosen in hopes it would be linked to Semlor's earlier accidental death, and the so-called pact with the devil."

I still didn't understand it all. "Simon, how could that thing have been placed in my coat, and why? I wasn't connected with these others. Why would Kiruna want to kill me?"

"He didn't, my friend. The disk was placed there only to frighten you and me away, if that became necessary later. As I said, it was triggered by accident tonight. As to how it was placed there, that could only have been done in this house, probably earlier today when Greta Blackmoor solicitously carried our coats to the other room. Cutting the thread, inserting the disk, and resewing the seam could have been accomplished in a moment's time."

The blood had drained from Greta's face, and now the coffee cup dropped from her fingers, bouncing on the carpet. "I—I didn't mean to—I didn't know he'd try to kill you too, Bertil! It was only supposed to be Arno—"

The following afternoon, as we arrived at the airport, I said, "No pact with the devil, no stalker of souls, only the eternal triangle and a woman who wanted her husband out of the way."

Simon Ark nodded. "Kiruna would have killed Millman to further the illusion. Perhaps he'd have gotten around to Hans Wahlstrom too. As for Greta, she wasn't all that innocent. Remember she was the one who sewed the disks into the coat collars of her husband, Millman, and yourself. And she was the one who brought up that pact with Satan, and the similarity to Semlor's death, in case the police missed the point. The disk had to be ripped from Arno's coat after he was killed, of course. That was why the police thought the first blow of the ax had hit his collar. Kiruna and Greta were both stalkers of souls, doing the devil's work."

I remembered the crystal I'd promised Shelly and bought it at the duty-free shop. Then we boarded the plane for a peaceful flight home.

Among Barry Malzberg's many considerable achievements—he's not only a fine novelist but a first-rate critic as well—is one book that should be of interest to all writers. *Herovit's World* is one of three novels that definitively describe the writer's world (the other two being Donald E. Westlake's *Adios, Scheherazade* and Wilfrid Sheed's *The Hack*). It is a dark and powerful and mesmerizing work and deserves a much larger audience than has yet discovered it.

———— 💀 ————

DARWINIAN FACTS

Barry N. Malzberg

Do you want to hear a story? Of course you do, your curiosity is limitless: here is a story. An assassin, let us call him Gregor Mendel, is summoned on special detail to track and kill an important man. Mendel is frightened by the orders, terrified by necessity, but he has a long history in this trade and is essentially unemployable outside of it; he adapts to the rigors of circumstance and he believes in following orders. Slowly, slowly the assassin narrows the circle of his own evasions, his own reluctance, conceals his dilemma (as everything else) from his wife, circumscribes his own evasions until he is convinced that this is not only an assignment but a great task. Like the alchemy of the Middle Ages, like the summoning of gold to lead, Mendel sees himself as gripped by destiny.

The transition to purpose is not immediate, it takes many months until Mendel can be really brought to the point of fiction. But at last then, at last, hand on heart, he solemnly nods, accepts the assignment, leaves the room. Heart on trigger, trigger to bolt, knowledge to destiny, Mendel *explodes* his high and perilous deed in a fireball of fond recrimination, tender retribution, and the target is ever so publicly, ever so finally dead. This is the sentimental part of the narrative: Mendel feels badly about this. He adores his wife and infant even though he cannot talk to or touch them; he knows himself to be a profound and feeling man, he is not touched lightly by the wicked temper of his time. Mendel weeps for the widow of his target, for the children of his quarry. Knowing the depths of loss, stunned by his own velocity of mourning, Mendel feels the burden of his duty as he is seized by huge and controlling hands, dragged away. He is entrapped and arrested, of course. Mendel had been assured of success, of an escape route, but they had lied to him as he rapidly discovers, and it is the work of few authorities to truncate his pathetic flight and drag him into custody.

Ah, Mendel! Too late, at last, he discovers that he has not only been a tool, he has acted as the only bridge between those who gave the orders and those who would find the truth. Only Mendel could connect the two. If Mendel is killed, his directors and caretakers will be invulnerable. Bridge, then, cat's-paw, our poor Mendel. Oh how his forehead burns, his eyes dazzle with the tears of his discovery! In the brief span now allotted, what rage and betrayal, what recrimination and pain for him as, carried in custody through the bowels of the police station, he is shot in the stomach.

It does not take him long to die. Even at the moment of death it is possible that Mendel has had little knowledge, although we cannot be sure of this. Ultimately, we can only infer his interior, his processes, we are not privy to them. His wife felt Mendel's engorged, raging tool within her spitting fire and yet he gave *her* no part of knowledge, how much less for the rest of us. Ultimately, layered within himself, Mendel dies, as we all must, some sooner, some much later, some clutching the cloak of judgment, others casting it.

You have heard the story. The essential outlines, anyway. This is the greater and cruder arc of narrative.

But, but, but there is a little more: here is the withheld denouement, the windup, the smash smasheroo, the old surprise end which can of course be no surprise because the least of you must have crafted your credulity toward this end. One more detail, thus, to clinch the matter.

No, I am not Mendel.

Nor the widow, nor his quarry. Mendel is dead and so is the quarry and the others will go on in one way or the other. Some will prosper. Others will change their names, unlearn the place of Mendel's grave. All will be changed in smaller or greater ways, but all will be unchanged in some more fundamental sense.

The ending is this: I am Mendel's assassin. I am the man who killed the man who killed. The hand of his undoing is mine. The betrayer and vindication of the assassin, both of them are mine.

That is the story in its center and its arc.

This amazing revelation, none of you could have suspected it, none of you would have known, this astonishing revelation given early rather than late . . . even that is not the totality, for here is a story with many, many endings, some of them unrevealed. One closes a box, opens another box; one ends a prayer, begins an imprecation, it is one of those Eastern voyages of discovery and memory which we calculate. The story is diverse, involuted. So here is yet another true conclusion: I have performed under instruction. Removing one bridge, *I* have become the bridge. I know those who created Mendel and sent him on his tasks, I can lead you straight toward them. It is within my power, if I say so, to pledge to you the full and desperate revelation of our time, and that is why I have offered you this story with many endings, a story that only I can transmogrify.

It is abominably cold in this place.

It is cold, I am dying, the freeze not from weather but from the cold and deadly fire with which they beam death into my bones, my burning and insubstantial soul. They have ordered me to death, they hurl cancer at me. Oh my soul, it is cold from my knowledge, their machination. Attend to the rays of death! Consider the condition of the dappled and complaisant Mendel as from his parapet he arches his back to the task, extends his arms, sighs, scratches himself, thinks of women, thinks of the small and florid spaces of his wife's cunt as he waits for the motorcade, the damned motorcade to plummet. Consider Mendel as he belches, squirms, adjusts his rifle, adjusts his underwear, flexes himself for his vault toward immortality, and consider me as well, emtombed in this cell, asking only the opportunity to share as one must the source of the commands that so spirited me here.

Oh, Dallas. I thought that Chicago was the center of darkness, that Chicago was the rock of our enchantment and entrapment, that it was at Chicago where the rolling continent ended and began but that was before I trundled south, found quarters in this deadly and constant city. It was in Dallas where I came to understand the true meaning of passage, the sheer *weight* and force of the continent as it caved toward crushing circumstance here and never got out. In Chicago I could smell the slaughterhouses all the time, the moaning and clatter of the beasts and their stink rose and rose into all of the parlors where I carried out my fate, I smelt the cattle all of the time, but the stockyards were nothing as against the deeper and richer stink of Dallas, not oil, not coastal waters, not the fumes of the derricks and the corruption, but something deeper, ever deeper, that seemed to carry me back further than I had ever before reached. In Chicago there were summers where I believed that I was on the arc of a death not so existential as personal and final (as some Midwest deaths need not be), the obliteration of all possibility in that most secret and concealed of all places, but oh boy, oh boy, Chicago was toy city, was Gang Expo as against Dallas. It was Dallas who taught me not to live, not to die, not exactly but rather that the two were indistinguishable. That like Mendel one could be placed in a circumstance where they became the same and one did not, ultimately, know in what state one might be. They taught a hard and final school in Dallas and then they locked up the boxes of the Stadium Club and put the real knives to bear. You hang around, you stay around, you place a bet or two, you follow the grind and the knives in your time and you learn a thing or three but you can never, truly learn enough. Murder exceeds knowledge by a sufficient factor, oh Macbeth.

Do you want to hear the domestic story? Do you want to hear the gentler and more sentimental, the linoleumed and porcelained interior of this narrative? Even assassins have home lives, you know, even assassins can cry at the more rending moments of certain films or at home movies of the Presidential candidate holding his daughter on his knee.

So consider this as part of the detritus of a life too, this affecting and personal side. Young Mendel, twenty-four years old and knowing more already than he ever dared to think was possible of pain and implication, young and thin Mendel, with his stunned eyes and rifle case stashed, kisses his young wife and infant daughter, bids them a tender farewell, adjusts his clothing, centers his cap (a recent affectation but one that he thinks makes him look rather dashing), and hugs them as he prepares to desert the apartment for his great task. Perhaps Mendel will never see them again. He has to commit himself to that possibility, certainly he cannot deny it. Not after the degree of obligation they have put upon him. "Goodbye," his young wife says. We will not give her a name just now, it is not necessary. It will make the matter *too* affecting, will break all of the circumstantial bounds. Call her Mrs. Mendel. That is what wives were called at that innocent time. "Goodbye, goodbye," Mrs. Mendel says. His daughter, too young for speech (as Mendel, stricken by sorrow and destiny, has become too old for speech, knows that not words but tragedy must ensue), waves a speechless little hand. Perhaps the baby gurgles. At such a distance, at such a remove from events, who can be sure. "Goo-by," Mrs. Mendel says, mimicking her daughter's sound. "Goo-by." She knows few words of English but she is capable of assessing moods, she is no fool, not insensitive, merely in over her head as almost everyone at this impossible time was. Gigantic events are created by those who are fundamentally unaware of their own significance. It is most distressing. Much of this gives me more pain than I can possibly say. It is all part of the circumstances in which we are plunged.

Think of Mendel. He is about to leave. He has coffee in his stomach, anticipation as well as dread in his bearing, he has been made sufficiently alert for the duties to come. Mrs. Mendel knows nothing of this assignment, is unaware of Mendel's destination or preparation, really understands only the imperatives of her own appetite, her daughter's appetite, her fear, but she can sense Mendel's tension and perhaps a little whiff of his thrall comes upon her. "Goo-by," she says again. Mendel stands at the door and waves. The M-1 is stashed in the warehouse. Dreaming of the M-1, thinking of this smuggled rifle which he has assembled from the cautious pieces his masters have sent from various widely dispersed military supply depots in this and other countries, Mendel sits at the window of the bus, rocking in the traffic, closing and opening his eyes convulsively. Soon the dreaming M-1 will be in his hand. He thinks of the slide of the barrel in his hand, the feel of his wife's thigh, the rapid swell and rise of her cunt as he slammed inside her, when, two days ago, perhaps three. The cunt and the rifle blend in his consciousness as such things are wont to do. The bus slams to a sickening jolt in heavy traffic, Mendel slides, desperately grips the railing. In his half-dream it is as if he has been shot, as if the jolt were a fatal wound. He thinks of Mrs. Mendel, the slide of her arm, touch of her lips, but the image is replaced by that of the President. Mendel deeply admires the President, envies him, would like to have his life. His assignment is nothing personal, as he keeps on reminding himself; he has a very high opinion of the President, as do many Americans of this time. Certainly nothing will be known of the President for years and years, of his secret life, hidden desire and when—long after the acts I am trying desperately to objectively describe here—it is revealed, it will have no bearing upon that sense of loss and mourning that will soon enough rack the nation. Dallas to Mendel's eyes could now be Chicago, it is indistinguishable from Chicago in his half-doze. These places torn from the continent, taken arbitrarily from the rock and the sluice, called "cities," given spaces where one could prosper, flourish, starve, or die, all at the same time, never knowing one another.

Mendel knows that he may never see his wife and child again. It is difficult, perilous for him to dwell on this, and so, to the best of his ability, he does not.

Here is my own revelation; here is my own detritus and admission: for years I had loved Mrs. Mendel, if only at a great distance and in a yearning and covert way. I loved the *idea* of her before I knew she existed; when I became aware of her reality my excitement quickened to force, to desperation. The love of most women is not for me, I have had my problems, have always had difficulty with the run of women produced by America at this part of the century . . . but the youth, vulnerability, lack of language, uncertainty, sheer *ignorance* of Mrs. Mendel inflamed me. Here at last was someone with whom I could deal, someone who I would know as she would know me. Now and then, through the course of my days, dealing with the beaten and insulting women who came to work for me, I would close my eyes and there would be Mrs. Mendel or someone very much like her. I would give her a first name, would characterize her as I must to draw her closer. Grace, I would call her. Oh Grace. "Oh Grace," I wanted to say, even as I took measurements from strippers and made arrangements for liquor deliveries, ignore this heavy and corrupt mask, this sagging tissue, this dispirited crown and sunken face, this is not the man but merely what Chicago beat into him, this rubble is a concealment of the man inside.

"Oh Grace," I would add to persaude her, "I am not

merely a functionary, not a running man for my masters and your husband's; I am a tender and sensitive man, I suffer. Grace, Grace," I would murmur to her, hoping that she could hear and on some level I am sure she did, "touch me and know my yearning, clasp me and know my burning, my yearning and my burning, my lust and my dust, my cry and my sigh," but I did not would not say things like this, I kept them inside.

Much be kept inside; Chicago taught me restraint and the heaviness, the weariness of a burdened body, tossed like a sack into Lake Michigan, sinking without a merry burble. "I am not the sort of man," I did not therefore say to her, "who looks capable of such speech, such yearning, but I know this, I will say this: Mendel cannot give you what you want, what you need. He has a small and crushed soul; he hasn't the breadth of spirit which I can give, don't you see that? Don't you know it?" Oh, I could have said and this much else to her; "I know your life is as stricken for love as mine and that with one another we can find the better parts of ourselves." But I said nothing. Business must prevail and the mask of circumstance.

Said nothing until that day when I was summoned to Carlos's presence and was then for the first time determined to speak my need. "I do love her," I said. "I have seen her picture, I have seen her on the streets. I love Grace Mendel. You must know this."

"It is all right," Carlos said. "You are free to speak. We are beyond love," he said. "We are into action now. You will be celebrated, you will be a national hero, you will be acclaimed and admired if you but do what we ask. You will be jailed, yes, of necessity, will serve a brief sentence and be released, they will strew flowers the day you walk out of the prison. Your memoirs can be sold for enormous sums to *Collier's*. Agents will bid for your likeness and the movie."

"Grace. This is what I want."

"Grace," Carlos said, shaking his head. "So be it then. What do I know? What do I know of women? That too, if you wish. We will arrange everything *por favor* if you insist, if you want. Do you understand?"

I am a fat man but I move with gentility and the arc of a dancer. This is my conception of myself: the dancer's vault. I looked at Carlos, brandished a hand. "They will jail me," I said. "There will be great notoriety, a huge trial. I am not a fool, I am not blinded by love. I know what will become of me. It will not be an easy task, it will not admit of resolution."

"Trust us."

"There is a craziness. There is a craziness in this country, in this time. You wish to make it worse yet and then you will put me at the center of it."

"You will end it," Carlos said. We were sitting in the nightclub in the afternoon, in the false light and streaming dust. There is nothing like a nightclub with the lights off on a sunny weekday afternoon in a fallen October. "You will be a hero because you will have killed the craziness that killed the craziness. And this woman, she will be yours."

"I don't know. I love her too much and she knows of me too little."

"Love," Carlos said. He spat in the dust, ran his toe on the wet spot. "What you Americans will not do for sense, you will do for love. So be it. Trust us. It will happen. All things will happen."

"I have seen Mendel. He is—"

"We will not talk of Mendel. He means nothing, he is already perished and *morte* in the run of history. It is you upon whom it depends. But you will do us this favor," Carlos said, "for without it nothing can happen at all. You owe us this," he said, "and now it is time for me to ask, to insist. You can refuse," he said. "That refusal is within your right."

I looked in his face and saw cast back to me the light of my own refusal and it was heavy, it was blunt, it was an ax in the darkness.

"No," I said, "I will not refuse."

"That is good," he said, "we would be most hurt or disappointed if that were indeed the case. This is a nation that flourishes on its disappointment, on the teasing of expectations. We do not wish to join them. It is this Grace you love? Then there will be an arrangement."

"It is not the woman," I said then. It was not insight but resignation then that leached from the pores of understanding. All of my life had been predicted upon denial, surely nothing now could change. "It is not the woman," I said again, pondering. "It cannot be for her, then. You know it is impossible between us. You know that for all my desire, she is merely a fiction."

In Carlos's presence I mimicked his speech, just as in the presence of masters in Chicago I spoke like Capone. In New Orleans I slid into an almost impenetrable Southern accent. This is one of my traits. There are those who say—do not, do not believe them!—that I am an empty man, that I am a bankrupt man, that there is nothing inside me other than an utter and credulous responsiveness and that I take on the sounds and speech of those whom I address. It is a temptation to think this way, even though I know that is not the case. I have an interior, I suffer, how could I speak to you like this were I not suffering?

"It will destroy us," I said to Carlos.

"Oh, no. You do not understand, still. There is nothing to be destroyed. You cannot abolish a nullity. You cannot eliminate a cipher. By subtraction you are participating in addition."

"I will do it," I said. This was another voice, a Chicago voice, a voice of the north, of stone and concrete, of rifle fire in garages. It was the voice that I had always known would emerge. "I will do it, I will kill the killer. I will destroy Mendel."

"This is good. I hope it is sincerely meant."

"Everything is sincerely meant," I said. There was more conversation to be sure, and I could, if I were to reach back to that time, find and record it, but what is the point? What is the point of any of this? The outlines of the discussion are clear, the difficult rim of necessity, the bowl of recollection filled. "I will do it," I must have added finally, "because I have no choice."

"Surely you do. We all have choice, right up to the lip of the grave."

"That is a Latinism," I said. "I reject that; I make no statement. I understand that there is nothing else to be done. Not for Grace Mendel then, no matter how I love her. Not for the nation. Not even for self or for old debts or for Chicago or fear. But because it must be done.

"As you wish," Carlos said. This must have been the next day. The conversation was spread, I think, over several days, perhaps I mean several months, as negotiations and calculations were made. One compresses for the sake of unity and recall, but nothing was so simple. (Except for Mendel's bus ride; that is exactly how it happened, how it must have happened.) "As you will," Carlos said. "As you want," Carlos added. He said other things as well, made many interesting brisk points and philosophical comments about the collapse of our civilization, but they are not to be reported, nor is the nature of my difficult obligation. That obligation was clear then, clear now, clear for all time, glinting at us through all the tunnels and tents of recall as I try to assure you of the seriousness of my position.

Poor Mendel. Have I constructed him as he has been presented or does he really exist in that way? How much of Mendel can be known outside of these calculations? Thinking of him, thinking of all that has happened, I wonder about this and other things, wonder if this "Mendel" I have created is not merely another aspect of this putrescent and dying self. Struggling to the sixth floor of the warehouse, thinking of his difficult and necessary obligation, did Mendel know what he was doing? Did he ever come to terms with its meaning? Or was it all mindless, circumstantial, arbitrary, operative, the cells moving toward their own completion? Does he do what he must for guile, or out of passion? Is it the President of whom he thinks at this moment? The President has consorted with evil, made perilous arrangements, indulged impossible risk, reparations are due. The "Mendel" I have conceived thinks of this and that as he hunches over his bologna sandwich on rye, his homemade lunch humbly packed by the unthinking Grace and placed in the rifle case, the bread crumbs scattered on the floor for future officers to marvel at. Sooner or later he would have had to die anyway, Mendel thinks or does not think. This is merely a matter of adding purpose, of granting structure, of ordering the mindless and unfiltered events of our lives toward some kind of outcome. And so thinking, he sighs, begins the final assembly, embarks wearily but with much dedication upon the great task. One must have sympathy for him. One must understand Gregor Mendel's position here. Nothing is easy for this tormented young man and matters will become only more difficult as the years go on and on and on.

Dallas was a fresh start, I thought. Dallas would enable me to reconstruct my life. Oh, I was a practical man when I headed for Dallas, truly I thought it would be different. How was I to know? How were any of us to know? Observe the earnestness of my voice, the earnestness of my eyes; I am not casual about this, I am giving you hard and real information here, slabs of life *cut* from the bleeding and necessitous whole.

So one can apprehend this as Mendel himself might have seen it then, peering over the rifle sight after the shot he could see the President's head explode through the force of that bullet, no, there is *another* bullet, that second shot placed with deadly and preventive force which breaks open the slab of skull, the blood leaping in a high, fine, weeping line from the interior of the skull. Mendel can see this (as I can) and he bellows, for all his fear, one astonished *ya-hoo! heigh-ho!* as that second, disappearing supplementary shot struck home, secret help from the secret masters, but no time for Mendel to relish this act of extirpation, no time at all. He must flee. He has been given strict orders, he knows what he must do next.

Ya-hoo! heigh-ho! and squirm on belly to the staircase, rising then only as the door is reached and so, so then the clumsy, shouting, excoriating events of that profound afternoon continue.

"Oh, if you could only know me, Grace," I want to say to her. "I'm a fat blur, a figure in black-and-white fleeing through the bottom of a screen and that is all I will ever be but I loved you, don't you know that? I loved you and what you became in a way that Mendel never could, you must understand, you must accept, you must pledge for my love." But to say this would be a craziness; even now, at this time, it is impossible for me to say this. Of all the things I have done or have not done, this begging, wailing appeal to Grace would be the maddest of all and so I will not, will never do this.

No, it is Carlos's business which I conduct, with more brutality and efficiency perhaps than anyone could have known, than *either* of us at that or any other time would have thought, and the extrapolate dimensions of this horror sprawl ever further. They let me in, they pushed me forward, they slid the little gun in my hand and helped me point it. They were huge and ever helpful as I knew they must be. First the confirming call from Carlos, just before these climactic events. "He is being transferred at eleven," Carlos had said. "He will make transversal through the basement, the information is excellent, be there on time and we will put everything in your hands." They put everything in my hands. "There will be no further instructions." There were no further instructions. "We will allow no margin whatsoever for your failure." There was no failure.

There was no failure; I did what had to be done, overtook with efficacy. Dare I say "overtook with Grace"? So, then, I overtook with grace. Falling away from me, falling in that place, that astonished look of recognition in his eyes for all (who could know) to see, Mendel fell and fell (and fell) away, his mouth pursed in an accusatory *O you!* much like his *ya-hoo! heigh-ho!* as he went down. "You, you have done this," he would have said more mildly, added in a tone shockingly like commendation, but there was no speech, only the withdrawal and the falling. Their hands upon me, the hands of the state were enormous, a deliverance, a speeding toward obsequy and conclusion, a voice in my ear then whispering *say nothing, say nothing* and so I was dragged, complaisant as Mendel, complaisant as the now dead President himself from that public and wretched space.

If I could tell you here and at this place what I wished to become of Grace and myself I would but I cannot; this is not at all possible. She would come, would come to me in love and tender searching, uttering my name, but I cannot divulge this, I cannot bear it, I cannot at the end come to terms with what cannot be but let it be known, let it be known that if it were other than what it must have been . . . we might have had that urgent and whispering closure in the dark.

Slowly, methodically, my bones are cooked by their secret and deadly rays into the froth of cancer.

"You fool," Mendel wants to point out, "you were worse than me; I knew that I was wretched and doomed from the beginning but I never thought that there was anything else. But you were like him, like the President, you *believed* everything you were told. You were even worse then: what I did was at least for passion, and history will make of me how and what it will but, *you*, you—

"I did it for passion," I wanted to say but did not. "My passion exceeded yours, it outgrew the sun, it was larger and burning ever brighter than yours. I am a ridiculous figure, yes, with a cocked hat and a fat belly, but inside I *suffer*, I am a man of some dimension and pity, consider what I have been able to establish for Mendel, how fair I have been.

*   *   *

No Grace, no light, only the cold and deadly force of their beams, burning, burning my bones, my light—

Do you want to hear a story? Everyone wants to hear a story, little children in their beds and grownups by the fire. But I cannot, will not tell you here; you have got to remove me, get me out of here, get me away so that I will tell you all of it, oh so much more than you have yet heard. Describe Carlos, tell you the shape of Grace's tits. What Mendel said to her in the dark. What the President planned for the Republic. Everyone knows me, everyone! *Everyone!*

Richard Laymon keeps trying to disgust, gross out, and otherwise repel decent upstanding middle-class readers who want a little shock but not enough volts to inflict death. What keeps Laymon from being just another splatterpunk is the human heart at the center of all his fiction. He writes with stone brilliance, for example, of the subtle shifting mores of high school life. And he seems to understand in some near profound way the ying and yang of contemporary marriage, which is particularly apparent in his forthcoming novel *The Stake* (St. Martins).

THE HUNT

Richard Laymon

Still there. Still staring at her.

Kim, seated on a plastic chair with her back to the wall, felt squirmy. Except for the door frame, the entire front of the laundromat was glass. The fluorescent lights overhead glared.

To the man in the car outside, it must have been like watching her on a drive-in movie screen.

She wished she'd worn more clothes. But it was a hot night and very late, and she'd postponed doing her laundry until nearly every stitch in her apartment needed a wash. So she'd come here in sneakers, her old gym shorts from high school, and a T-shirt.

Probably why the bastard's staring at me, she thought. Enjoying the free show.

No better than a peeping Tom, the way he just sits there, gazing in.

When Kim had first noticed him, she'd thought he was

the husband of one of the other women. Waiting and bored, choosing to spend his time in the comfort of his car, maybe so he could listen to the radio—or ogle her from a discreet distance.

Soon, however, two of the women left. The only one remaining was a husky middle-aged gal who kept complaining and giving orders to a fellow named Bill. The way Bill listened and obeyed, he had to be her husband.

Kim didn't think the stranger in the car was waiting for them.

They finished. They carried their baskets of clean clothes out to a station wagon, and drove off.

Kim was the only woman left.

The stranger stayed.

Every time she glanced his way, she saw him staring back. She couldn't actually see his eyes. They were masked in shadow. But she felt their steady gaze, felt them studying her.

Though she was unable to see his eyes, enough light reached him from the laundromat to show his thick neck, his shaved head. His head looked like a block of granite. He had a heavy brow, knobby cheekbones, a broad nose, full lips that never moved, a massive jaw.

Wouldn't be so bad, Kim had thought, if he looked like some kind of wimp. I could handle that. But this guy looked as if he ate bayonets for breakfast.

She'd wanted to move away from her chair near the front. Wait at the rear of the room. Hell, duck down out of sight behind the middle row of machines.

But if she did that, he might come in.

I'm all right as long as he stays in the car.

I'm probably all right as long as Jock's here.

She didn't know Jock's name, but he *was* one. The big guy might even be a match for the stranger. He appeared to be a couple of years younger than Kim—maybe nineteen or twenty. He had so much muscle that he couldn't touch his knees together if his life depended on it. Nor would his elbows ever rub against his sides. His sleeveless gray sweatshirt was cut off just below his chest. His red shorts were very much like Kim's, but a lot larger. He wore them over sweatpants.

She watched him, now, as he hopped down from one of the washers and strutted to a nearby machine. He thumped a button. The door of the front-loading dryer swung open. A white sock and a jockstrap fell to the floor.

Kim's stomach fluttered.

He's done.

She forced herself not to glance out the window. She forced herself not to hurry. She tried to look casual as she rose from her chair and strolled toward the crouching athlete.

"Hi," she said, stopping beside him.

He looked up at her and smiled. "Hello."

"I'm sorry to bother you, but I was wondering if you could do me a favor."

"Yeah?" His gaze slipped down Kim's body. When it returned to her face, she knew he would be willing to help. "What sort of favor?" he asked.

"It's nothing much, really. I just don't want to be left alone in here. I was wondering if you could stick around for a few minutes and keep me company until my clothes are finished. They're in the dryers now. It'll just be about ten more minutes."

He raised his eyebrows. "That's it?"

"Well, if you could walk me out to my car when I'm done."

"No problem."

"Thanks. I really appreciate it."

He stuffed the rest of his laundry into a canvas bag and tied the cord at the top. Standing up, he smiled again. "My name's Bradley."

"I'm Kim." She offered a hand, and he shook it. "I sure appreciate this."

"Like I told you, no problem."

Kim stepped to a washer across the aisle from him. He watched as she braced her hands on its edges and boosted herself up. Watched her breasts.

Maybe it wasn't such a hot idea asking him for help.

Don't worry, she told herself. He's just a normal guy.

She slumped forward slightly and cupped her knees to lossen the pull of the fabric across her chest.

"You live near here?" Bradley said.

"Yeah, a few blocks. Are you a student?"

"A sophomore. I live off-campus, though. I've got my own apartment. Do you come here often?"

"As un-often as possible."

He laughed softly. "Know what you mean. Chores. I hate them."

"Same here. Especially laundry. It gets kind of spooky here." Her head turned. She wanted to stop it, couldn't, kept turning until she saw the parked car and the grim face behind its windshield. She quickly looked back at Bradley.

"If you get spooked, why do you come here so late?" he asked.

"No waiting for machines." Then she added. "Famous last words."

Bradly frowned. "What is it?" He glanced toward the front, then scowled at her. "What's the matter?"

Kim felt her mouth stretch into a grimace. She shook her head. "Nothing."

"Is it that guy out there?"

"No, it's . . . He's been watching me. Ever since I got here. He just sits there, staring at me."

"Oh yeah?" Bradley glared in the man's direction.

"Don't! Jesus! Just pretend he's not there."

"Maybe I ought to go out and—"

"No!"

He turned to Kim. "You don't know who the guy is?"

"I've never seen him before."

"No wonder you're worried."

"I'm sure it's nothing," she said, beginning to tremble again. "He probably just likes to look at women."

"I like to look at women. That doesn't mean I hang around laundromats like a goddamn pervert."

"He's probably harmless."

"Doesn't look harmless to me. Who's to say he isn't some kind of freak like the Mount Bolton Butcher."

"Hey, come on . . ."

Bradley's face went pale. His eyes widened. They roamed down Kim, and returned to her face. "Christ," he muttered. "I hate to tell you this, but . . ." He hesitated.

The change in him frightened Kim. *"What?"*

"You . . . you're a dead match for his victim profile."

"What are you talking about?"

"The Mount Bolton Butcher. He's had eight victims, and they all . . . they were all eighteen to twenty-five years old, maybe not as pretty as you, but almost. And slim, and they all had long blond hair parted in the middle just like yours. You look so much like the others that you could all be sisters."

"Oh shit," Kim muttered.

"I was going with a girl who kind of fit the profile. Not as much as you do, but it had me worried. I was afraid, you know, she might end up raped and dismembered like . . . Is there a back way out of here?"

"Hey, come on. You're really—"

"I'm not kidding."

"I know, but . . . It probably isn't him, right? I mean, he hasn't . . ."

"He hasn't nailed anyone in two months, and the cops think he might've left the area, or died, or been jailed for something else. But they don't *know*. They're just trying to calm people down, saying stuff like that. Have you ever been up around Mount Bolton?"

Kim shook her head. It felt a little numb inside.

"I tell you, it's one big mean wilderness. A guy could hide out for years if he knew what he was doing. So maybe he laid low for a while, and maybe now the surge has gotten the best of him, and . . . Not much of anyone goes camping up there anymore. If he wanted a new victim, he might have to come down into town for one."

"This is really starting to give me the creeps."

"Just sit there a minute. I'll check the back."

Bradley walked up the aisle between the rows of silent washers and dryers. He stepped past the coin-operated vending machines where patrons could purchase drinks, snacks, detergent, or bleach. He tapped out a rhythm as he walked by a long, wooden table where people earlier had separated and folded their laundry. Then he disappeared into a recessed area at the rear of the room. He was out of sight for just a second.

When he stepped into the open again, he met Kim's eyes and shook his head.

Not once did he glance toward the man in the car as he came back to her. "Nothing but a utility room," he said. "The only way out is the front."

Kim nodded and tried to smile. She felt a corner of her mouth twitch.

"You think your stuff is about ready?"

"Close enough." She hopped off the washer. Bradley picked up his laundry bag and stayed at her side as she headed for the pair of dryers near the front.

"Your car's in the lot?" he asked.

"Yeah."

"I'll get in with you. If he thinks we're really together, maybe he won't try anything."

"Okay," Kim said. Both dryers were still running. She could see them vibrating, hear their motors and the thumps of the tennis shoes she'd tossed into the nearer of the two.

She swung her laundry basket off the top of that machine, set it at her feet, crouched, and opened the front panel. The motor went silent. Reaching inside, she lifted out a handful of warm clothes. They still felt a little damp, but she didn't care.

"If he follows us when we leave," Bradley said, "maybe we can lose him. But at least you won't be alone. As long as I'm with you, he'll think twice before he tries anything."

She dropped more clothes into the basket, and looked up at Bradley. "I really appreciate this."

"I'm just glad I'm here to help."

"Do you really think he might be the Butcher?"

"I hope we don't find out."

What if you're the Butcher?

The thought came suddenly, and seemed to turn her stomach cold inside.

No. That's ridiculous.

Looking away from him, she continued to unload the machine.

What's so ridiculous about it? Bradley seems to know a lot about the Butcher. And he wants me to take him in my car. Once we're alone . . .

For all I know, he's been lying from the start.

Maybe he's *with* the other guy. They might be working together.

Don't let him in the car, she told herself. Walk out with him, but—

"Oh shit," Bradley muttered.

Her head snapped toward him. He was standing rigid, eyes wide as he gazed toward the front.

Kim sprang up and whirled around.

The stranger filled the doorway. Then he was inside, striding toward them.

He wore a dark stocking cap. His face was streaked with black makeup. His black T-shirt looked swollen with mounds and slabs of muscle. The sling of a rifle crossed his chest. So did the straps of a harness that held a sheathed knife, handle down, against the left side of his rib cage. Circling his waist was a web belt loaded down with canvas cases, a canteen, and a holster. He wore baggy camouflage pants. Their cuffs were tucked into high-topped boots.

Bradley, fists up, stepped in front of him. His voice boomed out, "Stop right there, mister."

A blow to the midsection dropped Bradley to his knees. A knee to the forehead hurled him backward. He hit the floor sliding and lay limp at Kim's feet.

She whirled away and tried to run. A hand snagged the shoulder of her T-shirt. The fabric tugged at her, stretched, and ripped as she was twisted sideways. Her feet tangled. She crashed against the floor.

The man grabbed her ankles, tugged her flat. His weight came down on her back. An arm darted across her throat and squeezed.

Kim woke in total darkness. She lay curled on her side. Her head ached. At first she thought she was home in bed. But this didn't feel like a bed. She felt a blanket under her. The surface beneath the blanket was hard. It vibrated. Sometimes, it pounded against her.

She remembered the man.

Then she knew where she was.

To confirm her fears, she tried ro straighten her legs. Something stopped her feet. She reached out. Her fingers met hard, grooved rubber.

The spare tire.

The car stopped. Kim had no idea how long she had been trapped inside its trunk. Probably for an hour. That's about how long it should take, she knew, to drive from town to the wilderness surrounding Mount Bolton.

Ever since regaining consciousness and realizing she was in a trunk of the man's car, she had known where he was taking her. After a period of gasping panic, after prayers for God to save her, a numbness had settled into Kim. She knew she was going to die, and there was nothing she could do about it. She told herself that everyone dies. And this way, she would be spared such agonies as facing her parents' deaths, the deaths of other loved ones and friends, her own old age and maybe a lingering demise in the grip of cancer or some other horrible disease. Has its advantages.

God, I'm going to die!

And she knew what the butcher did to his victims: how he raped them, sodomized them, tortured them with knives and sticks and fire.

The panic came back. She was whimpering and trembling again by the time the car stopped.

She heard the engine quit. A door thudded shut. Seconds later, a muffled jangle of keys came from behind her. She heard the quiet clicks of a key sliding into the trunk lock. The clack of a latch. Then, the trunk lid swung up, squeaking on its hinges.

A hand pushed under her armpit. Another thrust between her legs and grabbed her thigh. She was lifted out of the trunk, swung clear of the car, and thrown to the ground. The forest floor was damp, springy with fallen pine needles. Sticks and cones dug against her as she rolled onto her back. She stared up at the dark shape of the man. He was a blur through her tears.

"Get up," he said.

Kim struggled to her feet. She sniffed and wiped her eyes. She lifted the front of her torn T-shirt, covering her right breast and holding the fabric to her shoulder.

"What's your name?" the man asked.

Kim straightened her back. "Fuck you," she said.

A corner of his mouth curled up. "Look around."

She turned slowly and found that she stood in a clearing surrounded by heavy timber. There was no sign of a road, though she suspected they couldn't be far from one. The car couldn't have traveled any great distance through the underbrush and trees. She faced the Butcher. "Yeah?"

"Do you know where you are?"

"Got a pretty good guess."

"You're a tough little thing, aren't you?"

"What've I got to lose?"

"Not a thing, bitch. Look to your right. There's a trail sign."

She looked. She spotted a small wooden sign on a post at the edge of the clearing.

"Stick to the trail," he said. "You'll make better time."

"What are you talking about?"

"You've got a five-minute head start." He raised an arm close to his face. With the other hand, he pushed a button to light the numbers on his wrist watch. "Go."

"What is this?"

"The hunt. And your time is running."

Kim swung around and dashed away from the man. She didn't head toward the trail sign. Instead, she ran for the end of the clearing. This was the way the car had come. She might reach a road.

He's not going to let me get away, she thought. This is just part of it. A goddamn game. I'm not going to get out of here alive.

That's what he thinks.

I haven't got a chance.

Oh yes I do, oh yes I do.

She dodged a bush, raced through the gap between two trees, and shortened her strides when she met a downslope.

Car couldn't have come this way, she realized. The bastard must've turned it around before he stopped. Knew I'd try this.

I'm running *away* from the road.

She wondered how much time had passed. Her five minutes couldn't be up yet.

He won't give me five, she thought. He's probably already after me.

But she couldn't hear anything back there. She heard only her huffing breath, her heartbeat, her shoes crunching pine needles and mashing cones and snapping twigs.

I'm making too much noise.

Then a foot slipped out from under her. She saw her leg fly up. Saw the treetops. Slammed the ground and slid on her back, forest debris raking her shirt up, scraping her skin. When the skid stopped, she lay sprawled and didn't move except to suck air into her lungs.

I can't run from him, Kim told herself. He'll catch me easy. Gotta sneak. Gotta hide.

Sitting up, she peered down the slope. It wasn't heavily wooded. The dense trees were off to the sides. She stood. She glanced toward the top. No sign of him yet. But time had to be running out.

In a low crouch, she traversed the slope. Soon, she left the moonlight behind. The dark of the forest felt wonderful—a sheltering blanket of night. She walked slowly, trying not to make a sound as she stepped around the trunks of spruce and fir trees, ducked under drooping branches.

The place smelled like Christmas.

Play it right, she told herself, and maybe you'll see another Christmas.

How good is this guy? she wondered. Is he good enough to track me through all this in the dark?

He wouldn't have let me go if he wasn't sure he'd find me.

There must be a way. I just have to be smarter than him.

He's after me by now, she thought. Even if he did wait the whole five minutes.

Kim had no idea how much time had gone by, but she guessed twenty minutes. Maybe a half hour.

If I haven't lost him, he's probably gaining on me.

Kim stopped behind a tree, turned around, and scanned the woods. Except for a few milky flecks of moonlight, the area was black and shades of gray. She saw the faint shapes of nearby trees and saplings. Nothing seemed to move.

You won't spot him till he's right on top of you, she realized, recalling his dark clothes and makeup.

She looked down at herself. Her legs were dim smears, her shorts dark, but her T-shirt almost seemed to glow. Muttering a curse, she pulled it off. She tucked it into the front of her shorts, so it hung from her waist. That was better. She was tanned except for her breats, and they weren't nearly as white as the shirt.

Turning around, Kim made her way toward a deadfall. The roots of the old tree formed a clump nearly as high as her head. Bushes and vines had grown around the trunk. She considered climbing over the dead tree, but decided to bypass it, instead.

As she neared the mound of dirt-clogged roots, she noticed a space between the trunk and the ground. Kneeling, she peered into the opening. It was exposed, but she would be out of sight if she squirmed to where a thick nest of bushes grew in front of the trunk.

The idea of being trapped beneath the dead tree didn't appeal to her. Probably a host of nasty creatures under there—ants, spiders, termites, slugs. They would crawl on her.

Besides, she told herself, if it looks like a good hiding place to me, it'll look like one to him. If he comes this way, he'll check it out. And he'll have me.

Forget it.

She hurried around the root cluster and headed to the right of the deadfall. With the barrier at her back, she broke into a run and didn't bother moving from tree to tree for concealment. She dashed as fast as she could, staying clear of trees, dodging occasional clusters of rock, circling patches of underbrush. At last, winded and aching, she ducked behind a trunk. She bent over and held her sweaty knees and gasped for air.

That little burst of speed, she thought, ought to put some ground between us. He can't run all-out, not if he's tracking me.

How can he track someone in the dark? she wondered. It wouldn't be easy, even in daylight, to follow her signs. What does he look for, anyway? Broken twigs?

Kim pulled the T-shirt from her waist band and mopped her wet face, her dripping sides, her neck and chest and belly. As she tucked the shirt into her shorts again, she wondered if the Butcher might have a night-vision device. Maybe an infrared scope, or something.

That would explain a lot.

He seemed so sure he'd find me.

Maybe took it out of his car while he was giving me the headstart.

How can I hide from something like that?

They pick up body heat? she wondered.

What if I bury myself?

That idea seemed just as bad as hiding under the deadfall.

Sighing, Kim leaned back against the tree. Its bark felt stiff and scratchy. A quiet scurrying sound made her flinch. But it came from above. Probably a squirrel up there, she thought.

What about climbing a tree?

She considered the idea. It seemed like a good one. Even if the Butcher figured out that she had gone up a tree to hide, there were thousands. She could climb high enough to be invisible from the ground. The limbs and foliage would offer some cover from a night scope, if he had such a thing.

If he does find me, Kim thought, he'll have a damn tough time getting to me.

He could probably shoot me out of it. That won't be easy if I'm high enough. And he might be afraid of the noise. The sound of gunfire would carry a long distance. Somebody might hear it.

Besides, I'd rather be shot than taken alive. Quick and clean.

If he doesn't shoot me down, his only other choice is to go up after me. That'll make *him* vulnerable.

"All *right!*" Kim whispered. "Let's make it even tougher."

She stepped out from under the tree. Crouching she studied the ground. Here and there, the faint gray shapes of rocks jutted through the mat of pine needles. She gathered several, choosing those that were large enough to fill her hand—large enough to do some real damage. When she had six, she spread her shirt on the ground. She piled them onto the shirt, brought up its corners, and knotted it to form a makeshift sack.

Swinging the load at her side, Kim wandered through the trees until she found a stand of five that were grouped very closely together. Their branches met and intertwined, forming a dark mass.

Perfect.

She hurried to the center tree, saw that it had no handholds within easy reach, and went to the tree beside it. The lowest limb of this one was level with Kim's face. After the first limb, it looked as if the going would be easy.

The shirt full of rocks presented a problem. Kim thought about it for a while. Then, she opened the knot and retied it so the untorn sleeve was free. She pushed her left hand through the neck hole and out the short sleeve, then slid the bundle up her arm. With the weight of the rocks tugging at her shoulder, she swung the load out of the way against the side of her back.

She shinnied up the trunk, struggled onto the limb, stood, and began climbing carefully from branch to branch. It wasn't as easy as she had supposed. Soon, her heart was slamming and she had to fight for air. Stopping to rest, she leaned away from the trunk and peered down. She couldn't see the ground—just a tangle of lower branches.

I'm pretty high, she thought.

Damn high. Jesus.

Her throat tightened. Her stomach fluttered. Her legs began to tremble. She turned suddenly and hugged the tree. I'm safe up here, she told herself. I'm not going to fall. She reminded herself of her days on the high school gymnastics team. That wasn't so long ago, she thought. This is no tougher than the uneven parallels. I've stayed in pretty good shape.

She still had to cling to the tree for a while before she found the nerve to relax her hold.

Just a little bit higher. Don't look down, and you'll be okay.

She got her knee onto the next branch, crawled up, stood on it, swung her foot around the trunk to another, pushed herself higher, and soon the process of climbing occupied all her thoughts, leaving no room for fears of falling.

When her movements began to sway the upper reaches of the tree, Kim knew she was high enough. She straddled a branch, scooted forward until she was tight against the trunk, and wrapped her legs around it.

For a long time, she stayed that way. Then, the rocks began to bother her. The sleeve of the T-shirt felt like a hand on her shoulder, trying to pull her backward. Rough edges of rock pushed against her skin through the fabric. Easing away from the trunk but still keeping it scissored between her legs, she swung the bag onto her lap. She draped it like saddlebags over a branch just overhead and to the right.

Relieved of the burden, she inched forward again and embraced the tree.

Kim dreamed she was falling, flinched awake, found herself slumping sideways, and clutched the trunk. Cheek pressed to the bark, she saw that morning had come. Dust motes floated in golden rays slanting down through the foliage. Out beyond the branches, she saw the bright green of nearby trees. Tilting her head back, she saw patches of blue, cloudless sky. She heard birds singing, a soft breeze whispering through the pine needles.

My Christ, she thought, I made it through the night.

She'd even, somehow, drifted off to sleep some time before dawn.

She felt numb from the waist down. Hanging onto an upper branch, she stood and held herself steady. Sensation returned to her legs and groin and rump, making them prickle with pins and needles. When they felt normal again, she removed her shorts, and climbed to a lower branch and urinated. Returning to her perch, she put her shorts back on. She sat down, one arm around the trunk, and let her legs dangle.

Now what? she wondered.

Obviously, she had eluded the Butcher. She wondered if he'd passed this way in the night, and kept on going. Maybe he'd never even come close.

Maybe he gave up, finally, and drove away.

That's wishful thinking, Kim warned herself. He won't give up. Not this easily. A: he wants me. B: I can identify him. He isn't going to let me waltz out of here.

On the other hand, he would've found me by now if he'd actually been able to follow my signs.

Maybe he *did,* she thought. Maybe right now he's taking a snooze under the tree.

No. If he knew I was up here, he would've tried to take me.

I lost the bastard.

The trick now, is to find my way back to civilization without running into him.

Trying it in daylight seemed foolhardy.

*   *   *

Waiting for nightfall was torture. There was no comfortable way to sit. Kim changed positions frequently, mostly sitting, sometimes standing, occasionally hanging by her hands from higher branches to stretch and take the weight off her legs.

Hunger gnawed at her, but thirst was far worse. She ached for a drink of water.

In spite of the shade provided by the upper areas of the tree, the heat of the day was brutal. Sweat dribbled down her face, stinging her eyes. It streamed down her body, tickling and making her squirm. Her skin felt slick and greasy. Her shorts felt as if they were pasted on.

For all the wetness on her skin, her mouth had none. As the day dragged on, her lips became rough and cracked. Her teeth felt like blocks of gritty stone. Her tongue seemed to be swelling, her throat closing so she had difficulty when she tried to swallow.

At times, she wondered if she could risk waiting for dark. Her strength seemed to be seeping away with the sweat pouring out of her skin. Spells of dizziness came and went. If I don't climb down pretty soon, she thought, I'm going to fall. But she held on.

Just a while longer, she told herself. Again and again.

Finally, dusk came. A refreshing breeze blew through the tree, swaying it gently, drying her sweat.

Darkness closed over the forest.

Kim began to climb down. She was ten or twelve feet below her perch when she remembered her T-shirt. She'd left it resting on a branch up there.

It seemed miles away.

But she couldn't return to civilization wearing nothing but her shorts.

She began to cry. She wanted to get down. She wanted to find water. It just wasn't fair, having to climb back up there again.

Weeping, she struggled upward. Finally, she tugged the loaded shirt off the branch. Didn't need the damn rocks anyway. She plucked open the knot and shook the shirt. The rocks fell, thumping against branches, swishing through pine needles. She stuffled the empty rag into the front of her shorts so she wouldn't lose it, then started her long climb to the forest floor.

When Kim dropped from the final limb, she had no clear memory of descent.

She found herself walking through the woods. Her hands felt heavy. She looked at them, and saw that each held a rock. She didn't remember picking them up. But she kept them.

Until she heard the soft, windy sound of rushing water. She tossed them down and ran.

Then she was kneeling in a stream, cupping cold water to her mouth, splashing her face with it, sprawling out so she was submerged, the icy current sliding over her body. She came up for air. She cupped more water to her mouth, swallowed, sighed.

Kim didn't think she had ever felt so wonderful in her life.

Her hair was grabbed from behind and she was jerked to her knees.

No! Not after all this!

Hands clutched her breasts, tugging her up and backward against her assailant. She squirmed and kicked as he hauled her to the bank. There, he threw himself down, slamming her against the ground. He writhed on top of her. His hands squeezed and twisted her breasts. He grunted as he sucked the side of her neck.

Reaching up, she caught hold of his ear. She yanked it. Heard tearing cartilage, felt a blast of breath against her neck as he cried out. His hands flew out from under her. He pounded the sides of her head.

Stunned by the blows, Kim was only vaguely aware of his weight leaving her body. She thought she should try to scurry up and run, but couldn't move. As if the punches had knocked the power out of her.

She felt her shorts being tugged down. She wanted to stop *that,* but still couldn't make her arms work. The shorts pulled at her ankles, lifted her feet, and released them. Her feet dropped and smacked the ground.

Rough hands rubbed the backs of her legs, her rump. She felt the press of a whiskered face. Lips. A tongue. The man grunted like a beast.

Then he grabbed her ankles, pulled and crossed her legs, flipping her over.

Kim stared up at the man.

He pulled a knife from his belt. Its blade gleamed in the moonlight. He clamped the knife between his teeth and started to unbutton his shirt.

She stared at him.

She tried to comprehend.

He was skinny, wearing jeans and a plaid shirt. His hair was a wild bush.

He's not the Butcher!

He pulled his shirt open.

A roar pounded Kim's ears. The man's head jerked as if he'd been kicked in the temple. A dark spray erupted from the other side. He stood above her for a second, still holding his shirt open, the knife still gripped in his teeth. Then he fell straight backward.

Kim's ears rang from the sound of the shot. She didn't hear anyone approach.

But then a man in baggy pants and black T-shirt was standing near her feet. He pointed a rifle down at the other man, and put three more rounds into him.

He slung the rifle onto his back. He crouched, picked up the body, and draped it over his shoulder. Turning to Kim, he said, "Get dressed. I'll give you a lift back to town."

"No way," she muttered.

"It's up to you."

He strode into the trees, carrying the body.

"Wait," Kim called, struggling to get up.

He halted. He turned around.

"*He's* the Butcher?" she asked.

"That's right."

"Who are you?"

"A hired hand."

"Why did you *do* this to me?" she blurted.

"Needed bait," he said. "You were it, bitch. I figured he'd sniff you out, sooner or later. He did, and I took him down. Simple as that."

"How did you find me?" Kim asked.

"Find you? I never lost you. Climbing the tree was a pretty good gimmick, I'll give you credit for that. Glad you dumped the rocks, though. Great timing. That's what brought him out of cover."

"Why didn't you shoot him right then?"

"Didn't feel like it. Coming?"

"Fuck you."

He left.

James Kisner has the distinction of being one of the nicest writers alive. Shocking as it may be, some writers are egomaniacs, others are strutting braggarts, and still more are whimpering megalomaniacs. Not Kisner. He always asks how *you're* doing, what *you're* writing, how *your* life is going. And despite these terrible lapses of taste and judgment, he still manages to be a damn fine writer, as most recently shown in his novel *Strands*.

MOTHER TUCKER

James Kisner

January: Abel Johnson's body was found over twenty feet from the burned ruins of his rig. He had been dead twelve hours.

Clinical detail: his left thumb was missing.

My name is Mother Tucker, I'm a mean motherfucker, and I hate truckers.

"Take that, bitch!" Randy Taggart growled at the CB and slammed his palm on the dashboard.

He pressed the accelerator pedal down, pushing the rig up past seventy. It was a clear summer night and there wasn't much traffic out on Interstate 65; he could get away with a little speed.

Mother Tucker came on again with the same message, delivered in the same singsong bitchy monotone.

"Mother Tucker, my ass," he snarled. "I get my hands on you, you'll be Mother Shit."

Randy didn't take it lightly when some asshole was razzing truckers on the CB, and tonight it was especially hard to endure. He'd been off the road a few months—laid up in the hospital from that accident back in December—and this was his first time out since coming home. He'd been looking forward to getting behind the wheel of the Kenworth again, but his joy was soured by having to listen to this "Mother Tucker" crap.

Randy switched channels, but Mother Tucker was still there, talking on another frequency. It was as if she were determined to get to him in particular.

Her voice was strident and harsh; it stung his ears. If only he could get his hands around her throat, he'd show her a person couldn't get away with badmouthing truckers, not even a woman.

That was just like a female to tease truckers like that, because a woman would think she wouldn't get stomped. Maybe she didn't know how some truckers didn't care about the sex, race, or nationality of the people they whipped. In fact, some of Randy's buddies would get off more if it was a woman, because that would show just how badass they really were.

And Randy could be as badass as the worst of them.

February: Ralph Corrigan's charred remains were dug out of the collapsed skeleton of his cab in bits and pieces. *Clinical detail:* both his legs were missing.

Randy was thirty-eight. He was working on his second old lady and had a few kids scattered about—some of whom he acknowledged and some he didn't. He was tall and somewhat leaner than usual, due to having been laid up so long. His hair was salt-and-pepper, mostly salt, and cut close to his skull, so it required little maintenance. He wore a cap, a short-sleeved shirt and Levi's. He had a self-inflicted tattoo on his left biceps that resembled a dragon trying to eat its own tail, though it was supposed to be a naked woman.

He was sweating despite the air conditioning and rolled down his window to let a little air in, though it didn't do much good. He was out of shape, not really ready to make the long run from Chicago to Nashville, but he wanted to get back to work before he went stir crazy.

Mother Tucker's obscene refrain assaulted him again on yet another channel.

"Fuck you!" he yelled into the CB mike. Then he turned it off and popped a tape in the cassette deck. David Allen Coe's raspy voice filled the cab, and Randy started to feel better—more like his old self again, shooting down the highway behind the wheel of a big rig, just breezing along in the darkness like a goddamn freight train, the power of several hundred horses pulsating throughout his whole body, especially athrob in his pecker.

But he couldn't blank Mother Tucker from his mind. He kept imagining her falling under the front wheels of the truck, her head popping like a ripe melon when thirty tons of freight ran over it, her body shredding like tangled spaghetti as he kept on rolling over her, and her guts just smearing down the road like a long goddamn wipe of dog shit.

His mind painted the picture vividly, though there was something askew about the vision. It was familiarity; that's what it was. Something like December, only the details were blurred and insubstantial.

"Damn!"

He turned the volume up and began to wail along with Coe, singing louder and louder, but he couldn't drown out the voice pounding relentlessly inside his head:

My name is Mother Tucker, I'm a mean motherfucker, and I hate truckers.

March: Much of Red Worley's remains were discovered in the back of his trailer, tossed among the boxes of snack cakes.

Clinical detail: only his legs, arms and head were found.

It was almost one thirty when Randy crossed the bridge over the Ohio River into Louisville. Hunger was gnawing at him, so he decided to get off the highway just south of the city to fuel up and fill up.

The truck stop Randy pulled into was on one of those big concrete plazas that covered a couple of acres. It was a kind of miniature city for truckers, with sleeping rooms and showers and good eats. There were also women hanging around, if a trucker felt an urge for the flesh. Some of the women even came right to a man's truck, to accommodate him, and they could be very accommodating for a few bucks.

Randy parked his rig, climbed out, and went into the restaurant. The place was jammed with other truckers, many of whom Randy knew. A few of them called out to him as he walked up to the counter. He sat next to another driver, a man he had seen frequently on this run.

"Hey, Bill," he said. "How's it hanging?"

"Where the fuck have you been?" Bill was drinking coffee and smoking Camel filters.

"Had an accident in December. Busted my leg."

"Just get back on the job?"

"Yep. First night. I sure missed it."

The waitress handed Randy a menu. He glanced at it perfunctorily and gave it back to her. "Honey, bring me biscuits and gravy, scrambled eggs, a piece of ham, and a big cup of black coffee."

"You want grits with that?"

"Might as well." He patted his stomach. "I lost a lot of weight when I was laid up. I got some catching up to do."

The waitress smiled, jotted his order down on her pad, and walked away.

"Nice ass."

"Yep," Bill said. "I guess you got to catch up on that too."

The two men laughed, then shot the shit until Randy's food came. He put it away quickly, pausing only to talk to Bill. He had even forgotten about Mother Tucker for the moment.

"I'm stuffed, man," Randy said as he sopped up the last of the gravy with a morsel of biscuit.

"Don't fall asleep behind the wheel." Bill stood up to leave. "I got to go now."

"Hey, Bill, before you go—have you heard that Mother Tucker bitch on the CB tonight?"

"No, can't say I have. I don't pay much attention to the CB."

"She comes on and says how she hates truckers. Real smartass, this one is. I'd like to kick her ass."

Bill laid a hand on Randy's shoulder. "Don't let that crap bother you, buddy. She'll get tired of jawing after a while."

"It gets on my nerves. Seems like she's on every channel."

"So don't listen to the CB."

"Yeah, sure." Randy turned back to his coffee, somewhat disappointed. "See ya."

"Catch ya later, ace."

Randy finished his third cup of coffee, paid his tab, and went outside. The food wasn't sitting well on his stomach, though he had eaten such fodder before and suffered no ill consequences.

It was that damn Mother Tucker. Talking about her had upset him, making the voice replay in his mind. God, how he wished he could find that bitch!

April: The corpse of truck driver Tyrone Watson was discovered in a ravine off Interstate 65 in Southern Indiana, where it had apparently lain for some days.

Clinical detail: his right arm was missing.

As Randy started to climb up in his truck, he saw a huddled form on the floor of the cab.

"What the hell?"

"Shh," a female voice cautioned.

Randy leaned forward but still couldn't see the person very well. "Hey, get out of there. I don't want none of that."

"I ain't no hooker."

"Who are you, then?"

"My name's Trish. Please, give me a ride." Her voice was

flavored with a distinct twang of Kentucky. "You got to help me."

He slid up the seat and shut the door. "No. It's against company policy. See that sticker—it says 'No Riders.' So get your ass out."

"Please. I'm in big trouble."

"What kind of trouble?"

"I can't tell you till we get on the road. I'll—I'll be awful grateful, if you can help."

"Get up here where I can see you."

The woman edged herself up on the seat next to him. She seemed to be about thirty-five or so. She was small and frail, with skinny legs and hardly any tits. Her complexion was yellowish and worn-looking. She wore a T-shirt, shorts, and a pair of rubber thongs. A fairly large canvas handbag was slung over one shoulder.

Her appearance screamed "truck stop hooker," no matter how much she denied it. She'd probably ask him for money once they got down the highway and offer to give him head while he drove.

It might not be too bad at that. "Well, you ain't much, but I guess you'll do.

"Then you'll take me along?"

"How far?"

"I got to get to Nashville. That's all."

"Okay, though I guess I'll regret it later. But this is just to help. You understand? I ain't got time for bullshit."

"Sure, I understand. I won't be no trouble."

"We'll see." He switched the engine on, shifted gears, and pulled out of the plaza.

Having company for the next couple of hours might be pleasant after all. It would help keep him awake, and it certainly would take his mind off that Mother Tucker.

But, Lord, why couldn't it be a woman with some jugs on her?

May: Pete Sloan's body was picked out of the twisted wreckage of his Peterbilt cab in several parts.

Clinical detail: his left arm was gone, but his left thumb was in his shirt pocket.

After three miles, Randy broke the silence. "Okay, we're on the road and there ain't nobody for miles. What's the big trouble I'm saving you from?"

She licked her lips and regarded him with desperate, wide eyes.

"It's the Mother."

"What you mean?"

"Mother Tucker. She's after me."

Randy allowed a couple of beats. He heard pavement crackling under his tires, clicking in a steady rhythm.

"You mean that Mother Tucker I been hearing on the CB?"

"Yep. That's the one. She's a motherfucker, just like she says. And she's after me."

"Now, why would she be after you, honey? You ain't no trucker."

"She's after me because I know who she is."

Randy took his eyes off the road momentarily to check her expression. She seemed genuinely frightened.

"You really know who that bitch is?"

"I surely do."

"Why does she get on the CB and say that shit? Don't she know she's making truckers mad at her?"

"She don't care. She wants them to be mad. I think—I think she's crazy."

"That ain't no shit. Anybody knows better than to fuck with truckers. Even a kid knows that much."

"That's right, but a crazy person don't know anything except to be crazy."

As the import of that seeped into Randy's mind, he realized his stomach was churning even more earnestly now; it was the battle of the grits against the gravy. He wished he had some Tums to chew on.

"So if you know who she is, why don't you turn her in?" The vision he had earlier flashed in his mind. "Or tell me

who she is and I'll see she don't hurt you." *Her head
popping like a ripe melon . . . her body shredding . . . her
guts . . . like a . . . wipe of dog shit . . .*

Oh, I couldn't do that. She'd cut me up—just like she did
the others—"

"What others?"

"Them truckers she got."

Randy forced his eyes on the road. Disturbing, blurred
images seemed to flit before him in the darkness. Or was it
bugs in the headlights? "What truckers? What're you talking about?"

Her voice grew stronger suddenly, acquiring an edge of
harshness. "Every month she goes after one and when she
gets him, she cuts something off him . . ."

Randy's stomach protested. Gravy was winning over grits;
something awful was happening inside him.

". . . like a thumb, or a leg, or something, then she leaves
the *rest* of him just laying there. You know, like leftovers."

"How come I never heard about this before?"

She ignored the question. "Then sometimes she sets his
truck on fire, just for plain meanness, as if killing him
wasn't meanness enough."

"How come nobody told me?" Randy stared at her
helplessly.

"Maybe you wasn't supposed to know." She seemed to be
enjoying making him squirm.

"I've been in the hospital, you know. Lost touch with
what was going on."

She laughed. "You sure did."

He gulped. "Why do you think she does them things?"

"She's a mean motherfucker."

"That ain't no answer."

"She hates truckers."

"Why, goddman it, why?" he shouted.

"I guess because of what one of them done to her."

"What could anybody do that would make her want to
kill them and—and cut—" He couldn't force himself to say
the words.

"Lots of things, but mostly it was what one of them truckers done when he ran her husband off the road, then run him down."

"What?" Bile burned the back of his throat.

"I hear that's what happened." She pulled her shoulder bag into her lap. "It was some son of a bitch who thought he owned the road just because he drove a truck."

"Now, I don't think . . ."

She unzipped the bag. "It was in December. The trucker was driving a big Kenworth, hauling about thirty tons. The husband was driving one of them little foreign cars and he wasn't going fast enough. The trucker forced him off the road and when he got out of the car to yell at the son of a bitch, the trucker came back and deliberately run over him. It caused his rig to jackknife and he got thrown out."

"I don't want to hear no more."

She reached into the bag. Randy could hear the chilling sound of metal clinking in there. "It was on this here highway it happened. The trucker said it was an accident, but it wasn't. But the worst part was when he run over her old man, all that was left was pieces, and the pieces was so small there wasn't nothing left to bury."

Randy swallowed. He looked at the speedometer: seventy-five. He had to slow down somehow.

"That fucking trucker that done it was laid up with a busted leg, but Mother Tucker had to do something." She was pulling something from the bag, slowly. "She knew all them truckers was bad, so she went after any trucker she could find until the guilty one got out. She had to collect—to collect *pieces*—like the pieces of her husband. She *needed* them."

The woman no longer seemed so small and frail. Randy cast his eyes down the road, searching for a good place to pull off. The darkness was suddenly impenetrable through his blurred vision.

"I've been waiting a long time," she said. "I knew you'd come through here—eventually."

"I didn't do it deliberate! I didn't." December replayed in

his memory: the man standing there next to the little car, shaking his fists and cursing, his eyes gleaming in the headlights of the Kenworth, then his head popping like a ripe melon when thirty tons of freight ran over it, his body shredding like tangled spaghetti as he kept on rolling over him, and his guts just smearing down the road like a long goddamn wipe of dog shit.

"My name is Mother Tucker."

Her hand darted from the bag, her finger gripped around a hypodermic. Randy screamed as she jammed it in his thigh.

"I'm a mean motherfucker . . ."

He went limp within seconds. She expertly took over the wheel and managed to slow down and ease the rig off the side of the road. Her hand reached back in the bag.

". . . and I hate truckers."

She brought out the meat cleaver.

Trish Tucker set fresh flowers over the spot where she had dug in the grave. She had deposited the last piece her husband needed to be whole. She had built a body for him, bit by bit, and now her work was finished.

It was a sunny morning. Off in the distance she could hear the cemetery maintenance man mowing the grass that grew over the sea of dead people. Now the grass could grow over Bobby, like it was supposed to.

She knelt and prayed. Bobby was at peace now. And she was too. She could go home and raise the baby with a clear conscience.

June: After hours of searching, Tennessee state police located the body of trucker Randy Taggart in a ditch off the Interstate just north of Nashville, half a mile from his burned abandoned rig.

Clinical detail: his head was missing.

At one time there was a theory that J. N. Williamson was actually several people. How else to account for the incredible amount of work attributed to the J. N. Williamson name? The truth is simpler, however—he's simply this imaginative, tireless writer who came late to writing and feels driven to make up for lost years. His best novel to date is *The Black School,* and his best work is characterized by a serious understanding of the occult and all of its machinations.

JEZEBEL

J. N. Williamson

Because of the way he breathed in her ear, she thought he was an obscene caller. Because of the way he started talking about heaven and hell, she thought he might be religious instead. She was correct on both counts, in a manner of speaking.

In a way, she was wrong both times. It was a matter of interpretation and where, or who, you were. And what.

"I saw you," he said after he had breathed and muttered things about Jesus awhile. "Right out there on the street, as clear as day. And we was close to one another, too. I loooooked, and we was near enough I could've reached out to touch you." Deep breath. He almost choked on it. "You was as close to me as the fires of hell, but that warn't the time"—gaaasp—"to meet. They's a time for all things, you know that? For *all* things under the sun."

She took a quick drag on the Pall Mall filter she'd lit when she thought it was Judd phoning, placed the cigarette carefully in a ceramic tray beside the telephone directory.

She knew better than to waste her time asking this person's name. His type never told, so perhaps they didn't have names and that was why they did this. Make X number of calls to strange females, scare them Y number of times, and you got a name of your own.

"I was only out once today," she informed him as if this could be a mistake that simple facts would set straight. "To the grocery." The notion of learning if he was a regular customer at Kroger's grew in steady, unrushed pace with her heartbeat, "Is that where you . . . saw me?"

"No, ma'am, it warn't." Was that excitement making him breathe in a gasp or did he have some kind of condition? Not out of loathing or much fear but because of an image she'd had of the stranger at the other end, fondling himself, she hoped it was the latter. "Ma'am, you stopped somewhere else."

"I didn't." That denial rose to her lips even as a hazy recollection of objects other than lines of gleaming coffee cans and bored people waiting to be checked out came to her thoughts. She elected to stick to her story, let him tell *her* if he could. If he would. "I bought some snacks and some Maxwell House and came straight home."

"Liar—Jezebel!" His voice seemed to get closer to her mind and she imagined moisture bubbling yellowly at the edges of his nostrils. The rancor became half-sniffle, half-giggle, as he showed off for her. "Home is 416 Capistrano Drive, apartment B-33, with womany white curtains at the windows that don't close far enough, so y'kin see all the way into your bedroom. From across the street." He had to inhale deeply then, and so did Alex. He knew her address, he had followed her. His voice retreated slightly, grew regretful, sounded disappointed. "Lordy! You sin so much you don't even recollect the truth yourself! Well," he hissed, stubbornly working to prove he knew all there was to know about her, "you was somewhere else afore goin *back* t'your place of sin. Now, think hard. Wasn't you at . . . the school?"

Alex almost blinked, made herself stare instead, as if she should not look frightened, or guilty. From the corner of

one eye she noticed the column of ash that had supported
her smoldering Pall Mall collapsing. She *had* paused a few
minutes outside the old-fashioned chainlink fence that squared
off the grade school like a huge bird cage. She had been
distantly aware of the building's age and deteriorating condition, how poor its students must be, and wondered why
she'd caught no glimpse of teachers; adults. The day was
dreary—rain had stopped or she wouldn't have done so,
arms wrapped round the Kroger sack until they began to
throb—and there'd been five or six children at desultory
play. At their feet tiny dust clouds burst when, dispiritedly,
unenthusiastically, they ran. Any games they'd played were
locked in their own minds beyond communication or the
thought of sharing, and she had decided she wanted Judd to
spend the night tonight.

And the man on the telephone must have seen her in the
grocery and trailed in her wake, sharklike, eyed her while
she clutched her sack to watch the children and wish she had
had one of her own when she had been young enough. But
why? Why had he picked *her* out? She wasn't pretty, wasn't
a girl any more. Phone calls like this—fear, terror being
seeded and starting to burst—they were for an earlier version of Alexis McCammon, a time when she had known she
was really desirable and had guarded against such dangers,
even worried now and then that she might someday be—

The temperature seemed to plummet ten degrees in apartment B-33, autumn left and baleful winter came. She shivered and realized the caller was awaiting her answer, thought
(with no conception of whether it made sense or not) that
each age a person lived had its own risks—its own way to be
hurt, even killed. And the unfairest thing in the world was
being threatened when that age's hazards were safely passed.

She started to hang up.

"—Don't *do* that, harlot," the voice said more loudly
than Alex would have considered possible with her arm
straightening out, her hand with the receiver inches from
the powder-blue Princess cradle. She froze. "I *seee* you."
He whispered it but the message reached her ears clearly,

distinctly. "I'll know *ever thing* you do. I'm judging you, Alex—from now on."

Her gaze of hopeful discontinuance swept over the middle room of the three-room flat to white curtains turning sere with evening's onset, breathing November air fitfully. The window was up only a few inches. She saw only the whole apartment building across from her; no light showed at any of the windows lapped by shadow tongues. Automatically, she stared down at her body, checked to see if she was descent, saw that she was but wondered wildly, *Am I—am I really decent? Decent enough?* She started to drop the phone and rush to the window to close, lock, and bolt it, knew the man would see her and not like that.

"Why?" she asked him. She spoke so softly it revealed an instant conviction that he was omniscient. *And what do you want?*

"This ain't the time," he said curtly.

Alex wasn't sure he had hung up until she'd waited long enough to feel completely stripped and colder than she had ever felt before.

She wasn't going to keep her date with Judd but the passing of almost two hours dimmed the details of the telephone conversation. When Judd came to pick her up, he was illimitedly more substantial, real, than the breathy, judgmental voice seemed by then. Loving Judd—forty-two; well over six feet tall with a paunch, but able to wear clothing tailored so perfectly that he simply appeared big, meaty—was the easiest thing a woman could do, and easy was what Alex McCammon wanted at this time. However, falling in love with him would've been like getting romantic over one's gynecologist and Alex's primary attribute in her self-circumscribed catalogue of good qualities was an inclination to laugh at foolishness, particularly hers. Sleeping with Judd (there were others but she never believed she was promiscuous, seldom spent the night with any man on whim) helped remind her of the requirement to laugh at life when she could. When Saturday came and they were fixing breakfast together in her small kitchen, she told him about the breather mostly to hear Judd say what she had been thinking.

People who bothered other people with anonymous telephone calls were more to be pitied than censured. Alex's man—she didn't like Judd referring to him that way—hadn't even been original or frank enough to be vividly obscene. Such persons, like Peeping Toms or transvestites, couldn't even qualify as real perverts! They moved languorously as ravenous hyenas from woman to woman, always at random, so there wasn't any special mystery about his selection of Al McCammon—anything she had done might've caught his passing attention. And all that meant he was probably making a pest of himself today with some other poor female, Alex a mere neurotic memory. "So long as the woman's alone," Judd explained before leaving. "These bastards are all scared shitless if you speak up to them."

And he didn't phone her again until Sunday afternoon. "After services," he said, "but I stood to recite your name. *Told* folks you was a Jezebel."

"You miserable bastard!"

"I reckon your kind don't ackshully want nobody t'witness for you, none of any kind."

"You discussed my life with a lot of other *strangers?*" Incredulous, she clutched the receiver tightly with both hands. A draft was on her fanny, getting colder, because she'd gotten out of the tub to answer the ring and this . . . this do-gooder, this busybody, had the gall to tell her what he had done! "How *dare* you?" she demanded. "Who the hell do you think you are?"

"Your towel." His lips were clearly pressed as close to the mouthpiece of his telephone as possible and his tone was virtually paternal. "It's slippin, Alex. Alex . . . you're exposed."

"*Exposed?*" She caught a deep breath, became furious. A busy schedule was lined up for Monday afternoon and this lunatic was moving into her private life as if he had some sort of right! "All right!" She turned quickly on bare feet to face the window. Without considering what she was doing, fed up, she let her enormous bath towel fall. Then she thrust her pelvis forward, wiggled her hips. "How do you like that, you sanctimonious creep!"

And the world became soundless. Mute. Instantly, the white curtains at the window raised slowly, ponderously. They billowed into the middle room of Alex's apartment as if someone right outside, someone with immense lung power, had exhaled his outrage and astonishment along with passions for which she knew no words. Regretting her brief impulse, reddening, she stooped quickly to retrieve her towel and wrap it with embarrassment around her nakedness.

"Well, I've had *all* I'm gonna have to do with *you* for now!" Obviously he was getting ready to hang up and was, amazingly, washing his hands of her. More astoundingly, Alex was filled with a sudden great need to keep him on the line somehow, with getting the stranger to change his opinion of her. When he spoke next, she was shaking her head and searching for the right words, and he sounded sadder than any man she had ever heard before. "It's a pure shame what has to happen to you." He gasped, regretfully, "I'm afeered you're Billy's, now."

And he was gone.

Not forgotten. (*Who is Billy?*) Not after the windows were secured, the door bolted with a chair slanted under the knob. (*What is Billy?*) Not after a phone call which found Judd, precisely as he had said he'd be, en route to San Diego with his wife Molly and the kids. Not after she tried to reach Karl or Adam What's-his-name without luck and smoked pot through the interminable hours; not during any of her sleepless night. (*All I'll have to do with you for* now?) Not in the morning when she attempted, in diametric opposition to Judd's wishes, to reach him at his hotel on the coast (*Billy who?*)

Nor when she left 416 Capistrano because she was out of Pall Mall filters and a killing afternoon was ahead of her, but didn't call a cab because these were modern times, he *wanted* her to behave like a scared rabbit; not when she seemed to be swimming in the fluorescent wash of the grocery store and pictured wild-eyed fanatics and rapists with sweating pores like silver dollars lurking behind every aisle.

Nor on her drained and nerve-jangling walk home, when she saw the century-old, fenced-in elementary school and also saw the small boy with his sallow moon face turned toward her. Expecting her, it appeared, to come his way this morning.

He was roughly eleven, possibly twelve, maybe no more than ten, with cheeks as round and puffy with baby fat as if he had tried to chew and eat it. Neither ugly nor attractive, the boy had wavy, wiglike auburn hair with an orange cast, because sunstream haloed it. Untentatively, he stood at the fence with his nostrils flaring as if he smelled something pervasively sour. His flat, knowing eyes were the color of hardening mud. The clothing he wore was frayed, cheap, too big and old for him. He could have been small for his age, had Alex known what that was, and ten pudgy fingers with schoolyard dirt caked under the much-munched nails worked, constantly. It was as though he were groping at something Alex couldn't make out that nonetheless kept him vertical. Recent spittle or drool glistened as stickily as honey on one wing of his drab shirt collar. On another morning, Alex probably would not have noticed him, definitely would have done no more than give him the dutiful vague smile one offered unlovely children as if it befitted some cosmic rank and its absence might be counted against her.

This Monday, sensing a need or desire in him and feeling miserably behind in her submissive column, Alex allowed her stride to lag, and hesitated. She smiled, nodded as well. When he did not respond she felt constrained to volunteer a cheery feminine "Hi," then knot the muscles of one leg in preparation for resuming her homeward trek. The leg started forward.

"*I'm* Billy." His tiny mouth—perhaps he had never smiled, to make it grow apace with the rest of him—didn't seem to widen when he spoke, to move from side to side or otherwise create a customary human expression. But he was just a child. The lips parted only at the center as if Alex were to poke a straw into the fleshy hole and feed him something tasty; mollifying. Alex had the impression it might be years before his voice began to change. After announcing himself, he stayed where he was.

Except, she saw, he stood at the gate of the fence and it wasn't locked. Behind him, kids who looked exactly like the children had when Alex first stopped outside the institution paid them no heed. Skipping pointlessly, unhurriedly—some hopping with precision and muttering chants as though they were casting curses—they made dust rise from the grassless plot beneath them like explosions, scaled-down. They were no part of the tableau she shared with the boy who said he was Billy, but they were central to it, like a backdrop someone had painted for the event a long time ago. Brick, a three-story, the old school showed no lights burning despite clouds that had taken sudden shape over the grounds, blighting the morning. Some windows on the topmost floor looked barred. Darkness darted or drifted beyond them but also appeared arranged and purposive as contrasted with any participation in that moment.

"You know who I am," Alex said measuredly.

"Sure. 416 Capistrano, apartment B-33. Yes, ma'am."

She stared at the aperture of his strange mouth. "Who told you? Your father, a brother?"

"Nobody told me." He pushed the tall gate wide. Instead of creaking because of little use, it swung soundlessly open. He walked out onto the sidewalk, his groping lifted fingers still wriggling. He drew closer. "I know ever thing."

She chilled but told herself to remain where she was. The grocery sack was becoming soggy, the cardboard edges of the red cigarette carton pressing through. "Billy," she said firmly, "you aren't old enough to . . . to understand what you were told."

"Yes, ma'am," he nodded in the unambivalent fashion of the young. He was as near Alex as possible without embracing or shoving her and his muddy eyes, this close, were all wrong. "I understand ever thing."

Fretfully, she leaned away from him and frowned. His breath stank. His ill-clad little chub's body reeked too. "Very well. What is it you think you know?"

"That you're a whore." He raised his plump hand but didn't strike her and did not quite place it on her arm. He let it hover there, fingers working, almost brushing one breast. "I know you sleep with married men and kill babies and use drugs. I know you're an evil Jezebel, a low and disgusting abomination in the sight of the Lord."

She had no will to retain her grip on the sack and it hit the pavement. Then she had turned to run, toward home, with no awareness of having made a choice to flee, and the child with the mudpie eyes was running after her, chasing her! "Harlot!" he cried, his voice a pig squeal. His heels kicked out behind him the way some girls' feet do when they run and he breathed hard, seemed incapable of sustaining Alex's pace. "Jezebelwhorebitch!" That was what preceded a Noah's flood of words remotely like the recitation of passages taken at random from various books of the Bible—except Billy couldn't know what they meant, he rushed them together in a mad syllabic series that perverted the words of love and divine wisdom into a terrible child's curse. Alex had heard kids do something of the sort as a girl, when they'd all learned to swear and applied the terms willynilly, regardless of the gender or particular guilt of the person to whom they were slurringly directed. Abruptly she remembered a fat boy, amazingly like Billy, that time he called her a "nigger prick" and it had stung, it had hurt and remained with Alex a long while even though there was no way in God's green world that either portion of his cruel taunt could have applied to little white her.

Glancing wildly around, she found no one breathing on her heels—nobody after her at all. Billy was nowhere in sight! *I did it,* she thought but kept jogging, her breath turning to short gasps. *I outdistanced the little creep!*

Face burning, sweaty, dimly aware the last block or so

that passerbys had gaped at the running woman with the spooked and guilt-ridden expression, she sped up the steps and shoved her way into the apartment building. Mortally shocked, she reached B-33 and stood on the landing fumbling with her keys until, alert for the clatter of feet on the stairs, she unlocked the door and stumbled wearily inside. At once, the phone rang. Heaving for breath, she hurried toward the phone desk without closing the door after her, reached tentatively for the receiver—

Froze. What if it were he—the boy's father, or whoever in hell he was? This could have been timed, maybe they didn't work alone any longer, maybe this was something new—members of some organized team that sought to frighten women, humiliate them any way they could. Perhaps they didn't choose their victims at random or did not always move hurriedly on to a different target. Maybe there were many of them everywhere—you couldn't be certain what new lunatic nightmare had sprung up overnight these days—and they no longer let it go after a mere heavy-breathing phone call or two. Perhaps . . . *anything*.

Her hand still lifted and trembling, she heard the noises from behind her and spun, knocking the receiver off the cradle like a hand grenade sailing toward its objective.

"Hello, Al? Alex?" Judd's voice rising from the floor, from the phone, but with a different quality to it.

She scarcely detected it. Billy was in the open doorway, hands clasped, appearing to pray. Pray at her, his pursed lips simultaneously sneering and chanting.

His mouth opened wider while he prayed, and edged inside.

"Get out of my home," Alex said. An hysterical note she heard added sharpness, command. "Billy, you'd better listen to me!"

He was still hunched in a pseudo-praying stance, muttering incomprehensively. The soprano litany was beyond human understanding, and it surely meant nothing to the boy either. But it was horrid, being stalked, being prayed at, it made her feel she had become an unclean leper or a demon

Jesus told to get out, and this place and this body were all she had.

"Help me, Alex," Judd cried. From the floor, his voice was tinny, tiny. Frightened. "Who *are* these damned children? They said you know them, Al, that you could tell me how the hell I got here. Dammit, what *is* this place?"

She tried to stop her ears and not to watch while other parts of Billy widened, grew, in addition to his mouth. His body filled out as if air were filling it. His round, stubby legs shoved the bigger body up, elongated it as the level of the soprano incantation lowered like a recording with the speed being reduced.

And the pace of the prayer also slowed, dragged audibly, became clearer, intelligible.

So were the mudpie eyes, now that Billy was grown and Alex was able to understand everything he chanted. Now that she realized he had been reciting the ancient and immortal message of love and wisdom backward.

He stopped finally, drew in a breath with great urgency. "Now, this here is the time," he intoned. His splitting mouth yawned to show Alex something mammoth, perfectly hollow. At its source was eternity and the barred windows of evil and insanity. His pudgy fingers—still upraised as he came close to her—went on working spasmodically, groping spastically. At last he touched her and his lips smiled. "Jezzzzebel," he said rackingly. "Welcome."

Michael Seidman is a literary man. He has been a critic, editor (magazine), editor (books), writer (nonfiction), writer (novel), and writer (Spur-
nominated short story, among many others). Presently, he is the editorial
director of Zebra books and in the spare moments that task leaves him,
he is a writer of great high style and real insight. As here.

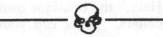

WHAT CHELSEA SAID

Michael Seidman

Bumbutt.

There was one thing you could say about Koenig: he
loved his daughter. Absolutely and completely. When she
was a baby, he'd hold her in his arms, rocking her as he sat
in the recliner, and coo at her, whisper to her, run his lips
across her little pot of a belly. "Who loves you, little Chelsea?" he'd ask, then purse his lips and vibrate them against
tender skin. "Who's going to eat you all up," he'd say, "all
up with little pliffle bites?" And Chelsea would coo right
back, and smile (it was never gas, of course, not little
Chelsea Koenig, not his little pliffle-love), and wave her
arms and fall asleep, all warm and sweet-smelling.

Big, glistening, fat, black Bumbutt.

Lavery walked down Broadway, his eyes shifting without
focus. He pulled the front of his sport jacket together, holding
the buttonless material tightly with one huge hand. Everything
about Lavery was huge, except for his clothes—pants cuff
above his ankles, jacket sleeves snugged against forearm.
The March wind wrapped itself around him and he shivered.

"Hey, Walker."

Lavery turned toward the voice and saw the owner of the small boutique waving him in. He smiled and waved, letting the old tweed jacket fall open again. It had been a long time since anyone had called him Lavery, but that was okay; he knew Walker meant him. That's what he did—walking.

"Hi, mister. Want a cup of coffee today?"

"Yeah, thanks. Here," the boutique owner said, handing him a couple of dollars, "get a cup yourself, too, while you're at it, okay?"

"Okay. Thank you, mister."

Walker folded the bills and put them carefully into his pants pocket, patting his thigh several times. *Coffee for mister, coffee for mister.* He repeated the words to himself as he continued along the street, crowded with Saturday shoppers.

By the time Walker reached the corner both he and the man who had given him the money had forgotten about the coffee.

Bumbutt was the first.

Walker didn't notice a lot of things anymore, so he didn't see how parents pulled their children closer when he approached. Sometimes he thought that he liked children, but he couldn't remember—that was part of the Lavery time; but that was also before everything happened. One of his doctors had told him that he used to be an artist, that he'd been married, but he didn't remember any of that.

At 74th Street, Walker saw two people picking through the supermarket dumpster. That was wrong; people shouldn't eat garbage. They should have food. He remembered eating earlier in the day, a hard-boiled egg and a piece of bread. That reminded him of why he was walking downtown: He wanted to go to the library on Amsterdam Avenue and find a recipe for the woman who'd given him the egg. He'd read it in a book a long time ago, a recipe for some kind of pork.

Lavery started walking faster, the cold curling around him. He held his jacket together with his left hand, his right going into his pants pocket. Good, he thought, I have some money left. Maybe I'll buy a hot dog or a cup of coffee. In the meantime, though, he walked, waving at people and saying hello.

When Chelsea was four years old, Koenig, knowing the value of both the quality and quantity of time, took her downtown to his office on a Saturday. It was a first subway ride, and as they waited for the downtown express, Chelsea looked around with glee and fascination. Koenig squatted next to her, haunches on heels, and answered all her questions, explaining almost everything. (He didn't talk about the scrawny kid trying to hide at the end of the platform, the kid with the skin magazine in one hand, a tissue in the other. Watching the scum, Koenig vowed that nothing would ever harm Chelsea, that if anyone did anything to her, he'd set things right. "I'll just be a bear and eat up anyone who tries to hurt you, Chells, I promise.")

On the other side of the station, an uptown local screeched in, and Chelsea pointed at it and laughed. "Look, Daddy," she said, "isn't that great? They paint each of the trains different. Ohh, that's so pretty." And Koenig almost cried with happiness, hugging his daughter and laughing with her and saying, "Oh, Chelsea, I love you. You say the most wonderful things, you're so clever, Chells."

The people who knew Thomas Franchi knew that in him the milk of human kindness had curdled into nothingness. He kept a cork bristling with straight pins on his desk and gave a pin to each new employee. "That's so when I tell you to move, you can stick that thing in your ass and get moving fast. If you don't move fast enough, *I'll* stick you." Newcomers only thought he was kidding for a couple of days. He looked like a granite-bound, old-fashioned, New England fire-and-brimstone preacher; instead he was a constipated businessman, owning seven stores on the West Side—a barber shop (not a salon), a pizza joint, assorted other businesses—raising rents regularly as the neighborhood improved, always finding new tenants, and running a deli.

Some of the people who knew Thomas Franchi figured that
he was into other things as well, but no one ever discussed
that.

He watched Walker strolling by the store, head down
against the wind, and thought about the meeting of the
Business Alliance he had attended last night. Things were
really getting bad: Verdi Square was turning into a little
slum, Riverside Park looked like a campground, there was
garbage walking the streets, litter blanketing the sidewalks.
How could he expect customers to want to come in and eat
with all those bums hanging around, trying to get handouts?
And that commie group, Give A Hand, wasn't helping
matters, what with their soup line across the street on the
corner of 72nd and Broadway, all those lazy bastards lining
up for handouts, shoveling down soup and bread and whatever else those ridiculous do-gooders were serving, then
throwing the plates and cups on the ground. It was bad now;
once summer hit, the place would stink for blocks around.

Franchi could cope with Walker (*God, his head's the size
of a basketball!*), guy always showed his money when he
came in, never hung around begging. He knew that some of
the other shopowners were giving him the money, but that
was their business; as long as the retardo spent it here, well
fine. But something was going to have to be done, and
soon. Hell, even the nigger drug dealers were coming back;
it had been a long time since anyone had called this neighborhood Needle Park; now, when he walked through the
streets at night, smoking his pipe, the vermin kept offering
him "something good to smoke in there, man." Bums,
junkies, and do-gooders. He shook his head in disbelief:
Who would have thought that those damned fools would
have come in and asked him to donate food for their "good
works."

"Food costs money," he'd said, looking through the young
woman they'd sent, her with her sweet Southern accent and
scrawny body. Why didn't she stay down wherever it was
she came from instead of coming up here with her begging.

"Yes, sir, I know. And we pay for as much as we can out

of our contributions and other funds, but there are just so many people to take care of—"

"They can take care of themselves, young lady, if they wanted to. And if you weren't feeding them, maybe they'd go someplace else, instead of waiting for you and your friends to feed them, dirtying up the neighborhood. No, I won't contribute anything to your cause."

The girl had smiled at him (*smiled!*), said, "God bless you," ordered a cup of tea to go, and left, closing the door carefully behind herself as he walked onto the street. He watched through a clear patch on the steamed window, saw her give the cup to some scruffy punk with a beard and matted hair. She looked back at Franchi over her shoulder, waved again, and disappeared. No, there was no question about it: At the next Alliance meeting, he was going to move that the group not be allowed to serve food on the streets. Let them invite the riffraff into their homes or into the church that was their headquarters; that was the way.

When Chelsea Koenig was nine, she was walking to the store with her father when, suddenly, she stopped, gasped, and pointed. "What is it, Chelsea, honey?" Koenig said, head swiveling in an attempt to find the danger.

"Look at that bum's butt, daddy."

Koenig looked. On a park bench in Verdi Square, a huge black woman sat, her pendulous breasts exposed behind a knit shawl, her skirt hiked up so that her behind stuck through the space between the seat slats and the back. Disgusting. They really should do something about all these people; this used to be such a nice area and now, even with the prices going up faster than anyone could deal with them, rents skyrocketing . . . with all of that, all these people living on the streets. There were some nights, coming home from work late (and later and later, because all the bright young things, the fair-haired boys and girls, working all kinds of hours, neglecting their lives for their jobs, were moving up behind him on the ladder, surrounding him, passing him), coming home from work, then, Koenig would be afraid, flinching when he saw shadows move, almost running so as not to hear the voices begging.

"Now Chelsea, honey, it's not nice to call that poor lady a bum. She may be sick" *she's probably a walking medical lab* "or something may have happened. You have to be understanding, Chelsea, not everyone is as lucky as you are.

"Now," he said, turning Chelsea away from the sight, "let's go get that sushi, okay?" He threw a handful of change into the hat lying next to the woman, but she didn't seem aware of it.

Chelsea shrugged. "Okay, Daddy." Koenig's perfect, clever, little girl hugged his arm, took his hand, and led her daddy across Amsterdam. She looked both ways before crossing, because he'd taught her to be careful, just in case he wasn't around to take care of her sometime.

Koenig laughed to himself. *Bumbutt. What a perfect pun. The things you say, Chelsea, and you don't even know it.* He whistled, and their arms swung between them.

Chelsea had the nightmare when she was ten. Koenig expected it: She was too young to have to think about divorces, about why Mommy, who said she loved her but obviously didn't, would go away. The thing that pleased Koenig was that he was in her room ten seconds before the screams began.

"No, no, sweetheart, don't worry. Daddy won't let anything hurt you," he said, giving her neck little pliffle-bites and kisses. "Anything tries to hurt you, Daddy'll just eat it right up, you know that."

Chelsea giggled. "Eat the bad dreams, Daddy. Make 'em go away."

Koenig opened his mouth wide, making chomping sounds over her head. "There they go, Chells. Yum-yum yummy in my tummy." He sat at the edge of her bed, holding her hand and humming the songs he'd hummed when she was an infant in his arms, until she was asleep.

He'd heard of things like that happening, of a parent knowing of trouble before it was real. Now he felt confident that he'd be able to protect her and not only protect her, but be there for her before anything happened, stopping the problem before it started. Hadn't he just done it? Yes, he had.

Koenig was wrong.

Lavery stood at the librarian's desk, wringing his weather-reddened hands. They knew him here; he spent a lot of time at the reading tables and never going to sleep or falling out of his chair the way so many of the street people did. He always took a book and read it, sometimes not moving until he'd finished it entirely. One of the workers had once asked him about the novel he was reading, and Lavery had responded intelligently. Such a waste, the librarian had thought at the time, and then recommended another book to him, a book he'd finished the next time he came in.

Now he was trying to tell her about the book he was looking for, he thought it had a recipe in it, a recipe for pork. He wanted to give it to the woman who'd given him the egg this morning, because she said that she was buying pork for dinner. "It was a long time ago, the story was, about men on a ship and an island." Lavery screwed his eyes tightly shut, thinking. "It was something they ate on the island. He was trying to see the words, the book, anything.

"Maybe it was *Hawaii*," the woman suggested. "or *Mutiny on the Bounty.*"

"I don't remember. It was a good book." Lavery sat down in the straight chair next to the desk and put his hands in his pockets. He felt the crumpled bills and thought about getting something to eat, then remembered that he had to bring mister some coffee. "I have to go now. Maybe I'll remember later."

He left, shoulders slumped, head down. As he walked into the deli, the name of the dish came to him. There was something special about it, something . . . "Long pig," he said, startling the man who was filling the two cardboard cups with coffee.

"Long pig. Do you have any of that? Any long pig?"

"Never heard of it Walker. Here's your coffee." Franchi

took the two singles the big man had put on the counter and replaced them with two dimes. But by the time he'd turned back from the cash register, Walker was gone, waving to people on the street. *Dummy.* He put the dimes in his pocket and stared blankly into his empty shop, waiting.

It was a sunny, warming Saturday afternoon when Chelsea came running into the apartment, her clothes torn, a bruise on her arm, tear tracks traced in the dirt on her face.

Koenig paled. He hadn't been there for her. *What happened?* "What happened, Chells, tell me, what happened, are you okay?" She was eleven years old, but looked older. Could she have been . . . ?"

Between sobs, Chelsea told him, told him about taking a walk to the 79th Street Boat Basin, walking back along the river, running around the track and, then, as she was leaving, having a man come out of the bushes, a guy with a beard, but not old, who jumped out and said, "I want you, pretty girl" and she had run away through the bushes and trees and fallen, and "I'm scared, Daddy, I don't want to go back to the park."

She's okay, just shook up. I should never have let her go alone. But there were so many people out, a beautiful spring day. It was safe there in the park on Saturday. All the kids went. Okay. "Okay, okay, you're okay Chelsea, Daddy's here, no one's going to hurt you." He gathered her in his arms as he knelt on the floor, hugging and rocking her. "I'm sorry, baby, I should have been there, I'm sorry, I'm sorry." He thought about going across the street to the park, but there were so many bums there now, how'd he ever find the right one? "Chells, Chells, everything's okay sweetie. I'm here. Daddy's with you now." He looked over her shoulder and through the window, looked at the park, one of the reasons the apartment had seemed like such a good idea when they'd moved in, when they'd been a "they," and saw the sky filled with pastels as the sun disappeared into New Jersey. "It's okay, Chelsea, you're okay. Daddy will take care of you. I promise."

* * *

Franchi took most of the large bills out of the cash drawer and put them in his money belt, leaving only enough in the till for the night crew to be able to work. He buttoned his coat against the cold and walked uptown on the west side of Broadway. The Walker was looking in the window of the art gallery, as if he could have any idea of what he was looking at. There was a long line in front of the theater, people freezing while waiting to see some dumb movie or another. Looking ahead, Franchi realized that he was going to have to walk under one of those construction walkways, meaning the street next to the Ansonia was going to be dark. There were enough people out, though. There, there was that girl, the one who wanted him to give away food. She was carrying a big, heavy shopping bag.

As he neared an empty storefront near the boutique, a voice called out, asking for money. Franchi turned toward the beggar and recognized the man who had gotten the cup of tea from the girl earlier. "Help me out, mister?"

"Why don't you go to work instead of begging, you bum you?" All of his anger and frustration were in his voice; it would take him a minute or two to realize that foot traffic had stopped, that people were looking at him.

The beggar was ready for the fight. "I would, if I could get a job, you old fart. Think you're so damned good."

Franchi spun around, attacking. "Can't get a job, huh? Probably couldn't hold on to one, you lazy bastard. Don't even bother looking. Rather let other people work and take from them, right? Go around mugging honest people, stealing. Goddamned slime. Why don't you find something useful to do, huh?" Spittle drooled down his chin. "Go beg somewhere else. That's private property you're on, I own it. Go away or I'll call a cop."

The girl stepped between them, taking the young man's arm. "C'mon, Roger. Don't you pay him no mind, hear. You just come with me." Gently, she tugged, leading the boy away, downtown, toward the church. "I'll get you something to eat. That old man, he's never been homeless or hungry, he doesn't know anything."

I don't, huh? We'll see. We'll just see. Then Franchi began to laugh because suddenly he remembered. He laughed so hard he didn't even see Bumbutt defecating in the doorway to his empty store.

"Daddy, it was awful, just awful. I was getting off the train and this guy, it was like Omigod, he just reached over and grabbed my bracelet. I was like 'no, no,' and I pulled and he called me a bitch, but then the doors closed." She sat in the living room, drinking from a bottle of lemon-flavored Perrier water. Koenig shook his head; he had accepted that he wasn't going to be able to protect Chelsea and Chelsea didn't expect it. She expected a lot of other things: Clothes, vacations, jewelry, fun and games.

Koenig had supplied them. His little daughter was growing up; she was fourteen and wouldn't let him give her little pliffle-kisses any more. That disappointed him, but he realized that he was beginning to, well . . . It wasn't healthy. He also didn't know how to tell her that he'd been fired. Two weeks. A decent settlement.

But he was in his mid-forties; all those fair-haired kids had packed around him. He was too high on the pyramid. Koenig was screwed. And what was he going to do, anyway, find the guy on a subway platform somewhere? Chew him up and spit him—?"

"Daddy, are you listening to Chells?" She finished her drink and put the bottle on the side table. "What's for dinner? I feel like going out, I'm so depressed."

Koenig smiled. "Sure thing, sweetheart. I'm sorry, babe." He couldn't tell her, not now. And anyway, he was going to take care of her. "Wear your warm jacket, Chelsea. It may be March, but spring hasn't sprung yet. We'll go to Shun Lee Palace, okay?"

"Oh great. I feel better already." She left to get ready, leaving the bottle for someone else to clear away. Koenig.

Franchi was on the phone, placing an order, and looking

at the late rush-hour foot traffic on Broadway when Walker
ambled by, staring at his feet. "Joey, hang on— No, wait,
I'll call you back later, there's something I have to do now."

He used the receiver to bang against the window, hoping
the retardo would hear it and turn. *Shit.* He ducked under
the counter and trotted into the street. "Hey, hey Walker,
come here."

Lavery turned slowly and waved. "Sure, mister. Want
some coffee today?" He hulked over Franchi, forcing him to
take a step back.

"No, no, that's not it. I sell the coffee, remember? You
buy the coffee from me.

"Come in for a minute, please. There's something I'd like
to propose— To talk to you about."

"Sure, mister. Can I have a cup of coffee?"

"Yes, Walker, anything you want."

Franchi leaned across the table. He didn't want to get too
close, but he didn't want to be overheard; he would have
enough trouble explaining why he was sitting back here with
the retardo if anyone had had the balls to ask him, but he
definitely didn't want anyone to hear what he was saying.
"Walker, remember when you came in the other day . . . ?"

When Lavery left, a cardboard cup of the soup of the day
in his hand, Franchi was smiling. He didn't know if it would
work, but if it did, if it did . . . It was all up to Walker now;
if he did his part, Thomas Franchi could do the rest. And if
he needed more help, he knew where to get it. It would
take a while, a couple of months to get Walker ready.
Everything else would fall into place.

Light jackets replaced coats to be replaced in turn by shirt
sleeves. Franchi had been right; the streets began to stink.
Koenig knew how badly, because he spent a lot of time on
them. There were no jobs, nothing permanent. A little of
this, a little of that thrown his way by old friends, but it
became less and less more and more quickly.

Koenig began to walk instead of taking a bus or subway;
saving two bucks a day, he could see, would soon make a
difference. There was still some money, enough, but it was

going fast: Chelsea was always running off someplace, going out with friends, needing something. He'd talked to her about maybe taking a job this summer, "things are tough right now, honey, you know," and all she'd said was that she'd think about it, but she was going over to Billy's house, "you know Billy, Dad, he's got the house up near Monticello. Maybe I can spend the summer up there with him," and then she was gone. She was always gone.

Koenig felt a small stone pressing against his foot, he'd have to get these shoes resoled soon. At least he still had a roof over his head. *Where am I?* He looked around; he'd walked down to 27th Street and Seventh Avenue. There was a restaurant near here that he had frequented back in the old days; checking his pockets, he found ten dollars. Not enough.

He walked along 27th Street, heading west, passing the campus of FIT, and staring at the girls sitting on the steps and benches, getting some sun. One of them, a little heavy, long, dirty-blond hair, sultry eyes, stared at him and he thought about going across the street to talk to her. He remembered being on the campus once, back in the mid-sixties, when he was a student; that girl hadn't even been born then. Koenig kept walking, going around the corner and looking into the window of Bogie's, at the people at the bar. "She wasn't even born yet and I'm thinking about trying to pick her up." That was when Koenig realized that he had started talking to himself.

He wiped his nose with the back of his hand and started walking faster. Where was Chelsea? Was she picking up men? Where did his pliffle-love spend all her time? Who was she—

"Help me out, mister? Some change so me and my kid can get somethin' to eat?" Koenig looked into a pair of dull eyes and shuddered. He found fifty cents in his pockets, dropped the quarters into the woman's dirty palm. Behind her a little girl clutched at the woman's skirt.

On the subway going uptown, Koenig heard himself say, "Help me out? Any spare change, please?" but wasn't certain whether or not he'd actually said it aloud. He knew, though, that his stomach ached.

At 72nd Street, Koenig looked at the clock on the bank: 4:45. 83 degrees. On the corner, people were lined up, taking food from the group that was feeding the homeless. Whatever it was, it smelled good. His stomach ached. He saw the guy they called Walker *he's a walker, I'm a walker, wouldn't you like to be a walker too?* talking to Bumbutt. *The things Chelsea said. She was such a wonderful kid. God, he loved her.* Bumbutt took her cup and plate and started walking down Broadway with the big man. Even they had someone to love. Koenig wondered if she was going to share her food with the big man. He wondered if she'd share with him.

"Hey mister, would you care to give me fifty cents so that I may complete the down payment on my condo? See, you're smiling. The *New York Times* said that I had one of the best lines on the street. So, what do you say?"

"I say the *Times* is right but I'm afraid I can't help you." Koenig smiled at the man, ignoring his profanity, but by the time he got home, he couldn't think of what was so funny. Here he was busting his butt trying to keep body and soul (and Chelsea) together, no job, no prospects, and these bums were complaining when he didn't give anything to them. Something had to be done.

Franchi was doing it. He'd contacted Give A Hand and told them that he'd contribute food, but he wanted his donation kept secret. The Southern girl, her name was Amy, she said, and she was from Georgia, told him not to worry. He did, anyway.

Bumbutt was the first to disappear.

Koenig looked around. He didn't think anyone he knew was around. He stood on the corner, watching the people line up for food; no one asked questions, they just served. He didn't remember getting *in* the line, but there he was, saying thank you as a pretty young woman gave him a plate with a sandwich—roast pork, mustard, lettuce—and a cup of thin soup. Koenig's stomach ached, but the food was good.

Roger was the next to disappear. No one missed them, not even Amy from Georgia, who had gotten used to the fact that street people come and go. She waved to Mr. Franchi, who wasn't so bad after all, even if he wouldn't acknowledge her greeting. As long as his delivery boy kept showing up with meat and bread, she'd keep his little secret. She looked into the eyes of the man in front of her now, looking so guilty about taking the food. She wanted to talk to him, he looked so lonely, looked like he wanted company. He looks familiar, Amy thought.

Koenig smiled at the young woman, looking so innocent and tired and filled with happiness at being able to help. Stay safe little girl, he thought. The food was good and it meant that tonight, when he took Chelsea to dinner, he wouldn't be hungry, he'd be able to have soup or something, save some money, but still let Chells have her treat. He looked at Amy, wondering if she'd like little pliffle-bites.

Chelsea noticed that Bumbutt was gone from her usual place in Verdi Square as they were crossing Broadway, but she only remembered her because she had given the fat old lady the nickname. She wrinkled her nose as they passed the soup line. "Boy, this place stinks. Why don't they clean up?"

Koenig hadn't noticed the smell in weeks, just the scent of food, fresh and good and filling and free. "Chelsea, you know these people have no place to go to bathe or wash or anything. They're not as lucky as we are" *were, this is the last month I know I can pay the rent* "and they clean up later, when the line closes, throw away the garbage" *and the people, I think. Bumbutt's gone* "and do what they can."

"I know what they can do, Daddy," Chelsea said, taking her father's hand, "they can feed the homeless to the hungry."

And Thomas Franchi, walking past them, started to laugh.

Trish Janeshutz is probably better known to you as T. J. MacGregor, author of several Ballantine suspense bestsellers, of which *Fevered* is generally considered the masterpiece in a field of six other strong contenders. Trish's work is filled with grace notes, those telling little moments—the right phrase, the right piece of dialogue, the right place description—that illuminate the pages of the very best kind of writing.

RIVEREÑOS

Trish Janeshutz

1

Eva waits on the upper deck for him, in the sweet lushness of the warm Peruvian night. There is enough starlight to see the black shape of the jungle on shore. She feels its weight pressing up against her, an impenetrable wall, impossibly rich and dense. Below her, the muddy Amazon rushes past, whispering in some ancient tongue, dark and seductive.

She isn't sure what she's doing here, waiting for a man who isn't her husband, a man she met, in fact, only yesterday, when she boarded the boat. This isn't something she has done before. She has been happily married for more than ten of her thirty-six years. She and her husband own an import shop on Miami Beach and she has been traveling through Colombia and Peru buying native art and crafts. A simple trip. Purposeful. But there's something about the heat and smells here in the upper Amazon that stirs a deep fever in the blood, a delirium of need, a certain eroticism that stalks the dormant self.

"One Pisco sour," says Pablo, coming up behind her.

His cool mouth brushes the back of her neck, and the bright burn of her betrayal blazes inside her as she turns, smiling, and takes the drink. It's a local whiskey concoction as mysterious and powerful as the river, and it scorches a path down her gullet.

"Any more of these and I won't be seeing tomorrow."

Pablo chuckles. "No problem. The doctor he has many cures for hangovers." Despite his accent, his voice is buttery and smooth and slides through her in much the same way the voice of the river does. He touches the small of her back and tilts his head toward the hammocks, an invitation that implies more than she may be willing to give. "It is more comfortable over there," he says.

She hesitates, but not for long, and moves toward the hammocks. They settle into the same one, both of them slipping toward the middle until their shoulders seam. He leans back and stretches out his legs, sandals pushing against the pole until the hammock starts to sway. His nearness, the heat of his skin, the boundless sky overhead: all of it makes her heart drum. She feels lightheaded, not quite herself, and sips quickly at her drink. Its chill paralyzes her esophagus, but her insides are as hot as the night air. Such extremes are symptomatic of something, but she isn't sure if it's physical or mental. Perhaps both.

She asks him to point out the Southern Cross. His arm lifts and a long finger points slightly off to her left. "There. See it?"

It takes her a few moments to find it. But detecting the cross is a bit like recognizing a fundamental truth: once she sees it, she can't imagine how she missed it before. It glistens against the black skin of the sky, a constellation unique to the southern hemisphere, a phenomenon as strange to her as the way water here, below the equator, swirls counterclockwise down a drain.

"It is not in the same place it was when I was a boy," he says.

She thinks he's joking and laughs. But his expression is so solemn, he reminds her of her husband when he's driving himself crazy during tax season, juggling the store's books within the parameters the tax code allows. An honest man, her husband, a prince whose world is as distant from Pablo's as Neptune is from the sun.

"Really. It is not a joke, Eva. All things here transform. The sky, jungle, the river, the animals. Everything. You know the pink dolphins we saw this morning?"

"Sure." The dolphins, pink as seashells, followed the ship for nearly an hour at dawn. They leaped from the muddy river in graceful, shimmering arcs, water shooting from their blowholes, then dived again. It was as if they were escorting the ship through a treacherous zone.

The pink dolphins, he explains, are the best known of the changers. Sometimes, when there are festivals in the villages, they come ashore as men. You can always tell a dolphin/man because he's wearing a white suit and a white hat that covers his blowhole. He dances with the prettiest woman, charming her, mesmerizing her, until she consents to go away with him. Then he whisks her to his underwater city and makes love to her. When her child is born, he too has the magic to transform. "This is the Amazon's way of keeping itself alive and vital, part of its web."

The dolphin did it: it sounds like a good way to explain an illegitimate birth so a woman doesn't lose respect in her village. But Eva keeps her opinion to herself because the myth is real to Pablo. It's an intimate part of his roots, roots that bind him despite his self-education, his contemporary veneer, his Westernization. He is, after all, an Indian who was born and raised on this river; perhaps that is the source of her attraction to him.

"What other creatures transform?" she asks.

He speaks softly, in the voice of the river. "Many. And they change in a variety of ways. We call them rivereños." She's heard the term. It refers to Peruvians who move back and forth between life on the river and life in the city, existing in two worlds, but belonging to neither.

Music blasts from the lower deck, something from an American tape. The Talking Heads. Pablo's foot taps to the rhythm. The music is out of place here, and irritates her, reminds her of home, of the husband whose face, even now, seems less clear than it was yesterday or even this morning. She tries to shut it out, to focus on the music of the river instead.

As this old ship, which once hauled rubber up and down the Amazon, moves deeper and deeper into the jungle, her other life seems to be fading, becoming less real. Perhaps, by the time they reach the city of Iquitos, she will have no memory at all of her former self; her conscience will be as flawless as an infant's. A nice thought, but she knows it won't happen. She has an excellent memory. She will recall every detail, every nuance of tonight—the sharp, bitter taste of the Pisco sours, the heat of his arm as it slides around her shoulders, the rich smell of the river, even the way the shape of his mouth changes as it seeks hers. Her memory, which has often been her salvation, will become her curse. Maybe in the end, she will be like the rivereños, resident of two worlds, citizen of neither.

She stares at herself in the tarnished mirror in her cabin's bedroom, expecting to see another woman looking back at her, a woman she has never met. But her face is the same. The dark eyes remain a shade too small, too widely set. The cheekbones are still prominent, the chin rounded, the nose too straight. Her features, in fact, seem clearly defined, oddly American, obvious. Only her hair looks different, the blond so pale it's nearly white, as if she's standing in a pool of jungle light.

She shucks her T-shirt and turns on the shower. There isn't much pressure, but the water is hot. She stands under the paltry spray longer than necessary, eyes squeezed shut against last night. But memories rise unbidden, a wild current of images and colors, scents and noises, and in the heart of it is her husband's face, a sharp picture, hurtful in its clarity. Her breath hitches in her chest. She presses her hands to her face, ashamed for her betrayal and her pleasure. She wants to cry, but can't. The pain isn't deep enough.

It lacks power, conviction, reality, because given her druthers, she would make the same choice again. And again.

Later, as she's drawing a comb through her wet hair, she notices a mark on her neck, a bruise, where he sucked at her skin. A *hicky,* she thinks, and starts to laugh, a quick, fluted sound, false. She pulls at the skin with her fingers, trying to get a better look at it. She hasn't had one of these since high school, when they were a statement of possession, of territory, like a ring hanging from a chain at your throat. How long will it take to fade anyway? Two days? Three? She will be back in the States the day after tomorrow. Steve, her husband, will notice it. He has always seen things that are not meant to be seen. He will comment on it, ask what it is, how she got it. A bite, she will say. Something bit her one night when they were out on the skiffs, in one of the black water tributaries. She will lie for the first time in ten years of marriage and he will believe her because he has no reason not to.

All day, the collar of her shirt is turned up so it hides the mark. She stays away from the other passengers, lost in a book in a hammock on the upper deck, her solitude a kind of penance.

2

"You avoid me," Pablo says.

It's just the two of them, sitting across from each other at the long wooden table in the dining room.

"What?" She laughs a little, as though she hasn't understood what he said. Dusk fills the windows in front of her and slides up against her back, warm, humid, beckoning. "You. Avoid. Me." His jaw is set, stubborn, and his face is hard, more Indian than she recalls. "Yes?"

"No, of course not. Why should I avoid you?"

Pablo covers her hand with his own, trapping it like a small bird, and strokes her knuckles with his thumb. Small, smooth strokes that promise more of last night, a universe of pleasure. She gently pulls her hand back.

"You will have my children, Eva." A smile shadows his mouth and his dark eyes are so intense, the back of her neck prickles with alarm. She pushes away from the table.

"I'm not having anyone's children." She hurries out of the dining room, and feels his gaze against her spine, a hot, relentless pulse.

3

The skiff putts through the still waters of a tributary as black as the sky, the din of its Suzuki motor competing with the jungle noises along the bank. They are out here looking for cayman, although Eva isn't sure what's supposed to happen if they spot one. Probably nothing. The point of the trip is to experience the river at night.

Eva and six other passengers are crowded together in the skiff, with a guide at the back who steers the boat and Pablo standing at the front like an Indian chief who's ferrying his tribe to a safer place. The beam of his flashlight dances across the shore. Branches close off the sky. The press of the jungle is oppressive, claustrophobic. She winces every time a branch brushes across her back. Her heart leaps when something splashes in the river several feet from the boat. The scent of insect repellent mixes with the smell of water and trees. The stuff coats her skin, her shoes and hair, her clothes, and radiates from everyone else as well, a ludicrous testimony of civilization. But all of them are immunized against yellow fever, diphtheria, typhoid. They have quinine tablets, Kaopectate, antibiotics. They drink bottled water and Pepsi without ice, and don't eat salads. They follow the rules. But what immunization is there, Eva wonders, for what ails her?

"There!" Pablo hisses, and the beam of light fixes on a pair of red orbs glowing from the dark wall of trees on shore. A cayman, Pablo whispers, and goosebumps erupt on her arms as the driver cuts the engine.

The sudden absence of sound is quickly filled by jungle noises. Frogs, screeches, rustling in the trees, fish splashing in the black waters. The red orbs vanish. Pablo's flashlight darts right, left, searching, finding nothing. He grabs onto a nearby branch, pulling the skiff closer to shore, then leaps off, bare feet sinking in the mud. The night sucks him into itself. For a few seconds, Eva hears him clicking his tongue against the roof of his mouth, as if he's calling to the cayman. Then she hears only the jungle and the excited murmurs of voices in the skiff.

Someone asks where Pablo went. The driver pats the air with his hands and whispers, "To find the cayman."

Now that the boat has stopped, mosquitos swarm around their heads. She slides the hood of her windbreaker over her hair, sprays herself with Off, then passes it on when someone asks for it. Something swoops low over the skiff and a woman on board yelps.

"Bats," exclaims one of the men.

"Ssshhh," scolds the driver.

A scuffling in the brush, a shriek, then laughter. Pablo and a man emerge from the trees. "Un amigo," Pablo shouts to the driver, slapping his companion on the back. "Un buen amigo."

"What happened to the cayman?" someone asks.

"He was too fast," Pablo replies as he and his companion climb aboard.

The stranger is tall, compact, muscular, with dark hair and the sharp features of an Indian. His eyes seem to glow in the dark.

All things here transform.

She stares at the stranger.

He's one of them.

No way.

A rivereño.

Hysteria bubbles in her throat as Pablo settles at the stern and the stranger sits across from her. She barely resists the urge to get up and move to the back of the skiff. She stares at her feet, hands clasped tightly in her lap, and forces herself to take long, deep breaths. She tries to conjure details from her other life—the color of her bedroom, the scent in the shop on Miami Beach, the shape of her husband's face—but the Amazon has swallowed all of it.

She hears Pablo say, "The insects they do not bother me," and looks up. He's holding the can of Off, her can, and now he tosses it toward her. "Catch, Eva."

She misses it. The damn thing rolls noisily across the floor of the skiff. She reaches for it, but the stranger plucks it up first and holds it out like an offering. She blinks and for an instant, sees a hand that is leathery, like a cayman's hide. She blinks again and sees skin. Her imagination. But if he *is* a cayman, then what is Pablo?

Stop it.

Pablo and the stranger are only men. She silently repeats this. *Men, they are men.* Her panic begins to ebb. She's tired, that's all, tired and confused and a little frightened. The jungle exhausts her. Makes her see things that aren't there.

She takes the Off from him and murmurs her thanks. For a beat or two, their eyes meet. His impale her. She looks quickly away and shoves the can in her bag. The mark at her neck burns and itches. The skiff rocks as the engine cranks up, and chugs farther into the tunnel of trees. The thick richness of the river fills her, intoxicating her. She's afraid to lift her gaze, to look closely at the stranger, but she can't resist the temptation to see if his eyes really glow or it was only another trick of the jungle, the dark. She raises her head. The stranger is already watching her, smiling as if he has been waiting for her to do exactly this, and for just an instant, his eyes burn pink.

Eva wrenches her gaze away and hugs her arms against her, air congealed in her lungs like blood.

4

Heat, so much heat. It blazes a path through the center of her being, baking her from the inside out, blackening her organs, her muscles and sinews, her skin. She's dreaming, she knows she is, but she can't break out of the dream, it has snared her, it holds her, it whispers to her in the voice of the river, the jungle. *You are mine, I have claimed you, you are mine mine.* The voice rises and falls inside her, echoing, and becomes Pablo's voice, *You will have my children . . .*

Now he moves through the steaming green of the jungle, coming for her. Eva can't see him, but she senses him, feels him advance through the trees, the underbrush. She catches his scent in the humid air, a wild, musky scent, not human.

She runs, crashing through the jungle. Branches snap back in her face. Roots spring from the black soil, tangled, gnarled, blocking her path. A monkey swings in front of her, chattering, teeth bared. She cuts left. Parrots squawk and fuss and a flock of them lift from the trees, wings beating the hot air. Her head jerks around. She still can't see him, but he's close, very close, she hears him breathing, hears the jungle opening up for him, helping him. Vines tangle in her hair and seize her ankles.

She stumbles and tries to catch herself, but pitches forward with a scream, into the dark, wet foliage. Leaves the size of cats slap wetly across her face, blinding her. They squeeze around her arms, trapping her, holding her against the ground. Branches clamp around her ankles like vises. Her legs snap open. Her clothes are gone. Insects scurry across her belly, her breasts, her face. Something squats on her eyelid. A worm burrows into her ear.

Mine, you are mine, you will have my children, he whispers in the voice of the jungle, the river, the wildness.

"Señora? Señora?"

Eva bolts forward, frantic, a scream already rolling down her tongue, and stares into the face of a pretty flight attendant. *I'm on the plane, on my way home.* Giddy with relief, she says she's okay, really she is, and asks for a glass of water. When the flight attendant has walked off, Eva's hands tighten against the arm rests. She smooths her palms over her slacks, touches her fingertips to the cool glass. Real, all of it is real.

She peers out into the endless blue sky, thinking of home, of her husband, of the life she can barely remember, but which she is nonetheless rushing back to claim. She will return to the woman she has been for the last ten years and everything will be fine, just fine. The memories of the jungle and the mark on her neck will fade.

They will.

They have to.

5

Her husband believes her story, that she was bitten by something. Maybe you should see a doctor, he says. No need, she replies, the mark is fading.

But it doesn't fade. Within seventy-two hours of her return, it seems to be swelling. She touches it during the day when she's at the shop, feels it a night when she lies awake in the dark, examines it every morning to see if it's larger or redder. Within a week, she feels a hardness just under the skin, a cyst, a knot, something that wasn't there yesterday.

She hurries into the bathroom at the back of the shop. Shuts the door. Locks it. She is trembling. She hears Pablo whispering of transformation, riverños, his voice slick and warm. She slaps her hands over her ears, struggling against the seduction of that voice, and when she's silent inside, she turns down her collar and scrutinizes her neck in the mirror.

She can see the lump. It fits perfectly within the borders of the red mark, a hard knob shaped like a jagged bullet. It looks like a birthmark or an allergy of some kind. But of course it isn't.

Her fingers touch it gently. It moves from side to side like a glob of fat in water. She presses her palm over it and feels heat, the intense jungle heat that steams, oppresses, stalks, kills. Something is inside her, he left something inside her, Jesus, she can feel it sinking deeper and deeper into her muscles, her tendons, taking root inside her.

6

"I want it cut out."

Her family doctor smiles and shakes his head. "I think that's a little drastic, Eva. It's a mosquito bite that's gotten infected. A good dose of penicillin should take care of it. I'm also going to give you a prescription for penicillin tablets."

"Okay. But I still want it cut out." She hears the quaver in her voice, the incipient hysteria. "I don't like it there."

"The cyst is just the infection, hon. Trust me, okay?"

She has known him for twenty years and of course she trusts him. He removed her tonsils, her appendix, has treated her for colds and the flu. Trust. He gives her an injection and writes the prescription, which she takes to the drug store next door to be filled. As she waits, she thinks about penicillin. The miracle drug. Can it battle jungle magic? Will it silence the soft whispers in her head? Will it obliterate the nightmares? The memories? The mark? Yes yes yes.

On her way back to the shop, the sweet beach air fills the car and the hot sun beats the hood and the penicillin rushes through her bloodstream, working miracles. She tells herself that the throb of her neck, the movement deep inside the cyst, is nothing but her imagination, and she almost believes it.

Almost.

7

Three days later, a Sunday. The weather is warm, the sky a clear, hot blue. She and Steve are playing softball with friends in a park near the house. She's the pitcher and Steve is coming to bat. He flashes her a grin as he steps up to the plate, a smile that challenges, and she grins back.

Her arm swings back and she lobs the ball. It arcs into the cobalt sky, high and smooth, and flies down across the plate. Steve smacks it. The crack echoes across the field and the ball zips toward her.

But before she can react, it slams into the side of her neck and the impack knocks her to the ground. Black dots swim in her eyes. Dust swirls in her nostrils. She's sprawled in the dirt. Her head aches. Her neck feels like it's been severed. People are shouting. She's trying to sit up.

Her hand jerks to her neck and she feels something warm and wet. When she brings her hand away, she screams. It's covered with them. Hundreds of them. *Spiders.* They scamper over her hand and up her arm and into her hair and down the front of her shirt and across her face. She screams and screams as she leaps up, trying to brush them away, to get them off. But there's so many of them and they keep pouring out of her neck, some of them covered with her blood, others as clear as cellophane. She claws at her neck, digs her fingers into the hole where they had nested, and scoops them out, her screams still shredding the air.

The breeze lifts the smallest ones. They trail bits of web as they rise into the sky like kites and even as she screams, Pablo's voice is everywhere, whispering, *You will have my children.*

Whispering.